Praise for Shirlee McCoy and her novels

"*The Guardian's Mission* is full of action
and romance."
—*RT Book Reviews*

"*The Protector's Promise* is an extremely suspenseful,
touching story. You'll want to put [this] book
on your keeper shelf."
—*RT Book Reviews*

"McCoy's characters are engaging,
as is the suspense."
—*RT Book Reviews* on *Defender for Hire*

"A page-turning read."
—*RT Book Reviews* on *Lone Defender*

"McCoy's writing is descriptive and contains
a well-balanced blend of action and romance."
—*RT Book Reviews* on *Tracking Justice*

D1479626

SHIRLEE McCOY

The Guardian's Mission

and

The Protector's Promise

◆ HARLEQUIN® LOVE INSPIRED® CLASSICS

If you purchased this book without a cover you should be aware that this book is stolen property. It was reported as "unsold and destroyed" to the publisher, and neither the author nor the publisher has received any payment for this "stripped book."

Recycling programs
for this product may
not exist in your area.

ISBN-13: 978-0-373-60605-4

THE GUARDIAN'S MISSION AND THE PROTECTOR'S PROMISE
Copyright © 2014 by Harlequin Books S.A.

The publisher acknowledges the copyright holder
of the individual works as follows:

THE GUARDIAN'S MISSION
Copyright © 2008 by Shirlee McCoy

THE PROTECTOR'S PROMISE
Copyright © 2008 by Shirlee McCoy

All rights reserved. Except for use in any review, the reproduction or utilization of this work in whole or in part in any form by any electronic, mechanical or other means, now known or hereafter invented, including xerography, photocopying and recording, or in any information storage or retrieval system, is forbidden without the written permission of the editorial office, Love Inspired Books, 233 Broadway, New York, NY 10279 U.S.A.

This is a work of fiction. Names, characters, places and incidents are either the product of the author's imagination or are used fictitiously, and any resemblance to actual persons, living or dead, business establishments, events or locales is entirely coincidental.

This edition published by arrangement with Love Inspired Books.

® and TM are trademarks of Love Inspired Books, used under license. Trademarks indicated with ® are registered in the United States Patent and Trademark Office, the Canadian Trade Marks Office and in other countries.

www.Harlequin.com

Printed in U.S.A.

CONTENTS

Books by Shirlee McCoy

Love Inspired

Love Inspired Single Title

SHIRLEE McCOY

has always loved making up stories. As a child, she day-dreamed about elaborate tales in which she was the heroine—gutsy, strong and invincible. Though she soon grew out of her superhero fantasies, her love for storytelling never diminished. She knew early that she wanted to write inspirational fiction, and she began writing her first novel when she was a teenager. Still, it wasn't until her third son was born that she truly began pursuing her dream of being published. Three years later, she sold her first book. Now a busy mother of five, Shirlee is a homeschooling mom by day and an inspirational author by night. She and her husband and children live in the Pacific Northwest and share their house with a dog, two cats and a bird. You can visit her website, www.shirleemccoy.com, or email her at shirlee@shirleemccoy.com.

The Guardian's Mission

Enter through the narrow gate. For wide is the gate and broad is the road that leads to destruction, and many enter through it. But small is the gate and narrow the road that leads to life, and only a few find it.

—*Matthew* 7:13–14

To my dear friend Darlene Martha Gabler. Though we are far apart, you are always in my thoughts and prayers.

ONE

First-aid kit?

Check.

Water? Protein bars? Check. Check.

Chocolate? More chocolate? Tissues? Triple check.

Not that Martha Gabler was going to need the tissues. She wasn't. She was over her crying jag and done feeling sorry for herself. It was time to move on, to embrace singleness with the same joyful excitement with which she'd embraced being a part of a couple.

The fact that in one year and three months she'd hit the magical age that separated young-enough-to-hope from too-old-to-keep-looking didn't matter at all. So what if women in Lakeview, Virginia, married young? So what if reaching thirty without heading down the aisle was tantamount to walking around town wearing a placard that read Past My Prime?

Did Martha care?

Yes!

She sighed, zipping her backpack and shoving a

baseball cap over her unruly curls. She'd come to the mountains to put the past behind her. She didn't plan to spend time dwelling on things that couldn't be changed.

Like her newly single status.

Outside Martha's Jeep, the day was as gray and gloomy as her mood, the deep oranges and brilliant reds of the fall foliage muted in the dreary morning light. Maybe visiting her father's hunting cabin could wait another week, another month. Another year.

No. It couldn't.

She hadn't been to the cabin since she started dating Brian two years ago. Now that he was out of her life, it was time to enjoy the things she'd loved before Brian had pulled her into his high-society world. Time to start fresh, to look with excitement at the new horizons stretching out before her.

Martha snorted and shoved open the Jeep door, stepping out into cool mountain air. Gravel crunched beneath her feet as she hoisted her pack onto her back and turned to survey her surroundings. The old gravel road she'd parked on dead-ended a hundred yards up. Beyond that, a dirt path wound its way up into the mountains. A steep and difficult climb led to the cabin, but Martha didn't mind. Some good hard labor would get her mind off Brian-the-jerk.

She started to close the Jeep door and jumped as her cell phone rang.

Dad.

For a split second she considered ignoring the call, but the thought of seventy-year-old Jesse Gabler hiking up to the cabin was enough to convince her otherwise.

She pressed the phone to her ear, hoping her voice wouldn't give away her emotions. More than anything else, she hated to worry her father, and if he thought she was upset, worried was exactly what he'd be. "I'm fine, Dad."

"Who said that's why I was calling?" Gravelly and gruff, his voice reminded her of all the triumphs and losses they'd faced together since her mother walked out when Martha was five.

"Dad, it's ten o'clock on a Friday morning. Why else would you be calling except to check up on me?"

"Maybe I'm just calling to say hi."

"Right. You can't stand it that I'm going to the cabin alone. Admit it."

"Marti, the cabin has been closed up for two years. It might not be habitable anymore."

"As long as it's still got a roof and four walls, I'll be fine. I don't need more than that."

"Need more for what? Grieving in private over that scumbag doctor? I knew he was no good the minute I met him. Wishy-washy, wimpy kid with a head too big for his scrawny little neck. If I'd had my way you would never have…" His voice trailed off and Marti could almost see his hazel eyes going dark with worry and regret. "Sorry, baby doll. You know how I am."

"Yeah, I know." Which was why she'd had to escape to the mountains. Between her father, her friends, her church and her community, Martha had nearly drowned in the outpouring of sympathy since she'd called off her engagement three days ago. That was the problem with living in a small town. Everyone knew everyone's business. Most of the time, Martha didn't mind, but right now she needed space.

She needed time.

She did *not* need to be smothered by well-meaning people who all claimed to have believed her relationship with Brian was doomed, but who hadn't bothered to tell *her* that.

Her father cleared his throat the way he always did when he wasn't sure what to say, then launched into a safer topic. "It's supposed to storm tonight. You know that, right? The creek might flood its banks. You might get stranded for a few days."

"A few days isn't going to kill me. Besides, I know how to handle myself out here. I was taught by the best."

"Glad to know I taught you something." *Since I obviously didn't teach you how to protect your heart from smooth-talking men.*

Martha could almost hear the words, though her father loved her too much to say them. "You taught me plenty, Dad. So, listen, you take Sue out this weekend, okay? Somewhere fancy."

"Why would I go and do a thing like that?"

"Because tomorrow is the three-year anniversary of your first date and she expects it."

"Three-year anniversary of our first date? Who keeps track of that kind of stuff?" As Martha had hoped, mention of his wife of eight months was enough to distract her father.

"Sue. She's been talking about it nonstop for two weeks. I'd have thought you'd have gotten the hint by now."

"You know I'm no good with hints. You could have given me a heads-up before now."

"Sorry, Dad. I just figured you knew."

"I guess I'd better get to work planning something. You be careful, you hear? And if you're not back by Sunday noon, I'm coming to get you. Love you, baby doll."

"Love you, too, Dad."

She started to shove the phone in her pocket, then thought better of it and tossed it into the glove compartment. Reception was poor in the mountains. Besides, she'd lost three phones in the past two years. A fact her ex-fiancé, Brian McMath, hadn't let her forget.

Not that she was going to think about Brian. Or their relationship. Or why she'd tried so hard to fulfill his definition of what a doctor's future wife should be.

Organized.

Efficient.

Sleek. Slim. Beautiful.

Martha stomped up the gravel road, forcing her mind away from her ex-fiancé. He'd been an arrogant jerk. She'd been too focused on trying to build the kind of family she'd always dreamed of to notice.

Enough said.

Rain began to fall, but she ignored it as she moved up the trail toward the hunting cabin. She *would* put her disastrous relationship with Brian behind her, and she would enjoy her weekend alone. Just Martha and the great outdoors. What could be better?

Forty minutes later, she was thinking there were plenty of things better than walking soaking wet through thick foliage, with chilly air cutting through her jacket and jeans. Panting hard, her heels burning with blisters from new boots, she splashed across a creek and muscled her way up a bank. All the physical exertion should have forced thoughts of Brian out of her mind, but they were still there.

Frustrated, she stomped up the cabin steps, pulled the key from her pocket and swung the door open. The place hadn't been used in a while, and watery light danced on dust motes as she hurried across the room to pull the curtains open. She'd barely touched the thick material, when she heard something behind her. Or maybe felt it. A subtle shifting in the air, a whisper of danger that electrified the room, made the hair on the back of her neck stand on end.

She wasn't alone.

Her heart pounded, her hand froze in place, her mind screamed directions that she couldn't quite follow.

Run!

No! Never run from a predator.

Walk *back out the open door. Pretend you don't know someone is here with you. Go. Go, go, go!*

Her legs were lead, the pack ten tons of brick as

she started toward the door. She'd barely taken a step when the door swung closed, cutting off light, sealing her in. It was like a nightmare, like a horror movie come to life. Dead silence. Pitch-blackness. Someone waiting in the darkness. Her heart thudded as terror pooled in her belly.

Please, God, I don't want to die like some clueless victim in a horror film.

She stepped backward, bumping into something hard, tall.

Human.

A scream ripped from her throat, but died abruptly as a hand slammed over her mouth.

"You don't want to do that." The growl rumbled in her ear; a warning, a threat. "Do you?"

Martha shook her head. Anything to get his hand off her mouth and give her another chance to scream. Not that it would do any good. There was no one around to hear. The cabin was miles from civilization.

"Good. Just keep quiet, do what I say and everything will be okay." As he spoke he moved backward, pulling her away from the door and farther into the darkness.

Don't just let yourself be accosted. Fight!

She slammed her elbow into his stomach, but his grip didn't loosen. "That wasn't smart, lady."

Maybe not, but she tried again anyway. This time slamming her foot down on his instep. He grunted, his grip loosening just enough for her to jerk from his hold. She lunged forward, yanking open the door, racing outside and slamming into a short, wiry man.

"Goin' somewhere, darlin'?" His eyes were pale, clear green, his lips thin and tilted up in a sneer. Freckles dotted his face, but they didn't make him look any less like a coldhearted killer. If death had a look, it was in his gaze. Martha shuddered, stepping back.

"I—"

"Nowhere without me. Right, Sunshine?" A hand dropped onto her shoulder and hard fingers urged her around to face the man who had followed her from the cabin.

Over six feet tall. Light hair. Hard features. Icy blue eyes filled with a message Martha couldn't decipher. He seemed to want her to agree, but Martha had no intention of going anywhere with him or his friend.

"No" was on the tip of her tongue, but before she could say it, the guy behind her spoke. "She's with you?"

"Sure is."

"Buddy won't like it."

"I don't see why he should care, but if it's going to be a problem, maybe I'll take my business elsewhere." He grabbed Martha's hand and pulled her down the porch steps, tension seeping through his palm and into hers. That only added to her anxiety and fear. Whatever was going on couldn't be good, and the sooner she escaped, the better.

"Hey, now wait just a minute." The smaller man

hurried up beside Martha, his eyes darting from her to her captor and back again. "I didn't say Buddy would care. I said he might not like it. But that's your problem. My problem is getting you to the meeting place. So let's go."

"Ready, Sunshine?" Her captor cupped Martha's chin, nudging her head up, gently but firmly forcing her to look into his eyes. Silvery-blue eyes that flashed with anger and something else, something softer, but just as fierce. Concern?

Martha blinked. No. That couldn't be right.

"I said, *are you ready?*" There was an edge to his voice, a warning, and Marti nodded because at the moment, she didn't have a choice. Eventually though, she would. And when she did, she'd take it.

Her gaze jumped away from his fierce intensity, landing on the thin man standing a few feet away.

He was still as stone, his empty eyes locked on Martha. Dead eyes. She wasn't sure how she knew that. Maybe some primal instinct kicking in, warning her. Whatever the case, she was sure the guy would kill her in a heartbeat if she gave him a reason. As if he sensed her thoughts, he smiled, his thin lips twisting up into something that should have been friendly but wasn't.

She looked away, meeting the other man's eyes, her heart beating so fast she thought it would leap from her chest. "Where are we going?"

"For a walk. Just relax and enjoy the scenery." He tightened his grip on her hand until it was just short of painful. He clearly didn't plan to let her go, but Martha didn't get the same sense of danger from him that she got from his friend.

She resisted the urge to pull away from his hold and make a run for it. After all, the key to winning a battle didn't lie in acting quickly. It lay in weighing the enemy's strengths, finding his weaknesses and exploiting them. Her father had told her that a hundred times, and she'd rolled her eyes just as many. Now what had seemed like useless information had value. She'd have to thank her father when she saw him again.

If she saw him again.

She shied away from the grim thought and focused her attention on the shorter of the two men. He had a cigarette pack sticking out of his pocket and was panting for breath as he hurried them toward a dirt road. Obviously out of shape, probably smoker's lungs. Martha figured she could beat him in a footrace.

The man holding her hand was another story. Tall, well muscled, long-legged, he was not even breathing deeply let alone panting. From where Martha was standing, he didn't seem to have any weaknesses. That could be a problem.

She stumbled over a root, rain slashing against her face and stinging her eyes as her captor's grip loosened a fraction, his hand sliding against hers.

Forget about looking for his weakness. Run!

She didn't consider the odds of success. As soon as she regained her footing, she yanked hard, her wet skin slipping from his grip, and ran toward the trees.

TWO

"Hey! What's going on? Why's she running?" Gordon Johnson's question was one Tristan Sinclair could have answered easily—the woman was running because she'd walked into a cabin she'd thought was empty and into a man she didn't know. She was terrified and trying to escape.

He *could* have answered, but he didn't.

Instead, he raced after the woman, determined to regain control of a mission that, until five minutes ago, had seemed ordinary.

Meet Johnson at an abandoned cabin near the base of the mountain. Follow him to an undisclosed location. Bring down one of the biggest illegal weapons rings in the country.

Piece of cake. Or as close to one as any mission like this could be.

So how had things gone so wrong so fast?

Tristan scowled as he closed in on the fleeing woman.

She was fast, dodging around trees and doing her

best to evade capture. Still, he managed to catch her easily, snagging the back of her pack and praying she wouldn't start screaming. Johnson had a reputation for acting first and thinking later, and there was no doubt the gunrunner would be carrying a weapon. One bullet, that's all it would take to spill innocent life out onto the rain-soaked earth. Tristan could only prevent that from happening if the woman cooperated. Judging from the expression in her eyes, that wasn't going to happen.

She swung a fist in his direction, and he grabbed it, tugging her so close he could feel her body trembling with fear. He wanted to tell her it was okay, that he was one of the good guys and that he'd make sure she got out of this alive, but Johnson was jogging toward them, and Tristan had no choice but to play the part he'd been perfecting for months.

He gave her a little shake, hoping to convey the urgency of the situation. "What's the deal with trying to run off on me, Sunshine? I thought you were over our little spat."

"Let me go—" She jerked against his hold, and he tightened his grip, afraid he might leave a bruise, but figuring a bruise was better than a bullet.

"I guess you're still mad. Which is too bad, because difficult women aren't my thing. For you, though, I might make an exception."

"You're insane. I don't kn—"

He pressed his lips to hers, cutting off her words in the only way he could think of that wouldn't make Johnson suspicious. Warmth, softness, the sweet scent of chocolate. He inhaled, drinking in the scent, the sound of rain fading, his heart leaping.

Pain shot up his leg as she slammed her foot down on his instep.

Again.

He maintained his grip, but jerked back, staring down into her eyes, surprised by his own reaction to the kiss and to the woman. Johnson was hovering near his back, just waiting to pull his weapon. There was no time for wondering about the woman who was staring up at him. No time for anything but action.

He leaned forward, holding her tight when she would have wrestled out of his grasp, and whispered in her ear, "If you don't want the day to get a whole lot worse, calm down and play along. Otherwise, we'll both be six feet under come daybreak. Understand?"

She didn't, of course. She'd wandered into her worst nightmare and all she'd be thinking about was escape.

Tristan, on the other hand, was thinking about turning potential failure into success. As long as Johnson didn't suspect the truth, the woman would be fine, the mission could continue and nearly a year working undercover and playing a role he had no liking for wouldn't go to waste.

"Do you understand?" He hissed the question into her ear, hoping she'd sense just how important the right answer was.

Maybe she did. Or maybe she was too scared to

argue. She nodded, her eyes wide with fear, sandy curls plastered to her cheeks, the baseball cap she wore sodden and dripping. She looked young, vulnerable, scared.

"Good." He kept his voice low so that it barely carried above the rain. "Here's how we're playing it. I'm Sky. You're my girlfriend. Got it?"

She nodded again, her gaze darting toward Johnson who was moving closer, apparently trying to hear their conversation.

"Whatever you say, *Sky*." Her voice shook, but she looked right into his eyes.

"Good," he said, speaking louder for Johnson's benefit. "Like I told you before, we've got this gig this afternoon. The rest of the night is ours." He squeezed her hand, hoping she'd take it as it was meant—a gesture of reassurance.

"You didn't tell me the *gig* would involve hiking in the rain. I came here to have fun. I'm not having fun. I'm going home." She huffed the words, managing to sound irritated and angry rather than scared. As if she really had been out on a lark with him and was annoyed that things weren't going the way she'd expected.

Not only did she seem to be gaining control of her emotions, she also seemed to be trying to take control of the situation. She'd offered a plausible explanation for walking away. Maybe Johnson would believe it and let her leave. "Go, but don't think I'll be calling tonight. I've got better things to do with my time than chase after a fickle woman." Tristan pulled keys from his pocket and tossed them her way, trying to play the part well enough to be convincing.

She caught them, her eyes widening a fraction. "I wasn't planning on waiting by the phone. See you around, Sky."

She pivoted away, the picture of an irritated woman, and Tristan started to believe they'd won this round. She'd return to civilization, report what had happened to the authorities. By that time, the raid would be over and the police would be able to tell her what she'd walked into and how close to death she'd been. Maybe she'd think twice the next time she went hiking through the Blue Ridge Mountains alone.

He should have known things wouldn't be so easy.

"You're not going nowhere. You wanted to come along. You're coming." Johnson moved in close, pulling a gun and pointing it at the woman, then Tristan. He'd use it, too. Kill them both the same way another person might swat a fly.

In other circumstances, Tristan would have tried to disarm him, but these weren't other circumstances. There was an innocent civilian to worry about, and he couldn't take chances with her life. "Cool it with the gun, man. You keep swinging it like that and someone could get hurt."

"Your lady friend keeps causing trouble and someone will."

"I'm not causing trouble. I'm saying I want to go home, but if you're going to get hot about it, I'll tag along with you two instead." She shrugged as if she really didn't care, her movements confident and easy as they started moving again.

Who was she? Not your typical civilian, that was for sure. No panic. No begging or pleading. If Tristan hadn't known better, he would have thought she was a fellow agent. He took a harder look. Short. Pretty. Athletic build. Dressed in jeans, a nylon jacket and hiking boots, she looked like any other weekend camper, but most normal people were tucked inside cozy houses sitting beside blazing fires, not traipsing through the mountains in frigid rain.

Normal?

As if he knew what that was anymore.

Living undercover didn't leave room for normal. It only left room for the job. And right now the job suddenly included the woman trudging along beside him. He kept a firm grip on her arm as they walked. No way could he let her go running off again. Not when he knew Johnson was just waiting for an opportunity to get rid of her. Permanently.

She slipped and nearly went down on her knees, but he managed to tug her up before she landed. "Careful. The leaves are making things dangerous."

She laughed, the sound choking out and cutting off almost before it had begun.

Surprised, Tristan scanned her face. Rainwater slid down smooth cheeks, freckles dotted her pale cheeks, gold and green mixed in the depth of her eyes, soft lips pressed together.

Lips he'd kissed.

Lips that had been softer and warmer than he'd expected.

Whoa! That wasn't the direction his thoughts should be heading. He forced his attention back to the moment, to the mission, to his role. "I'm glad you're keeping your sense of humor, Sunshine. It makes life a lot easier."

"I wouldn't call it humor."

"No?"

"No. I'd call it hysteria, and if I wasn't afraid your friend would pull out his gun and shoot me dead for it, I'd probably be laughing uncontrollably right now."

"You're right to be worried about that. Johnson isn't known for his self-control."

"Maybe if you'd tell me what's going on—"

He pressed a finger to her lips, cutting off her words before she could say something that would get them both in trouble. Johnson might seem oblivious to the conversation, but Tristan knew him well enough to know he didn't miss much. Not when it had to do with the business he was in. The business of death. "Nothing is going on that we haven't already discussed. You need to relax and enjoy the experience."

"Right. Sure. Enjoy it." She wiped rain from her eyes, or maybe those were tears. It was hard to tell with so much water pouring from the sky.

Up ahead, Johnson was shoving through more brush, leading them northwest toward the abandoned logging camp that served as meeting place and auction house for Johnson's boss Buddy Nichols's gun-running activities. There'd been other auctions before today, other buyers leaving with weapons meant to kill and maim, weapons that even the most sophisticated armor couldn't stop.

Today, though, was going to be different. Johnson might think Tristan was clueless about their destination, but informants had been willing to leak the auction's location to the ATF for a price. A few hours. That's all that stood between the men who were dealing in illegal weapons and justice.

Tristan smiled with grim satisfaction, holding a thorny branch back and motioning for the woman to step past. One gunrunner, one gang leader, one weapon at a time, he was doing what he'd pledged to do after his brother had been shot and almost killed—evening the odds, adding one more good guy to the fight against the bad guys. Now, though, he had something else to think about. Some*one* else. An unknown player in an unpredictable game.

As if she sensed his thoughts, the woman glanced his way, her expression hiding whatever she felt. "How much farther?"

"Not much."

"Which could mean anything." She frowned, wiping at her face again. Rain. Not tears. Tristan was pretty sure of that.

"Which means we'll be there soon. Then this will be over and we'll be out of here." Anything else was unacceptable. Anything else could leave one or both of them dead. "Just keep your head together, Sunshine, and everything will be fine."

"Hurry it up, you two. We've got places to be." Johnson shot a look over his shoulder, his flat eyes settling on the woman.

Tristan didn't like the surge of interest that blazed in his eyes, the flash of heat that brought the only hint of life he'd ever seen into Johnson's gaze.

He dropped his arm across Sunshine's shoulder, praying she wouldn't jerk away and give Johnson something else to speculate on. "Pick up the pace then. We'll keep up."

As Johnson turned away again, Tristan let his arm slip from Sunshine's shoulders, grabbing her hand instead, squeezing gently and silently sealing their partnership. Whether she liked it or not, they were in this together. Lord willing, they'd make it out together, too.

THREE

Martha told herself she shouldn't be comforted by the warm, callused palm pressing against hers, or by the well-muscled arm brushing her shoulder. Somehow though, she was. Which proved just how scared she was. She didn't know Sky, and she didn't trust him.

What she did trust were her instincts, and right now they were telling her that flat-eyed, freckle-faced Johnson was a killer. The gun he'd pulled had been a Glock 22, a weapon so powerful that the bullet would kill her before she had time to realize she was dying.

The thought made her shiver.

She didn't want to die today. She wasn't *going* to die. She had too many things she still wanted to accomplish. That cross-stitch project she'd planned to make for Dad and Sue's anniversary but had never finished. The missions trip to Mexico. The vacation to Australia she'd been dreaming about since she was old enough to have dreams. The ten pounds she wanted to lose so she could fit into flirty little summer dresses.

Not that her size was going to matter when she was lying inside a coffin.

Don't even go there, Marti.

You are not *going to die.*

At least, she hoped she wasn't going to die. Who knew what God's plans were? She sure didn't. Every time she thought she had a handle on what He wanted for her life, He spun her around and started her in a new direction. Case in point—Brian. She'd been so sure he was the one, so certain God had brought them together. Funny how easy it was to believe something was right when you wanted it badly enough. Even funnier how little all of that mattered in light of the fact that she might not survive the next few hours.

Rain continued to fall as they picked their way along an overgrown road, the raindrops like tears that streaked the earth and trees, muddling the colors so that they blended and bled. Probably washing away any evidence that Martha and the two men had passed this way, too. She glanced around, trying to get her bearings, and realized with a start that they were heading toward an abandoned logging camp. She and her dad had hiked this way many times before, even staying overnight in the cabin that had once served as an office. There wasn't much left of the place—a couple of rusted trailers, the cabin. Another half century and the entire place would be overgrown and covered with vegetation.

What kind of business would take place so far from civilization?

What kind of men would be there?

Not the kind of business she wanted to be involved in. Not the kind of men she should be around.

Yet here she was, going where she didn't want to go, with men she shouldn't be with, and she had absolutely no idea how to get out of the situation.

Any time you're ready, Lord, I'm open for suggestions.

She hoped for sudden inspiration, a quick solution to her troubles. She got nothing.

Her fingers itched to unzip her pack and pull out one of her chocolate bars. A little sugar, a little energy and maybe her brain would start functioning and she could figure a way out of the situation. She started to shrug out of the pack, but froze as Sky speared her with a hard stare. "What are you doing?"

Johnson must have heard because he turned, his dead eyes jumping from Martha to Sky and back again. "What's going on?"

Don't panic. Be a ditzy, stupid woman who thought it would be adventurous to wander through the Blue Ridge Mountains with Sky and his friends.

She forced herself to let the pack slide the rest of the way down her arms. "Just thinking I'd have a snack."

"A snack?" Sky's jaw twitched, his blue eyes boring into hers.

She forced strength back into legs that had gone wobbly and did her best to act as if she didn't know how much danger she was in. "Yes. A snack. A girl's got to eat. Right? It's not like you gave me a chance to have lunch before we left."

"Let me give you a hand with that." Johnson yanked the pack from her hands, his eyes gleaming with the hard gaze of a predator and filling Martha with cold dread.

"Knock yourself out."

He rifled through the pack, then thrust it at Sky. "No more stops."

"Or else" hung in the air, unspoken, but Martha heard it clearly enough. She was also pretty sure that if she looked hard enough, she could see the outline of Johnson's gun beneath the lightweight jacket he wore. It would take only seconds for him to pull it, fire it and wash his probably-already-stained-with-blood hands of the situation.

Fear loosened her muscles and joints and made walking almost impossible. Only Sky's firm grip on her hand kept her going. She wanted to go home to her little cottage in the woods, sit on the front porch and watch the sunset behind the mountains one last time; bask in the colors, the feel, the scent of it. Crisp, cool, alive. She wanted to hug her father, tell him she loved him, kiss his leathery cheek just *once* more. Wanted to go out with her girlfriends, have a slice of Doris's apple pie, inhale the scent of laughter, the heady aroma of joy.

Hot tears worked their way down her cheek, mixing with cold rain.

"Chocolate?" Sky's question pulled her away from her maudlin thoughts.

She glanced at the candy bar he was holding out and knew she'd choke if she tried to eat it. "I changed my mind."

"A little energy will do you good." He unwrapped the chocolate, pressed the bar into her hand. "Eat and stop worrying."

To her surprise, he wiped the hot tears from her cheeks, pressing his palm against her chilled flesh, his voice warm as a spring day. "Everything will be okay. I promise."

"Promises are a dime a dozen."

"Not mine. You *will* be okay. There is no other option." He stared into her eyes as if he could pass his confidence to her with a look.

Then the moment was gone. He reached for the candy bar, broke a piece of chocolate off and popped it into his mouth. "Looks like we've reached our destination. Showtime."

With that, he hiked her pack onto his back and pulled her toward the skeletal remains of the logging camp.

Fear was a terrible thing. It made thinking impossible. It made smart people act dumb. And that's exactly what it was doing to Martha. She wanted to yank her hand from Sky's and run, but that would not only be the stupidest decision of her life, it would also be her last. Sky would catch her before she got three feet away if Johnson's bullet hadn't already knocked her to the ground.

The way Martha saw it, she'd done enough stupid things in the past few months to last a lifetime. First she'd dated a guy who had a reputation for being arrogant and thoughtless. Second, she'd continued to date him even after she'd begun to suspect those rumors were true. Third, she'd decided to run and hide rather than face more pity from her friends and family when she'd finally broken things off with the jerk.

Now she was officially done with stupidity.

It was time to be smart. That meant waiting no matter how much she wanted to run. Eventually she'd have a chance to escape. She had to believe that.

Up ahead, thick trees opened into an overgrown field filled with the remnants of a once bustling logging camp. Martha hadn't been there in years, but from what she remembered, things hadn't changed much. The place was just a little older, a little more overgrown, a lot more creepy. Then again, maybe Martha was just more creeped out. To the left, an old trailer sat atop a cinder-block foundation, graffiti bleeding down the side in reds and blues and greens. Stumps and fallen logs stood to one side, skeletons of the life that had once been there.

In the distance, the clapboard cabin where Martha and her father used to stay stood blurry and gray in the pouring rain. Several men moved toward it ahead of Martha and her escorts, their tension filling the clearing and adding to Martha's fear. She didn't much care for the men she'd already met. She definitely didn't want to meet more.

"Maybe I'll wait out here." She tugged against

Sky's hold, but he didn't loosen his grip. Nor did he slow his pace. They were heading toward the kind of trouble Martha had never dreamed she would find herself in, and it didn't seem as though there was much she could do about it.

"You'll wait where I tell you to wait. Right in that trailer over there. After me and your friend are finished with business, we'll decide what to do with you." Johnson speared her with a cold, hard glare, his voice chilling in its callousness.

What to do with her? As if she were some disposable thing. Martha's heart raced, her breath came in short, shallow spurts. *This* was terror. Pure and stark and ugly. She forced it back, not wanting Johnson to see just how scared she was. "I'd rather—"

"I don't care what you'd rather. In the trailer. Now."

Johnson pulled his gun, pointed it at her chest.

"Cool it, Johnson." Sky stepped between Martha and the gun, his hand still wrapped around Martha's wrist.

"Do we have a problem?" The words were smooth as honey and cold as ice. A new voice, a new player, another danger. Marti didn't need to see the man to know it, she could hear it in his voice.

"Nothing that isn't being dealt with." Johnson still had his gun out, but his focus had shifted, his eyes on the man who was walking toward them— medium height, well dressed. Power. Wealth. Danger. They oozed off him. It was his eyes, though, that turned Martha's insides to mush. If Johnson's eyes were dead, this guy's eyes were *death*. There was evil there, a blackness that no amount of polish could hide.

He moved toward them, his gaze resting on Martha briefly before he turned his attention to Sky. "You're Sky Davis. We were wondering if you'd show up."

"I got a little sidetracked."

"So I see." Soulless eyes rested on Martha again, and she resisted the urge to look away. "I'm Buddy. You'll have to forgive Johnson's overreaction to your friend. He's very zealous about his job. We've got client confidentiality to protect."

"Understood." Sky spoke before Martha could. Which was for the best as she could think of nothing to say.

"Then maybe next time you won't bring a... friend." He glanced at Martha again. "It makes things complicated."

"She's a member of the Blue Ridge Mountains Militia. I'm teaching her the ropes."

"Not here you're not. She'll have to wait in the trailer. We'll deal with her after we've concluded our business." He nodded toward Johnson who strode forward, grabbing her arm.

"Hold on a minute." Sky pulled her back toward him, and she was sure he was going to protest, come up with some reason they had to stay together.

Instead, he pulled her close, leaning forward, staring into her eyes. "Don't worry, Sunshine. This won't take long."

He pressed his lips to the sensitive flesh behind her ear, his words barely a whisper. "Sorry about this."

Then he kissed her.

Not the bland, almost sterile kind of kiss Brian usually offered. Not a hard, quick kiss to silence her. A searing kiss that burned its way down her spine. A toe-curling, heart-pounding, honest-to-goodness, Prince-Charming-I'm-gonna-love-you-forever-type kiss.

Too bad the guy was a stranger.

Too bad Martha was scared out of her mind.

Too bad.

Because if he wasn't, if she hadn't been, she just might have enjoyed it.

"Mr. Davis." Buddy's voice drawled into the moment, cold and slithery as a snake. "Sorry to interrupt your moment, but we've got business to attend."

Sky released his hold on Martha and she nearly fell.

He didn't give her another look, just walked toward the cabin with Buddy, while Johnson moved closer to Martha, waving the gun toward the trailer. "Let's go."

He grabbed her arm and yanked her forward, nearly dragging her the few yards to the trailer, his grip painfully tight. She didn't complain, though. No way would she give him that power over her. Let him think she was tough, that what he was doing didn't scare her. Let him think that she really was Sky's girlfriend, out for a jaunt and too dense to realize she wasn't going to survive it.

Please, Lord, let him think that.

Because if he did, if they all did, then they wouldn't be expecting her to escape—they wouldn't waste the time and effort guarding her, and she just might have a chance.

Johnson opened the trailer door and shoved her with enough force to send her sprawling on a pile of dirt, trash and other things she'd rather not examine. Before she could right herself, the door slammed shut, cutting off light. A key scraped in a lock, and Martha heard a bolt slide home.

Obviously, Marti wasn't the first to be locked in here. She'd be the last, though, because once she escaped, she was going to the authorities and she was going to shut down whatever illegal activities were going on here.

Her eyes adjusted to the darkness, and she surveyed the room. Trash. Debris. Probably snakes, rats and mice, too. Not her favorite things to share space with, but a lot better than the men outside.

And at least here she wasn't in danger of having a bullet put through her heart.

The thought got her moving across the room to a plywood board that she was sure covered a window. All she had to do was pry it off, slip out the opening and run. She searched the debris for a tool, her mind ticking away the seconds and telling her she was running out of time. Finally, desperate, she wedged her fingernails under the board and pulled.

Pain speared through her hands, her nails bending back as the board gave slightly. Blood seeped from the wounds, but she ignored it, shoving her fingers into the wider space she'd created.

"Please, Lord. Please let this work."

She braced her legs, yanking against the plywood with all her strength. It gave with a crack, and she tumbled backward, landing hard on a pile of garbage. Stunned, she lay still for a moment, her pulse racing frantically, demanding that she get up and go. Now. Before someone decided to check on her.

She stood, her thoughts jumping forward, planning a path through the forest that wouldn't be easy to follow, but that would lead her back to her Jeep and her cell phone quickly. She'd call for help while she was driving away.

Her keys!

They were in her backpack. The one with an identification card that listed her name and address. The one that Sky had taken from her. The one that Johnson could just as easily take from him.

This wasn't good. It wasn't good at all.

For a moment she didn't move, just stood frozen in place unsure of what to do.

"Don't be an idiot. Of course you're sure. If you don't get out of here soon, Johnson won't have to use the identification card to find you, because you'll be dead." She muttered the words as she hurried to the window and peered outside.

Rain still poured from the steel-gray sky, the sound masking any noise she might make as she dropped to the ground. For a moment she hesitated, her mind conjuring an image of Sky as he'd looked when he'd stood between Johnson's gun and Martha. Fierce, protective. Heroic. Would he be blamed for Martha's escape? Would he be hurt because of her?

She shook her head, forcing the thoughts away. Sky knew what he was doing, and whatever it was had only become more complicated because of Martha's presence. Without her to worry about, he could easily do whatever it took to survive. She knew it as surely as she knew that staying and waiting for him to return might get them both killed.

She eyed the tufts of overgrown grass that were fifteen feet below, scanned the area, then hoisted herself onto the window ledge.

"Lord, I just need a little head start. Can You help me with that? Because I'm pretty sure that on my own, I'm in big trouble. And while You're at it, could You watch out for Sky, too?" She whispered the prayer as she twisted, grabbed the windowsill and slid out into the rain. Suspended by her throbbing fingers, she took a deep breath and willed herself to drop.

FOUR

Tristan glanced at his watch as Buddy pulled a sleek M16 from a box Johnson handed him and held it up for his audience—a ragtag group of militia men from various organizations around the area. The auction was underway and in two minutes an organized team of law enforcement officials would stream from the woods and take everyone present into custody. It was what Tristan had spent months working toward. Knowing it was about to happen should have filled him with satisfaction. Instead, he was worried. If guns were fired, if bullets flew, Martha Gabler was a sitting duck. The trailer she was in offered about as much protection from Buddy's arsenal of weapons as a sheet of aluminum foil.

He waited until Johnson stepped into a back room to retrieve another case of weapons, then slipped from his position at the back of the crowd and walked out the open cabin door. By the time Johnson realized he was gone, Tristan would have Martha out of the trailer and to safety.

That was the plan anyway. Tristan prayed it would go off without a hitch.

He jogged across the clearing, planning to open the front door of the trailer and hustle Martha out. Before he reached the steps, a muffled scream and quiet splash sounded above the pouring rain.

Apparently the woman he'd dubbed Sunshine hadn't needed his help escaping after all.

Tristan switched directions, racing around the side of the trailer just in time to see Martha struggling to her feet. He didn't give her time to react, just lunged forward, grabbing her arm and tugging her toward the trees. "Next time you attempt an escape, you might want to keep the volume down."

"There isn't going to be a next time, because if I live through this one I'm never leaving my house again." Her teeth chattered on the last word, her face devoid of color.

"You're going to be fine, Sunshine." He'd barely gotten the words out when the world exploded. Gunfire. Shouts. White-hot pain sliced through his upper arm, warm blood seeping down his bicep. Dark figures swarmed from the trees, surrounding them as Martha screamed.

"Freeze! Police! Hands on your head. Down on the ground. Down! Down! Do it now."

Tristan did as he was commanded, pulling Martha with him. Cold, wet earth seeping through his clothes. It was over. Martha was alive. He was alive. God had gotten them both through. The rest was gravy.

An officer frisked him, cuffed him and pulled him to his feet, calling in a request for hospital transport as he eyed the blood seeping down Tristan's arm. Tristan barely heard. He was looking around, searching for something he didn't see. *Someone* he didn't see. Martha stood a few feet away surrounded by uniformed men and women. Her baseball cap gone, her hair plastered against her pale face, mud streaking her cheeks. She must have sensed his gaze, because she met his eyes, tried to smile, but failed.

Tristan wasn't smiling, either.

Something was wrong. Really wrong.

No way had law enforcement started the gunfight. Someone else had pulled a weapon, and Tristan was certain he knew who that someone was. Gordon Johnson had no qualms about shooting a man in the back. No doubt he'd been intent on doing just that. And no doubt he would have been successful if his aim hadn't been ruined by…what? A gunshot wound?

Tristan turned to the police officer. "Who started the gunfight? Your men? Did they shoot someone?"

"We're the ones asking the questions here."

The officer shoved Tristan forward, apparently not knowing Tristan was one of the good guys and not caring that blood was seeping down his arm, or that the bone was most likely broken.

Tristan couldn't say he blamed the guy. The guns being auctioned today were the latest in advanced armor-busting weaponry. The kind that killed cops.

"Look, if the guy who shot me isn't in custody,

you'd better make sure you find him. He's Buddy's right-hand man. If he escapes, there's going to be trouble."

The officer stopped walking and turned to Tristan, something flashing in his eyes. Maybe concern. Maybe recognition of Tristan's humanity. Whatever it was, he shrugged. "The guy was coming around the trailer with his gun drawn as we were moving in. Must have seen something that spooked him because he jumped back behind it just as he fired."

"And he's not in custody?"

"Couldn't tell you. Seems to me, though, that you should be a little bit more concerned about yourself and less concerned about your buddy."

"He's not my buddy." Tristan couldn't say more. Not here. Maintaining cover until he was brought away in handcuffs was part of his job. If the wrong person saw him being chummy with cops, he'd have a difficult time working undercover again.

"Right." The officer said something to one of the other uniforms, and walked away.

Tristan tried to relax. Tried to tell himself that he'd accomplished his goal—Martha was safe.

He didn't believe it. Not if Johnson had escaped. The man didn't believe in leaving loose ends, and Martha was definitely that.

He grimaced at the thought, blood seeping in warm rivulets into his palm, his head swimming as the officer he'd been left with marched him toward the other handcuffed felons in the center of the clearing.

Officers and agents milled around, relaxed. Smiling. Box after box of weapons were being numbered and photographed. Thousands of dollars' worth of death confiscated. Hundreds of lives saved. The raid had been a success. A huge one.

Tristan should be happy. He wasn't.

It was over, but not over.

The knowledge edged out pain and frustration, his worry throbbing hotly as he was escorted to an ATV and taken to the main road.

It was over. Marti told herself that again and again as she sat in a small room at the Lynchburg Police Department, visions of cold-eyed killers and blood filling her head. Her hands trembled as she lifted the cup of coffee a female officer had brought in forty minutes ago. Forty minutes. It seemed like hours.

She stood, testing her still-shaky legs as she moved to the door. They held her weight. Barely. Since the moment she'd turned and seen blood seeping from Sky's upper arm, her body seemed to have a mind of its own, her muscles loose, her limbs ungainly. Shaky, unsure, out of sync with her brain. It was like walking in a dream or a nightmare. Only she wasn't asleep.

A soft knock sounded at the door and Martha stepped back as a stocky, dark-haired man strode into the room, his expression neutral. "Ms. Gabler? I'm Officer Miller. Sorry for keeping you waiting."

"It's okay."

"Can I get you something else to drink? A soda? Water?"

"No. Thanks. I'd just like to go home."

"We'll let you go soon. Right now, I need you to tell me what happened this afternoon."

Tell him what happened? Martha wasn't even sure she *knew* what had happened. One minute she'd been stepping into her dad's hunting cabin, the next she'd been running. Guns going off, men shouting. Total chaos. Sky bleeding. She shuddered, taking a seat again. "I just wanted to spend a weekend in the mountains."

She told the rest as quickly as she could, filling in as many details as she remembered until her words ran out and she had nothing more to say. "That's it."

"Great." Officer Miller looked up from the notebook he was scribbling in. "I think that's all I need. Let me just check on a few more things and we'll get you out of here."

"Before you go, I was wondering, is Sky okay?"

"Sky?"

"He was shot in the arm."

"Sky. Right. He should be fine."

"*Should* be fine? How bad was his injury?"

"As far as I know, it's not life-threatening."

"But—"

"Ma'am, you've had a long day. I'm sure you're anxious to get home. Give me a few minutes and I'll make sure that happens." He cut her off, closing the notebook and leaving the room, firmly ending the conversation.

Which should have been fine with Martha.

After all, he'd said Sky's injuries weren't life-threatening. She didn't need any more information than that. As long as he hadn't died trying to save her, she should be willing to let the matter drop.

She wasn't. She wanted to know more. Was Sky in jail? Was he going to be charged with a felony?

How had a guy who'd willingly risked his life for a stranger ended up a criminal? It took uncommon courage to step between a bullet and another person. It took valor. Heroism. It took the kind of grit most people didn't have.

Sky had it, yet he'd been in the mountains to buy illegal weapons. That's what Martha had been told by police, and she'd seen the evidence of those weapons as officers led her to waiting vehicles. Still, the gunrunning militia member didn't seem to mesh with the courageous hero, and the dichotomy bothered Martha.

She shook her head, forcing her mind away from Sky Davis. Hero or not, he'd committed a crime. He was going to pay for it, and *she* was going to forget him and move on with her life.

She really was.

She was still telling herself that as Officer Miller returned and escorted her outside into the cool gray evening. Her car was still parked in the mountains where she'd left it, so she accepted Miller's offer of a ride. Her only other choice was to call her father or a friend, and either of those options would have involved explaining everything that had happened.

She didn't want to go there again tonight.

Tomorrow, she'd find someone to help her get her car.

Tomorrow, she'd tell everyone about her experience.

Tonight, she'd just pretend that her life hadn't changed. That she hadn't become a different person. A person who suddenly understood her own limitations. Her own mortality.

Dusk tinged the white siding of Martha's story-and-a-half blue-gray Victorian and shadowed the small front porch with darkness as Officer Miller pulled up the dirt driveway. Cute and quaint when the sun was bright, the place looked lonely and old in the twilight.

Martha hesitated as Miller pulled her door open, suddenly not so sure she wanted to be alone.

"You live here by yourself?"

"Yes."

"Maybe I should call someone to come stay with you. A friend? Relative? Boyfriend?" His dark eyes scanned her face, and Martha wondered what he saw. Certainly not the delicate fragility that embodied so many of her female friends. She was more likely to be called tough than vulnerable, strong than weak. Sometimes she thought that was a good thing. She didn't want or need to be taken care of by anyone. Other times, like now, she wished she looked a little more like a delicate rose than a hardy dandelion. Then maybe Officer Miller would have taken the decision out of her hands instead of giving her a choice.

Because, really, there was no choice. Dad had taught her to face her fears head-on, not to rely on others when she could just as easily depend on herself. She'd learned the lesson well. "No, I'll be fine. Thanks for the ride."

"All right. Here's my business card. Call me if you have any questions." He walked her to the door, watching as she lifted the welcome mat and pulled out the spare key.

"Might be best not to leave that there anymore. It's the first place an intruder will look if he's trying to get in."

Twenty-four hours ago, Marti would have scoffed at the idea of someone wanting to break into her modest home. Now, she could imagine it happening; imagine a man skulking in the nearby woods, waiting until the lights went out and then creeping up onto the porch. She shuddered. "I won't."

Her hand shook as she shoved the key into the lock and pushed the door open. Safely inside, she offered Officer Miller a quick wave, then shut the door and locked it again. Maybe she should put the couch in front of it, too. Just for a little added security.

Of course, that would mean she'd also need to block all the windows. And the back door. Maybe even the chimney.

"You are not going to turn paranoid because of what happened. You're *not*."

She spoke out loud as she turned on the table lamps, letting their bright yellow glow chase away some of the shadows. This was her house. Her safe haven. A place she'd bought because of its peaceful ambience and tranquil setting. She wasn't going to let Gordon Johnson or his boss take that away from her.

Tomorrow would be a whole new day. The sun would come up. The sky would lighten, and today's nightmare would fade from memory. Until then, she'd just cling to the knowledge that God was with her, that He hadn't saved her life for nothing. He'd keep her safe. No matter how dark the night, or how dangerous the monsters that lurked in it.

FIVE

The phone rang just after seven Sunday morning, dragging Marti from restless, nightmare-filled sleep. She scowled as the answering machine picked up and Jennifer Gardner's soft Southern drawl filled the room. "Marti? Jenny, here. I heard what happened Friday and was calling to see if you needed me to fill in on nursery duty for you. Adam and I just got back from Cancún. It was absolutely the most relaxing, fantastic place to honeymoon. Maybe you and Brian... Oh, I am *so* sorry. I did hear that the two of you broke up." Her pause was dramatic and typical Jennifer. Marti could almost imagine the dark-haired beauty pressing the phone close to her ear, hoping Marti would feel compelled to answer.

She didn't.

She'd spent the previous day fielding calls from friends, acquaintances, local newspaper reporters. She did not plan to add to that by explaining the situation to Jennifer, who, if she'd taken the time to check things out, would have realized that Martha had found someone to replace her in the nursery as soon as she'd decided to spend the weekend in the mountains.

"Marti? Are you there? You do know you're signed up to work in the toddler nursery, don't you?"

"Yes. I know. And, no, I don't need anyone to fill in for me. Even if I did, I wouldn't ask a lacquer-nailed, overly hair-sprayed former homecoming queen who knows as much about kids as I do about curling irons." Marti muttered the words as she turned down the volume of the answering machine, muting the rest of Jennifer's long message.

Her attitude stunk, and Martha knew it, but she seemed helpless to get a handle on her irritation. Chalk it up to lack of sleep, or too many nightmares. Whatever the case, there was no way she planned to spend another day answering the phone and being nice to people who were more interested in gossip than in her well-being. She was going out. Not just out. She was going to church. At least there most of the people truly cared about how she was doing.

She grabbed a dress from her closet, barely noticing the color or style as she hurried to shower and change. Her ears strained for sounds that didn't belong, her heart pounding a quick, erratic beat. No matter how many times she told herself she was safe, she couldn't seem to shake the fear that had been nipping at her heels all weekend.

When she was a kid, she hadn't been afraid of monsters under the bed or bogeymen in closets. It seemed ironic that she was now. Every noise, every shadow made her jump. Every night was filled with potential danger.

Worse, her hands were still shaking, her pulled-back nails throbbing as she grabbed a brush and raked it through her hair. The pain reminded her of the desperate moments in the trailer; the danger just outside the metal prison she'd been trapped in. Johnson's dead eyes staring at her. Memorizing her.

Her heart leaped at the thought, and she took a deep breath. Johnson was surely in jail now. She would never see him again. The thought should have been comforting, but wasn't. She swept blush across her cheeks, hoping to liven her pale face. It didn't help. She still looked pale. Still looked scared. But she was going to church.

Because there was no way she was going to let fear control her. She smiled at her reflection. There. That was better. All she had to do was pretend she was fine. Eventually, she'd believe it.

She grabbed her purse and Bible. A few hours away from the house would be good for her. Maybe after church she'd visit Sue and Dad, beg a home-cooked meal off them. At least then she wouldn't have to be alone.

Until tonight. When it was dark again and memories of gunshots and blood filled her dreams.

She shuddered, stepping out into cool, crisp air.

"You clean up good, Sunshine." The deep rumble cut through the morning quiet, and Marti whirled toward the speaker. Tall. Light hair. Icy blue eyes that raked her from head to toe. A slight smile curving firm lips. Left arm in a sling that couldn't hide the thick muscles of biceps and shoulders.

"Sky?"

"Actually, it's Tristan. Tristan Sinclair." He moved up the porch stairs, and Marti took a step back, not sure if she should run into the house or stand her ground. He'd saved her life, but he'd also been responsible for dragging her through the mountains with Gordon Johnson. He was a militia member. A man who dealt in illegal weapons. Who hung out with murderers and felons. Who was supposed to be in jail.

"What do you want? Why aren't you in prison?"

"To make sure you're safe, and because I didn't commit a crime."

"You were in the mountains to buy illegal weapons. That's a felony."

"It would be if that's what I had been doing."

"So you're saying you weren't?"

"I'm saying things aren't always what they seem. Now, how about we go inside to discuss this?"

"Anything we need to say can be said out here."

"It can be, but that might not be for the best. You're not safe, Sunshine. The sooner you realize that, the better."

"Is that a threat?" Her heart slammed a quick, hard beat as she reached for the doorknob. He was close, but not so close that she couldn't get inside the house and lock the door before he grabbed her. She hoped.

"It's a warning. Gordon Johnson escaped into the mountains Friday. He still hasn't been apprehended."

Johnson had escaped? A shiver of fear raced up Marti's spine. "Why didn't the police tell me this?"

"You'll have to ask them that."

"I will." The hollow thud of her heart echoed in her ears as she turned and shoved the door open. Of all the men she'd run into Friday, Johnson was the one she most feared. The one whose lifeless eyes haunted her dreams. If he was really out there somewhere, she wanted to know. She'd call Officer Miller. He'd be able to tell her what was going on.

The soft click of the door and the quiet slide of the bolt pulled her from numb fear. Or maybe *dumb* fear was a better term. She'd just let the man who'd kidnapped her walk into her house!

She whirled to face Tristan.

He stood just a few feet away, leaning against the door, blocking her escape. She could run for the back door, but he'd be on her before then.

The phone! Grab the phone and call for help.

She lifted the receiver. "I'm calling the police."

"Good idea. Tell Officer Miller I found your place just fine."

Marti hesitated with the phone halfway to her ear. "You spoke to him?"

"He said you were asking about my injury." He flashed white teeth, but Marti wouldn't exactly call the expression a smile. "He also said you lived off the beaten path at the end of a dead-end street. Not the most secure house in the world. He was right."

He was telling the truth. She knew it. What she didn't know was why he was in her house and not in jail. She hung up the phone. "Who are you? And I don't mean your name."

"Tristan Sinclair. ATF agent. I was working undercover the day we ran into each other."

ATF? It made sense. A sick, crazy kind of sense. "Ran into each other? You kidnapped me and pulled me into the biggest illegal firearms raid in a decade." Something the newscasters had made mention of over and over again as they'd covered the story. Something everyone but Marti seemed to find fascinating.

"I kept you safe until reinforcements could come in and bring you out."

And he'd saved her life. He didn't point that out. Brian would have. He would have been announcing his feat to the world, making appointments with television shows and radio programs, planning a book and movie deal, telling Marti again and again how fortunate she was to have him.

"Sorry if I sounded ungrateful. You saved my life, and I really do appreciate it. Thanks."

"You saved yourself, Sunshine. I just helped a little."

"And got shot doing it. How's your arm?"

"Better."

"Than?"

"Than being dead." He smiled, but Martha didn't think Tristan's potential death was amusing.

"That's not funny."

"No, but I'm celebrating survival, so I'm trying to find a lot to smile about." He smiled again, and some of the tension that had been coiled inside Martha eased. It felt good to be talking to someone who knew what had happened to her and didn't need to ask questions about it. Someone who had shared her experience and could show her how to put it in perspective.

"I guess if you can smile about it, I can, too."

"And you should. You've got a beautiful smile." His gaze dropped to her lips, lingered there for a moment before he met her eyes again.

Her cheeks flamed, her heart jumped, and she resisted the urge to smooth her hair, fidget with her dress. She did not need to look good for Tristan Sinclair. Sure, he'd saved her life, but he was still a man. And men were something she'd decided less than a week ago that she could do without.

She needed to keep that in mind, or she might end up exactly where she didn't want to be—nursing a broken heart and mourning the death of her dreams. Again. It was time to put some distance between herself and Tristan.

"Look, I hate to shove you out, but I've got to be at church in less than thirty minutes."

"Good. Let's go." He took her arm, started walking toward the door.

That was easy. A lot easier than Martha had expected it to be. Relieved, she allowed herself to be ushered out the door and down the porch steps.

A cool breeze carried the scent of Tristan's after-shave. Pine needles and campfire smoke, crisp fall air and winter wind. Everything outdoorsy and good. All the things Marti loved most about God's creation.

"Thanks again for saving my life, Tristan. I know you said I saved myself, but we both know it's not true."

"Do we?" He took the keys from her hand, unlocked the door and carried the key chain with him as he rounded the car.

"Hey! I need those if I'm going to get to church."

"I know. I'll give them back to you in a second." He opened the passenger door, slid into the car and held the keys out to her, a grin easing the hard angles of his face.

Her heart leaped, her brain froze. He was in her car. In. Her. Car. And she had absolutely no idea what to do about it. She leaned in the open door, stared him in the eye, hoping she looked less flustered than she felt. "What are you doing?"

"Making sure you get to church in one piece."

"I've been driving to church on my own for years. I'm sure I can manage it today."

"Unless you run into Johnson."

"He won't try anything in the middle of broad daylight when anyone might see him." At least, she didn't think he would.

"Sunshine, you don't know much about men like Johnson. He's not going to just forget that you saw him Friday, that you heard his name, that you could sit in court and identify him. He and I both saw your name on the card inside your pack. There's no way he forgot it. He's going to come after you and he's not going to wait until it's dark, or you're alone, or until some time when it's convenient for you. He'll strike when he's good and ready. For all either of us know, he's ready now. Until he's caught, you need to be careful."

"I know I need to be careful. And I will, but that doesn't mean having a personal bodyguard."

"I think it does." He grabbed her hand, tugged her farther into the car. "And since I took a bullet for you, I think I should have some say in these things."

"I can't believe you're using that against me after you said I saved my own life."

"Whatever works, Sunshine." He tugged hard, and she almost tumbled across the seat and into his lap.

"It's Marti, not Sunshine." She muttered the words as she pulled away from his grip and settled into the driver's seat.

"Right. Martha Darlene Gabler. Born September 18. Twenty-eight years old. Two and a half years of college. Working as a veterinary technician at Lakeview Veterinary Clinic. Recently engaged. Even more recently no longer engaged."

"I'm not even surprised you know all that about me."

"There's more."

"Of course there's more. Since I know myself pretty well, and you now seem to know everything about me, let's save some time and not rehash all the details of my boring life."

"Who said anything about boring?"

"Compared to yours—"

"Why would you? Compare your life to mine, I mean?" He watched her with those striking eyes, leaning toward her, his body language, his posture saying he was really listening. That he really wanted to hear what she had to say.

Which was, of course, part of the courting game and meant absolutely nothing.

Courting?

As if.

Men like Tristan Sinclair did not notice women like Marti, let alone court them.

"I'm not comparing. I'm just saying that my life is pretty mundane and yours…well, yours isn't."

"I've got news for you, Marti. Your life is anything but mundane right now. And, by the time this is all over, you're going to be wishing for boring." The words were a grim reminder that Gordon Johnson was free, and Marti's hands tightened into fists around the steering wheel.

"You really think Johnson is coming after me?"

"I don't think it. I know it. Johnson is a lot of things, but stupid isn't one of them. He knows you're bound to be the state's key witness against Buddy and him. He's going to make it his goal to keep you from testifying."

"That's not very comforting."

"Good. The less comfortable you are, the happier I'll be."

"Gee, thanks." She shoved the keys in the ignition, but he put a hand over hers before she could start the car.

"Johnson is a cold-blooded killer, Marti. If making you uncomfortable keeps you safe from him, that's exactly what I want to do."

"Look, Tristan, I know you're trying to help, but—"

"I'm not *trying* to do anything. I'm doing it." He squeezed her hand, the gesture easy and warm. "Now, let's go. We don't want to be late."

She should keep arguing, tell him to get out, remind him that she was a grown woman capable of taking care of herself, but something told her that Tristan Sinclair was not going to be dissuaded and that short of getting out and walking to church, Marti had no choice but to accept her unwanted passenger.

Or maybe not so unwanted.

The fact was, having Tristan around didn't seem like such a bad thing. As she pulled up her long driveway, she imagined a million eyes watching from the woods that lined the street, a million dangers lurking just out of sight. Silly, she knew, but as real as the air she was breathing. Anyone could be hiding in the thick fall foliage, ready to jump in front of the car, shoot out a tire, force her to a stop. And if that anyone happened to be Gordon Johnson, Marti figured that having Tristan in her car might not be such a bad idea after all.

SIX

Chocolate. Cinnamon. The warmth of family mixed with the cool, crisp fall breeze.

Tristan had smelled more exotic perfumes, but none had tugged at his awareness the way Martha's scent did. It hovered around her as he escorted her through the church parking lot and made him want to inhale, to hold the fragrance deep in his lungs, let it fill the part of him that had been emptied during the months he'd worked undercover.

A time of renewal.

He needed that as much as he needed to get the cast off his arm and get himself back into working shape.

"I'll be fine from here." Marti spoke quietly as they approached the church's open front door. It seemed she actually thought he was going to leave her there.

"I know, but I think I'll join you anyway."

"You might want to rethink that. I'm planning to volunteer in the toddler nursery." They might not need her there, but at least closed in the nursery, Martha knew she could avoid the questions her women's Sunday School class was bound to ask.

"And you think that will scare me away?"

"I've seen lesser men felled by the prospect."

Tristan laughed, the sound dry and a little harsh. It had been a while since he'd found anything to be truly amused about. Life as Sky Davis hadn't been something to laugh at. "Good thing I'm not lesser men."

She leaned back, giving him a slow appraising look that was more joke than flirtation. "Yes, it is."

He laughed again, hooking his good arm around her waist and tugging her the last few feet to the church door. "Thanks for the laugh, Sunshine."

"Thanks for playing bodyguard. Of course you know that as soon as church is over, I'm sending you on your way."

"I know you'll try."

"Martha!" The strident male voice greeted them as they stepped into the building. The speaker, a lean blonde with hard eyes and a weak jaw, hurried toward them, his gaze on Martha. "I've been trying to call you all weekend."

Marti stiffened as he approached, but her smile was pleasant. Unless Tristan missed his guess, this was the fiancé. The ex-fiancé.

"Yes. I know."

"And you didn't think it necessary to answer the phone, or to return the calls?"

"A lot of people were calling me, Brian. I couldn't get to everyone."

Brian. Yep, the ex-fiancé.

"If you organized your time better that wouldn't be a problem. What you should have done was make a list and—"

"Prioritize. Yes, Brian. I know. Fortunately, that's not something you need to concern yourself about anymore." Marti smiled again, her teeth gritted in an obvious effort to keep from saying something she'd regret.

Tristan had no such compunction. "I'm sure you did prioritize, Sunshine. There's no doubt in my mind you managed to contact the people who warranted it."

Brian frowned, seeming to notice Tristan for the first time since the conversation had begun. His dark gaze dropped to the arm Tristan had wrapped around Marti's waist, his frown deepening. "I don't think we've met."

"You're right. We haven't. I'm Tristan Sinclair." He offered his hand, not surprised that Brian put a little too much strength in the shake. He was a man who seemed determined to be the top dog. Unfortunately, he was probably closer to being the runt of the litter.

"Brian McMath. Martha's *good* friend."

"I wouldn't exactly call us friends, Brian."

"Of course we're friends. Just because we broke up doesn't mean we don't still care about each other. As a matter of fact, I've been thinking that we could—"

"Don't we need to get to the nursery?" Tristan cut off what threatened to be a long-winded attempt to win Martha back.

"Yes, we do. Nice seeing you, Brian." Martha moved away, and Tristan started to follow only to be pulled up short by Brian's hand on his shoulder.

"I think we need to talk."

"Do you?" Tristan eyed the other man, wondering what Martha had seen in him. Obviously he had an overblown sense of importance and a penchant for cutting people down.

"You may not know this, but Martha and I were engaged."

"I'd heard talk of it." While Tristan lay in a hospital bed recovering from surgery on his arm, his brother Grayson had spent the previous day gathering information. A Lakeview local who'd transplanted from their childhood home in Forest, Virginia, Grayson was a lawyer and good at getting the information he wanted.

"Good. Then you'll understand my concern. She's vulnerable right now. It's going to take her a while to get over our breakup."

"I heard Martha broke up with you. I doubt it'll take her long to recover from that."

Brian's face went scarlet and his eyes flashed. "No one broke up with anyone. It was a mutual decision."

"If that's the way you want to see it." Tristan didn't know why he felt the urge to needle the man.

Sure, the guy was arrogant, but most of the time Tristan ignored people like him. Then again, most of the time, he didn't have to deal with arrogant jerks masquerading as caring Christians.

"Look, my point is that Martha needs time to recover from everything that's happened to her. A relationship at this point would only be a rebound reaction to her loss. It's probably best if you give her some space."

Space? Not likely. At least, not until Johnson was found. "I think I'll let her tell me that. If you'll excuse me, I promised to help her this morning." He strode away before McMath could respond, just catching sight of Martha's deep blue dress as she hurried into a room at the end of the hall.

Tristan followed, peering into the nursery and grimacing as he caught sight of his worst nightmare—fifteen kids the size of peanuts waddling around crying, giggling and babbling. Cute, but dangerous. He'd learned that the hard way on more than one occasion.

He stepped inside, closing the door firmly behind him. Three women eyed him with curiosity. The fourth studiously avoided glancing in his direction. Too bad. He wouldn't mind getting another look in Martha's gold-green eyes.

"Ladies." He tipped his head in greeting and used his good arm to lift a rambunctious little girl from the floor. The angelic-looking kid gave him an impish grin and popped him in the nose. "Hey, that hurt!"

"Better watch out for that one. She's got a reputation for making boys cry." An older lady with salt-and-pepper hair and amused blue eyes pulled the little girl from his arm. "I'm Anna Patrick."

"Tristan Sinclair."

"Nice to meet you, Tristan, but I don't think you're on the nursery roster for this morning."

"I'm with Martha."

"With Martha?" Anna and the other women glanced in Martha's direction.

Martha's face went three shades of red, but she managed a smile. "We're…friends. Tristan offered to lend a hand in here today."

"*A* hand is right." A thirty-something blond woman with bright brown eyes and a quick smile gestured to Tristan's sling. "You're going to have a hard time with only one hand. This is a busy bunch of kids."

"He looks like the kind of guy who can handle anything." A sharp-faced brunette eyed Tristan from a rocking chair across the room. He recognized the interest in her gaze, the sharp gleam of a huntress on the prowl. He'd met plenty of women like her, had even dated a few. But women like her weren't what he was looking for. Not anymore. Now, he thought he might like to find someone more solid, more down-to-earth.

More like…well, Martha.

There. It was out. A truth he'd been avoiding since he'd awakened after surgery on his arm. Martha had been the first one he'd thought of. The only one he'd really wanted to see. Sure, he'd made conversation with his parents, his brothers and sister, the doctors and nurses and coworkers who'd been a streaming distraction while he lay in the hospital bed, but it had been Martha he'd wondered about. Martha he'd pictured over and over again. Gold-green eyes, wild curls. Strength and determination, wrapped up in a very attractive package. Thinking about Martha, wondering how she'd fared after the raid, had provided Tristan with more of a distraction than any of his visitors. Much as he might tell himself he was here to catch Johnson, the truth was a little more complicated. Sure, he wanted to stop Johnson, but he also wanted to keep Martha safe.

And get to know her.

No matter how bad of an idea it might be.

And it *was* a bad idea. The life he led didn't lend itself to family. It was stressful and hard. Not just on the men and women who worked the job, but on their families, as well

"Why don't you come have a seat in one of the rocking chairs." The brunette waved him over. "You can tell us how you and Martha met."

"Thanks, but I've had a few too many days of forced rest. I think I'll stand for a while."

"Did you break your arm?" The brunette didn't seem to be getting the hint that Tristan wasn't interested, and Martha seemed determined to ignore them both rather than join in the conversation.

"Yes." He didn't add that a bullet had shattered

the bone and that rods and pins were currently keeping things in place.

"You're probably one of those extreme-sports junkies. Skydiving. Snowboarding. That kind of stuff."

"Actually, I prefer long hikes in the mountains." He crossed the room and knelt on the floor next to Martha who was building a block tower with one of the toddlers.

She met his gaze, acknowledging his comment with a smile. There were freckles on her nose and cheeks that he'd noticed the first time he'd seen her. Cute freckles to go with the curls that were escaping the sleek hairstyle she'd managed.

"What?" She brushed a hand down her cheek. "Is there something on my face?"

"Just freckles."

She wrinkled her nose. "Don't remind me. They were the bane of my elementary-school years. Jeremiah Bentley used to call me Paint Splatter. Eventually that was shortened to Splat."

"Jeremiah must have had a serious crush on you."

"Jeremiah was a pest. Until tenth grade. Then he was captain of the football team. At that point I decided it was better to have him call me Splat than to not have him call me at all."

He chuckled, pulling a little boy away from another child's toy. "Captain of the football team, huh? And you were what? Head cheerleader?"

"Cheerleader? Hardly. I was more likely to be hiking through the woods than dancing and flipping in front of a crowd." Martha didn't add what she was thinking—that she'd never been one of the popular crowd, and that growing up without a mother had made it difficult to figure out the kind of girlie things that were so valued in high school. Makeup, hair, clothes. She'd learned them all by trial and error. And, she had to admit, there'd been a lot more error than success.

"Martha, a cheerleader? You don't know how funny that is." Jenny Gardner brushed a thick wave of dark hair from her forehead and stood, moving across the room, her hips swaying in her perfectly fitting knee-length skirt. She looked good and she knew it. But then, Jenny had never had a bad hair day in her life. Or at least, not in the fifteen years Martha had known her.

"Funny? Why?"

Of course, Tristan had to ask, and, of course, Jenny was more than willing to answer. Martha had seen the way she'd been eyeing the man in their midst. Like a chocoholic at a candy buffet.

"Martha was a science geek. Always outside traipsing around in the forest, coming into school with twigs and leaves in her hair, mud from feet to knees. I don't think she'd have ever cleaned up enough to be in a cheerleader uniform."

"A science geek, huh?" Tristan met Marti's gaze, his eyes bright blue and assessing, scanning her face, touching on the freckles that she had always hated. Under his intense but clearly approving stare, they didn't seem quite so bad.

"Half the time the poor dear looked more like a guy than a girl with her baggy pants and hooded sweatshirts."

Martha's cheeks heated, but she refused to be pulled into Jenny's grade-school behavior. Sure, she'd been a geek, but that was years ago. Now she was an accomplished, confident adult. Really. She was. "That was a long time ago, Jenny."

"True, but you still do love to wander around in the woods. That is how you ended up involved in that…incident…Friday, isn't it?"

"Incident? Marti could have been killed! I'd call that a little more than an incident." Anna jumped into the conversation, and Martha let her take over. She was too tired to go a verbal round with Jenny.

Martha stood, brushing off her dress. Deep sapphire blue, it had been a spur-of-the-moment purchase. One she'd regretted immediately. Brian had liked it, of course. The slim-fitting sheath had an air of sophistication that made her seem almost elegant. Almost.

And that was the problem. No matter how hard she tried, she could never measure up to women like Jenny who oozed style from every pore. In her opinion, it was better not to try at all than to end up looking like a want-to-be fashionista.

She sighed, gently tugged a toddler from the nursery door. Why she was even thinking about her lack of style, she didn't know. She'd accepted herself for who she was long ago and didn't bother making apologies for it. So she liked to hike and camp more than she liked to shop for clothes. Was that a crime?

"You and I have a lot in common." Tristan moved up beside her, a pigtailed little girl in his arm.

"Do we?"

"I was a science geek, too."

"You? No way." She laughed, sure he only said that because he thought Jenny's comments had bothered her. They hadn't. Much.

"I was president of the science club three years running."

"Not four?"

"I would have been, but Sheryl Greeson wanted the position and I decided she could have it."

"She was cute?"

"Beautiful. And smart. Of course, she only had eyes for the captain of the football team. I wound up going to the prom with a cheerleader who had a thing for geeks."

She doubted it was Tristan's "geekiness" that had appealed to his prom date. "Well, I can one-up you on that. I didn't go to the prom."

The words slipped out before she thought them through, and she winced. She'd made herself seem pathetic.

Before she could try to rectify the error, Jenny spoke up. "Marti was too busy working. She was always one of those goody-goody daddy-girls. Too busy helping out at her father's store to cut loose and have a little fun."

"Some kids have to work, Jenny. That's just the way it is."

Cries filled the room as one toddler after another

decided to take up a chorus of tears. Much as Marti hated to hear them cry, at least the sound kept Jenny from commenting further.

Or Marti from saying anything else that might give Tristan the idea that she'd been a pitifully awkward teen.

Not that it mattered what ideas he had. She'd dated enough to know that she didn't want to waste more of her time mooning over a man. She'd been engaged long enough to know that it wasn't worth the hassle. No, from this point forward, she was man free and happy about it.

Tristan caught her eye as she scooped up one of the criers and smiled the kind of smile meant to melt female hearts. Marti's heart didn't melt, though. Maybe it softened a little, but it definitely didn't melt.

Because she really *was* happy about not having a man in her life. And she really planned on staying that way.

SEVEN

Church service started peacefully enough. Aside from the fact that Marti was sitting next to the best-looking man in the building, the day seemed like any other Sunday. If she tried hard enough, and avoided looking at Tristan, she might even be able to forget that she'd almost been killed two days before, that a murderer was wandering free and that he might be coming to find her.

"Doll! I thought you were staying home today." The raspy sound of her father's voice made Marti smile, and she stood to greet him as he moved down the aisle toward her. Though he'd been to her house the previous day, his eyes were lit as if he and Marti hadn't seen each other in months.

That was her dad. Her biggest fan. Her only fan.

"I thought I was, too, but I changed my mind at the last minute." Marti leaned forward and kissed him on the cheek, the leathery warmth of his skin as familiar as sunrise. "Where's your better half?"

"Chatting with some friends out in the hall. She'll

be glad to see that you're okay. She's been worrying something fierce. We both have."

"There was no need. I'm right as rain."

"Doesn't matter. I still worry. That's what fathers are supposed to do." His gaze shifted to the region beyond Marti's shoulder, and she had a feeling she knew what he was looking at. *Who* he was looking at.

She turned and saw that Tristan had moved up behind her, his silvery eyes focused on her father.

"Dad, I want you to meet Tristan Sinclair. He's a…friend of mine. Tristan, this is my father, Jesse Gabler."

"Nice to meet you, Mr. Gabler." Tristan extended a hand, his arm brushing Martha's as he leaned past her, the warmth of his body seeping through her dress and making Martha's cheeks heat.

"Call me Jesse. Most everyone does. You're a friend of Marti's, huh?"

"That's right."

"Where'd you meet?"

"Dad, the service is about to start. We don't have time for the third degree." She cut the conversation off before it could take wing. Knowing her father, he'd push for as many details as Tristan was willing to give. Right now, she didn't want him to give any. As soon as Dad found out who Tristan was, there'd be an explosion of questions. Maybe even of temper. Her dad was a lot of things, but meek and mild-mannered wasn't one of them.

"Then we'll talk about it over lunch. You are planning to join us for lunch, Tristan?"

"I'm sure he's got other plans." Martha shot Tristan a look that she hoped would convey her feelings about lunch—she didn't want to have it with him.

Either he misinterpreted her look, or he didn't care. "Actually, I don't. I'd love to have lunch with your family."

"Glad to hear it. Sue is always excited about an extra mouth to feed. Speaking of which, here she comes."

Sure enough, Sue was barreling toward them, her lively green eyes riveted on Tristan, her squarish frame nearly humming with energy. Where Jesse was reserved and slow to act, Sue was outgoing and quick to rush into things.

She was also quick to speak, and Martha didn't think that now was a good time to have a conversation.

Martha took a step back, bumping into Tristan, her cheeks heating again as his hand cupped her shoulder and stayed there. What was with her? She was a grown woman. Not a kid with a crush. "Sorry. The music is starting. I think we'd better sit down."

"No one else is."

True. As was usual, the congregation of Grace Christian Church was too busy catching up on the week's events to settle quickly. "They will be."

She nudged him in the stomach with her elbow, and this time he got the hint, moving back into the pew without further comment. And just in time. The air turned thick with the flowery scent of Sue's perfume as Martha's stepmother settled into the pew beside her. "Martha, dear, I'm so glad you're here. I've been up all night worrying. I was just so sure Jesse and I should have stayed over at your house last night."

As always, words poured from Sue like bees from a hive, thick and quick and charming in their artlessness.

"I know and I appreciated the offer."

"Did you sleep well? You do look a little tired."

"I'm fine."

"So, no nightmares? You know, my mother used to make me a glass of warm milk before bed. She insisted that it would chase away any and all bad dreams."

"Maybe I'll try that tonight."

"You should. You really should. Now—" Sue peered around Martha, giving Tristan a more thorough look "—who are you, young man? A friend of Martha's?"

"Tristan Sinclair, ma'am."

"It's good that you can be with our Martha during this terrible time. She did tell you what happened Friday, didn't she?"

"Actually—"

"Service is starting." Martha cut Tristan off.

Tristan leaned close, his lips brushing her ear as he whispered, "Chicken."

"I am not. I just don't think now is the time to tell my father you were the man who kidnapped me." She hissed her reply, sure she'd fallen into an alternate reality. One minute, she'd been engaged to a doctor, doing her best to fit the impossibly polished shoes the position demanded. The next, she'd been a kidnapping victim, fighting for her life. And now, well, now, she was sitting in church with her father, her stepmother and a man who'd caught the attention of every single woman in the congregation.

Obviously her life had taken a wrong turn somewhere in the past week. She needed to figure out where she'd gone wrong and get back on course. Quickly.

Tristan's hand covered hers, stopping the unconscious tapping she'd been doing. Warm and calloused, his palm pressed against her knuckles, his fingers linking with hers, deeply tan against her paler skin. He squeezed gently and released his hold, but the warmth of his touch remained.

She glanced his way, but his focus was on the pulpit and Pastor Avery, who'd begun to make the morning announcements. She knew her attention should be there as well, but she had trouble concentrating as announcements gave way to a hymn and then to the sermon.

The pastor's words of faith during adversity washed over Martha and through her, but she felt disconnected from the message. As much as she tried to concentrate, she couldn't hold on to anything the pastor said for longer than the few seconds it took him to say it. It didn't help that Sue's perfume was strong enough to clog her lungs and steal her breath. Halfway through the sermon Martha's eyes started to water. Her nose itched, and the urge to cough nearly overwhelmed her.

When the music minister stood to lead the last hymn, Martha eased past Sue and her father and hurried out the sanctuary door. The air outside was fresh and clean, the loamy scent of dying leaves and moist earth a welcome relief. Martha took a deep breath, trying to clear her lungs and her head.

"Next time, let me know before you go running off." Tristan's words made her jump, and she whirled to face him.

"You nearly gave me heart failure. Warn a girl next time."

"That's better than what Johnson would have given you if he'd found you out here alone."

"There's no way he'd know to find me here." She tried to sound confident, but Tristan's warning was one she knew she should heed. Going outside alone when a crazy man wanted her dead probably wasn't the best idea she'd ever had.

Tristan touched her arm, his fingers warm through the silky material of her dress. "Listen, Sunshine, I can do my job better if you cooperate. No more going outside without me. Okay?"

"Okay."

"Good. Sounds like the service has ended. How about we go have that lunch your dad promised me?"

"I'm still not sure I want you having lunch with us. There's no telling what my father will do when he finds out—"

"That I kidnapped you?" He grinned, his eyes the bright blue of the autumn sky.

She couldn't stop her answering grin. "Exactly. Of course, I'll also have to tell him that you saved my life, so that should even things out."

"Martha!" Sue bustled toward them, weaving her way through the crowd exiting the church. "Is everything okay? I was worried when you left so suddenly, but since Tristan followed you out, I knew you'd be fine."

"You were right. I was. I just needed a breath of fresh air."

"After all you've been through, dear, I'm not surprised." Her gaze drifted from Martha's face to Tristan's hand, which was still resting on Martha's arm. "You know, if you two were planning a special date, we can skip lunch—"

"A date? Us? No way." Martha nearly snorted at the thought.

"Don't sound so amused by the idea, Sunshine. It could happen."

"Not in this lifetime."

"Never say never, Martha." Sue smiled, looking more than happy to be witness to the interplay between them. "But since it isn't happening today, I'm glad to have you both for some good old-fashioned Southern-fried chicken and potato salad. *And* your dad started some of those yeast rolls you love so much, dear."

"It sounds wonderful. I can't wait to eat." But for the first time in as long as Martha could remember, the thought of food didn't appeal. It was amazing how almost getting killed could ruin a person's appetite.

"We'll see you at your dad's place in a few minutes then. You, too, Tristan. Bring your appetite. What with my boys all grown and gone, I've always got way too much food left over."

"I'm more than willing to do my part to rectify that situation, ma'am."

"Call me Sue. 'Ma'am' makes me feel old. Now, I'm going to find Jesse and get him moving. Otherwise, lunch won't be ready until suppertime! You two get a move on, and I'll see you at the house."

"I guess we've got our orders." Tristan cupped Martha's elbow, merging into a crowd of people moving toward their cars. He scanned the parking lot as he moved, looking for danger but not finding it.

"And I'm sure we'll get more before the day is through. Sue is a steel magnolia." Martha smiled up into his eyes, her lips curving.

And Tristan's mind jumped back forty-eight hours, remembering cool rain washing down his face as he leaned toward Martha, felt the softness of her lips, breathed in chocolate and cinnamon. It had been an action designed to fool Gordon Johnson. But it had pulled him in, become more. That was something Tristan couldn't quite understand.

He'd met a lot of women during his years working for the ATF. Many of them were from the darker side of life; some, like Martha, were innocents who had been drawn into circumstances beyond their control. None of them had affected him the way Martha did.

Maybe she sensed the direction of his thoughts, because she stiffened, her muscles tensing under his hand. "You know, you don't really have to come to lunch, Tristan. I'm sure you've got other plans, and I know I'll be safe inside Dad and Sue's place. As a matter of fact, I'll even promise to stay away from the windows."

"Thanks, but you are the only thing I have planned for this weekend. Actually, for the week." Maybe longer if that's what it took to bring Johnson in and ensure Martha's safety.

"You're not serious."

"Sunshine, I'm more than serious. Until Johnson is found, you and I are going to be joined at the hip."

"Eventually you'll have to go home and get back to work."

"I'm on medical leave. For now, keeping you safe is my work."

"Tristan—"

"How about we discuss it after lunch? I don't know about you, but I think better on a full stomach." He cut her off before she could argue more. It would be a waste of both their energy. He'd already made up his mind. Whether Martha liked it or not, he was sticking around. He'd told his boss that, had even asked for backup, but Daniel Sampson hadn't been convinced that Johnson would make a move against Martha.

Tristan was. The sole civilian witness to his

crimes and Buddy's, Martha was the state's key witness. Johnson would definitely try to get rid of her. It was just a matter of time.

EIGHT

Martha knew that having lunch with Tristan, Sue and her dad wasn't a good idea. There were just too many things that could go wrong. Dad could lay into Tristan, accusing him of reckless endangerment when he found out the role Tristan had played in Friday's trouble. Worse, he could break out Martha's baby pictures and brag about what a cute kid she'd been. Sue could fill Tristan in on all the details of Martha's relationship with Brian, explaining in excruciating detail her opinions on why things had gone wrong. Tristan could...well...he could be Tristan. Handsome, confident. Admirable. And Dad could start getting ideas about marriage and grandkids.

Five minutes passed as fried chicken was piled onto plates, potato salad and dinner rolls made their rounds and Sue regaled her guests with stories of her volunteer work at the hospital. The flow of conversation took on an easy, comfortable feel, and Martha started to relax, to believe that the meal might pass without any of the things she'd been worried about.

She should have known better.

"So, Tristan, tell us, how did you and Marti meet?" Sue's bright tone belied the intense curiosity in her gaze. The poor woman just couldn't help it. She was a born gossip. Or maybe collector of information was a better name for it. She might spread the information she gathered, but never with malicious intent.

"We met in the mountains on Friday."

"What?" Jesse set his fork down on the table, and sent a hard look in Martha's direction.

"I was working the gun raid."

"He's the man I told you about. Sky Davis. Remember?"

"The criminal? The guy who kidnapped you? Sitting at my table?" Jesse stood, and Martha had a quick vision of her father lunging for Tristan.

"Actually, Mr. Gabler, I'm an ATF agent. I was working undercover when Martha and I met."

"You nearly got my daughter killed!"

"Dad, he saved my life. I told you that."

"Sit down, Jesse. Sit down right now and eat. I won't have you ruining my meal with your temper. Tristan, I can't tell you how glad I am that you were there the day Martha ran into her trouble." Sue took a sip of sweet tea, her bright eyes filled with excitement. Martha could almost imagine her cataloguing Tristan's words, filing them under "juicy tidbits."

"I'm glad I was there, too." Tristan met Martha's eyes, and she was sure she saw humor in his gaze.

"Martha said you were shot trying to protect her. Is that where you got your arm injury? From the bullet?"

"I'm afraid so."

"And now you're in town to make sure Martha's okay? That's just so romanti—"

"Sue, I'm sure Tristan didn't come here to answer a hundred questions." Martha tried to stop the flow of conversation, but like the tide, it just kept rolling in.

"Actually, Sue, one of our perpetrators escaped Friday."

"This just keeps getting better and better. First I meet the man who nearly got my daughter killed—"

"He saved my life, Dad," Martha repeated.

"And now I find out a criminal mastermind is on the loose."

"Not for long, Mr. Gabler. We'll have him in custody soon."

"Says the man who nearly got my—"

"Dad!"

Jesse scowled. "Sorry, doll, but it's the way I see it."

"I'd see it the same way if it were my daughter." Tristan's words seemed to mollify Jesse, and he settled back into his chair.

"You think this guy is coming to Lakeview? Coming after Martha?"

"It's a good possibility."

"Well, put her in one of those witness protection

programs, then. A safe house. Someplace where the guy won't find her."

"I tried. My boss isn't convinced she's in danger."

"Give me his number. I'll call and make sure he is."

"You're welcome to try. I've already spent hours doing the same. Now I'm here, and I'll do everything in my power to make sure your daughter stays safe."

"Everything in your power. You want to explain what that means? Twenty-four-hour guard? Patrol cars in front of her place? What?"

Marti sighed. It was going to be a long afternoon. "I'm going to clean the kitchen."

She grabbed her plate and exited the room, relieved when Sue didn't follow her into the kitchen. Not that she'd expected her stepmother to. The conversation at the table was a lot more interesting than loading a dishwasher. Though, for her part, Martha could think of a lot of things she'd rather do than discuss scary possibilities and twenty-four-hour guards.

She grabbed a pan from the stove, scraped the contents into Sue's compost bucket and did the same with several bowls. Ten minutes later, she'd managed to empty the dishwasher, fill it again and wipe down the counters, but the conversation in the dining room was still going strong. She could hear just enough of it to know that her name was being mentioned over and over again. If Martha were brave enough, she'd march back into the room and tell all three of them that she'd prefer a change in subject.

She wasn't, so she'd just wait things out and deal with her father, Sue and Tristan one at a time. Starting with Tristan. If his boss didn't think Martha was in danger, then there was no reason for Tristan to play bodyguard. She'd tell him that on the way back to her place.

Just the thought made her feel better than she had all day. Once she sent Tristan on his way, she could get back to her normal routine. Tomorrow she'd go to work, immerse herself in her job and forget Friday had ever happened. Eventually the nightmares would go away and she'd stop jumping at shadows.

She grabbed the compost bucket and opened the back door. Outside, cold sunlight shone off dry grass and colorful leaves. The air was sweet with autumn, the sky vividly blue. In years past, the Gablers' corner lot had been scraggly and neglected. Sue had changed that, surrounding the large yard with a five-foot fence that she'd painted white, planting vegetable and flower gardens, creating order out of disorder. Marti smiled a little as she carried the bucket toward the compost pile at the back edge of the yard. Sue and Jesse Gabler were an unlikely pair, but a good one, and she was glad her father had finally found someone he could trust with his heart.

"At least *he* won't be spending the rest of his days alone." She dumped the compost on top of the pile, and turned toward the house just as an engine roared to life. A dark blue pickup drove by, U-turned in a neighbor's driveway and started back, picking up speed as it went. Surprised, Martha turned to watch its approach. A kid, probably. No one else would drive that fast through the neighborhood.

The truck jumped the curb, heading right toward the fence, not slowing as it ran over the grass.

"Get out of the way!" Tristan's warning barely registered as Martha jumped back, tumbling in her haste, landing on the ground and rolling away as metal and wood collided. Fence planks snapped; shards of lumber rained down.

"Stay down!" Tristan shouted the order as Martha struggled to her knees, his arms wrapping around her waist as he pressed her back onto the ground, holding her still when she would have levered up.

They stayed that way, his chest against her back, his lips close to her ear as wood crunched, tires squealed and the sound of the engine faded away.

In the stillness that followed, Martha could hear nothing but her frantically pounding heart and the harsh rasp of her breath. Then other things registered—Tristan's more controlled breathing, Sue's cries of alarm, her father's heavy footfall as he crossed the yard.

"What's going on? What happened?" Her father's raspy voice seemed to break through the terror that held Martha immobile. She shifted, and Tristan moved with her, standing and pulling her to her feet.

"Are you okay?" He brushed hair from her eyes and framed her face with his hands, his palms warm against her icy skin.

"I think so." Though she wasn't sure her shaking legs would hold her much longer.

"Can someone please tell me what's going on?" Martha's father raked a hand through his thinning hair, his gaze skimming over the broken fence before settling on Martha.

"A truck driver lost control and rammed the fence," she said.

"The driver did not lose control." Tristan's voice was harsh.

"What are you saying?" Sue nearly squeaked the question, but Tristan didn't respond.

His focus was on Martha, his eyes a deep, stormy blue. "What were you doing out here by yourself? I thought we agreed you'd stay inside."

"I was putting scraps in the compost pile. And this *is* inside. Or pretty close to it. The entire yard is fenced."

"Which is about as useful as a piece of paper for protecting a person from a bullet."

"No one shot at me. Someone drove into a fence. For all we know, it was an accident."

"It wasn't an accident." Tristan bit out each word, clearly enunciating, as if doing so would convince Martha.

But she didn't want to be convinced, because that would mean admitting Johnson had found her. "He couldn't have found Dad's house so quickly."

"He could. He did." Tristan's words were harsh, his grip tight as he hurried her back to the house.

"I'm going to call the police." Sue hurried inside, and Martha glanced at the broken fence, her heart still beating too fast. *Had* Johnson been at the wheel of the truck? Things had happened too fast for Martha to see. She couldn't say for sure that he hadn't been.

"Someone is going to pay for this." Her father pushed at splintered wood with his foot, but he sounded more worried than angry.

"Dad? Are you coming inside?"

"Yes, then I'm going out. I've got some business to attend to."

"What kind of business, Mr. Gabler?" Tristan nudged Martha inside the house. Her father followed them.

"I'm going to find that truck. I caught a good look at it. Dark blue Chevy. Two-door. It's got to have some scratches on the front bumper."

"I got a good look at it, too, and saw what direction it went in. If you stay here and wait for the police, I'll take Martha's car and go look."

"I think I'd rather go looking."

"Then who'll be here with Martha and Sue?"

"You should *both* stay here with us and wait for the police." The thought of either man chasing after Johnson made Martha's stomach churn.

"Babe, I *am* the police." Tristan snagged Martha's keys from the hall table where she'd dropped them when she'd arrived.

"The one-armed police."

"So?"

"So, I don't want you to get hurt again."

"I won't." He stepped out the front door, and short of grabbing the keys from his hands, there wasn't a lot Martha could do to stop him.

"Tristan, I really don't like this."

"Neither do I. Do me a favor and stay inside this time. I don't want anything to happen to you while I'm gone."

"You listen to him, doll. I come back and find out you're out looking for trouble and my heart might give out."

"I think you'd better stay and keep an eye on her, Mr. Gabler."

"Jesse. And I'm going. With you or on my own. Your choice."

Tristan hesitated, then nodded. "Then we'll go together."

"Let's get going then. We'll take my car." Jesse kissed Martha on the cheek and hurried outside.

Tristan followed, tucking Martha's keys into his pocket as he went. Obviously, he had every intention of making sure she didn't join the hunt. He hadn't bothered putting on his jacket, and the white straps of his sling were visible against his dark shirt. How much of a chance would he have against Johnson? Not enough. And having her seventy-year-old father along for the ride didn't increase his odds of success.

"Tristan?"

He paused with his hand on the car door. "Yeah?"

"Are you left-handed or right-handed?"

He laughed, shook his head. "I'm ambidextrous. Now go inside."

She did. Closed the door, turned the lock. "Lord, please keep them safe."

She whispered the prayer as she walked down the hall, wishing she could do more. Prayer was good, but sometimes life demanded action. Unfortunately, in this case action wasn't a possibility. She had to wait. Wait for the police. Wait for Tristan and her father to return. Wait to see how it all unfolded.

"Your father went off with him, didn't he?" Sue grabbed Martha's arm as she walked back into the kitchen.

"Yes."

"He's a brave man, your dad, but he's not as young as he used to be. And when he gets back I'm going to tell him exactly what I think of him going off after a killer." Her voice broke, and Martha put her hand on Sue's shoulder.

"It'll be okay. They'll be back before we know it."

"I hope so."

"I know so. Sit down. I'll make us some tea while we wait."

"That sounds lovely, dear."

Lovely. Definitely not a term Martha would use to describe anything about the day. She bit back a sigh, set the kettle on to boil and waited, her mind filling with images—the smashed fence and speeding truck, Tristan's arm dripping blood as men raced through the trees. Johnson's cold gaze.

He'd kill anyone who got in his way. Tristan. Martha's father.

Anyone.

Much as Martha wanted him off the streets, she wanted Tristan and her father safe more. She couldn't help praying that if it really had been Johnson in the truck, they wouldn't find him.

NINE

Time ticked by slowly as Martha waited.

Really slowly.

The police came and went. Martha drank two cups of tea and ate three chocolate-chip cookies. Sue made five phone calls. And still Tristan and Jesse didn't return. Finally, Martha couldn't take it anymore. She grabbed another chocolate-chip cookie, pilfered her spare keys from the kitchen drawer where her father kept them and eased open the front door.

She probably shouldn't be doing this. She probably should stay in the house where it was safe and listen to another few hours of Sue going over all the details of what had happened with friends, family and acquaintances. She probably should, but she couldn't. The men had been gone for three hours. That was a long time to be out searching for a truck. Something must have happened. They could have been in an accident. The car may have broken down. Or worse, they might have found what they were looking for. Just the thought of her father getting close to Johnson made Martha shiver as she got in her car.

She glanced in the rearview mirror and started backing out of the driveway, but slammed on the brakes when a car pulled in behind her. Her father's car. Finally. Relief filled her as Tristan got out of the vehicle and stalked to her door, pulling it open and tugging her out before she even had a chance to turn off the engine.

"Didn't I tell you to stay inside?" He barked the question, his scowl storm-cloud dark.

"You've been gone three hours. *Three.*"

"I don't care if it was a hundred. You shouldn't have come out here."

"What was I supposed to do? Sit in the house and wait forever for you two to come back?"

"If that's what it took, yeah." He ran a hand over his hair, obviously trying to rein in his temper before he spoke again.

"Well, I couldn't. I was worried. I needed to know that you guys were okay."

"We're grown men, Sunshine. Perfectly capable of taking care of ourselves."

"And I'm a grown woman. Also capable of taking care of myself."

"You're also the one Johnson wants dead."

"I doubt he's got any fondness for you, either."

"If he thinks I'm in jail, I'm safe."

"If. That's not very likely."

He shook his head, a half smile chasing some of the anger from his face. "You need to stop worrying so much about me and start worrying about yourself. Where'd you get the keys to your car?"

"I had a spare set. Should have thought of that before I left." Jesse spoke as he moved up beside Tristan. "Of course, I didn't expect Martha to come traipsing outside like there was nothing to worry about. This Johnson guy, he doesn't play games, doll. He's a cold-blooded killer." Obviously, Jesse and Tristan had done a lot of talking during the past hours and were now in complete agreement on the situation.

"Don't worry, Dad. I know."

"Good. Now I'd better go inside and apologize to Sue. I doubt she's happy that I went off without telling her what I was doing." He pushed open the front door and disappeared inside, leaving Martha and Tristan standing beside Martha's car. Just the two of them. Again. It seemed they kept returning to that.

"I guess you didn't find him." Martha knew that wasn't good, but she was too relieved that her father and Tristan were okay to dwell on it.

"No, but not for lack of trying. We drove through the neighborhood, knocked on doors, talked to people. A few saw the truck. None noticed who was in the driver's seat."

"Thanks for trying."

"I'd thank you for staying where I left you, but since you didn't, I won't."

"I'm not good at sitting around waiting."

"Yeah. I'm getting that. You know, Sunshine, you're more trouble than I bargained for when I went into those mountains on Friday." Tristan looked down into her face, studying it, searching it. She wasn't sure what he was looking for, but she doubted he'd find it. She was who she was. There was nothing hidden or mysterious about her.

"At least you were bargaining on trouble. I was looking for a nice peaceful getaway."

"Nice and peaceful, huh?" His fingers curled around her elbow, and he urged her to get back in the car. "I thought you said your life was mundane. Seems like there'd be plenty of peace in that."

"The past week has been hectic."

"You mean because you broke up with that Brian guy."

Surprised, she met Tristan's eyes. "How'd you know we broke up this week?"

"People talk. Give them an opportunity and they'll tell you just about anything you want to know."

"I suppose there's a reason you're telling me this."

"It isn't going to be hard for Johnson to find out everything he wants to about your life and your habits. He saw your name and address in your backpack. A few questions to the right people and he'll be staking out every place you go."

"Every place I go? You're talking work, home, the movies, the local diner. He won't have any trouble at all finding me." Despite the seriousness of the situation, Martha laughed. Nerves did that to her. And she was nervous. Scared. Anxious.

She caught her breath, wiped at eyes that were streaming and met Tristan's gaze. *He* wasn't laughing. That much was for sure.

"Sorry about that. Sometimes I laugh when I'm scared."

"You don't have to apologize. You just have to take the danger seriously."

"Trust me, I do. I saw Johnson's eyes. There was nothing human there."

"You've hit the nail on the head, Martha. He's got no conscience. Nothing to keep him from doing things most of us wouldn't even imagine." He cupped her jaw, stared into her eyes, and she found herself sinking into his gaze.

"I know."

"So next time, do what I say, okay? It's the only way to make sure you stay safe. And I do want you safe." His eyes were almost hypnotic, his voice soothing, cajoling. Martha imagined most women would do exactly what he asked simply because he was the one asking.

She blinked and pulled away from his touch, starting the engine and driving toward home, determined not to fall for his charm. "You're good at getting what you want, Tristan Sinclair."

"Thanks. I've had a lot of practice."

"You date a lot?"

He laughed, the warmth of it rumbling out into the car and chasing away some of Martha's fear. "I actually practiced on my parents. I have three brothers and a sister. I learned young that getting what I wanted involved finesse rather than fit-throwing."

"So you were one of those spoiled golden boys?

The kind who always got what he wanted because he was charming?"

"Hardly, but I sure gave it a run for the money. I used to keep a scorecard—how many times I convinced my parents to let me have my way as opposed to how many times my brothers or sister did."

"You did not!" She met his gaze, saw the laughter in his eyes.

"I did."

"So, did you get your way the most?"

"Not even close. My brother Grayson, he took the lead. Followed by my sister."

"I'm surprised your sister wasn't the clear winner what with her being the only girl."

"Don't be. My brother grew up to become a lawyer. He puts his persuasive skills to good use every day."

"Good career choice."

"We thought so."

"And you became an ATF agent so you could force people to do what you wanted."

"Actually, I became an ATF agent to change the world. Sometimes I think I just might be doing that." He spoke quietly, and Martha dared a look in his direction. He was staring out the window, scanning the trees that lined her long driveway. Looking for signs Johnson was there waiting for a chance to strike.

"Do you think he's out there?"

"No, but let's not take chances. Park close to the porch."

Martha did as he said, opening the door and running inside, Tristan right beside her. "Thanks for the escort, Tristan."

"No problem. And, Sunshine?" He grabbed her hand and pulled her to a stop.

"Yes?" She turned, her breath hitching as she met his gaze.

"For the record, I've gotten a whole lot better at getting what I want."

Her cheeks flamed and her heart did a strange little dance. She told herself it had more to do with fatigue than with the man who was staring down into her eyes. "I'll keep that in mind."

"You do that." He released her hand, pushed the front door open again. "I'll see you in the morning."

"You're going home?" *You're leaving me here alone when Johnson might be lurking in the woods just out of sight?* That's what she was really thinking. Thank goodness she had enough self-control not to say it.

"Actually, I'll be outside in my car. That's where I'm camping out until Johnson is caught."

"Your car?"

"I can't stay in here. Your father wouldn't approve."

"You're actually planning to sleep out there in your car?"

"I've slept in a lot worse places over the years."

"But—"

"You're a half mile from your nearest neighbor, Martha. You don't have a security system. Your phone lines are so easy to cut a child could do it. If

Johnson decides to come calling, I don't want you to be alone."

That was great, because she didn't want to be alone either. "Look, if you're really set on staying…" Her voice trailed off as she realized what she was about to say. What she was about to offer.

"What?"

Don't do it. Do *not* offer him the apartment over the garage. That will just make things too convenient and cozy. "There's an efficiency over the garage. The previous owner used to rent it to college students. It's empty. If you want, you can use it."

Of course, she did exactly what she shouldn't and offered him the place.

"How far is it from the house?"

"Not far. It's just out back." She led him out back to the square two-story building. A 1960s addition to Martha's turn-of-the-century home, the single-car garage stood less than a hundred feet from the back of the house. It had been a while since Martha had been inside the efficiency, and it took her a few seconds to find the key. When she did, the door squeaked open, the sound shivering along her nerves. Night hadn't fallen yet, but it would soon. She wanted to be locked in the house with every light on before then.

"Here it is. Like I said, it's not much. I don't even have furniture in here." She stepped into the large room, and Tristan followed, his arm brushing against her shoulder as he moved past her.

"I don't need furniture tonight. Maybe tomorrow I can get my brother to bring me a few things."

"Your brother is in the area?"

"Grayson lives about ten minutes away in a huge house filled with stuff he's not using. I don't think he'll miss a futon and a couple of pots and pans." As he spoke, Tristan strode across the room and pulled a dusty curtain back from one of the windows. "There's a good view of your back door from here." He seemed to be speaking more to himself than to Martha, but she crossed the room anyway, looking out onto her backyard.

"Do you want to stay here?"

"It beats sleeping in my car."

"I'll bring you a sleeping bag and a radio so it won't be too quiet out here."

"Quiet is good, so don't bother with the radio. I wouldn't mind a couple of aspirin, though."

"Is your arm bothering you?"

"Yeah."

"A lot?"

"Like a hot iron is being poked through it."

"Ouch."

"Exactly. Come on, let's go." He took her hand, his fingers warm and rough against her softer skin. Funny, Martha had never thought of herself as feminine and petite, but Tristan made her feel small and delicate.

Delicate? She almost snorted at the thought. She'd never been delicate, and she never would be.

"Stay here. It will only take me a minute to get

the stuff." She tried to tug away from his hand, but he held firm.

"I think we'll do this my way instead."

"What way is that?"

"We'll go together."

"That's really—"

"Not necessary?"

"Okay. Maybe it is, but it does seem a little bit like overkill, don't you think?"

"What's overkill? Me walking back to the house with you?"

"It's a ten-second walk."

"A lot can happen in ten seconds, Martha. You saw that truck today. It jumped the curb and hit your father's fence in the blink of an eye."

He was right. A lot *could* happen in ten seconds. An engagement could be broken. A mother could abandon her child. A life could be snuffed out.

And a woman who'd said she'd never have anything to do with men again could find herself falling into deep blue eyes. Again.

TEN

Knowing Tristan was sleeping a hundred feet from the house should have made it easier for Martha to rest, but at 2:00 a.m. she was still awake. Every time she closed her eyes, she saw Gordon Johnson. And looking into his face wasn't restful. She supposed she could try counting sheep, but that would require closing her eyes and she'd already decided against that. Turning on the television and watching reruns of sitcoms was another option, but she was afraid the sound would mask other things. Like someone cutting out a pane of glass, turning the lock of the window and opening it. Easing inside. Creeping down the hall.

Martha shivered and shoved aside the blanket she'd been burrowing under. She was not going to spend the hours until sunrise imagining the worst. If she couldn't sleep, she might as well do something constructive. Like find chocolate. One good thing about living alone—there was no one she needed to explain an early-morning chocolate raid to. No one to witness a bad case of bed head, two-sizes-too-big flannel pajamas or floppy pink bunny slippers. No one to keep awake with her restless fear.

No one to share her worries.

To tell her everything was going to be all right.

She shook her head, knowing that wasn't the truth. She wasn't alone. God was with her. She could share her worries with Him, and she could trust that He'd take care of her. She knew that, but sometimes it was hard to feel the emptiness of the house and know that it might always be the same. Just Martha. No husband. No kids. No busy days wrapped around a life of domesticity.

Maybe it was silly to want those things, but she did.

More than that, though, she wanted what God intended for her life. After her experience with Brian, she was pretty certain that marriage wasn't what He had planned. That was okay, because as much as she might want a forever-after kind of relationship, she wasn't sure how good she'd be at it. Her parents hadn't been a great example of how to make things work. And her mother certainly hadn't shown Martha how to mother a child, unless walking out on your kid when she was five was the way to do it.

She flicked on the light in the kitchen, scrounged through the cupboards in search of her chocolate fix. Her supply was sparse. Two chocolate bars. A bag of M&Ms with peanuts. A few Hershey's Kisses. She unwrapped one, popping it in her mouth as she set the teakettle to boil. So what if she couldn't sleep? It wasn't the end of the world. Plenty of people suffered from insomnia. As a matter of fact, she was sure if she went online she'd find a support group for people who couldn't sleep. And one for people who'd dumped their fiancés. Maybe even one for women who were being stalked by killers.

A soft tap sounded at the back door, and Martha nearly dropped her teacup. For a moment she wasn't sure what to do. Ask who was there? Turn off the light and hide? Call the police?

The knock sounded again, this time more insistent. She grabbed a steak knife and crept toward the door, her heart racing. "Who's there?"

"Tristan."

She nearly sagged with relief, her heart slowing, and then jumping again as she opened the door and met Tristan's vivid blue gaze. "You're supposed to be in the garage apartment."

"And you're supposed to be asleep. Apparently neither of us are doing what we're supposed to."

"Is everything okay?"

"That's what I was going to ask you. When I saw your light go on, I thought I'd better come over and make sure you were okay."

"I'm fine. Just having trouble sleeping."

"So you're wandering around the house with a steak knife in your hand and pink bunny slippers on your feet?" A hint of a smile eased the harsh angles of his face, his gaze dropping from her eyes to her feet and back again.

"They seemed like a good idea at the time."

"When was that?"

"When I didn't think there'd be anyone in the house at two in the morning to see them." She placed the knife on the counter as his warm laughter filled the room, resisting the urge to smooth her hair. There was no way she could fix the mess she knew it to be, so there was no sense drawing more attention to it.

"I guess we've both been surprised, then, because I wasn't expecting to see a light on in your house at two in the morning." He smiled again, grabbing a Hershey's Kiss from the counter, his presence reminding Martha of all the things she needed to forget—namely, how nice it was to have someone to count on. Someone stronger, tougher, more able to fight if fighting needed doing. Not that Brian had been much of a fighter. He'd been more likely to argue and complain.

She really needed to stop comparing Tristan and Brian, because doing so only painted Tristan in a more positive light than she wanted to see him. As she watched, he grabbed another chocolate, denting her limited supply.

See? Selfish. She'd known if she'd look hard enough she could find something negative about him. "Those chocolates are mine, you know."

"Didn't anyone ever teach you to share?" He popped the candy into his mouth and took a seat at the table.

"Didn't anyone ever teach you to ask?"

He laughed, grabbing another candy and eating it before Martha could snatch it from his hand. "I've got four siblings, remember? We all learned to grab what we could while we could. Besides, I'm hungry. I need to stock the fridge in the apartment tomorrow."

"If you're hungry, I've got sandwich makings in the fridge. Just leave my chocolate alone."

"Chocolate is a girl's best friend?"

"Absolutely."

"But it's not such good company at two in the morning, is it?" He looked up into her eyes, compassion shining from his gaze.

But she didn't want his compassion, because if she accepted it, she'd also be accepting his presence in her life. A presence that was becoming much too familiar much too quickly.

She turned away, pouring water over a tea bag, trying to put distance between them. "Want some tea?"

"No, thanks. I wouldn't mind a soda, though, if you have any."

"Soda at two in the morning?"

"Why not?"

"Good question." She grabbed a can of soda from the fridge, set it down in front of Tristan. Efficient. Businesslike. That was the way to handle this situation. "You asked me why I was up, but you didn't mention why you were."

"Probably the same reason you are—I'm worried."

"Because of what happened today?"

"Because of what happened Friday, what happened today. What might happen tomorrow and the next day." He ran his hand down his jaw and shook his head. "I know worry doesn't do any good, but my mind is running around in circles trying to figure out what Johnson's next move is going to be."

"I don't think anyone can do that."

"Maybe not, but I'm going to try." He stood, pacing across the room. He wasn't wearing his sling, and he held his injured arm close to his waist, shrugging his shoulder as if trying to relieve tension.

He might be saying he couldn't sleep because he was worried, but Martha wondered if the reason had a more physical cause. "Is your arm bothering you?"

"It's not too bad."

"That's not an answer."

"It hurts. Happy now?" He scowled, taking a sip of soda and eyeing Martha with an intensity that made her squirm.

"No, I'm not happy. I haven't been happy since Friday." Actually, she hadn't been happy in a couple of months. As much as she'd told herself she was, as much as she'd tried to pretend excitement over wedding preparation and engagement parties, there'd been a hollow ache in her chest that no amount of self-talk or pretend enthusiasm could fill.

She turned away from Tristan's gaze, grabbing a bottle of Tylenol from the cupboard and opening it. "Here, take these."

"Thanks." His fingers brushed her palm as he took the medicine, and she was sure they lingered for a moment longer than necessary. No. She had to have been wrong about that. There was nothing between Tristan and herself but the need to find Johnson and put him in jail.

She needed to keep that in mind.

In the distance, a car engine chugged along, growing closer. So close that Martha stiffened, cocking her head and straining to hear more. "I think someone is coming up my driveway."

"Sounds like it."

"You don't seem concerned."

"I called the local sheriff a few hours ago. He agreed to send patrol cars out as often as possible. It's probably one of them. Stay here while I make sure that's who it is."

"But—"

"Are you going fight me on everything, Sunshine?"

"No, I just—"

"Good. I'll be back in a minute." He pulled a gun that Martha hadn't even realized he was carrying, and her heart froze in her chest.

"What are you doing?"

"Taking care of things. Stay here." He strode away, not giving Martha a chance to ask more questions, or demand answers. The soft hum of the engine came closer, and Martha knew the car would be passing the house, U-turning at the dead end, moving by again. Or would it? Maybe it would stop. Maybe the sharp, quick blast of bullets would fill the silence.

Legs trembling, she grabbed the phone, ready to call 911 at the first hint of trouble.

Then she followed Tristan. He might not like it,

but he couldn't change it, and there was no way in the world she was going to cower in the kitchen while he faced danger alone. It wasn't what her father had raised her to do.

Be tough. Be strong. The world's gonna knock you down. You got to learn to bounce back up again.

She could almost hear him saying the words, could picture his gnarled hands pulling back branches as he led her on long hikes through the woods, teaching her about survival and about life. Too bad he hadn't told her what to do if a murderer came knocking on the door.

She moved silently, easing down the hallway, making sure that she avoided loose floorboards. The last thing she wanted to do was distract Tristan.

The darkness of the living room was as oppressive as her fear, sucking away her confidence and making her want to slink back into the kitchen and do exactly what she'd decided she wouldn't. Hide from the trouble. Let Tristan take control.

At the window, a shade darker than the room, Tristan stood pressed against the wall with his broken arm holding back the curtain, his good arm holding the gun. Focused. Intent. "I told you to stay in the kitchen."

She hadn't made a sound, but somehow Tristan had known she was there. "I thought you might need some help."

"Looking outside?" He didn't turn toward her as he spoke, just continued to stare out the window.

"Calling the police."

"Thanks, but if Johnson had been out there, I'd have acted first and called the police later."

"But he wasn't."

"No, he wasn't. But that doesn't mean he won't be next time."

"I know."

"Do you, Sunshine? Because you sure don't act like it." He dropped the curtain and tucked the gun out of sight again.

"How should I act? Like a damsel in distress who needs a prince to run to her rescue?"

"Like a woman who'd rather be alive than dead." Even in the darkness, she could see his eyes flashing with irritation.

"Of course I'd rather be alive."

"Then maybe next time I tell you to stay put, you'll do it."

"And maybe next time you'll actually give me something to do besides sitting around twiddling my thumbs."

He stared at her for a moment, his grim expression slowly easing into a smile. "You're stubborn as a mule, Sunshine, you know that?"

"How could I not? Brian told me that just about every day for eighteen months." The words slipped out and Martha blushed. Fortunately, it was too dark for Tristan to see.

"Brian is a real winner."

"That and a few other things." Like arrogant. Self-centered. Thoughtless.

"But you almost married the guy anyway?"

Ouch! That hurt, but she refused to let Tristan know it. "I like to call our engagement nine months of temporary insanity."

"Nine *months* of temporary insanity?"

"Yes. Fortunately, I'm over it now."

He chuckled, but Martha wasn't amused. She really had been out of her mind to consider marriage to a guy like Brian. Not that he was a bad guy. It was more that he wasn't the kind of guy who'd ever put another person's needs above his own. He was the kind who'd demand more and more and never be satisfied. The kind of person her mother had been.

She'd learned her lesson. There'd be no more trying to be someone she wasn't. The thought of the months she'd wasted doing just that made her feel more tired than she had all weekend. "It's late. We should both probably try to get some sleep."

"You're right, but there's something I want to ask you first." Tristan grabbed her wrist before she could take a step away, his thumb pressed against the pulse point there. Could he feel the way her heart jumped? The sudden speeding of her pulse?

She sure could, and she didn't like it.

If men could still be heroes, if chivalry were still practiced and dragons were still in need of slaying, Tristan would be in the front line of every battle; the knight that every maiden wanted as her champion. A guardian of truth, a protector of the innocent. A man who made women swoon and other men jealous. Someone who could be very, very dangerous to

Martha's heart if she let him. She had no intention of letting him. "What's that?"

"How is it that a woman like you ended up engaged to a guy like Brian?"

"The same way any woman ends up engaged to any man. Brian asked. I said yes."

"That's not what I mean, and you know it."

"Maybe, but your question is presumptuous and *you* know it. We barely know each other. Neither of us should be asking questions about the other's relationships."

"You're wrong there, Sunshine. We know each other a lot more than 'barely.' After what happened Friday, I'd say we know each other well."

"Why? Because you kissed me?" Twice. Not that she'd been counting.

"Actually, I hadn't thought about that, but thanks for the reminder."

Martha's cheeks heated. "We didn't even know each other's names Friday, let alone anything else."

"I knew your name. I saw it in your backpack, remember? I also saw that you were strong, independent. A fighter. That you pack more chocolate than protein bars when you hike through the woods, and that when the going gets tough you just keep going. Oh yeah—" he leaned in close, inhaling deeply "—I learned that you smell like a memory and a promise—chocolate and cinnamon all rolled into one."

There went her heart again, skipping and jumping and acting more foolish than it ever had when she'd been around Brian. "Tristan—"

"You deserve a lot better than a man like Brian, Sunshine. I'm glad you realized it." His lips touched hers, the contact so brief Martha could almost believe she'd imagined it. Almost.

"Lock the door." He left before Martha could respond, moving through the room and disappearing out the back door as quickly as he'd arrived, the house falling silent behind him.

Alone again.

Just the way she should want it.

She turned off the kitchen light and retreated to her bedroom. It had been a long day. Tomorrow would be longer. The best thing she could do was forget her worries and concentrate on getting the rest she needed. But as she settled into her bed, she couldn't deny the truth. As much as she might want to convince herself otherwise, alone really wasn't what she wanted to be.

ELEVEN

Tristan's cell phone rang at a little past seven in the morning. He'd been awake for an hour by then, and he scowled as he saw his older brother Grayson's phone number on the display. "It's seven o'clock."

"And?"

"And you said you'd give me a six o'clock wake-up call."

"You want a wake-up call, go stay in a hotel."

"I can't stay in a hotel and do my job at the same time."

"What job? You're on medical leave."

"That doesn't mean I'm not working."

"You shouldn't be." The oldest of the five Sinclair siblings, Grayson had definite ideas about what his brothers and sister should and should not do.

"That's my choice to make."

"That doesn't mean I have to like it."

"You're trying to tell me you're worried?" Tristan nearly snorted at the thought. Grayson was a lot of things, but he wasn't a worrier. As a matter of fact, he'd talked Tristan into more than his fair share of trouble when they were teens.

"*Mom* is worried. I'm just disgusted that you'd go to such great lengths to get out of painting our parents' house."

"It's that time already?" They'd been helping their father paint the hundred-year-old farmhouse they'd grown up in since they were old enough to lift a brush. Every three years they'd congregate at the old house and enjoy each other's company while they made sure the house looked bright and cheerful as per their mother's orders.

"First weekend in November, just like always."

"I thought we painted two years ago."

"Three. We painted the year I met..." He didn't finish, but Tristan knew exactly what he was going to say—the year he'd met Maria. A woman Tristan had never liked, and who, he had to admit, he was glad his brother had decided not to marry.

"That's right. I forgot. I may be able to make it if things here wrap up quickly."

"Somehow I don't think that's going to happen."

"Why not? Gordon Johnson isn't known for patience."

"He's also not known for stupidity." Grayson had good reason to know. A state prosecutor, he knew plenty about Gordon Johnson and his boss.

"True. One way or another, though, I'll be around when he decides to make his move." Tristan crossed the room and looked out the window. Martha's house shone brilliant white in the first rays of morning light, the windows reflecting the navy blue sky and the gold and red leaves of the trees that surrounded the property. A wide creek, filled from the fall rain, meandered through autumn-brown grass. At another time, Tristan would have appreciated the quiet beauty and peaceful tranquillity of the place. Now all he could do was see the potential for danger.

"Just be careful, bro. Johnson and Buddy have avoided prosecution for a long time. There's no way either plans to have that change now."

"Understood."

"Good. Do you need anything for your late-night stakeouts?"

"A futon. A chair. Some groceries."

"Seems like a lot to fit in one car."

"Martha's got an apartment over her garage. She offered it to me."

"And you accepted?"

"Yeah. Is there a problem with that?"

"No. I've just never known you to take the easy path in anything."

"What's easy about sleeping on the floor?"

"Good point. Listen, I've got an early meeting, so I've got to run. Give me the address and I'll drop off the stuff you need later in the day."

Tristan rattled off the house number and street address, then hung up and stepped outside. His arm throbbed and his body ached, but talking to his brother had lightened his mood. A mood that had been storm-cloud dark since he'd learned that Johnson had eluded capture. He'd wanted the man behind bars in a big way. Buddy might be the boss, but it was Johnson who carried out the orders. In Tristan's mind, that made him just as dangerous. Maybe more so.

Dry grass crunched under his feet as Tristan rounded the corner of the house and surveyed the front yard. Somewhere overhead a hawk called, the sound haunting in the still morning air. This was what life should be about—the beauty of God's creation. The harmony of nature. The peace that came from enjoying the bountiful gifts of the Creator.

Should be, but wasn't.

Much as he might appreciate the scenery, Tristan knew how fleeting peace was. Evil tainted every picturesque landscape. He'd seen it over and over again, and wouldn't be lulled into complacency by the sweet serenity the morning offered. That, he knew, was a surefire way to get killed.

A soft sound broke the stillness, and Tristan tensed, scanning the yard. Everything looked as it should, the rustle of leaves in the breeze the only movement. Maybe he'd imagined the sound.

Maybe.

And maybe something ugly was hidden behind nature's splendor. He pulled his gun, the cool metal a comforting weight in his hand. There it was again. The snap of a twig, the crunch of grass. Something big, but not Johnson. No way would the gunrunner announce his presence that way.

Tristan slid the weapon back into its holster, watching and waiting as the sounds drew closer.

A figure stepped out from the thick stand of trees. Short. Athletic build. Wearing a bright green jacket, jeans and hiking boots. Martha. Tristan scowled as she moved into the clearing, completely oblivious to his presence, her focus on something she held in a towel.

Sunlight danced off golden hair and highlighted the smoothness of her skin. Cheeks pink from the cold, her hair a mop of wild curls, she looked pretty and compelling and much too vulnerable for Tristan's comfort.

"What are you doing out here?" His tone was harsher than he intended, his frustration and his worry coming out in a near bark that made Martha jump and spin toward him. "Tristan! You nearly scared the life out of me."

"Better to have it scared out of you than choked out of you. I thought we agreed that you weren't going to wander around alone."

"I'm not alone." She glanced over her shoulder, looked confused for a moment, then shrugged. "At least, I wasn't. I guess Eldridge got sidetracked somewhere."

"Eldridge?" She'd been out taking a walk in the early-morning hours with a *man.* Tristan knew he should be happy that she hadn't been outside alone, but the thought of her taking a romantic stroll with another man didn't do much to his happy meter.

"My mailman."

Could it get any better? If Tristan's arm hadn't been throbbing so badly he might have laughed.

"You and your mailman are in the habit of taking early-morning strolls together?"

"Eldridge lives across the creek on the other side of the woods. *He's* in the habit of taking early-morning strolls and sometimes he stops here for coffee before he goes home."

"I see." And he didn't like it. Martha and her mail carrier out on romantic hikes through the woods. No, he didn't like it at all.

"Today he found this little guy." She moved toward Tristan, peeling back the towel and revealing a scrawny cat whose torn ear and feral hiss made Tristan want to pull the creature from Martha's hands and let it go back to whatever back alley it had come from.

"He looks mean."

"He's hurt. Eldridge asked me to help catch him so I could take him to the vet clinic." She dropped the towel back over the cat's head, bright red scratches visible on her knuckles and wrist.

Tristan grabbed her hand, tugging her close so that he could examine the wounds, his fingers wrapped around warm, soft flesh. "These need to be cleaned and bandaged."

"I'll do it after I get a carrier for Fluffy."

"Fluffy? That cat is scrawnier than a scarecrow without stuffing."

"He won't be once we get him cleaned up and treated, and put some groceries in him."

Tristan wasn't convinced, but decided not to say as much. Standing out front of Martha's house chatting about the rehabilitation of a scruffy cat wasn't high on his list of safe things to do. "Where's the carrier?"

"I've got three or four out in the garage." She started around the side of the house, but Tristan pulled her up short.

"I'll take the cat and get the carrier. You go inside and take care of those scratches."

"I can't let you lug around a squirming cat when you've got a broken arm."

"Who said anything about letting me? Give me the cat and go inside. It's not safe out here."

"Everything okay?" A man stepped out from the trees, his dark gaze dropping from Tristan's face to his hand, which was still on Martha's arm.

"Fine." Martha smiled warmly, her eyes glowing vivid green and burnished gold. "Come over and meet Tristan. He's the agent I was telling you about."

"The one that's staying out in the apartment?" The man moved toward them. Tall. A few years older than Tristan, he had a guarded smile and was carrying a handful of bright orange and yellow leaves.

"That's right. Tristan, this is Eldridge Grady. Mail carrier and distant neighbor. Eldridge, Tristan Sinclair. ATF agent."

"Good to meet you." Tristan offered his hand and was surprised by Eldridge's firm shake. Not aggressive or territorial as some men got when a woman they were interested in was close by.

"You, too. Thanks for taking care of Marti. My

wife and I have been worried about her since she had that run-in with trouble Friday."

Wife? Apparently Tristan had completely mis-read the situation. Suddenly, his bottom-of-the-barrel mood lifted. "I'm worried about her, too. That's why I was asking her to go inside. Until we capture the man I'm looking for, Martha needs to stay behind closed doors as much as possible."

Eldridge turned his attention to Martha, scowl-ing darkly. "Why didn't you tell me you were still in danger? I never would have asked for your help if I'd known."

"I—"

"Give me the cat and get yourself inside. Mary won't ever forgive me if something happens to you because I couldn't catch a mangy cat myself." El-dridge grabbed the cat from her hands.

"Fluffy isn't—"

"Go inside." Tristan turned to Eldridge as Marti finally disappeared inside the house. "Is she always this stubborn?"

"More, but she's got a good heart. Not enough people in this world are like that. You stickin' around for a while?"

"Until I'm a hundred percent convinced Martha will be safe if I leave."

"Good to know. Come on. Let's get this feral beast into a carrier before he decides to start fighting for freedom again and I drop precious cargo."

"I wouldn't call that cat precious."

"I'm talking about the leaves, man. If I go home

without them I'll be in the doghouse for a month." Eldridge nodded toward the leaves he still clutched in his hand.

"Your wife collects leaves?" Tristan took the bundle of gold and red foliage from Eldridge.

"Nah. She's got a fall project planned for her kindergarten class and she needs leaves for it. And don't ask me what the project is. She was telling me during the Cowboys game yesterday and the information got lost somewhere in translation."

"You're a Cowboys fan?"

"Is there any other football team?"

"I could name a few." Tristan tried the garage door, frowning when it opened easily. "Martha needs to be more careful."

"I've been telling her that since she moved out here, but she hasn't listened. I can't tell you the number of times I've delivered mail and found her windows opened."

"Tell me you're kidding."

"Would I kid you about something like that?"

"I guess not. Which carrier do you want? Red? Green? Purple?"

"One is as good as another. I don't think the cat is gonna care. Just grab something, quick. My wife is probably staring at the clock thinking she's going to be late to work if I don't hurry it up."

"Then Fluffy gets purple." Tristan set the leaves down, opened the carrier door. "Here you go."

Eldridge maneuvered the cat in and closed the door. "There. He's ready for transport."

"Thanks for your help."

"I did it for Martha. She's a great lady. I'd hate to see her get hurt."

"I feel the same."

"Yeah?" Eldridge reached down and grabbed the leaves before spearing Tristan with a hard, dark look. "Well, there are all different ways of hurting people, aren't there? Keep that in mind, will you, Sinclair? Martha's had a rough life. She doesn't need any more trouble in it." He strode away before Tristan could respond.

It was for the best.

There wasn't a whole lot Tristan could say. He knew a warning when he heard it, and telling Eldridge he had no intention of hurting Martha wouldn't make any difference. People said things like that all the time. It was their actions that mattered. And Tristan had every intention of taking action. Martha would be safe. He'd make sure of that.

The cat yowled, pulling Tristan from his thoughts.

Time to go. The clock was ticking. Johnson was getting closer. And knowing Martha, she was already heading back outside.

TWELVE

The veterinary clinic's waiting room was crowded when Martha arrived at work. She wasn't surprised. People in Lakeview were curious. Some would say downright nosy. Dogs barked, cats hissed and yowled, people stared and whispered as she moved through the room.

Martha was almost glad Tristan was with her. At least people were getting their money's worth. They'd leave with a story to tell—Martha Gabler escorted by a hunky ATF agent.

She was *almost* glad, but not quite. Because eventually, Lord willing, the nightmare she was living would be over. Tristan would go back to his life. She'd return to hers. Martha could almost hear the conversations that would take place when that happened. All of them would begin with "poor Martha," end with "poor Martha" and have "poor Martha" sprinkled liberally in between.

And she didn't want to be "poor" Martha. Pitied Martha. Martha who'd grown up without a mother.

Martha who'd had to help at her father's shop instead of hanging out with other kids during high school. She frowned, pushing open the door that separated the waiting area from the offices and exam rooms beyond. She'd thought she'd gotten over that years ago. Apparently too little sleep and too much fear were affecting her more than she'd thought they would.

"Martha, thank goodness you're here. The phones are ringing off the hook. The exam rooms are full. And to top it all off, Jessa McBride brought in her three dogs for a walk-in. I tried to tell her we were too busy, but she made such a fuss that I put her in room nine just to keep her from bothering our other clients. You'd think that woman was royalty the way she demands…" Lauren Parker's voice trailed off as she caught sight of Tristan and the cat carrier he held.

"Oh, sorry, I didn't realize you'd brought a patient back with you."

"I didn't. This is…" Who should she say Tristan was? A friend? A bodyguard? The man who'd saved her life? "Tristan Sinclair. He's helping me bring in a wounded cat. If you take care of Fluffy, I'll take care of Jessa." Martha took the carrier from Tristan and handed it over the counter before Lauren could ask questions she didn't want to answer.

"Fine by me. I'd rather deal with a feral cat than that woman." Lauren was still eyeing Tristan with blatant interest.

And why wouldn't she be? He was probably the best-looking man to set foot in the clinic since the doors opened three years ago.

Martha knew she shouldn't be bothered by Lauren's interest. After all, she had no claim on Tristan. Somehow, though, she was.

"Is Tori in yet?" Her question succeeded in drawing Lauren's attention away from Tristan.

"Her baby was fussy, so she's running a few minutes late. I told her we could handle things until she got here, but I didn't know things were going to be so hectic."

"How about Dr. Gerald?"

"He's not due in until ten. By that time, we'll have half the population of Lakeview complaining about our service."

"The good news is, our closest competitor is thirty miles away. Even if our clients are unhappy, they've got nowhere else to go." Martha attempted a smile as she hurried past the receptionist's desk and into a corridor lined with doors, doing her best to act as if this was any other day at work.

Of course it wasn't.

Tristan was right behind her, his presence impossible to ignore. Not just because Martha could hear his quiet footfall, but because she could feel him there.

Warmth. Strength. Confidence. They were as tangible and real as the first rays of sunlight after a storm. And just as welcome, even though she knew she shouldn't feel that way.

If she was smart, she'd turn around and tell him to go. Apparently, though, her brain cells weren't functioning today, because she couldn't muster the gumption to do it. Instead, she let him follow as she knocked on the door to room nine, braced herself and stepped inside. Three ratlike dogs rushed toward her, growling and barking in a high-pitched frenzy. Martha stood her ground. She'd dealt with Jessa's spoiled pooches enough to know they were all bark.

"Sheba, Sherry, Shelby! Cease!" Jessa walked toward Martha. No. She didn't walk. She glided, her head high, her dark skirt and pink blouse flawlessly tailored. Perfectly arched brows highlighted eyes that were blue today and might be green, purple or violet on her next visit. Collagen lips, Botox-smooth forehead, skin that was just a little too tight across her cheekbones and at the corner of her eyes, Jessa might have been forty or seventy.

Martha pegged her for mid-sixties and a lesson in what not to do as she grew older. Some things were meant to be—lines and wrinkles were two of them. "Jessa, how are you today?"

"It's not my health that's an issue."

"Lauren said this was an emergency visit. What's going on with the girls?"

"I'm surprised you need to ask. Can't you hear the problem?" Her gaze skittered from Martha to Tristan, her eyes widening. "Oh my. I didn't realize you had someone with you, Martha. Are you a new vet tech? Or perhaps a veterinarian? I didn't realize Tori was hiring someone else."

"Actually, ma'am, I'm neither of those. I'm here with Martha." Tristan's voice rumbled out and even the dogs seemed affected by it. They stilled, their beady little eyes riveted to the man in their midst.

Was no female immune to his charms?

Jessa obviously wasn't. She stepped closer, batting her fake eyelashes. "You're with Martha? As in—the two of you are together? What a surprise so soon after her engagement ended. And what a shock that was. We'd all hoped she'd finally found the man of her dreams."

"Brian wasn't nearly good enough for her, so I can't see how her breaking up with him would have surprised anyone."

Martha's cheeks heated, and she knew if she looked, she'd see amusement in Tristan's eyes. She chose not to look. "What he means is—"

"Exactly what I said."

"Oh my." Jessa's gaze jumped from Tristan to Martha and back again, and it was obvious she was already spinning the tale she'd tell her bridge club friends. "Well, then. I guess since things are so busy here today, I'll take my leave. You can set up an appointment for tomorrow, Martha, can't you? First thing in the morning, if you will. The girls are on their best behavior right after breakfast."

"Of course."

"I'll see you then, my dear." Jessa gathered her dogs' leashes, glided across the room to grab her purse, then returned to Martha's side, her long-nailed age-spot-free hand gripping Martha's bicep. "Do try to hold on to this one, Martha. You're not getting any younger, and soon the only catches you'll make will be old men or fathers of little hoodlums."

"Jessa!"

But Jessa was already heading down the corridor, her dogs barking and growling beside her.

"She's quite a lady." Tristan had moved closer, so close his breath ruffled Martha's hair as he spoke. If she turned, she'd be nose to nose with him. Or, rather, forehead to chin. Which was really close to lips to lips. Which was way too close for comfort.

"Yes. She is." And Tristan was quite a guy. A fact that Martha decided not to comment on.

She stepped away, moving down the corridor to the next door and pulling a file from the pocket there. Taylor Murphy and his guinea pig, Mop. "I'm going to check on the next patient. You can make yourself comfortable in the waiting area."

"I don't think so."

"So you're planning on following me around all day?"

"I am."

"I think that's unnecessary."

"I don't, so let's just play it my way and see how things go."

"Fine, but don't blame me if you're bored out of your mind inside of an hour."

"Sunshine, I could never be bored hanging out with you." He smiled, that easy, warm grin that made his eyes glow and his face soften, and Martha's traitorous heart did a little happy dance.

Who was she kidding?

It was a happy jig. A big one. The kind that was accompanied by bells and whistles and shooting stars. The kind it had done when Tristan had kissed her.

Three times.

Which was three times too many. She did not need a man in her life. The sooner her heart realized that, the happier she'd be. With that in mind, she did what any clear-thinking, romance-avoiding, smitten-with-a-guy-who'd-last-as-long-as-a-warm-day-in-the-Arctic woman would do. She ran, pushing open the door of the exam room and turning all her attention to Taylor and his pet.

Eight hours later, Martha had managed to answer several dozen questions regarding her health and well-being, field way too many questions about the illegal-weapons raid she'd been part of, assure dozens of well-meaning people that she was just fine and almost get used to Tristan's presence.

Almost.

She'd just filed the last chart and grabbed her jacket from a hook in the back room when her cell phone rang. She glanced at the number. "It's my dad. I'll just pick up the call. Then we can head out."

"Take your time. I'm in no hurry." Tristan leaned a shoulder against the wall and managed to look sincere, though Martha was sure he'd been ready to leave an hour after they'd arrived. Not that he'd complained. No, that would have made him too human.

And much less attractive.

She turned away from his steady gaze and answered the phone. "Hey, Dad. What's up?"

"Sue and I are going to be in your neighborhood tonight. We thought it might be nice to have dinner together."

"Dad, I'm a little tired."

"Too tired to spend time with your old man?"

"You're not old."

"Maybe not, but I'm pushing it. So, what do you say? Sue suggested we pick up Chinese food."

"Really, Dad, I've barely slept in three days, and I'm not sure I have the energy for company."

"Funny you should say that, I heard that you had plenty of energy for company last night."

"What?" Obviously, fatigue was playing tricks on her mind, because she was sure she must have misunderstood her father's words.

"Mary Grady saw Sue at the grocery store. She said you had a friend over last night. A male friend."

"Not a friend, Dad. Tristan."

"Thanks a lot." Tristan whispered the words so close to her ear, Martha felt the warmth of his breath.

She ignored him. At least, she tried to. "And I didn't have him over. I let him stay in the garage apartment. It was either that or leave him to sleep in his car."

"I'm glad to hear it, doll. I don't mind saying I'm worried about you. Having Tristan around makes me feel better."

"You don't need to worry Dad."

"Of course I do. I'm your father. It's my job."

"You're my father, and you taught me how to take care of myself."

"You keep bringing that up."

"Because it's true, Dad." Martha sighed, knowing that dinner with her father and Sue was inevitable. No way could she refuse. "Tell Sue Chinese food sounds great."

"You're sure?"

"Sure."

"Great. We'll see you in an hour."

"Right. Great." She mumbled the words as she tossed the phone into her purse.

"I take it we're having dinner with your dad and Sue."

"*We're* not having dinner with anyone. I'm having dinner. You're going to do whatever it is you feel like doing after I'm safe inside my house." She knew she sounded waspish, and tried to curb her irritable mood, brushing back curls that had escaped their clip and meeting Tristan's eyes. "Sorry. That didn't come out the way I meant it."

"No need to apologize." He took her hand, his fingers linking with hers. "It's been a long day, but it's over. Now we can go home, have some Chinese food with your folks, enjoy a few hours of normalcy."

"Nothing about the last few days has been normal."

"No? It's been a while since I've lived anything close to what most people would consider a normal life, but I'd say spending time with people who care about you is about as normal as it gets." His fingers tightened around hers as he escorted her outside, and Martha couldn't help wondering what it was like to live undercover, how it was possible to be one person at the same time you were another.

Who was the real Tristan Sinclair?

What would it be like to discover the things that made him that person?

She pulled her thoughts away from dangerous territory. She did not want to know anything more about Tristan than she already did. Too much knowledge would only lead to eventual disappointment. Or worse. Expectations. And in that direction lay the path to heartache. Of that Martha was very, very sure.

She tugged her hand away from his, and climbed into her car. Being vulnerable stunk, and that's exactly how she felt. Vulnerable because her dream of marriage and family was gone. Vulnerable because she was about to be relegated to the position of old maid and she wasn't even thirty.

Vulnerable because Gordon Johnson wanted her dead.

Vulnerable because Tristan made her want to do exactly what she'd been raised not to do—rely on someone else.

Vulnerable.

Yeah, it stunk.

What stunk even more was that until Johnson was caught, she'd just have to keep on feeling that way. And maybe that was the point. Maybe God wanted her to realize she really couldn't do everything on her own. Maybe He wanted her to rely less on herself and more on Him. There was a lesson to be learned through the trials she was undergoing. She was sure of that. Eventually she'd figure out what it was.

If she lived long enough.

That unhappy thought followed her all the way back to her peaceful cottage in the woods.

THIRTEEN

Dinner was more comfortable than Martha expected. Sure, her father shot looks in Tristan's direction every few minutes, but Sue kept up a steady patter of conversation, and Tristan seemed happy enough to join in.

All in all, things went a lot better than Martha thought they would. By the time Sue served coffee and homemade sugar cookies, Martha was relaxed enough to enjoy her stepmother's less than subtle questioning of Tristan. It was nice to have her ATF agent bodyguard on the spot for a change. Not that Tristan seemed to mind. He answered every question, telling stories about his family, his childhood, his faith, his job.

The fact that he didn't get frustrated or annoyed with Sue would have raised him to the top of Martha's acceptable-husband-material list if she'd had one. Which she didn't.

Maybe that had been her problem all along.

Maybe if she had a list of acceptable characteristics, she wouldn't have spent so much time with Brian, whose brisk, sometimes irritated attitude toward Martha's family should have been the first clue as to where their relationship was headed.

Nowhere.

"Well, doll, this has been fun, but I've got to get Sue home. She turns into a pumpkin if we're out past ten."

"Me? You're the one who can't keep your eyes open after a good meal." Sue patted her husband's arm, her round face as comfortable and kind as an old friend. After all his years of being alone, Jesse seemed to be settling into married life with ease. Martha smiled as the two bantered back and forth, her gaze drifting to Tristan.

He met her eyes, his expression guarded, his gaze intense and searching. As if he could see something in her that others couldn't. As if he might know more than she wanted him to.

She stood, turning away from his probing gaze. "All right. Enough bickering about which one of you is more decrepit. You're both perfect. This really was a great evening. Thanks for coming over."

"You're right. It was fun, doll." Her father pulled her into a bear hug and kissed her cheek. "Thank you for letting us come."

"Letting you? You know you're always welcome here, Dad."

"I know I'm an old busybody who can't stand not knowing what's going on in his daughter's life. That's what I know. And I know you're a good daughter for putting up with me."

"I'm not putting up with anything. I love having you and Sue over. Whether I issue an invitation or not."

"Just as long as we don't wear out our welcome. Sue, you want to grab your purse and jacket and we'll get out of Marti's hair?" He strode down the hall and pulled the door open, draping an arm around Martha's shoulder and pulling her in for one last hug.

"Get away from the door. You're backlit." Tristan's sharp words were cut off as something slammed into Martha's shoulder. She spun sideways, blood spraying her face, her father shouting, shoving her hard, then falling beside her. Sue screamed. Tristan shouted again.

Glass shattered. Pain roared through Martha, but she barely felt it over the wild pounding of fear. Johnson had come for her, just as Tristan had said he would, and the world as she knew it was over. The thoughts were quick staccato beats in her mind, the lights, the sounds, the smells all searing into her brain.

"Dad." She tried to sit up, but Tristan shoved her back down, covering her body with his own. A gun in his hand pointed out the open door. Firing. Once. Twice. Then there was silence, so deep, so black it stole Martha's breath.

"Don't move." Tristan's lips pressed against her ear as he levered forward and pushed the door shut. The soft click seemed to echo in Martha's head, spiraling in circles of color that made her stomach heave. She pushed up onto her elbows, and saw her father lying in a pool of blood, his chest covered in deep red as his life poured out.

"Dad!"

"I said, don't move." Tristan barked the command as he pressed his jacket against Jesse's chest. "Sue, call 911. Tell the dispatcher we need a Life Flight."

Life Flight. The words registered, but Martha couldn't allow herself to think about what they meant. She *wouldn't* allow herself to think about them, but they were there anyway, staining the wood floor, darkening the grain. Blood. Life. Oozing from her father.

She struggled to her knees, ignoring Tristan's next sharp command, to lean over her father, seeing his hazel eyes deep in a face so pale Martha thought he might already be gone.

"Don't worry, doll, I'll be fine." He wheezed the words out, and Martha's heart clenched.

"Of course you will. Just be quiet for now. Save your energy."

"For what? I don't think I'm gonna be doing much of anything for a while." He grinned, but his smile seemed to fade as his colorless face shrank in on itself, his eyes closing.

"Dad?"

"Lie down, Sunshine, before you fall down." Tristan growled the words, barking for towels in the same breath. Blood seeping over his hand, bubbling up from the dark, ugly wound in her father's chest.

Light faded. Sound diminished. Then returned. Louder. Brighter. Hands pressed Martha down. Concerned faces peered into hers. People shouted. Sirens blared. Mayhem and order all at the same time. Somewhere close by, a woman sobbed, the broken sound carrying over the cacophony of noise. Martha levered up, caught sight of Sue standing alone in the crowd, her face pale and streaked with tears.

"Sue—"

"You need to lie still, ma'am." Firm hands pressed Martha back down, and she looked up into concerned brown eyes.

"Is my father going to be okay?"

"They're airlifting him out."

Which wasn't an answer. Martha's brain was working enough for her to know that. "But is he going to be okay?"

"They'll do everything they can for him." The paramedic pressed another bandage to Martha's shoulder, holding it in place as he asked question after question that didn't matter until she finally shoved his hand away, and stood on shaky legs.

"Ma'am, you need to—"

"Find out what's going on with my father." Because he was the only real family she had. The one person who knew her and accepted her for who she was. The person who'd taught her what it meant to persist, to work hard, to have faith. To believe. In God. In people. In herself. And she wasn't going let them put him on a helicopter and fly him away before she said goodbye.

"Martha, it is Martha, right? You're going to do your father more harm than good if you get in the way of the medics who are treating him." The paramedic said something to the young woman next to him, and she nodded, moving toward Martha, speaking in the calm, soothing tones usually reserved for overwrought children. None of her words registered. None of what she said mattered. What mattered was seeing her father again. Just in case.

In case it was the last time. In case she never saw him alive again.

The ugly thought wouldn't leave, and Martha turned, her mind fuzzy as she tried to see past the people crowded around her father.

"Life Flight is two minutes out. Let's roll." A flurry of activity followed the shouted words, Sue's loud wail joining the frenzy of noise and activity.

Now Martha could see the stretcher being wheeled away. The small figure on it was the man who'd sung her lullabies in a rusty voice, who'd walked her to school on the first day of kindergarten, who'd dried her tears when she'd cried. Who'd been there when her mother had not. Steady. Sure. Unchanging through all the years of trouble they'd faced together.

"Can I just say goodbye?" The words barely escaped her dry throat, and she knew that no one heard them. That her father would be wheeled away, his life in the hands of doctors and nurses. And God.

Please, just let him be okay, Lord.

"Sunshine?" Tristan was suddenly in front of her, his eyes filled with worry, his harsh features softened with compassion. "You've got thirty seconds with your dad." He grabbed her hand, leading her through the crowd that parted as easily as it had closed ranks against her.

Her father lay pale and unmoving on the stretcher, his eyes closed, his breathing shallow. If she could have spoken, Martha would have told him everything would be okay, but she couldn't speak past the tears in her throat. She just leaned forward, pressed a kiss to his forehead. "I love you, Daddy."

His eyes flickered open, his lips twitched into a smile. "Love you, too. Don't miss me too much, doll. You hear?"

Then they were rushing him away, toward the main road and the helicopter's thunderous approach.

"We need to take you to Lakeview Memorial, Martha. Let me help you onto the stretcher and we'll get going." The female paramedic put a hand on her arm, urging her toward another stretcher.

"Where are they taking my father?"

"Lynchburg General. It's farther away, but it's got a Level I trauma center."

"Then that's where I'm going, too." She shrugged away from the woman's hold. No way did she plan on going anywhere but where her father was.

"You're going to the hospital that's closest, Sunshine. When the doctor releases you, I'll take you to your dad."

"It might be too late by then." Martha's voice broke, and Tristan pulled her into his arms, feeling warm blood soaking through his shirt. She was still bleeding; not like her father, but enough for concern.

He stepped toward the stretcher, maneuvering her backward, wishing he had two good arms and not just one. "It won't be too late. Your dad is a tough guy. If anyone can pull through this he can."

"I need to be with him, Tristan. He's the only family I've got."

"Not now. Now he needs to be with the surgeons who are going to treat him."

"I can't just…let him go."

"No one is asking you to. We're just asking you to make sure that you're ready to help him when he needs it."

"Would you feel the same if it was your father they'd just taken away?" She looked up into his eyes, and he saw shock and a hollowness that he'd seen in the eyes of every victim he'd ever met. It made him cold with rage and with remorse. He should have warned Martha and her dad before they went to the front door. Should have been there in front of them, making sure Johnson didn't have his chance to steal one of their lives. He tamped down the emotions. He had to get Martha to the hospital. Then he'd go after Johnson and make sure he paid for what he'd done.

"I'd feel the way you do, babe. Scared and worried, but hopefully I'd have friends who'd make sure I got the treatment I needed anyway."

"This shouldn't have happened. How did it happen?"

"I don't know." He'd known Johnson would act,

but he hadn't suspected the gunrunner would do so when there was so much room for error. With Tristan in the house. With witnesses around. With plenty of ways he could be seen or caught.

He should have known.

"But I do know this, I'm going to find Gordon Johnson, and I'm going to make sure he pays."

"It won't matter if my father dies."

"He won't." But even as he said it, Tristan knew that the chances of Jesse Gabler surviving were slim. The bullet had pierced his lung. Tristan had heard it in every gasping breath Martha's father had taken.

"Maybe I do need to go to the hospital." Martha swayed, and Tristan pulled her close, supporting her weight with one arm as paramedics rushed forward, lifting her, settling her onto the stretcher. Blood streamed from her shoulder, pooling beneath her and dripping onto the ground. Not as bad as her father, but bad enough.

It should not have happened.

He shouldn't have let it happen.

He clenched his jaw, shoving aside his anger. At himself. At Gordon Johnson. At his boss for not putting Martha in a safe house days ago.

"You're going to be okay, Sunshine." He brushed hair off her forehead, and was relieved when she opened her eyes.

She glanced over at her stepmother who was being given oxygen. "Will you take Sue to Lynchburg General and stay with her until we know what's happening with Dad?"

The desire to stay with Martha was so overpowering, Tristan almost said no. But the desperation in her eyes kept him silent. There were police everywhere, easing through grass and brush, searching for evidence that would lead to Johnson. Martha would be safe enough without him, but leaving her bleeding and scared was one of the hardest things he'd ever done.

"Whatever you need, Sunshine."

"That's what I need."

"Then I'll go. If you promise to stay at Lakeview Memorial until I can come get you."

"I promise."

"I'm going to hold you up to that." He trailed his knuckles across her cheekbone. Her skin was icy, but she forced a smile.

"Call me when you know something."

"I will." He let his hand drop, reluctantly moving away from Martha as they took her to the ambulance. When the doors to the ambulance closed, he turned to Sue, easing down onto the step beside her, covering her hand with his.

"Are you okay?"

"I don't know."

"Martha wants me to bring you to Lynchburg General. Are you up to it?"

"Yes. Thank you, Tristan."

He stood, offering his hand and gently pulling her to her feet. He'd do what he'd told Martha he would. He just prayed that when he called her he'd have good news rather than bad. He had to believe that's what he'd have. The world was full of ugliness, but sometimes there was a glimmer of beauty that couldn't be denied. A miracle that refused to be ignored. This was going to be one of those times. It had to be.

Lord, this time, let it be. Place Your hand upon Jesse Gabler so that he can return safely home to his wife. To Martha.

Tristan silently prayed as he escorted Sue to his car and drove her toward the hospital.

FOURTEEN

Martha prayed on her way to the hospital. She prayed as she was X-rayed and examined and as the deep gouge across the fleshy part of her shoulder was cleaned and stitched. She prayed while she was being questioned by the police and when she was left alone in a dimly lit hospital room, a television playing endless reruns.

And then she prayed some more while she waited, and waited and waited.

Please, God, let my father be okay. Please, God, let him live. Please let Tristan call me soon.

Please.

She pulled back the curtain and stared outside, smiling grimly when she realized she'd been put in a room that looked onto the roof of another part of the building. Four stories up. It would be all but impossible for Johnson to take a shot at her through the window. Obviously the police thought they were keeping her safe. If only they'd been as concerned about that *before* her father had been shot, then maybe he would have stayed safe.

Seconds ticked into minutes. Then into an hour. Then two. No one entered the room. The phone didn't ring. And like a prisoner waiting for release, Martha did nothing but pace and wonder if she'd ever get out. Her shoulder was numb, but her head ached with an insistent throbbing that made her stomach twist. Fear was a horrible beast, robbing the brain of the ability to think and the body of the ability to act. Martha knew she should do something, but couldn't decide what. Instead of calling Lynchburg General, or dialing Sue's cell phone, or calling friends who might come to keep her company, she paced the room. Scared of what a phone call might reveal, afraid that having friends close might put them in danger.

"I know you're with me, Lord, but I have never felt so alone in my life." She whispered the words as she settled onto the edge of the bed, her muscles so tense and sore that she felt closer to a hundred years old than to thirty.

A soft knock sounded on the door, and Martha braced herself for bad news as a police officer peered into the room. Older, maybe in his early sixties, his eyes were deep brown in nutmeg skin and so filled with compassion, Martha's throat tightened with tears she knew she couldn't allow herself to shed. Once she started crying, there was no way she'd be able to stop.

"Ms. Gabler? Dr. Brian McMath is asking to see you. He says he's a friend of yours. Do you know him?"

"Yes."

"Are you up to a visitor? Or would you rather I send him away?"

Under normal circumstances, Brian was the last person she would want to see, but these circumstances weren't normal and she wasn't sure what to do about his visit. Half of her wanted to send him away. The other half, the half that was terrified and lonely and unsure, wanted company no matter who that company might be.

"I...have you heard anything about my father?"

He shook his head. "I'm sorry. I haven't. I'll let you know if I do."

"Thank you."

"Should I send Dr. McMath away?"

There it was again. The same question that she hadn't known how to answer and still didn't. When had she forgotten how to make simple decisions? Probably at the same time she'd watched her father's blood seep out onto the floor. She shuddered. "No. That's okay. He can come in."

"All right. I'll be outside your room for the rest of the night, so if you need anything, just let me know."

"I will." But all she needed was to know that her father was okay and to hear that Johnson was behind bars, and no matter how hard she prayed, she just wasn't sure she would be hearing either any time soon.

The officer stepped back from the door, spoke quietly to someone else and then Brian walked into the room, his lab coat over a pristine shirt and muted tie, his hair perfectly combed and parted. Typical

Brian. No matter how late the hour or busy the day, he always looked perfect.

"How are you feeling, Martha?" He spoke quietly, his words softer than she'd expected.

"I'm okay."

"I talked to your attending physician. You should be able to leave in the morning."

"Good."

"I also put in a call to Lynchburg General. Your father is in surgery. It may be hours before he's out."

Surprised, Martha met his gaze. "Thank you for checking on him for me."

"It's the least I could do under the circumstances." He cleared his throat, took a seat on the bed next to her. "Listen, I'm really sorry this happened to you and your dad. I know we had our differences while we were dating, but I only ever wanted the best for you. Sometimes my way of expressing that leaves something to be desired."

An apology? From Brian? Like everything else that had happened, it seemed unreal. Part of a strange dream that Martha wanted to wake from but couldn't. "It's okay."

"It isn't, really." He sighed and stood. "Look, I just wanted to tell you I'm here if you need anything. And that I'll try to keep you updated on your father. I'm praying things go okay with the surgery, but I want you to know that it's going to be touch-and-go. Your father is older. He's in grave condition. You should prepare yourself."

Now he sounded more like the Brian she knew.

Stating the facts with blunt disregard to her feelings. Much as she knew she needed to hear the truth, she wouldn't have minded having it couched in some pretty words of comfort. "How does a person prepare for something like this?"

He blinked, shook his head. "If I knew that, I'd be able to make things easier for a lot of people. Call my cell if you need anything."

He walked away, closing the door with a soft click and leaving Martha in silent darkness, his words hanging in the air.

Grave condition.

Touch-and-go.

She'd known it before Brian had said the words, but hearing them made it so much more real. More final. As if her father's death were a done deal. Over already while she sat twiddling her thumbs waiting for news. A hot tear escaped and slid down her cheek. She ignored it, holding herself still, holding her emotions in, trying to pretend the world wasn't falling apart while the pieces of it tumbled soundlessly around her.

"Lord, I really need to know that You're here. That everything will be okay. That I'm not as alone as I feel." She spoke the prayer out loud, her voice raspy and dry. Until now, she'd thought her faith capable of withstanding whatever the world might throw at it, but suddenly she wasn't quite as certain. It would be nice to have a sign, some tangible proof that God was intervening in ways she couldn't see.

She flopped onto her back, staring up at the ceiling and wishing she was as sure of things as she'd been a week ago. There was something to be said for going through life naively believing things would always stay the same. Of course, she'd known they'd change. She'd just never imagined they'd change like this. That during the course of a few days, everything she held dear could be threatened.

On the far wall a clock ticked the endless minutes as Martha waited for news. Twice, she placed a call to Lynchburg General. Twice, she was told her father was still in surgery. That was better than the alternative. Much better. But Martha could take little comfort in it. Anything could happen in surgery. As Brian had said, her father was older, less hardy than someone a decade or two younger. And he'd lost so much blood. If she closed her eyes, she could see it, oozing out onto the floor, bubbling up between Tristan's fingers.

Marti gagged, then sat up, letting her head drop down to her knees.

She barely heard the door when it opened, and didn't bother to look up to greet her visitor. A nurse, probably. Or a doctor. Or Brian, back to tell her something else she didn't want to hear.

"Hey, babe. How are you holding up?" Tristan's voice should have pulled her from the fog she was in, made her leap from the bed and rush forward to demand answers, but she couldn't make herself look up, let alone stand. She was afraid. Afraid of what she might see in his face and in his eyes.

The mattress dipped under his weight as he sat beside her. Close. So close she could feel the cold chill of fall that he'd carried in. He brushed hair from her neck, his hand sliding across her skin.

"Sunshine?" He pulled her in, wrapping her in autumn mist and strength. "Your dad is out of surgery. He's alive."

At his words the tension that held her upright seeped out, and she sagged against him, her arms wrapping around his waist, her face buried against his shoulder. She wanted to ask questions, but her body shook with fatigue, with relief, with fear that still thrummed through her, and she couldn't get the words out.

"It's okay. Everything is going to be okay." Tristan smoothed her hair, pressed her closer to his chest. She could feel his heart beat, the steady rhythm clashing with her frantic pulse. The tears she'd been trying so hard to hold at bay escaped, rolling down her cheeks, spilling onto Tristan's shirt. She let them fall, too drained to wipe them away. Her father was alive. For now, that was all she would think about. For now, that would have to be enough.

FIFTEEN

Tristan grabbed a blanket from the end of the bed and pulled it around Martha's shoulders, wishing he could offer her more.

He couldn't give her what he wanted—a promise that her father would live and that he'd fully recover. The doctors were giving Jesse Gabler a forty percent chance of survival. But doctors didn't know everything. Only God could determine whether the man would live or die.

"How bad is he?" Martha lifted her head, looking at him for the first time since he'd entered the room. Her face was stark white in the darkness, her eyes feverishly bright.

"He's bad, Sunshine, but not so bad that he can't survive."

"But will he?" She straightened, tugging the blanket close around her chest. She looked young, vulnerable and scared. If he could have, he would have hidden the truth from her, let her think for just a little while that the picture wasn't as grim as doctors were painting it. But he couldn't. No matter how young Martha looked, she was an adult. She had the right to know the truth.

"The doctors are giving him a forty percent chance of making it."

She nodded, let the blanket drop and stood. "That's better than I thought. I'm going to see him."

She took a step away, her movements unsteady enough to make Tristan wonder just how far she'd be able to go.

He jumped up, wrapping his good arm around her waist and adding his support to her trembling legs. "Slow down, babe. You're not going anywhere if you end up on the floor."

"So you're not going to tell me I can't go?"

"He's your father. I'd never tell you that."

She offered a shaky smile. "Okay. Then maybe I'd better sit down for a minute, because things are starting to fade."

"You lost a lot of blood." Too much blood. On Martha. Jesse. The floor. The walls. Everywhere. Because Tristan hadn't thought Johnson would be so brazen. Because he hadn't been careful enough.

Tristan pushed the thoughts away. He needed to focus on the present, not obsess on the past and its mistakes. He helped Martha sit down, poured water from a plastic carafe on the bedside table and held the cup out to her, letting himself think only of now. This moment. Making sure Martha was okay. "Drink this. I'm going to find a wheelchair."

His tone was harsher than he'd intended, and Martha grabbed his hand, holding him in place when he would have walked away. "It wasn't your fault, you know."

Surprised that she'd read him so easily, he squeezed her fingers. "I was there to protect you. I failed. In the process I nearly got your father killed."

"It *wasn't* your fault."

"Sunshine—"

"Don't say it. Don't say that you should have been more careful, or you should have known that Johnson would be there, or that you could have prevented what happened. Because if it's true about you, it's just as true about me. I knew Johnson was a killer. I never should have let Dad come near me. If this is your fault, then we share the blame equally." She looked away as she spoke, and he knew that she believed what she was saying.

"You couldn't have known, and so you couldn't have prevented it."

"Then neither could you." She took a deep, shuddering breath that tore at Tristan's heart. He wanted to make things right. Wanted to be an epic hero, a man who could defeat every monster, even those that couldn't be seen. Like worry. Like fear. Like guilt and self-blame.

He caught her tear with his thumb, wiping it away, his pulse leaping at the contact. He wasn't sure how he felt about that. For years, he'd avoided serious relationships. He'd known too many ATF agents whose marriages had crumbled under the strain of long work hours and uncertain futures. He'd always thought it better to be alone than to risk creating something that wouldn't last. He never went out with a woman more than three times. Any more than that and he risked falling into something he absolutely wanted to avoid.

Lately, though, reassessing his relationship rules seemed like a good idea. Lately, forever seemed like it might just be a possibility. Martha's strength, her independence, her optimism and faith reminded him that as many women as there were who couldn't handle being with a man whose job demanded so much, there were just as many who could.

And only one that he might be willing to try it with.

He forced the thought to the back of his mind, and let his hand fall away from Martha's cheek. "I'll be back with the wheelchair in a minute."

She nodded, but didn't speak. He couldn't blame her. It was nearly four in the morning. If she was feeling as tired as he was, she was probably too exhausted to speak. He did his best to be quick as he found the wheelchair and a nurse who gave him permission to use it. Then he informed the officer on guard duty that Martha was leaving.

Tristan had already spoken to his boss, arranged a safe house for her to stay in until Johnson was caught. There would be no more chances taken. No more opportunities for Johnson to silence Martha.

Now all he needed to do was get Martha out of the hospital under Johnson's radar. He pulled his cell phone out and dialed Grayson's number, relieved when he heard his brother's harsh greeting.

"What?"

"I've got a problem and I need your help."

"At four in the morning?"

"It's a big one."

"Tell me."

"I'm at Lakeview Memorial. Martha and her father were shot last night."

"How come I didn't hear about this?" Grayson's harsh grumble had been replaced by cold, precise questions. He was in lawyer mode—logical, savvy. Someone Tristan needed on his team.

"We're keeping it quiet. Trying to keep as much information out of Johnson's hands as possible, but I'm not convinced that's kept him from finding her here."

"What do you need me to do?"

"Do you know the all-night convenience store a block west of the hospital?"

"Yeah."

"I need you to meet me there. Martha's father is in bad shape. He's at the Lynchburg trauma center."

"You want me to give you a ride?"

"I do, but it could be dangerous. You need to know that ahead of time."

"And?"

"And there's a potential that someone could get hurt."

"When isn't there? Give me fifteen minutes, and I'll be there." Grayson hung up in typical Grayson style, quickly with no goodbye. As if he didn't have time to waste on such things.

This time, he didn't. They had to move fast. Keep one step ahead of Johnson.

Tristan strode back to Martha's room, expecting to find her seated on the bed just where he'd left her.

Why he'd expected that, he didn't know.

Since he'd met her there hadn't been one time when she'd stayed where he'd asked her to. This time wasn't any different. Instead of sitting meekly on the bed, she was hovering in the doorway, staring down the police officer assigned to guard her as he blocked her path to the hallway.

He stepped aside as Tristan approached, and Martha moved into the hallway dressed in the same dark jeans she'd been wearing earlier, her shirt replaced by a hospital gown. Thick bandages peeked out from beneath the short sleeve of the gown and blood stained her hands.

Had she noticed?

"I thought you were never coming back."

"I tried to be quick. Sit down before you fall down." He took her elbow, urging her into the chair. She was still trembling, but not as violently. Dark crescents shadowed her eyes and her skin was colorless, her lips as pale as her cheeks, her freckles dark specks on white canvas.

Despite that, she looked ready to fight, ready to face whatever would come. "I'm sitting. So, let's go."

"I'll push her." The officer stepped forward. "Which direction?"

"We'll take the service elevator to the basement and go out the delivery bay. I've arranged transportation."

It didn't take long to make it down to the basement. Getting outside took a little longer. Undercover officers searched the perimeter of the building and cleared it before they called for Tristan to move out. He borrowed a heavy jacket from a housekeeper, helped Martha ease her arms into it. Then accepted a jacket the officer who'd accompanied them held out.

He pulled it on, covering his cast. "Thanks for your help. Do you mind bringing the wheelchair back up?"

The officer shook his head. "Not at all. You planning on coming back here tonight?"

No, but that was need-to-know information, and as much as the officer had helped, Martha's whereabouts and schedule were things he didn't need to know. "I'm not sure. We'll call your office if we do."

"Good. You have a good day." The officer wheeled the chair away and disappeared from view.

"Can we go now?" Martha shifted impatiently. Obviously, she was as anxious as Tristan to be on their way. No doubt the same clock that was ticking the minutes away in Tristan's head was ticking in hers.

"If you're ready."

"I've been ready." Martha looked determined, but there was no mistaking the fear in her eyes.

"We don't have to do this, Sunshine. Sue is with your dad. He's not alone. If you don't want to—"

"I said, I'm ready. Is our ride right outside?"

"Johnson will be expecting you to catch a ride from here if you leave. My brother is waiting a block away."

"A block." She straightened her spine, lifted her chin and nodded. "I can make it."

"I knew you'd say that. You're tougher than most of the men I know."

"If that's a compliment, thank you. If it's not, I don't want to know." She smiled, pulling the hood of the jacket over her hair. Her curls peeked out from underneath, brushing against her cheek and neck. Despite her fatigue, she looked beautiful, her eyes gold-green fire.

"It's definitely a compliment." He leaned toward her, knowing he shouldn't do it. Telling himself it wasn't the time or the place. Ignoring his own advice as he inhaled the antiseptic hospital scent that clung to Martha and the more subtle scent of chocolate that was like coming home.

Her eyes widened as his lips brushed hers.

Warm silk.

Sweet honey.

Promises.

He meant the kiss to be brief, but it lingered, the world fading…then coming into sharp focus as footsteps sounded somewhere behind them. He jerked back, glancing over his shoulder. A janitor pushed a cart into a storage closet, then moved away.

"We'd better go." Martha spoke quietly, and Tristan turned back to face her.

She looked the way he felt—surprised.

Worried.

Intrigued.

There was something between them. Something he hadn't expected, but that he wouldn't deny.

Possibilities.

He shouldn't want to explore them, but he did.

There was a reason for that, he thought. God didn't bring people into each other's lives without a purpose. He and Martha had met during difficult circumstances, but circumstances changed and eventually Tristan would have time to decide what direction he wanted their relationship to go. If it was going to go anywhere.

And he had a feeling it was.

He pushed open the service door and led Martha out into the cold, dark morning.

SIXTEEN

Grayson Sinclair was nothing like Tristan and everything like him. Both men were tall, broad-shouldered and handsome, but if Tristan was fire, Grayson was ice. While Tristan moved with a lithe and deadly grace, Grayson's movements were sharp, precise and to the point as he ushered Martha into the backseat of his dark sedan, and then turned to his brother. "Glad you finally showed up. I was beginning to think I'd have to come running to rescue you."

"When have you ever had to do that?" Tristan settled into the seat beside Martha, his large frame taking up more than its fair share of space. Or maybe it just felt that way because Martha was so aware of him. His short hair mussed, his chin shadowed with the beginnings of a beard, he looked tough, even dangerous, yet sitting next to him made Martha feel safer than she'd felt all night. She shoved the thought to the back of her mind. Later, she'd pull it out and examine it more closely. For now, all she could think about was getting to her father's side. Everything else was secondary to that.

"I could name a few, but I wouldn't want to embarrass you in front of your friend." Grayson slid in behind the steering wheel, meeting Martha's eyes in the rearview mirror, his expression somber. "Since I was just sitting twiddling my thumbs waiting for my slowpoke brother, I decided to make good use of my time. I called the hospital to check on your dad."

At his words, Martha tensed, her heart jumping with anxiety. At any second she expected to hear the news that her father had passed away. The moment he'd been shot had been replaying in her mind for hours. All that blood. Her father's blood. His sunken eyes. His labored breath.

Don't miss me too much, doll.

The words echoed in her head, but she shoved them away, not wanting to think that he might have been saying goodbye forever. "How is he?"

"Holding his own."

That seemed like a catchphrase for "he's alive for now, but may not be for long." "Did they say if he's awake?"

"Sorry. I was lucky to get that much information out of them." He pulled out onto the nearly empty road, the car picking up speed, but not going nearly fast enough for Martha's taste. She wasn't one to break traffic laws, but in this instance ten or fifteen or twenty miles an hour above the speed limit didn't seem like such a bad thing.

Twenty miles. That's how far it was to the hospital. Martha had been there enough times to know they should be there in a half hour.

Not long.

Still, it seemed like an eternity. Anything could happen in that amount of time. Her father's heart could stop. He could have a stroke, a blood clot, or simply slip quietly from this world into the next. Worse, Gordon Johnson could find his way into his room and finish what he'd started.

Her hands clenched at the thought, her fingers curling into tight fists. Of course, Johnson wouldn't go after her father. Why would he? It was Martha he wanted to get rid of. But what if he did? What if he tried to kidnap Dad to get Martha to cooperate and killed him in the process? What if—

"Relax. We'll be there soon." Tristan covered her hand with his, gently prying open her fingers and smoothing his thumbs over the crescent-shaped gouges on her palms. Something shivered to life inside her. Something she acknowledged even as she shoved it to the farthest reaches of her mind.

"I just hope *soon* is soon enough."

"Lynchburg General is a good hospital with an outstanding trauma team. They'll do everything they can for your father. He's in good hands." Grayson cut into the conversation, his smooth tenor very different from his brother's gritty baritone.

"I know, but I can't help worrying. Dad's not as young as he used to be."

"But he's tough. Strong. In good shape for his age." Tristan squeezed her hand, offering comfort that Martha shouldn't want. Hadn't she just been telling herself that she didn't need a man in her life? That she was perfectly capable of going it alone? That the only person she needed to depend on was herself?

Of course she had. Yet here she was, allowing Tristan to take care of her, to hold her hand, to offer comfort. Alarm bells should be shrieking inside her, screaming that the barriers around her heart were being breached. Instead, all she heard was the sluggish throb of her pulse and the grinding worry in her stomach.

Oh, yeah. She also heard her brain telling her that if she was going to depend on a guy, Tristan was the kind of guy she could depend on. The *only* guy she'd want to depend on.

Not good, but Martha was too tired and too worried to think about it, or to pull her hand away from his, or to even pretend that she didn't need him sitting beside her telling her everything was going to be okay.

"When I was a kid, I thought my dad could do anything. Leap over buildings, outrun bullets, stop a speeding train. It didn't take me long to realize he couldn't actually do all those things, but in my mind he was still invincible." She spoke quietly, sharing with Tristan in a way she never had with Brian.

"I guess most kids think that about their parents."

"I guess they do." She smiled, remembering the hikes she and her dad had been on, the camping trips, the hours spent working in his store. "With

Dad and me, though, everything was a team effort. There couldn't be one of us without the other. Where he went, I went. To his store, on hunting trips, hiking, camping, fishing. Now that he's getting older, I realize our time together is limited. I accept that, but I guess I'm just not ready to say goodbye."

"You're not going to have to, Sunshine. God didn't save your father's life on the operating table so He could take it in the ICU."

"I want to believe that, but no matter how much I trust that God is in control and that He'll work everything out, I also know that bad things can happen. They *do* happen. I'm not immune to them. None of us are."

"That doesn't mean they'll happen this time."

"It doesn't. It also doesn't mean they won't. I need to be prepared for that."

"There's no doubt in my mind that whatever happens, you'll handle it. You're a strong woman, Martha. It's one of the things I admire about you. When things get tough, that's when you shine. And you'll shine this time. No matter what."

No matter what. No matter if her father lived or died. No matter if Johnson came after Martha again. She'd be fine. She really wanted to believe Tristan was right, and that she'd hold up under whatever trouble came her way. She wanted to believe it, but she felt shaky, unsure. As if the world had tilted and she'd tilted with it. Off balance, she couldn't quite grasp the determination that usually brought her through tough situations.

She sighed, leaning her head back against the seat, Tristan's finger still linked with hers, his hand anchoring her. To reality. To hope. To the faith that suddenly seemed as elusive as a dream.

What do You want me to learn from this, Lord? There must be something. Some life lesson that will hurt, but that will help my faith grow.

The prayer whispered through her mind, but Martha felt no peace. Eventually, she'd be able to look back and see things clearly, but right now everything that had happened in the past few days seemed surreal and confusing. No matter how hard she tried, she couldn't quite wrap her mind around the fact that someone wanted her dead. Dead! And that in trying to kill her, that man had almost killed her father.

"We're here. Want me to pull up in front of the main entrance?" Grayson's words broke the silence, pulling Martha from her circling thoughts.

"Drive around the back. I've got some people waiting to make sure we get inside safely."

"You think Johnson is going to show up here?" If Grayson was worried by the thought, his tone didn't show it. He sounded as relaxed and untroubled as he had when they'd been introduced.

"Not if he thinks Martha is still at Lakeview Memorial. Since there's no guarantee he does, I'm erring on the side of caution."

"I taught you well, little brother."

"Little? Last time I checked, I was an inch taller than you."

The banter between brothers continued as Grayson drove to the back of the building. Several police cars were parked there, angled close to the hospital, but Martha knew they'd be a flimsy barrier against a barrage of bullets. And it wasn't like there weren't plenty of places for Johnson to take aim from. A parking garage hulked above the back lot, three stories tall and dark despite numerous lights. A great place for a killer to stay hidden until he was ready to make his move.

Uniformed officers were stationed near a back door, their faces shadowed by hats, their guns in holsters at their waists. It looked like a scene out of an action flick, but it was real. Too real.

Martha's stomach clenched, her breath catching in her throat as Grayson stopped the car. The engine died, the silence deafening.

Open the door, Marti. Get out of the car. Go in the building. Find your father.

But no matter how many times the words raced through her mind, Martha couldn't seem to move. She was frozen in place, her fear sapping her strength, stealing her ability to move.

Gunshots.

Blood.

Death just a heartbeat away.

Did she really want to step outside and live it all again?

An officer pulled open her door, several others standing beside him, forming a wall of protection that looked even less effective than the police cars.

"Ms. Gabler? If you're ready to go in, we've cleared everything for you to go up and see your father."

Cleared everything with the doctors, or cleared the halls to make sure Johnson wasn't lurking somewhere? Martha's mouth was too dry to ask, and instead of taking the officer's hand and allowing him to pull her from the car, she stayed put, her mind screaming for her to grab the door and slam it shut.

"You're not chickening out on me, are you, Sunshine?" Tristan whispered in her ear, his words spurring her to action.

"No." She took the officer's hand, and was pulled out into the cold morning air. Several pairs of eyes watched as she took a shaky step away from the car. Could they see how scared she was?

She felt dizzy, her ears buzzing, her heart slushing through her veins but apparently not bringing much oxygen to her brain. If she collapsed, one of the officers would feel obligated to catch her. That would be bad. She really needed to lose a few pounds before some poor guy had to lift her off the pavement. The inane thought ran through her mind as she swayed, stars dancing in front of her eyes. Apparently, she'd lost more blood than she should have, because no matter how hard she tried, she couldn't quite keep the world steady beneath her feet.

"Are you okay?" Tristan wrapped an arm around her waist, saving her from doing a face-plant onto the ground, and saving his friends from having to peel her off it. Then again, maybe he was saving himself. One arm or not, Martha had a feeling he'd be the first to attempt to hoist her up if she went down.

Which she was not going to do.

She'd lost a little blood. Big deal. People lost blood all the time. Her father was in the hospital. She was going to walk in on her own two feet and see him. Nothing could keep her from doing that. Not Gordon Johnson and not a pint or so of lost blood.

"Martha?" Tristan stopped walking and looked down into her eyes, concern etching fine lines near the corners of his eyes. "Do you want me to have someone get a wheelchair for you?"

"No way. I'm right as rain." Kind of.

"You're sure?"

"Of course I'm sure." To prove her point she took a quick step forward and felt the earth tilt again, this time too far. And she tilted with it, falling into blackness as the world disappeared.

SEVENTEEN

Tristan paced the hall outside the room where they'd brought Martha twenty minutes earlier, adrenaline humming through him and begging for release. Despite nearly twenty-four hours without sleep, he wasn't tired. Instead, he felt wound up, energized. Ready to go. In other circumstances, he'd be out on the hunt, searching for Johnson, knowing he was close and not giving up until they were face-to-face. But these weren't other circumstances, and his need to find Johnson was outweighed by his need to make sure Martha and her father were okay. It hadn't been a good night for the Gabler family. Tristan intended to do everything in his power to make sure the new day was a better one.

"Is Martha okay? One of the nurses told me they had to bring her in on a stretcher. I should have found a ride to Lakeview General while Jesse was in surgery. Martha shouldn't have gone through all this alone. It was too much for her." Sue hurried down the hall toward him, her words spilling out in frantic staccato beats, her round face creased with time and worry.

Hours ago, she'd seemed vibrant and lively. Now she was drained, her face gray and worn. Grief stole life as brutally as any disease. Tristan had seen it enough to know that for sure.

"It wasn't too much for her, Sue, and she wouldn't have wanted you to leave Jesse here alone."

"I hope you're right. I really do. Jesse and I haven't been married long, and I want so badly to be the mother that Martha never had. What if she thinks I was wrong to stay here, or expected me to come with her? What if she's angry with me and we never speak again? These things happen all the time, Tristan. They do. I've seen it on *Oprah*."

Tristan put a hand on her shoulder, hoping to stop the flow of words. "They're not going to happen this time. Martha isn't that kind of person. Besides, I know for a fact that she was relieved to have you here with her father. How is he doing, by the way?" Refocus her thoughts. Make her talk about something else. That was the goal, though Tristan wasn't sure he'd be successful. Sue was a great lady, but he had a feeling that refocusing her attention wasn't always easy.

"The same. He still hasn't opened his eyes. When he finally does, I'm going to have a thing or two to say about how badly he scared me." Despite the upbeat words, her eyes were red from tears, her lips trembling as if she was holding in much greater emotion.

"Sometimes it takes a while for a patient to come out of the anesthesia completely."

"That's what the doctors are telling me, but it doesn't make me feel much better." She paused, wiping away a tear that slid down her cheek. "He looks bad. Really bad."

"Tomorrow, he'll look better."

"The doctors told me that, too." She sighed and knocked on the door to Martha's room.

The door swung open, and Tristan was relieved to see Martha lying on a bed, her wild curls spiraling in every direction, her eyes flashing green-gold fire. She looked ready to do battle, which was a whole lot better than how she'd looked when she'd nearly collapsed at his feet. "Tristan, please tell the nurse that I am perfectly capable of going to see my father in the ICU."

"Please tell Ms. Gabler that this isn't about being capable. This is about common sense. The last thing her father needs is for his daughter to pass out while she's visiting him." The nurse who'd opened the door looked dour and disapproving, her eyes bright with irritation as she speared Tristan with a look meant to force cooperation.

Too bad he wasn't in the mood to cooperate.

No matter how much he wanted to believe Jesse would be okay, he couldn't be sure what the next few hours would bring. If Martha didn't see her father now, she might never see him alive again. No way would he be part of letting that happen. "She's come all the way from Lakeview General to be with her father. I'm sure we can find a way to get her into his room without her passing out again."

"I do understand the situation. I know she wants to see her father, but he's not conscious yet, so I really think it's best if Martha rests for a few hours before we bring her upstairs."

"What if her father doesn't have a few hours left?" He spoke quietly, knowing Martha and Sue were listening, but not willing to sugarcoat the truth of the situation.

The nurse's lips tightened, her scowl deepening, but she nodded. "All right. I'll get a wheelchair and we'll take her to ICU, but when she's done there, she's to come directly back to her room. The doctor wants her admitted. If her blood count doesn't come up, we may need to do a transfusion."

A transfusion? It was Tristan's turn to scowl. Obviously, Martha had lost more blood than he'd realized. There'd been plenty of it on the floor at her house, plenty of it on him. He'd assumed most of it was Jesse's, and had focused on that. Solve the bigger, more deadly problem first. Then take care of the less dangerous situation. It had been a knee-jerk reaction born of training and years of facing tough multifaceted problems. But even while he'd tended to Jesse, his mind had been shouting that he should be helping Martha.

"Hey! I'm right here, guys. I can speak for myself, or at least participate in the conversation," Martha said as she eased to the edge of the bed, placing her feet on the floor and looking as if she had every intention of getting up and walking to the door.

"I wouldn't do that if I were you, Sunshine. You end up on the floor, and there will be no way you'll be able to convince anyone that you're strong enough to see your dad."

She frowned, but didn't make any more effort to stand.

"Martha! Thank goodness you're okay!" Sue rushed forward as the nurse left the room, throwing her arms around Martha and hugging her vigorously.

Tristan gave the two women a few minutes to discuss Jesse's injuries and prognosis before doing what he'd been wanting to all along—move toward the bed.

Martha smiled as he approached, a sweet, gentle curve of her lips that welcomed him into her circle of family, her hair curling softly around her face, begging him to touch the silky strands. He shouldn't. There were too many other things he should be doing. Like checking in with his boss, making sure there were men stationed at both hospitals ready to bring Johnson in if he should dare to show his face.

"You're looking grim, Tristan."

"It's been a grim night. How are you feeling?"

"Dandy."

"You're not in any pain?"

"If I am, it's completely overshadowed by the pain of embarrassment I'm feeling."

"What's to be embarrassed about?" He gave in to temptation and lifted a heavy lock of her hair, letting it slide through his fingers, the smooth texture feeling like the finest silk against his callused skin.

"I passed out in front of a bunch of strangers and had to be scraped off the pavement. What's not to be embarrassed about?"

Tristan couldn't help chuckling. "You didn't exactly fall onto the pavement, so no scraping was required."

"Someone caught me before I fell?"

"Yes." *He* had, but he doubted Martha wanted details. Her independent nature was one of her greatest gifts, but also one of her most serious weaknesses. To be tough, a person had to be willing to be weak. He doubted Martha had learned to do that yet.

"Even worse."

"You'd rather have ended up on the ground?"

"I'd rather it not have happened at all."

"Your ride is here." The nurse stepped back into the room, pushing a wheelchair in front of her.

"Thank you." Martha eased into the chair, biting her lip as the nurse pushed her out into the hall. She was anxious. Tristan could see it in the way she clenched her fists and sat stiffly in the chair. He wanted to reach out and squeeze her shoulder, offer her silent support, but the nurse was moving away, taking her toward the bank of elevators at the far end of the hall with short, quick steps that refused interference.

Probably she wanted Tristan and Sue to stay in Martha's room and wait for their return. She was going to be disappointed. No way was Tristan going to let Martha out of his sight again. The police might be on the ball, making sure that Johnson wouldn't get into the hospital and get to Martha, but Tristan wasn't leaving her safety to someone else. He'd already failed her and her father once. He didn't plan to do it again.

The nurse shot him a look as he and Sue stepped onto the elevator, but she didn't tell him to return to the room. Not that he would have listened if she had.

He leaned his shoulder against the wall as the nurse gave Martha instructions. "As you know, your father is quite weak. He's hooked up to a lot of machines, and he's unconscious. That doesn't mean he can't hear you. When you go in to see him, make sure you talk to him and let him know you're there."

"All right."

"Don't be nervous about what you see. The machines are serving a vital purpose." The nurse pushed Martha out onto the third level of the building and headed in the direction of a large sign that pointed out the ICU.

"I understand."

"Good. Some family members get a little panicky when they see someone they love hooked up to monitors and machines."

"I'm not the panicky type."

"Then you'll be just fine. Just talk calmly to your dad, tell him he's going to be fine. When your time is up, I'll come in and get you to bring you back to your room. Please don't try to get down there on your own."

"I won't. When do you think my father will re-gain consciousness?"

"No one can say. I know it's hard to do, but in situations like this, the best thing is to just take it a day at a time and be there for your dad." For the first time since the door to Martha's room had opened, the nurse looked compassionate and kind.

"I will. Thank you."

"You can only visit for ten minutes every half hour. And only one at a time, so I'm afraid you and your mother will have to take turns."

At the word *mother* Martha stiffened, but she didn't correct the mistake. Neither did Sue. It seemed there was an unspoken understanding that in this situation, they were family. No matter how new the relationship or fragile the bond.

"I understand." Martha glanced at Sue, then Tristan, her eyes filled with a million worries. Tristan wanted to tell her everything was going to be fine, that her dad would be up and around sooner than she imagined, and that Johnson would be behind bars before she stepped out of the hospital again. But there were no guarantees in life, and no matter how badly he wanted those things to be true, he knew that only time would tell for certain.

"Here we are. You two can wait in our lounge while Martha visits her dad." The nurse pointed to a door that led off the hallway. Tristan hesitated. He knew what he'd find inside—grief. Thick. Hard. Ugly.

He'd been there before. In rooms just like that one.

Faced family members of fallen agents and seen the ravages of grief, the horror of loss. He'd rather stand eye to eye with a hundred cold-blooded killers than see one mother crying over her wounded child, one wife grieving for a husband she had to let go, one husband trying to comfort his children. That's what he worked so hard for. Get the bad guys off the street so that fewer people had to deal with the horror of losing someone they loved. It was another reason he'd never committed to a relationship. Never considered marriage, kids, family. He didn't want his wife, his kids, sitting in a room like that one, waiting, wondering. Crying.

No, he did not want to go into that room and see the harsh side of life. The alternative, though, was leaving Martha on the third floor and waiting down in her room for her return. That wasn't an option, so he took a deep breath, braced himself and stepped into the maelstrom of emotion.

EIGHTEEN

Martha had expected her father to look bad. She thought she'd braced herself for it, but seeing him lying in bed, tubes and wires snaking around him, was harder than she'd imagined. The nurse wheeled her close, positioning the wheelchair at the head of the bed, so that Martha could reach out and touch his leathery cheek.

"Dad, it's Martha. Can you hear me? Sorry it took me so long to get here, but you know what they say—better late than never. I've been praying for you, and Tristan is doing everything he can to get the guy who did this."

"That's exactly what you need to do, Martha." The nurse spoke briskly as Martha took her father's limp hand in hers. "Just talk to him like it's any other day."

Any other day? Any other nightmare was more like it. Martha's hand shook as she brushed it over her father's wiry hair. He looked shrunken, older than his seventy years, all his vibrancy, all his life gone.

Please don't let it be gone.

"Will you be okay in here on your own? Is there anything I can get you?" Nurse Ratched hovered near the door, watching with a worried expression. The first one Martha had seen from her since she'd arrived. Maybe she'd pegged the nurse all wrong. Maybe the woman wasn't a brute who loved throwing her weight around. Maybe she really was concerned about Martha's well-being.

"Martha?" Apparently, she'd taken too long to answer. The nurse was moving toward her again, looking as if she was ready to wheel Martha out into the hall.

"I'm fine. I don't need anything. Unless…" She stopped herself before she could say what she'd been thinking.

"What?"

Don't say it, Martha. You don't need Tristan in here with you. You're fine on your own. You're independent. Strong. Able to face whatever may come on your own.

"Would it be okay if Tristan came in here with me? My friend who brought me in, I mean."

Way to listen to your own advice.

"I'm sorry. The rules—"

"I know. It's okay. I'm fine."

The nurse eyed her for a moment, then nodded and stepped into the hall. It was for the best. Martha really didn't want Tristan with her. Okay. She did. But she didn't *want* to want him with her. That had to count for something.

She brushed a hand against her father's cheek,

feeling the dry warmth of his skin. He'd always seemed so young. Now he looked like an aged husk of the person he'd once been. How could it be that a man who'd been so filled with life could suddenly be so close to death?

One moment.

One heartbeat of time.

That was all it had taken.

And all it would take for him to drift out of her reach. "Dad, if you can hear me, I want you to know how much I love you. I know it wasn't easy raising me alone, but you did a great job."

Her voice broke on the words, tears slipping down her cheeks. This was her fault. All her fault. If she hadn't gone into the mountains to nurse her pride, if she hadn't dated a man who'd been so obviously wrong for her, if she hadn't wanted so much more out of life than what she had, then her father would still be fine.

The soft click of the door told her someone had entered the room. Probably the nurse coming to check on her. She didn't look up, just kept her eyes trained on her father, hoping her tears were hidden by the hair that fell across her cheek.

Someone touched the back of her head, wove fingers through her hair and let them rest at the base of her skull, the touch soft as a butterfly's kiss.

Her heart leaped in acknowledgment even before Tristan spoke.

"Everything will be okay." His words washed over

her, his hand lifting, then smoothing down her cheek to brush her tears away.

She didn't resist as he tugged her to her feet and wrapped her in his arms, his hand pressing against her back, his summer-blue eyes probing hers. "The nurse said you wanted me in here with you."

"She told me it was against the rules."

"I guess she decided she could bend them for once."

"Dad looks terrible."

"I know."

"It's all my fault."

"Not even close."

"It is. I was such an idiot. Dating Brian when everyone told me how arrogant and self-serving he was. If I'd listened to them, Dad wouldn't be here right now."

"Weren't you just telling me that I couldn't have known what would happen? That I couldn't have prevented it?"

"That's different."

"Because it's me and not you?" He sighed, his breath ruffling her hair. "I've been thinking about this a lot the last few hours. Sometimes things happen in a way no one can predict or prevent. If we could both go back and make different decisions to change the outcome, we would—but we can't. So we've just got to hold on tight and pray that when we get to the end of the journey, we'll understand why things happened the way they did."

He was right. Marti's head knew it, but her heart

was telling her something different. Her heart was telling her that she could have saved her father a lot of pain and trauma if she'd made better choices.

As if sensing her thoughts, Tristan tugged her even closer, pressing her head to his chest, his warmth, his strength, easing the icy fear that ran through Martha's veins.

She should put some distance between them, tell him that she was okay and didn't need his support, but she didn't. Her arms wound around his waist, her hands fisted in his shirt as her entire body shouted that she was exactly where she was supposed to be.

And the truth hit her like a ton of bricks.

She needed Tristan. *Needed* him. Not like she'd needed Brian—as a means to an end, a way to get one step closer to the family she'd always longed for. With Tristan, it was different. It was the kind of need that said—when you're with me, the world is a better place. When you're with me, I'm not alone anymore. When you're with me, all I want is for you to stay.

The kind of need that made a person vulnerable.

The kind of need she'd never, ever imagined she'd feel.

This was bad. Really, really bad.

She stepped away, avoiding Tristan's eyes, not wanting him to see what she was feeling. "How is Sue holding up? I didn't even think to ask her."

"She's doing okay. One of her sons is flying in to stay with her. He'll be here in the morning."

Martha nodded, putting a little more distance between them as she leaned over her father and lifted his hand. "Hey, Dad, it's me again, Martha. Anytime you're ready, you can open your eyes and let me know you're in there. I'm starting to worry that you've landed on that tropical island you always dreamed about visiting and you've decided to stay."

He didn't even twitch, his gray-tinged face lifeless, his eyes closed.

"Sue is worried about you, too. Neither of us knows what we'll do if you're not up and around in time to put up the Christmas lights. Remember last year? How you decided to outdo your neighbors? There was so much light pouring off your house, Darrel James called the sheriff and complained." The memory made her smile through the tears that were falling again.

Good times. Lots of them. No matter what happened, at least she'd have those.

"It's almost time to leave, babe." Tristan spoke quietly, his words reminding her of what she'd wanted to avoid. Him. His presence. The aching need inside that said being with him was much better than being without.

"I just want to pray for him before I go." She put a hand on her father's shoulder, feeling muscle and bone. Life and strength along with fragility she hadn't noticed before. Had he always been like that and she'd just not seen it?

Tristan leaned close, his chest pressing against her back as he placed his hand over hers. There. With her. Supporting her in a way no other person ever had. Not her mother who'd run from responsibility.

Not even her father who had always loved her un-conditionally, but who had hurt too much when she was hurt for Martha to ever want to share all her burdens with him.

She took a deep breath, closing her eyes, forcing her mind away from Tristan and back where it belonged—with her father. "Lord, I know You're here with us, and that You're in control of the situation. I pray for Your healing hand on my father. In the same way You made the blind see and the lame walk, I pray that You'll return Dad's strength to him. I trust that Your will will be worked out in Your perfect time, and I ask for Your comfort for Sue and me as we face whatever is to come. Amen."

"Amen." Tristan's agreement rumbled out, his thumb gently caressing her knuckles as he pulled his hand away. "Ready to go back to the room?"

"Do I have a choice?" she asked, though no matter what his answer was, she knew she didn't. Her mind was fuzzy, the room swimming, colors blurring. She needed to sit down now before she fell down.

"No."

"Then I'm ready. I'll be back in a little bit, Dad. Stay strong. I love you." She leaned over, placing a kiss on his parchment skin, then straightened, black-ness edging at her vision at the quick movement.

Tristan must have noticed, because he grabbed her arm, holding her steady as she sat in the wheel-chair again. She felt weak. Weaker than she ever had before. As if someone had taken her energy and sucked it out, leaving her empty and wanting. Getting shot stunk.

Watching your father get shot, that was even worse.

Seeing your father lying in a hospital hooked to machines that beeped and buzzed and breathed for him, that was worst of all.

But things would get better. What choice did they have? Trouble couldn't last forever. Her father had told her that often enough. It was a motto he lived by, and one Martha had learned before she could read.

All she had to do was keep her chin up, keep believing that God was in control and keep hoping that no matter what the next day brought, He'd get her through it.

That's all she had to do, but right now, as Tristan wheeled her out of the ICU, it felt like a lot more than she could handle.

NINETEEN

Martha didn't plan to sleep when she returned to her room. She had too much on her mind. When Tristan stepped into the hall to make a phone call, she leaned back against the hospital pillows and tried to make a mental list of things she needed to get done. Call the church and put Dad on the prayer list. Get someone to feed Sue's cat. Call a cleaning company who specialized in removing bloodstains.

That one made her shudder.

What else?

Call work. Let them know she wouldn't be in for a day or two. Find out who her father's doctor was and discuss the prognosis with him. Maybe that one should be at the top of the list.

She yawned, her eyes closing despite her best efforts to keep them open. Just for a minute. That's all she needed. A minute or two of shut-eye and she'd be good as new.

Blood-red sky. Deep black clouds. Rain falling like tears. Dad, lying on cold gray stone, his eyes open, but unseeing. Johnson, gun drawn, a feral smile on his face, pointing the gun at Martha, pulling the trigger. But she wasn't the one falling with a bullet hole in her. Tristan was. Tumbling onto the ground, sprawling lifeless next to Martha's father as Johnson's laughter filled the air.

Martha jerked awake, her heart slamming in her chest, her breath heaving out as she tried to remember where she was, how she'd gotten there, what was going on.

Johnson. The hospital. Her father lying nearly lifeless in ICU.

She swung her legs over the side of the bed, wincing as her body protested the sudden movement. She felt as if she'd been run over by a truck. Every muscle in her body ached, her shoulder throbbed and she was pretty sure that things wouldn't feel any better once she was on her feet.

She was going to get to her feet, though. She didn't know how long she'd been asleep, but it was long enough that the sun streaming in through the window seemed muted, casting long shadows. According to the clock, it was just past three. She'd been sleeping for hours while her father struggled for life.

She shifted her weight, determined to ignore the pain and get up. It's what her father would have expected, and what she expected from herself.

"Going somewhere?" Tristan's voice came from behind her, and she screamed, whirling to face him.

"Tristan! I didn't realize you were here."

"Sorry about that. I didn't mean to scare you. I

decided to catnap in the chair while you were sleeping. You and I both needed some rest."

"*Some* rest. I've been sleeping for hours."

"Like I said, we both needed it. With Johnson still on the loose, we've got to stay on top of our game. That means getting the rest we need."

"But my father—"

"Is being well taken care of." Tristan ran a hand down his jaw.

"I need to see him."

"I'll bring you up." He didn't even hesitate, just pushed the wheelchair to the bed, and gestured for her to take a seat.

"I don't think I need that this time. I'm feeling about two hundred times better." If she excluded the pain, and she thought she would. After all, a little pain was a lot better than being dead.

He looked as though he was going to argue, then changed his mind, shrugging broad shoulders and offering a half smile. "Suit yourself, Sunshine, but if you get halfway to your father and pass out, I'll be forced to perform a fireman's carry to get you upstairs."

"At least it would give the nurses something to talk about."

"And Brian McMath." His words were tight as he mentioned Martha's ex, his expression guarded.

"What does Brian have to do with anything?"

"He's been in here twice while you were asleep."

Ugh. That wasn't a pleasant thought. Brian Mc-Math hanging over her while she snored the day away. Worse, Tristan sitting in a chair watching her while she snored.

Had she snored?

The thought was appalling, and Martha's cheeks heated. "Did he say what he wanted?"

"I didn't ask."

"So, what did you do, stare each other down to prove who was the most manly?"

He chuckled, his hand resting on the small of her back as they stepped out of the room. "Thanks for the laugh. I needed that."

"Did something happen while I was sleeping?"

"Something didn't happen. Johnson is still on the loose."

"Maybe he left town."

"Not Johnson. He's got a mission. He's going to follow through. Get you out of the picture so you can't testify. It might take him a day, a week or a month, but Johnson has the kind of patience that allows him to wait things out rather than rush in."

"That's not a comforting thought."

"No, but at least we can be pretty confident that he won't go into hiding until he's achieved his goal. As long as he's not in hiding, we should be able to find him."

"I guess that's going to have to be good enough."

"For now." Tristan led her to the elevator doors and pushed the button to open them. "Sue's son arrived a few hours ago. He's up in the waiting room with her, and he plans to stay until your father is released from the hospital."

"That's really good of him."

"Yeah, I'm glad he's here, since you won't be." He said it so matter-of-factly, the words almost didn't register.

When they did, Martha stiffened, turning to face him. "I *am* going to be here, Tristan. I don't know where you got the idea that I wouldn't."

"From my boss who's finally managed to arrange a safe house for you until Johnson is caught."

"You're kidding, right?"

"I wouldn't kid about something like that." The elevator door slid open again, and Tristan stepped out, grabbing Martha's arm and pulling her with him when she hesitated.

"You may not be kidding, but there is no way I'll leave this hospital until I know my father is going to be okay."

"You don't have a choice, Martha. Johnson wants you dead. He's already made that more than clear."

"We knew he wanted me dead before he tried to kill me. I don't see how last night changes anything."

"It changes plenty because now I'm not the only one who believes he's coming after you. You're a key witness in this case. No way does the ATF want to lose you."

"I don't particularly want to be lost, but I'm not leaving my father."

"Like I said, you don't have a choice." The words were final, and Martha had the feeling that no matter what she said, how she tried to argue, Tristan would say the same.

She didn't care. She'd continue to argue her point. If push came to shove, she'd simply refuse to leave the hospital.

Sure she would.

She couldn't imagine facing down Tristan, let alone the police, the ATF and whatever other government agencies might want to have a part in finding Gordon Johnson.

So she'd deal with that when the time came.

Right now, she needed to see her father and make sure he was okay.

They walked into the room, and Martha's heart sank. She didn't know what she'd been expecting or hoping for, but it wasn't what she was seeing—her father looking exactly the same as he had when she'd been in earlier. "He still doesn't look good."

"Give it time."

"How much? A day? A week? Shouldn't there be some improvement by now?" She spoke quietly as she lifted her father's hand. "Dad? Can you hear me? It's Martha again."

To her surprise, his eyes blinked open, the usual bright hazel, muted and muddy. A tube in his throat prevented him from speaking, but he squeezed her hand, his grip weak.

"Dad! You *are* in there. I was beginning to wonder. How are you feeling?"

He frowned, gesturing toward a pad of paper and pen sitting on the table next to his bed. Once she handed both to him, he wrote slowly, his hand shaking, the letters wobbly and light. Barely legible. But at least he was communicating. That had to be a good sign.

He held the paper up, and Martha squinted, trying to make out the words. "I look awful, and you want me to go get some sleep?"

She smiled, shaking her head at her father. "I can't believe you're worried about me at a time like this."

"I'll make sure she gets the rest she needs, Jesse. You just worry about getting yourself healthy." Tristan moved smoothly into the conversation, his arm brushing hers as he leaned closer to the bed.

Martha's dad nodded, closing his eyes again. A man who'd worked hard his whole life, who could stay on his feet for twelve hours straight, tired after lifting a pen.

Martha lifted his hand again, trying to will some warmth into his cool skin. "Are you cold, Dad? Do you need another blanket?"

He didn't respond, and she squeezed gently, praying that he'd open his eyes again. "Dad?"

"Let him rest, Sunshine. He needs that more than you need him to talk." Tristan spoke quietly, and Martha knew he was right. Still, she wanted to know that he was getting better, that he was heading further away from the precipice he'd been hovering at the edge of.

"I need to speak to his doctor."

"Let's go find someone who can tell us who his doctor is."

Us.

She liked the sound of that but knew she shouldn't.

Tristan was dangerous. Too much time with him and she might just start imagining that there was more to their relationship than Gordon Johnson. "Why don't you wait here with Dad in case he wakes up again. I'll go find a nurse."

"I don't think so."

"Okay, then you go. I'll stay."

"I don't think you understand the way things are going to be. Once we talk to the doctor, we're leaving here and going directly to the safe house my boss has arranged. You're staying there until Johnson is caught."

"I think you're the one who doesn't understand, Tristan. I'm an adult. I make my own decisions. And I'm deciding right now that I'm not leaving this hospital until my father is off the ventilator and close to going home."

"You made your own decisions until you walked in on a gun raid and became the state's key witness. Now things are different. You may as well get used to the idea." His eyes flashed, his jaw tight with frustration, but Martha didn't care. Short of carrying her out of the hospital, there was no way anyone from any agency was going to get her to leave.

She planned to tell Tristan exactly that, but her father made a soft noise, drawing her attention away from the argument and back to the bed.

"Hey, you're awake again. Are you—" Before she could ask if he was in pain, if he needed something, if she should go get the nurse, he gestured toward the pad of paper and pen.

As soon as she handed them to him, he scribbled a message and held it up for her to see. *Stop arguing and go.*

"You can't be serious, Dad. You were shot. You were almost killed. I'm not going to…" Her voice trailed off as he started writing again.

If something happens to you it will *kill me.*

"Nothing is going to happen to me."

Go. It will be better for both of us.

"How can it be better for both of us if you're sick and I'm off who knows where not knowing what's going on?" But it seemed her father's strength had run out. His grip on the pen slackened and it rolled onto the blanket.

"I think what your father is trying to tell you is that he'll worry too much if you don't go to the safe house. In his condition, that kind of worry is the last thing he needs." Tristan spoke into the silence, and her dad gave a subtle nod of agreement.

"You don't have to worry, Dad. I'm going to be fine."

"Because you're going to do what your father and I are suggesting, and go to the safe house." Tristan leaned past her to squeeze her father's hand. "Don't worry, Jesse, I'll take care of your daughter. Before you know it, we'll all be sitting down to another one of Sue's fine meals together."

Her father blinked twice, then closed his eyes, his face sinking in on itself. What little animation had been there was gone. If anything, he looked worse than when she'd walked in. Had she done that to him? No. No. Of course she hadn't, but Tristan was right. Her dad didn't need the extra stress that worrying about her would cause. Whether she liked it or not, the best thing she could do for him was go somewhere safe and wait things out.

And she didn't like it.

What if she went off to the safe house and he got worse? "Will I be able to call the hospital from the safe house?"

"We'll make sure you're updated on your father's condition as frequently as we are."

"We?"

"A female agent will be staying with you."

"Oh." So she wouldn't be Tristan's responsibility anymore. That was good. So why did she feel so lousy about it?

Because she was leaving her father, that was why.

And if she kept telling herself that she might start to believe it.

She leaned down and placed a kiss on her father's forehead. "I'm going, Dad, but if you get worse I'm coming back, so you'd better just keep on getting better if you want me to stay away."

She thought he might be trying to smile as Tristan took her arm and led her out of the room.

TWENTY

The safe house wasn't anything like Martha imagined it would be. Not that she'd spent much time imagining it. She'd been too busy worrying about the doctor's guarded prognosis regarding her father's health to give anything else more than a cursory thought. Twenty miles from town, tucked away on a gravel road deep in the Blue Ridge Mountains, the house Tristan pulled up in front of was a charming villa that overlooked stunning views. Several acres of yard surrounded it, free of trees, shrubs or any other potential hiding place. Aside from that, the place didn't look any more safe than Martha's house.

"This is it?"

"Yep." Tristan stopped the engine and turned to face her. Two days without shaving had given him a rough, hard look that shouldn't have appealed to Martha. After all, she'd only ever been attracted to clean-shaven men. Men like Brian who were smooth, polished, restrained and predictable. Those were the kind of guys who were safe, easy. Tristan would never be either of those things.

Somehow that didn't seem to matter to Martha's treacherous heart. Not only did she find Tristan extremely attractive, but she was pretty sure safe and predictable would never appeal to her again. Good thing she'd decided before she'd met him that relationships weren't for her, or she might be having thoughts she shouldn't.

She cleared her throat, turning to look out the car window, avoiding Tristan's probing gaze. "It's a pretty house, but it doesn't look particularly safe."

"It's safe. Trust me on that." Tristan rounded the side of the car and pulled open her door. "Come on. Rayne has probably paced a hole through the floor already."

"Rayne is the agent who's staying with me?"

"She'll be the one you're dealing with, and she's not so good at waiting." He led her to the front door, knocked once and walked inside.

"You were supposed to be here two hours ago." A tall blonde moved across the two-story foyer. Mid-twenties. Dancer slim. Indigo-blue eyes in porcelain skin.

She was an agent?

As if she sensed Martha's doubts, Rayne met her eyes, letting her gaze drop to the bloodstained jeans and sneakers Martha wore. "You're Martha Gabler."

It wasn't a question, but Martha nodded anyway. "That's right."

"I'm Rayne Steward. I'm sorry about your dad. I know it must be hard to leave him behind."

"Thanks. It is."

"He's in good hands."

And if Martha had a dollar for every time someone had said that to her in the past twelve hours—

"But I'm sure you've heard that way too many times, so let's just get you up to your room. You're probably anxious to get cleaned up. Personally, I think a hot shower can wash away a boatload of trouble."

A shower sounded good. Great even. But Tristan would probably leave while she was trying, without success, to wash away her problems.

She might not want to need him.

She might not want to want him around, but she did. Chalk it up to fatigue and injury, but the thought of not having Tristan close by filled her with dread. "It's okay. I can wait for a while."

"Go on, Sunshine. I've got a couple calls to make before I head out of here. Then we need to talk about the rules." Tristan nudged her toward Rayne.

"Rules?"

"Did you think I was going to leave you here without some? Who knows what kind of trouble you'd get yourself into." He smiled, and Martha wanted to throw herself into his arms, beg him not to leave her in the middle of the mountains with a stranger.

Dumb.

Really dumb.

She did not need Tristan to stay. She would not

beg him to stay. She wouldn't even indicate that she wanted him to stay. She wasn't a toddler, after all. She was a grown woman, perfectly capable of taking care of herself. Hadn't she hiked into the mountains on her own just a few short days ago? Hadn't she been planning on spending a weekend completely by herself?

What had happened to the strong, independent woman she'd been?

She hadn't died, that was for sure, so there was no way Martha was going to act like a whiny, weak damsel in distress, willing to let the knight fight her battles while she hid inside the castle. She straightened her spine, stiffened her shoulders. "Just so you know, me being given rules doesn't mean I'll follow them. I need to hear what they are before I commit to them."

"You'll follow them, Martha. Otherwise how can we make sure you stay safe?" Rayne's words were calm with barely any inflection, but there was a hard edge to her tone, a sharp look in her eyes.

Definitely an agent and not a paid babysitter. And definitely someone Martha wanted to avoid crossing. For now she'd let the rule battle go. She had a feeling there'd be plenty of other things to battle over during the next few hours. Like visits to her father. Tristan might think she'd given up on the idea, but that was far from true.

She followed Rayne upstairs into a large room decorated in soft yellows. The curtains and shades were drawn, and she started to open them, stopping when Rayne put a hand on her arm.

"That's probably not the best idea." Because if Gordon Johnson is out in the wilderness with a sniper rifle you might not live to see tomorrow. Rayne didn't add the last, but Martha heard the words as clearly as if she had.

"Oh. Sorry."

"No problem. Everything in the room was brought in for you. We couldn't grab stuff from your place, but Tristan gave us sizes and color preferences. Go ahead and take a look. Make sure he got it right. You know how men are. Give them an easy job and they'll find a way to mess it up." She pulled open a dresser drawer and gestured for Martha to look inside.

Shirts, jeans, sweaters in deep purples, bright blues and vivid yellows. All in her sizes. "These look good."

"TV works. I brought a couple of old movies. Musicals. Tristan said you'd probably enjoy that more than thrillers or action flicks."

"He's right." Though how he'd known that much about her, she didn't know.

"He didn't mess that up, then. Tristan brought your purse. I left your cell phone in it, but don't use it."

"You went through my purse."

"It's what I do." She smiled, but it didn't reach her eyes. "Why don't you go ahead and check things out. Take a shower. Freshen up. Put on some clean clothes. Take your time. Tristan and I have a few things to discuss."

"All right. Thanks."

"Don't thank me. This is my job. It's what I get paid for. Just stay put until Tristan or I come up to get you, okay?"

Obviously, she wanted Martha to stay upstairs for a while. Was there some kind of secret-agent stuff that had to be discussed while she wasn't around? Some bad news Rayne didn't want her to hear?

She didn't ask. Mostly because she wasn't sure she wanted to hear the answer. She might have slept for a few hours, but she felt sick with exhaustion and pain. A shower sounded good, and she was going to take one while the taking was good, because who knew what the next few hours would bring. For all she knew, Johnson would show up here and she'd be off running through the forest trying to escape him.

Or she'd be dead.

She grimaced at the thought. "Okay."

Rayne nodded, stepped out of the room, closed the door and left Martha alone.

Silence pressed in, and she moved to the dresser, pulling out clothes. Her body was humming with nerves but dragging with fatigue. She felt drained. The truth was, she'd felt that way before Friday. It was one of the reasons she'd run to the cabin after she'd broken up with Brian. Somehow in the past few years she'd lost her focus. In pursuing her dreams, she'd forgotten to pursue her purpose.

And, she realized, those two things were not the same.

Really, would God want her to change who she was and what she believed about life and relationships so that she could have a family? Of course He wouldn't. He'd much rather she use her gifts and talents for Him. She knew that. Had always known it, but somehow the family she'd wanted, the relationship, the happy home she'd dreamed of had made her forget it for a while.

"Whatever You want my life to be, Lord. That's going to be good enough for me from now on."

An open door led to a large bathroom, its earthy tones exactly what Martha would have chosen had she been the one to decorate. Double sinks. Huge soaking tub. Separate shower. For a safe house, the place was fancy.

Martha, on the other hand, wasn't looking so hot.

She scowled at her reflection. Frizzy curly hair, dark circles under her eyes, pale skin that seemed to have taken on a greenish tinge. The jacket Tristan had borrowed for her hung over her shoulders, but didn't hide the blue hospital gown or the dirty blood-stained jeans Martha wore. Her own blood. Her father's.

Martha grimaced, running hot water into the shower so that steam filled the room and masked her reflection as she searched for something to cover the stitches in her shoulder.

Fifteen minutes later, she'd dressed in clean clothes and was running a brush through her hair, wishing she had a little makeup to liven up her pale cheeks. All her purse had yielded was a tube of

ChapStick. Oh well, at least she didn't look quite as sickly as she had before her shower. She grabbed a bottle of lotion from the sink, rubbing it into her hands, smiling a little when she realized it was chocolate-scented. It didn't seem like the kind of thing Rayne would pick out. Maybe she had a soft side.

"Martha?" Tristan called through the closed bedroom door. Martha hurried to open it, her heart doing the same happy dance it did every time he was around.

"I was starting to wonder if you were going to leave without saying goodbye." The words slipped out and her cheeks heated. Why oh why had she inherited her father's fair skin?

"And miss my opportunity to remind you of the rules?"

"Remind me? You haven't told them to me yet."

"Sure I have, you've just chosen not to follow them." He smiled, pulling her out into the hallway. He'd changed into dark jeans and a navy T-shirt, and the scent of soap and shampoo clung to him. She wanted to cling to him, too, wrap her arms around his waist and beg him not to go.

Fatigue. That had to be the reason. In the two years she'd known Brian, she'd never once felt the urge to ask him to stay longer than he'd planned. "Go ahead and give me the list."

"There are only two. First one—stay inside unless Rayne is with you. Second one—do everything you're told when you're told without arguing."

"That sounds like more than two."

"Count them however you want, Sunshine, but for once, follow them. It could make the difference between living and dying. Not just for you, but for anyone protecting you."

His words were a harsh reminder that Martha wasn't at a fall retreat, that the beautiful house and awesome landscape were a temporary prison designed not just to keep her in, but to keep Gordon Johnson out. "I will."

"Promise me." He placed a hand against her cheek, staring into her eyes. For a moment she forget everything—guns, blood, death dogging her.

"I promise."

"Good." He leaned in, inhaled. "Chocolate. One of my favorite things."

"It's hand lotion. I guess Rayne picked it out."

"Actually, *I* did. In the gift shop at the hospital. I saw it and thought of the day we met. You smelled like rain and chocolate." His lips brushed hers, a second of barely there contact that curled her toes and made her pulse race.

And then he stepped away, shooting a hard look in her direction. "Don't forget your promise."

Before she could respond, he'd moved down the steps and out the front door.

TWENTY-ONE

Three in the morning.

And she was sleepless. Again.

Martha paced the length of her room for the millionth time and scowled at the numbers glowing red on the bedside clock. She'd known that napping in the afternoon was a bad idea, but there hadn't been a whole lot else to do besides watching television, and daytime dramas really weren't her cup of tea.

What she'd really wanted was to get in a car—any car, she wasn't picky—and drive back to Lynchburg General. That hadn't been possible, not just because Rayne Steward was pacing the downstairs like a caged animal, but because she'd promised Tristan she wouldn't.

Unlike a lot of the people in her life, Martha believed in keeping her promises. Though right about now, she was thinking breaking one might not be such a bad thing.

Where was Tristan? At the hospital with her dad? Pursuing a lead that might bring him to Johnson?

Sleeping?

He'd better not be sleeping.

If she had to be awake pacing the floor, so did he.

Which, she realized, was a very selfish thought.

Unfortunately, at three in the morning, she wasn't feeling very altruistic.

The soft chime of her cell phone startled her out of her thoughts, and she rushed to her purse, grabbing the phone and staring at the caller ID. Lynchburg General. She answered without a thought, only remembering Rayne's warning not to use the phone after she was speaking into it. "Hello?"

"Martha Gabler?"

"Yes."

"This is Louise Gilmore from Lynchburg General. I've been trying to reach you for several hours. Your stepmother was finally able to remember this number."

"Is my father okay?" Martha's heart beat a sickening rhythm in her chest, her mind racing through a million things that might have gone wrong.

"I'm afraid he's taken a turn for the worse. You'll want to get here as soon as possible."

"A turn for the worse, how?"

"The doctor will explain everything, but, really, it would be for the best if you come now. He's not doing well. It may only be a matter of hours."

Hours?

She'd thought she'd have decades left with him. Now that time had been reduced to fragments of a day. She wasn't going to waste it trying to get permission to leave the safe house. She was going. Whether Rayne liked it or not. Whether Tristan liked it or not. She might be a state's witness, but she was also a daughter. She would not be denied the opportunity to say goodbye to the man who'd raised her.

Promises or no promises.

She grabbed a thick sweater from the drawer, wincing as she pulled it on over the T-shirt she wore. Her shoulder throbbed with every movement, but she worked quickly, pulling on sneakers she found in the closet. Her size exactly. Was that Tristan's doing?

Her promise to Tristan whispered through her mind as she grabbed her purse. The straightforward approach was best. Down the stairs. Out the front door. If Rayne tried to stop her, she'd just…

Well, she wasn't sure what she'd do, but she'd do something.

The hall was dark, the house silent as she hurried down the stairs. Her hand trembled as she grabbed the door knob and paused.

And then what?

She didn't have a car.

"I'm pretty sure you aren't supposed to be going outside." Rayne appeared at the top of the stairs, dressed in a black shirt and jeans, her hair pulled back from her face.

"I just got a call from the hospital. My dad isn't doing well."

"I don't think so."

"Why would I make something like that up?"

"I'm not saying you did. I'm just saying that if

your dad had taken a turn for the worse, I would have already heard about it." She leaned her hip against the railing, her expression bland.

"Look, Rayne, I don't have time to argue with you about this. My dad's health is failing—"

"Who'd you talk to? What was his name?"

"Her name was Louise something. I didn't catch the last name."

"And she called your cell phone?"

"Yes."

"Let me call the hospital from the secure line. See what I can find out."

"We don't have time for that. She said my dad might only have hours left." Martha's voice broke on the words, and she pressed her lips together. The last thing she wanted to do was break down in front of Rayne.

"Look, Martha, I sympathize with what you're going through, but rushing over there before we check the situation out could be dangerous. Gordon Johnson wants you dead in a bad way. He'll go to any lengths to accomplish his goal."

"He couldn't pretend to be a woman and call me on a number he doesn't have."

"No, but he could bribe someone to help him get what he needs. I've seen it happen before. I lost a good friend that way."

"I'm sorry."

"Yeah. Me, too, and I'm not willing to risk having it happen again. Five minutes to make sure the call was on the up and up. That's not much time."

Not when you had years to play with, but when you only had hours, those five minutes seemed huge.

Martha hovered near the doorway as Rayne disappeared into a room off the foyer. Several minutes later she returned, a frown line marring her smooth forehead. "Good news and bad news. Your father is doing better, not worse. That means Johnson was trying to find you."

"Louise said she got my cell-phone number from my stepmother."

"Maybe. Maybe not. Unless we can figure out who she was, we won't know for sure."

"What now?"

"We wait for Tristan. He's on his way over."

"At three in the morning?"

"Yeah. There's been a change in plans. My boss has decided you need to go back to your father's side."

"You're kidding, right?"

"I'm afraid not. We need to bring Johnson to justice. Sooner rather than later."

"You're going to use me as bait."

"For the greater good, Martha. The longer he's on the streets, the more likely it is that someone else will get hurt. Maybe even killed."

"I don't think I like this idea."

"I don't think anyone does, but Johnson is getting antsy. He may be getting desperate. That's making the situation more and more dangerous. We need to deal with him now."

Deal with him now or spend days, weeks, maybe

even months hiding from him. Martha thought she'd rather do the first. No matter how frightening it sounded. "All right."

"Don't worry. We've done this before. Most of the time, the sharks don't get the bait." She grinned, but Martha didn't think the comment was amusing.

Shark and bait? Definitely not something she wanted to dwell on. Of course she *did* dwell on it anyway, and by the time Tristan stepped into the house, her heart was galloping and she felt physically ill.

"Hey, Sunshine." He pulled her close, wrapping her in his arms. "Another long night, heh?"

"Were you at the hospital?"

"No. I was following up on a few leads. Looks like the best one just came from your cell phone." He released his hold, turning his attention to Rayne. "You talked to Sampson?"

"Yeah."

"So you know the plan."

"Bring Martha to the hospital. Give Johnson a chance to go after her."

"For the record, I'm not too fond of the plan."

"For the record, I don't think your fondness or lack thereof matters. We need to get this guy off the streets, Tristan. We need to do it now."

"Not if it means risking a civilian's life."

"We're risking civilian lives if we don't act."

"I disagree."

"You won't when he goes after Martha's father or stepmother. Or when some poor nurse or doctor is killed so he can get the old man and use him to draw Martha out."

"My dad isn't an old man."

"Sorry, I meant no offense. My point is simply that Johnson is a cold-blooded killer who is desperate to keep you from testifying against him. If that means killing a few innocent people who happen to get in his way—so be it."

"We'll get someone to fill in and pretend to be Martha."

"He may be a killer, but he's not stupid." Rayne frowned, her frustration obvious.

"I—"

"We're wasting time." Martha interrupted Tristan's words. She wanted Johnson off the streets as badly as they did, and as far as she was concerned, if going back to the hospital accomplished the goal, she'd do it. "I'm ready to go get this done."

"Do you realize how dangerous this could be?" Tristan's expression was thunderous, his eyes flashing blue fire.

"Name one thing that's happened in the past few days that hasn't been dangerous."

He scowled, pacing across the foyer. "Look, you're safe here. I want you to stay that way."

"So do I, but I also want to go back to my life. I want to be able to be there for my dad while he's recovering. I do not want to spend days, weeks or months here. I'd go crazy."

"Crazy is better than the alternative."

"We could stand here all day arguing, but it's

not going to accomplish anything. I've got orders to bring Martha to the hospital." Rayne grabbed a jacket from the coat closet. "That's what I plan to do. Unless you want to do it for me."

"*You're* supposed to bring me?" Surprised, Martha turned her attention to Rayne.

"Tristan is on medical leave. He's not supposed to be doing anything more strenuous than lifting a can of soda."

"I'm taking her to the hospital."

"You sure you can handle it, Sinclair?" Rayne sent a mocking smile in his direction.

"Has there ever been any doubt about it before?"

"No, but I'm starting to think you're getting soft, and getting soft is a precursor to dying."

"Thank you, Ms. Mary Sunshine."

"Hey, I'm just saying." She paused, glanced at her watch. "Sampson will have men in place at the hospital by now. If you're taking Martha, you'd better go. If Johnson really is waiting, he'll take off if Martha doesn't get there in a reasonable amount of time."

Tristan nodded, took Martha's arm. "You ready?"

"Yes."

"Put this on under your jacket." Rayne handed her a heavy black vest. "Of course, knowing the kind of guns and weapons Johnson and Buddy have been putting out on the street, there's no guarantee that this will protect you."

Marti didn't like the sound of that, but she tugged on her vest anyway, gritting her teeth as she tried to pull the vest over her aching shoulder.

"Here—" Tristan leaned close "—let me help." His breath whispered against her hair as he eased the vest over her bad shoulder, his fingers brushing against her neck. She shivered.

"Do you think Johnson is waiting?"

"I think there's a good chance."

"Then let's go find him."

Us. The two of them together.

Despite her fear and worry, Martha couldn't help thinking that she liked the sound of that.

TWENTY-TWO

Tristan didn't like the situation. He didn't like it at all. It had been one thing to expose Martha to danger when she'd walked into his raid Friday afternoon. He'd had no choice then. Now, he did, and using her as bait to bring Gordon Johnson in was not a choice he would ever have made.

Unfortunately, it wasn't his decision, and what he liked or didn't like didn't figure into the equation. At least not as far as his boss, Daniel Sampson, was concerned. Tristan had argued with him for the fifteen minutes it had taken to drive to the safe house, but Sampson had remained unmoved. Risking one life to save hundreds, maybe even thousands, made sense. Even without Buddy, Johnson was capable of continuing to trade in illegal weapons. He had the connections, the know-how. He needed to be off the streets. Now. Not weeks or months from now.

As far as Sampson was concerned, the worst-case scenario was that Johnson would ambush Martha and kill her before they could stop him. They'd be out a witness, but there was enough manpower at the hospital to ensure Johnson's capture. Best-case scenario, one of the officers patrolling the hospital would spot Johnson before that happened. Either way, a gunrunner would be behind bars. In Sampson's mind it was a win-win situation. And, Tristan had to cut the guy some slack, he really did believe they'd be able to keep Martha from being hurt again.

Tristan thought they could, too, but that didn't mean he liked the idea any better. Martha should be tucked away in the safe house under Rayne's watchful eye, not riding into Johnson's line of fire. His grip tightened on the steering wheel, and he wondered how many years he'd get if he kidnapped the state's key witness, took her somewhere far away and kept her there until Johnson was caught.

"Don't worry, Tristan. Everything will be fine." Martha spoke quietly, her words barely carrying over the rumbling chug of the engine.

"Aren't I supposed to be the one saying that?"

"Yeah, but seeing as how you look like you're going to tear the steering wheel to pieces, I thought I'd better say it first."

"You're something else, Sunshine."

"Something good, or something bad?"

"Definitely good." He patted her knee, some of his anxiety easing. She was right. Everything *would* be okay. He'd played out these kinds of scenarios dozens of times in the past years, and they usually ran like clockwork. There was no reason to expect this to go any differently.

"What's going to happen when we get to the hospital?" Martha sounded much calmer than Tristan felt.

"We're going to get out of the car and walk into the building like we haven't got a worry in the world."

"You don't think Johnson will realize he's being set up?"

"I do. I think that's the whole point. He's trying to get you out in the open and he doesn't care if we know it. His arrogance is going to be his undoing."

"So he's going to be waiting for me to arrive? Just waiting there even though he knows half the state police are going to be at the hospital?" She couldn't seem to wrap her mind around it, but, then, she was a nice person, a law-abiding citizen. Someone who probably felt guilty if she went a mile an hour above the posted speed limit.

"He doesn't think he'll get caught, babe. That's the thing with men like Gordon. They've gotten away with so much, they think they can get away with anything. In the end, that's what always brings them down."

"Yeah, but how many innocent people do they bring down with them?"

"Too many. That's why my boss wants to make sure we get Johnson tonight."

"The good of the individual sacrificed for the good of the many?"

"Something like that. Only don't think of yourself as a sacrifice. You're more like a carrot held out in front of a donkey's nose. Motivation, but never meant to be eaten."

"A carrot. Make it a huge chocolate-chip cookie hanging from a treadmill, and I just might get into the imagery."

He cast a quick glance in her direction, surprised to see that she was smiling. A tense, tight smile, but it was there, her resilience carrying her through again. She'd pulled her hair into two low ponytails that fell in soft curls near her ears, and he wanted to weave his fingers through them, let the silky softness slide across his skin. Beautiful. Funny. Intelligent. She was a compelling combination. But there was something more. An indefinable something that tugged at Tristan's heart every time he was near her. No matter how much he wanted to ignore it, wanted to pretend it was nothing, the truth was that Martha was becoming part of his life. A big part. Not because she was the key to finding and capturing Johnson, but because she offered something he'd never found with another woman—a sense of belonging. As if being with Martha made him more alive, more complete.

If any of his brothers heard him say that, they'd laugh, but truth was truth. And the truth was, when he was with Martha, he felt like he was home. A strange idea, but one he hadn't been able to shake no matter how hard he'd tried.

"Sometimes I don't understand why God doesn't just reach down and fix things. You know, make life easier for us. He could. A whispered word and Johnson could be in custody without any trouble at all."

Martha's words pulled Tristan from his thoughts, and he glanced her way again. She was still smiling, but there was a sadness to it that made him wish he could take the nearest exit to wherever and hope for the best.

"It would make life easier, but I don't know if it would make things better. A placid lake is nice, but an ocean squall is a lot more interesting."

"Yeah? Well, I've had about enough of squalls. I want placid for a while."

"Eventually, we'll get there, babe. For now, we just have to hold on tight and trust that God will get us through in one piece."

"I know. I just…"

"What?"

"Like to have a little more control over things."

"I get that about you."

She laughed, a soft sound that made him want to turn and look at her again. See the laughter as it played across her face. "I guess it's pretty obvious. I don't mean to be difficult—"

"Who said anything about difficult?"

"I'm sure people have thought it."

"People like Brian?" The more he heard the guy's name, the less he liked him. As a matter of fact, it had been all he could do not to tell the doctor to get lost and stay lost when he'd stopped in to check on Martha at the hospital.

"People. The thing is, I've just learned how important it is to take care of myself and be responsible for my own decisions. Besides my father, I've never had anyone else to lean on. I've never needed anyone else."

"That's admirable, Martha, but sometimes we do need someone to lean on. Sometimes we really can't go it alone."

"Yeah, I think I'm starting to get that." She was silent for a minute, then she shrugged, her arm brushing against his. "I'd still rather do it on my own. It's easier that way."

"It's always easier to guard our hearts than to open them up to pain, but without pain how would we ever know what joy was?" He spoke as he pulled into the hospital parking lot, his gaze scanning cars, probing shadows. The hair on the back of his neck stood on end, his body humming with adrenaline. Johnson was out there somewhere, and Tristan could almost guarantee he was close.

"Do you think he's here?" Martha whispered as if afraid Johnson would hear her.

"Yeah, but don't worry, we're ready for him." Dozens of officers and agents were stationed around the hospital, ready. Waiting. At least, that was the plan. In all the years he'd worked for the ATF, he'd never doubted that all the players would be in place when a mission began. He trusted his team. But this time, he didn't want to leave things in anyone else's hands.

"Good. Let's get going. As long as we're here, I may as well spend some time with my father." Martha didn't seem at all worried to be stepping out of the car and into danger, and Tristan leaned in, star-

ing into her eyes and trying to convey the seriousness of the situation.

"For someone who may be about to walk into a
gunfight, you seem awfully calm, Sunshine."

"Calm? I'm scared out of my mind."

"Good. That'll keep you safe."

"It doesn't feel good. Now, let's get out of here before I chicken out and decide I'd rather not be shark
bait." She put her hand on the door handle, but he
grabbed her arm, stopping her before she could push
it open.

"Wait until I come around."

"Okay."

"And remember, whatever I tell you—"

"Do it. No questions asked. No arguments."

"You know, Sunshine, I think you're finally getting the hang of things." He chucked her under the
chin, meaning the gesture to be friendly, brotherly,
encouraging. Somehow his hand lingered, his fingers caressing the soft skin beneath her jaw, circling
around of their own accord until he was cupping her
neck, pulling her in close.

Chocolate. Sunshine. Sweet summer and cool
calm fall.

They enveloped him, tempted him.

Her eyes widened, but she didn't pull away as
he did what he knew he shouldn't and kissed her. It
didn't matter that a handful of police officers and
federal agents were watching. It didn't matter that
Gordon Johnson might be lurking nearby. It didn't
even matter that Tristan had told himself he could

never offer a woman the kind of stable life she deserved.

What mattered was seizing the moment, knowing that the moment was all they might have.

Finally, he backed away, catching his breath, wondering when he'd lost his mind to this woman. Or maybe it wasn't his mind he'd lost at all. Maybe it was his heart.

She blinked, put a hand to her lips. "I don't think you should have done that."

"No? I guess we can debate that later. Right now, I need to get you inside that hospital in one piece. Ready?"

"As I'll ever be."

"Then let's do it." He stepped out of the car, letting the cold air slap some sense into him as he pulled Martha's door open and helped her out, shielding her body the best he could, knowing that might not be good enough. His nerves were alive, every sense heightened as he waited for the first bullet to fly. It never did. They stepped across the parking lot, moved toward the hospital doors. No one else approached. No patients. No visitors. At three-thirty in the morning, the hospital was eerily silent. Unnaturally silent. As if it were holding its breath and waiting.

A hundred yards. Fifty. Martha's feet padded against the ground, and Tristan was sure he could hear her teeth chattering, but she continued walking.

Thirty yards. If Johnson planned to make a move, he'd do it soon or he wouldn't do it at all.

Okay, Lord, it's in Your hands. Let us get this guy tonight, before he hurts anyone else. And keep Martha safe through it all. Preserve her life so that she may continue to serve You.

The prayer raced through his mind as he led Martha closer to the doors, and he could almost picture it rising on the cold night air, flying to the heavens on wings of faith. God knew what would happen in the next few hours. He'd work His will out in the way He'd predestined before time began. Tristan believed that, had always believed it. That's what kept him going even when evil seemed to prevail. It's what motivated him, spurred him on. Darkness lived in the world, but would never overcome it. Christ, the great overcomer, had already won the war. People like Gordon Johnson just hadn't realized it yet.

Lord willing, tonight one more bad guy would realize the futility of fighting a battle that had already been lost.

TWENTY-THREE

Nothing happened.

Martha expected it to. She almost hoped it would. If it meant getting Gordon Johnson off the streets and ending her nightmare, she was willing to walk through a hailstorm of bullets. Hopefully the vest she wore would keep her alive during the onslaught.

But Johnson didn't fire. Not even one shot, and before Martha could hyperventilate from anticipation and fear, she and Tristan were in the warm quiet of the hospital lobby.

"That didn't go well." She spoke more to herself than to Tristan, but he responded anyway, taking her arm and leading her to the bank of elevators that lined one wall.

"Or it went very well, depending on your perspective."

"He's still out there somewhere."

"And you're still alive. I'm more than willing to trade one for the other."

"Did you really think he might succeed in killing me?"

"If I did, I would have done what I wanted to—taken the next road to nowhere and helped you disappear."

"You're not serious. You'd lose your job for that."

"And?" He turned to her as the elevator doors closed, his eyes blazing from his hard face.

"I wouldn't want you to lose your job for helping me."

"I wouldn't want you to lose your life so I could keep my job. If that meant kidnapping you and taking you somewhere safe, that's what I'd do."

"You weren't really thinking about kidnapping me?"

"I was." He meant it. The truth was in his eyes and in the intensity of his gaze.

"That would not have been a good idea." But it was an intriguing one. Going off to some unknown destination with a man determined to protect her. A fairy tale come to life. Only this wasn't a fairy tale and the chance of a happy ending was slim to none. "I guess we'll just have to be thankful it didn't come down to that."

"I don't know, Sunshine. I don't think I'd mind spending a few weeks in an exotic location keeping an eye on you."

Her cheeks heated at his words, and he grinned, the flirty mischief in his gaze enough to make her pulse race. She really needed to get a grip. She really needed to focus. Someone wanted her dead and she was mooning over an ATF agent she'd known for less than a week. The door to the elevator slid open and she rushed out into the hall, nearly falling backward as Tristan yanked her to a stop.

"Let me lead, okay?" All the humor was gone from his face and from his eyes. In its place was grim determination and the hard, implacable expression she'd seen at the cabin in the mountains.

"There's no way Gordon could be in here. There are police officers stationed all over this wing. It's impossible."

"I've seen the impossible happen more times than I'd care to remember. Besides, someone called from the hospital. That person may or not be dangerous to you." He led her to the nurses' station, the quiet of the ICU broken by the beep and hum of machinery that supported the lives of the patients there. Tristan spoke to the nurse on duty, but his words didn't register. Martha's heart was beating too hard and too fast, her blood sloshing in her ears.

No matter how many times she told herself not to be afraid, she was. The terror clawed at her, threatening to turn her into a blubbering mass of hysteria if she let it. She was not going to let it. She'd held herself together this long, she was not going to fall apart now.

Keep telling yourself that, Martha. Eventually your racing heart might believe it.

She frowned as Tristan stopped in her father's doorway. "What's wrong?"

"Just making sure nothing is out of place."

"Out of place? There's nothing in there but my dad and a bunch of machines."

"Exactly. So if there is something else lying around—a box, a bag, a duffel—it would be worth checking out."

"A bomb?" She whispered the words as if that could make them less real.

"I doubt it, but it's always better to be cautious." He moved silently, making a circuit of the room, glancing behind machines, under the bed, behind the door. Then, finally, gestured for her to enter. "It's okay. Come on in."

Relieved, she hurried to her father's sidc. There was some color in his cheeks now, but he still looked awful—tubes and wires snaking out from his mouth, his nose, his chest. "You look like the Bionic Man before he got all his new parts, Dad. Remember how we used to watch that show together while we worked in the store? You had that little black-and-white television, and we'd sit in front of it, watching until a customer came in. Then we'd argue over who was going to ring up the order. You always won, and I always ended up missing half the program." She squeezed his hand, was surprised to feel the pressure returned. "You can hear me, huh?"

He opened his eyes, tried to nod.

"You're supposed to be sleeping."

He gestured for the pad and pen, and scribbled a note. *Better-looking than the Bionic Man. Was sleeping until you came in and woke me.*

Martha laughed. This was her father. Funny.

Tough. And she knew in that moment that he was going to make it. "Glad to have you back."

Won't be back until the lung is healed. But getting there.

"Get there fast, because I'm counting on you being out of the hospital by Thanksgiving. Sue puts on a great spread, and I wouldn't want her too distracted to cook."

Thanksgiving. The four of us. It's a date.

"Four?"

Her father's gaze jumped to Tristan who'd moved up beside Martha.

"I'm sure Tristan has plans with his family."

"Do I? And here I was thinking I had plans with *your* family. Now that I'm thinking about it, we could invite the whole clan to my brother Grayson's house. My folks, my siblings, your family. It's the perfect time for everyone to meet." Tristan smiled, and Martha's heart did its crazy little dance again.

"Meet?"

"Sure. If you can survive being stalked by Gordon Johnson, you can survive meeting my family."

"But—"

"I've already met yours, Sunshine. So I'm at an unfair advantage. Once you meet my family, that'll put things on more even footing."

"What things?"

Jesse scribbled on his pad, motioned for Tristan to take it. He read the words, laughing as he met Martha's eyes. "Your dad says I'm going to have my hands full with you."

"I…" She shook her head and gave up. What was the sense in arguing with the two of them? There was no way she could win. "Fine. We'll do Thanksgiving your way if Dad is out of the hospital."

"So you've got plenty of incentive to get better, Jesse." Tristan placed the paper back on the bedside table and took Martha's arm. "To that end, I think our ten minutes are up. I'll bring Martha back as soon as it's possible."

Jesse nodded, his sharp gaze sending a silent message that Martha couldn't decipher. Tristan seemed to understand it. He nodded, patting her dad's hand. "We'll talk more when you're feeling better."

Talk more? About what?

Honestly, it was like they were planning a siege, and she was the enemy. Or maybe she was the princess standing on the other side of the city wall they wanted to batter down.

Either way, she didn't like it.

She waited until they were out of her father's hearing, before turning on Tristan. "Look, I don't know what you and my father are planning, but I don't like it."

"How do you know you don't like it if you don't know what it is?"

"Because it involves talking about me, and I don't like the idea of you two plotting things I don't know about."

"Trust me, Martha, what we're plotting is something you know about." He smiled, but his eyes burned into hers, intense, probing.

She knew, all right. Knew enough to turn tail and run as soon as she got the opportunity. Tristan was a great guy, but he wasn't the right guy for her. No one was. She'd already decided she was going to be the neighborhood cat lady. No strong, determined, compassionate, good-looking hero was going to change her mind.

She'd forgotten to say "kind." Tristan was that. And loyal, faithful, moral: an all-around good guy. The kind of guy that was hard to come by in this day and age. The kind of guy any woman would be beating down doors to have interested in her.

But Martha wasn't any woman.

She'd learned young that relationships couldn't last. She'd still tried to make it work with Brian. Thank goodness that had ended before they'd taken vows. For better, for worse, in sickness and health. Brian hadn't been able to be with her in the *good* times. There was no way she'd have ever been able to count on him in the bad ones.

Tristan, on the other hand, had only ever been with her in bad times. When good times came, he'd probably move on to the next distressed damsel, the next battle against evil. Not because he'd want to hurt Martha, but because it was what he did. He was one of those rare people who gave everything to others. His passion was for justice. She doubted there could be room for much else. The thought was a lot more depressing than it should have been, and Martha shoved it aside as Tristan led her back outside.

The sun had set and stars dotted the black sky—a

field of wishes waiting to be harvested. Martha imagined reaching up, pulling one toward her, reciting that childhood rhyme her father had taught her. Star light, star bright, first star I see tonight, I wish I may, I wish I might, have the wish I wish tonight. What would her wish be? That her father get better quickly? That her life go back to normal?

That Tristan stay?

It didn't matter. Wishes were only hopes given voice, they had no power. Power lay with God, and only He could fulfill the desires of the heart.

Soon this would be over. She'd go back to her life. Tristan would go back to his. The world would right itself again, and she'd find her balance. Then she'd look back and laugh at how her heart had seemed to beat in time with Tristan's, at how her pulse raced when she looked into his eyes. At how much she seemed to belong when she was with him.

Tristan pulled the car door open, his hand on her waist, steadying her as she slid inside. "Buckle up, this could be a wild ride."

"A wild ride? I thought the worst was over."

"It may be, but Johnson isn't one to give up. He was too smart to try anything here, and smart enough to know that we're most vulnerable when we're on the road. If we leave here without an escort, he just might make his move."

"So we're on our own from here on out?"

"We're never on our own, babe."

"I know, but I'd feel a little better if we had some

tangible proof of God's protection. Like maybe an armored car, or a military escort."

"We've got backup standing by in various locations on our route. It'll be okay."

"For someone who thinks that, you sure don't look happy."

"I'm never happy when I'm dragging an innocent person into something dangerous. The fact that it's you I'm dragging only makes it worse."

"You still have to do your job. It's who you are."

"You're right about that, babe. I have to do it, but I don't have to like it." Grim-faced, he started the car and pulled out of the parking lot, leaving the relative safety of the hospital behind them.

They drove in silence. No radio. No conversation. Tristan's tension filled the car, and Martha's joined it, welling up and out until it seemed to steal the oxygen. She took a deep, shaky breath, forcing herself to relax.

Five minutes passed. Then ten. Cars and trucks passed them on their way into the Blue Ridge Mountains. Despite the hour, the road was busy, and Martha started to relax. To believe that Johnson had given up, that he'd decided killing her wasn't worth taking a chance. Tristan wound his way up into the mountains, leaving Lynchburg behind, the sheer drop below shrouded by darkness.

Ten minutes. The traffic thinned a little as they drove along Blue Ridge Parkway, but was still heavy enough that Martha felt confident Johnson wouldn't strike. Five more minutes and they'd reach the turn-off that led to the safe house.

"Here he comes."

"What? How do you—" Before she could finish, they were hit from behind. The sedan slid sideways toward a sheer drop.

Martha screamed, her hands clutching the dashboard as she imagined plummeting a hundred feet to the ground below. She'd always loved the Blue Ridge Parkway, but if she made it off this road alive, she would never, ever drive on it again.

Tristan righted the wheels, stepping on the accelerator and racing ahead of the vehicle behind them. Fifty miles an hour. Sixty. Seventy. Eighty. Martha's heart beat so hard, she thought it would jump out of her chest. Johnson wasn't going to have to hit them again, they were going to lose control and die without any help from him at all.

"Hang on." Tristan took a corner so fast, Martha's head slammed into the side window and she saw stars. When she could see again, she realized they were on a dirt road rather than the gravel road that led to the safe house. Not where they should be, but at least they weren't racing along a sheer drop.

Tristan eased his foot from the accelerator, his speed dropping to thirty. Martha barely had time to thank God for that, when they were hit again, this time with more force. The car spun off the road, tumbling sideways, sliding into trees. Snapping. Crashing. Crunching. Glass shattering. Air bags popping. Blood. Pain.

Silence as still as death.

Not a breath. Not a sound.

She wanted to believe it was over. Wanted to think it was the end, but her heart knew the truth. Gordon Johnson was right outside the car, and any minute he'd pull open her door and finish what he'd started.

"You okay?" Tristan pressed a palm against her cheek, and she nodded, wanting to press her hand over his, force him to maintain contact, but her arm wouldn't listen to the command her brain issued. "Good. I tried to slow down to keep the damage at a minimum, but he was still coming fast."

"Is he out there?"

"Oh, yeah, he's out there. And he and I are about to have a little face-to-face." His hand dropped away, and this time Martha managed to grab it.

"You can't go out there."

"Sure I can. It's what I'm trained to do."

"But he's got a gun."

"Yeah? So do I."

"So let's wait longer. Eventually, your backup will arrive. They can take care of Johnson."

"That's not how it works, Sunshine. I've got our perp close enough to take down. I'm not going to risk letting him get away."

"But—"

"We rolled down a slope and through some thick foliage. It's going to take a little time for him to get down here. You stay put while I go find him."

"Tristan, I really don't like this plan."

"I know, but you've got to trust me on this, babe.

It's the only way. Stay here." His voice had softened, and his fingers skimmed across her brow, down her cheek, touching her lips briefly before slipping away. "Promise me, Sunshine. No matter what, you won't get out of this car. You've got to trust me to take care of this situation."

"I can't."

"Then I can't go looking for Johnson. I won't leave you here knowing you might walk right into danger." He was serious. He really wasn't going to leave. Martha sensed it in the stiff way he settled back into his seat, the tense way he held his body.

"Go. I'll stay here."

"Promise." It was a demand rather than a request, but Martha couldn't deny it. Couldn't deny who Tristan was, or ask him to do it. He was meant for this job. No matter what, she had to trust him and let him do it.

"I promise."

He leaned in, and she could smell soap and shampoo and autumn cold as he pressed his lips to her forehead. "Don't take this the wrong way, babe, but I think I'm falling for you."

Then he was gone, sliding out the window and into the predawn, not even a rustle of leaves letting her know which direction he'd gone.

And Martha was alone. A sitting duck waiting for a wolf to move in for the kill.

TWENTY-FOUR

At first all she could hear was her rushing pulse, but as minutes passed and nothing happened, she began to hear other things. Leaves whispering. The first bright trills of a songbird. Cars somewhere in the distance. Life going on while she sat and waited for death.

Well, she was done waiting. Gordon Johnson might want her dead, but that didn't mean she had to make it easy for him. She slid across the seat, her head butting against the crushed roof, her arm throbbing with a deep insistent pain that was nearly impossible to ignore.

It didn't matter. All that mattered was sliding out of the window, fading into the shadows and finding a place to hide from the Grim Reaper. She shifted her weight, almost had her head out the window, when she heard Tristan's words, clear as a bell ringing in her ears. A memory, but so vivid she could almost believe he was beside her again. "Promise me, Sunshine. No matter what, you won't get out of this car. You've got to trust me to take care of this situation."

And then, whisper soft, echoing in her heart—
"don't take this the wrong way, babe, but I think I'm
falling for you."

Falling for her.

With those simple words, he'd tied her hands.
Made her a prisoner to her promise. She couldn't
betray a man who believed in her, who was counting on her. If she got out of the car and put Tristan
in danger, she'd never forgive herself.

She sank back into the car, tears streaming down
her cheeks. Helpless. Angry. But more than that,
afraid. Afraid that everything she'd ever wanted had
just stepped out into the darkness and she'd been too
foolish to believe in it, too cowardly to go after it.

"Lord, please keep Tristan safe. Keep me safe. I
realize now the gift that You've given me. I realize
now that I can't be too afraid to take it. Please, let
everything turn out okay."

Branches cracked nearby. Heavy footfalls. A muffled curse. Not Tristan. Gordon Johnson. She didn't
need to see his face to picture him. Red hair. Pale
eyes. Death in his cold, unfeeling gaze.

She shuddered, her mind screaming for her to run,
to slide out the window and take off before Johnson
found her. Her heart wouldn't let her do it.

Her treacherous, traitorous heart.

The one that refused to believe in love.

The one that insisted fairy tales were nothing
more than fantasy.

The one that had already created a neighborhood
cat-lady existence for herself, wouldn't let her betray
Tristan or his trust in her.

So she waited, as the footfalls grew nearer, the curses grew louder, until finally, branches were pulled away from the car, and Gordon Johnson was inches from her face.

"Where's your friend?" He growled the question, turning to the left, then the right, a gun in his hand. Not the gun he'd had in the mountains. A different gun. One with a silencer.

Lord, please, please let Tristan be around. I don't want to die. I really, really don't.

"I'm alone." She managed to squeak the word out as her mind made plans for escape. Not that she'd get far before Johnson put a bullet in her back, but if she was going down, she was going down fighting.

"You're not alone. You got a friend with you. He was driving. And I'm thinking it might be my old buddy Sky Davis, so tell me where he is now, and I can finish my business with you and be on my way."

"I said—"

He lifted the gun, pointed it at her forehead, and she knew she was going to die. Knew it in the deepest part of her soul. No husband. No kids. Not even any cats. If she hadn't been so scared she would have cried, maybe even begged for her life.

"Looking for me?" Tristan's voice came from out of the darkness, and Johnson whirled toward the sound.

"Come on out here where I can see you, Davis. I got a score to settle with you. I gave you my trust. You repaid me with a betrayal."

"You're scum, Gordon. A lackey working for someone else because you don't have the brains to do the job yourself."

"I got news for you, Davis. I'm not the one sitting behind bars. Buddy is. So, who's the one with less brains?"

"I'd say neither of you have much, because you're going to be joining your boss soon."

"Not if I have anything to say about it." Johnson fired a shot, a pop and a flash of light that disappeared almost before Martha could see it.

Her heart jumped, her stomach churning. Where was Tristan's backup? Where was the cavalry? Shouldn't someone be riding to the rescue by now?

"Put the gun down, Gordon. You've lost this battle. You'll get to fight another one in court."

"You're wrong, Davis. I haven't lost anything." He grabbed Martha's hair, pulling her halfway out of the car. "Come on out now, before I make hamburger out of your girlfriend's face." Johnson lifted the gun, aimed it at Martha's face while she struggled against his iron grip on her hair.

Would it be quick?

Would she feel anything?

Was God already opening His arms to welcome her home?

The thoughts hammered through her mind, beating with the loud, horrifying thump of her heart.

No. Tristan wasn't going to let her die. He was going to—

A loud crack split the silence, and Johnson cursed, his grip on her hair going lax. She scrambled back, away from the shattered window and the killer outside. Her fingers clawing at the far door, her shoulder slamming into it as she tried to get it open.

Stuck tight.

Her breath heaved out in great, gasping sobs as branches cracked, sirens blared, men shouted and the world spun crazily in its orbit.

A dark shadow loomed in front of her, and Martha screamed, lurching back.

"Hey, it's okay." Tristan yanked hard on the crushed door, pulling it open and climbing into the car, enveloping her in his strength.

She wrapped her arms around him, her fingers fisted in his shirt. "I've never been so scared in my life."

"Me neither. I thought I was going to lose you before I ever even had you." His voice was steady, but his heart was racing wildly against her ear.

"Is Johnson—"

"Alive. Justice is better served that way."

"But you did shoot him?"

"His arm. Paramedics are already treating him. Come on. Let's get you out of here."

He started to move away, but Martha tightened her grip. "I don't think I can move. My legs aren't working. Can we sit for a little while longer?"

"We can sit for as long as you want."

"Don't say that. I might stay here forever."

"From where I'm sitting, that doesn't seem like such a bad thing." She could feel his smile against her hair, feel his heart slowing and her heart responding. Her pulse eased, her breathing calmed, her tense muscles relaxed as if they knew the truth she hadn't wanted to accept—that Tristan was exactly what she'd always been looking for. Home. Belonging. Family.

She sighed, wishing she *could* stay there with him forever, cocooned in his arms, and forget everything but this moment. Good things never lasted and tomorrow Tristan might be gone.

Outside the car, men and women called to each other, flashlights danced along the ground. A cool breeze blew moisture through the trees. Twenty miles away, her father lay in intensive care, struggling to survive.

And Martha knew she needed to step back into the world again. She loosened her grip on Tristan and leaned back, putting some distance between them. "I guess I can go to the hospital and be with my father now."

"I guess you can."

"And I guess you won't be needing that apartment over my garage anymore."

"I guess not."

"So, I guess this is probably goodbye."

He chuckled, shook his head. "Haven't you been listening to a word I've said, Sunshine? I'm not going anywhere."

"But it's over. I'm safe."

"So we've made it through the bad times together. How about we start making it through some good times?"

"Like Thanksgiving with both families?"

"For a start."

"What if your family doesn't like me?"

"Grayson likes you. If you meet with his approval,

you're a shoo-in with everyone else. Besides, I'm past the age where I need my family's approval."

"What if you decide I'm too stubborn for my own good and get sick of being around me?"

"What if you decide my job takes me away too much and you get tired of having me gone?"

"Your job is what you're meant to do, Tristan. I would never resent you for that."

"And your determination is what makes you a strong, independent woman. The way I see it, if anyone can handle being with someone whose job takes him away more than he's home, you can."

"So we're on for Thanksgiving?"

"And for painting my parents' house, if you're up to it."

"Painting their house?"

"Yep. An old Victorian lady that gets her hair and nails done the first weekend in November every three years. We can always use an extra set of hands. And don't think you'll get out of painting because you've been shot. It's all hands on deck when it comes to the job."

"It sounds like…" Like fun, like family, like everything she'd dreamed of when she was a kid.

"Like what?"

"Like good times."

"Then it's a date?" He held out his hand, and she took a deep breath, then did what her heart was telling her to, and took it.

"It's a date."

Tristan's smile warmed her as he tugged her out of the car.

EPILOGUE

"You missed a spot." Martha couldn't hide her smile as Tristan glanced down from the scaffold he was perched on. A paintbrush in his good hand, a scowl on his face, he looked like a knight braced for battle rather than a man painting a three-story Victorian monstrosity.

Her knight.

She smiled again.

Being independent and capable was great. She highly recommended it, but she had to admit, being cherished and taken care of wasn't such a bad thing either. Especially when the guy doing the cherishing was Tristan.

"Did one of my brothers send you over here to tell me that? Because if it was Grayson—"

"Actually, I discovered the problem all by myself."

"Did you? Well, far be it from me to do a less than perfect job. Come on up here and tell me where it is, and I'll fix the problem. For a price."

"A price?"

"A kiss. Or two." He grinned, and Martha's heart jumped in response.

No matter how many times she looked into his eyes, no matter how many smiles they shared, how much laughter passed between them, it always felt like the best of surprises; the most wonderful of gifts.

"I'd love to, but your father expressly forbid me to climb up any ladders for fear that I'd reinjure my shoulder."

"Funny, he didn't seem nearly as concerned about my injury. As a matter of fact, he told me I'd better not think I could slack off because of a little gunshot wound."

"Then maybe you shouldn't have told him *I* couldn't paint."

"Piper's been talking to you, hasn't she? Why won't she just have the kid already so she can stop causing trouble?" He smiled as he said it, and Martha laughed, moving closer as Tristan climbed down from the scaffold.

"I like your family."

"I knew you would."

"I especially like them because they're not making *me* paint."

"Keep it up, Sunshine, and I'll tell your dad you're not treating me right."

"You may be his favorite son, but I'm still his little princess. Your whining won't do any good."

"Brat."

She laughed again, and he pressed his lips to hers, drinking in her joy, sharing it with her.

Breathless, she stepped back. "We're really going to make this work, aren't we?"

"This, as in you and me?"

"What else?"

"Yeah, Sunshine, we really are."

"You know, just a few short weeks ago, I was sure I'd wind up being the neighborhood cat lady. You know the one. Tucked away in her house with twenty cats and no friends, overgrown bushes blocking out the sunlight."

"I couldn't imagine that happening to you even if I tried." He brushed stray curls from her cheek, his eyes the deep blue of summer sunsets.

"That's because you see something in me no one else ever has."

"It's because I see *you*. The person God created. Sweet and gentle, but with a spine of steel. You were meant to have a family, Martha."

"Maybe, but I'm scared."

"Of me?"

"Of *me*. What if I'm like my mother? What if, as soon as things get tough, I take off running? What if we create something really good together and I mess it up?"

"You've got too much love in you to ever do that."

"But—"

"You worry too much, you know that?"

"I just don't want to be disappointed."

"I will never disappoint you, Sunshine. And you'll never disappoint yourself. God planned this out from the very beginning. From the moment you walked into the cabin in the mountains, I knew there would be something between us. I felt it in my soul. We were meant to meet that day. We're meant to be to-gether now. We're meant to have a future together. I believe that or I wouldn't be standing here with you now." He stared into her eyes as if he could will his confidence into her.

But he didn't need to.

She felt it. Just as he'd said. Deep inside, where the quiet voice of the Spirit whispered truth. Where God spoke to her heart, telling her that He'd planned it all before her life began. "You know what?" She pulled his head down for a kiss. "I believe it, too."

"That is exactly what I was hoping to hear." He claimed her lips again, pulling her in, promising her what she'd always longed for and had been so afraid she'd never have.

"Hey! I'm hard at work on the west side and I come over here and find my brother being distracted by one of the prettiest women in the house. That doesn't seem right." Grayson's voice cut through the haze of Martha's emotions, and she jerked back, her cheeks heating as Tristan chuckled.

"You're just jealous."

"Jealous that you're succumbing to the love bug? I don't think so. I've been there. Done that. As far as I'm concerned, that's enough for one lifetime." He turned away, calling over his shoulder as he went. "Mom just told me lunch is on the table. You're wel-come to stay out here as long as you want, but don't expect me to save you any of the good stuff. And that includes the cherry cobbler she made."

"We'd better hurry." Martha started after Grayson, but Tristan pulled her up short.

"Let's take our time. The way I see it, I've got something a lot sweeter than Mom's cherry cobbler right here beside me." His eyes were filled with humor, his stride easy as he wrapped his arm around Martha's waist and led her into their future.

* * * * *

Dear Reader,

Life is filled with choices. When we take time to pray and seek God's will, we have peace that comes from knowing we're walking in God's will. When we don't, we find ourselves at crossroads, unsure of which direction to go. Martha Gabler is in just such a place. Desperate to be married, she allows herself to be pulled into a relationship that isn't God's plan. When she finally realizes her mistake, she hikes into the Blue Ridge Mountains, planning to spend time praying about God's will for her life. Instead, she finds danger and intrigue and learns that God's vision for her life is much better than anything she could have imagined or dreamed.

I hope you enjoy Martha's story, and I pray that whatever choices you're faced with, you will find the peace that comes from seeking God's plan for your life.

In Him,

Shirlee McCoy

Questions for Discussion

1. After breaking up with Brian, Martha realizes a relationship with him wasn't the best thing for her. Why doesn't she realize this before becoming engaged to him?

2. How does knowing this make her feel?

3. Have you made decisions that you've convinced yourself were right, then discovered they were mistakes? Why do you think this happened?

4. Martha's childhood impacts the way she looks at the world and at herself. What are her feelings about marriage and motherhood? How do they change over the course of the story?

5. How has your childhood experience impacted your life? How does faith change the way you look at the world?

6. What is Tristan's motivation for going to Lakeview? Does this change during the story?

7. Martha is strong, determined and not necessarily in need of a hero. Somehow, though, Tristan fills a place in her life that's been empty. What is it about Tristan that appeals to Martha?

8. What is it about Martha that Tristan finds attractive?

9. Trusting God isn't always easy for Martha. What is it in her personality that makes sitting back and waiting so hard?

10. Tristan seems like the perfect hero, but Martha doesn't want to believe that he might become something more than that to her. Why?

11. When given a choice between taking action and waiting on God's will, Martha is more likely to act than to wait. Can you identify with this? What things in your life have you had to wait on?

12. It is difficult for Martha to accept help from others. She's been taught to take care of herself. Do you have difficulty accepting help from those around you? How does this affect your life?

13. Vulnerability is often seen as a weakness, but Martha learns that to be strong we must sometimes allow ourselves to be weak. How does being vulnerable before God make us stronger?

The Protector's Promise

For when your faith is tested, your endurance
has a chance to grow. So let it grow, for when
your endurance is fully developed, you will be
strong in character and ready for anything.
—*James* 1:3–4

To Sara. The darker the night,
the more beautiful the sunrise.
And in loving memory of Willetta Ruth Pothier,
who once told me that I had capable hands.
I didn't understand then. I do now. May I prove
to be as capable of sacrifice, of service
and of love as she was.

ONE

Something woke Honor Malone from deep sleep, the scratchy scrape of it pulling her from dreams of the green hills and cool mists of her native Ireland. She lay silent for a moment, listening to the old bungalow settling and to the quiet whisper of her daughter's breath. Neither was the thing that had woken her. Something else had dragged her from peaceful sleep. She sat up, her heart pounding, her mind racing with images she'd rather forget—a dark shadow, a knife, blood.

The past, she reminded herself. That was in the past, now.

She was in a new home in a new neighborhood. There was nothing to be afraid of. No way that the ugliness that had touched her life could have followed her from St. Louis. She probed the shadows anyway, searching the room for anything out of place. Moving boxes stood against one wall waiting to be unpacked. Her nurse's uniform hung from a hook on the closed bedroom door. Outside, the wind howled, pushing through the cracks in the house's old windowpanes and leaving the air in the room chilly and damp.

Honor shoved aside the heavy quilt her mother had sent as a housewarming gift and stood shivering in her flannel pajamas. Her daughter lay in the bed across the room, and Honor went to her, wanting to assure herself that the four-year-old was okay. Lily lay on her side, sleeping deeply. Safe. Cocooned in blankets and sheets. Just as she should be.

A soft scraping sound froze Honor in place, the noise discordant against the backdrop of wind. Scrape. Tap. Scrape. Like a stick scratching against the window.

Or a knife.

Fear raced up her spine and refused to leave, no matter how many times she told herself that the sound was nothing but the branch of one of the old rosebushes butting up against the window. Her feet moved in slow motion as she walked toward the sound, her stomach hollow with terror. She wanted to climb back into bed, pull the thick comforter over her head and pretend she hadn't heard anything, but she had a family—her daughter and her sister-in-law—to protect. She'd face anything to keep them safe.

Her hand shook as she eased back the curtains and peered outside, bracing herself for whatever she might see. All she saw was darkness pressing against the glass and wispy tendrils of fog that danced eerily in the yard, swirling and swaying, concealing and revealing as the wind blew them away.

Was something else moving out there?

Honor leaned close to the window, squinting as she tried to find substance in the mist.

Scrape.

She jumped back, her heart racing so fast she was surprised it didn't leap from her chest.

Scrape. Tap.

A branch. It had to be. She hadn't seen anything else at the window. She pulled back the curtains again, this time looking down. Overgrown rosebushes brushed against the house with every gust of wind, their gnarled branches tapping against the aluminum siding. That's what she'd heard. Nothing sinister. Nothing frightening. Nothing to get herself worked up about.

She sighed, dropping the curtains and crossing the room. Her shift at Lakeview Haven Assisted Living facility had ended at two, and she'd been home fifteen minutes later. Exhausted, she should have been asleep as soon as her head hit the pillow, but Honor had tossed and turned until after three. Now, it was nearly six and she was awake again.

She knew she should climb back into bed and try to get back to sleep, but the dream had reminded her of things she'd rather forget. Longings and disappointments. Joy and bitter sorrow.

She eased open the bedroom door, closing it quietly before crossing the hall and hesitating in front of her sister-in-law's room. Candace was years past needing to be checked on. But knowing that didn't keep Honor from pushing open the door and peeking into the room. The golden glow of a night-light illuminated the bed where Candace lay. At eighteen, she should have been too old to need the light, but she'd never outgrown it. Despite her maturity, Candy's childhood still haunted her dreams. Honor had given up trying to broach the subject. Instead, she'd done what Candace preferred and learned to pretend that the past wasn't still alive in her sister-in-law's mind.

Honor retreated, closing the door and walking down the hall, knowing she wouldn't be getting any more sleep. The past month had been filled with traumas large and small. Honor had hoped that moving to Lakeview, Virginia, would help settle the family back into the normal rhythm of life, but leaving St. Louis had been much harder than she'd expected.

Harder on Honor.

Harder on Candy.

Harder on Lily, who had only ever known their tiny apartment in the busy city. Lily, who thought that everyone should marry a prince and live in a castle. Lily who had her father's dreams shining in her eyes.

The thought had the same bitter sting it always did, but Honor pushed it aside. She didn't have time to waste mourning the past. Her girls were her priority. Her job, her faith were what pulled them all through the difficult times. This time would be no different.

She turned on the light in the small outdated kitchen, moving quietly as she put a kettle of water on the stove and pulled a tea bag from the canister on the counter. The window above the sink looked over the backyard, and again and again her eyes were drawn to the gray predawn scene. In the city, there had always been light and noise. Here, it was almost too quiet. Too dark. She'd get used to it eventually, she supposed. Just as she'd adapted to city life after living for years in the lush Irish countryside.

She smiled a little as she remembered the childhood years she'd spent exploring the beauty of God's creation with her friends. Those memories were one of the reasons she'd moved to a small town in a rural area. The other reason was Candace's decision to attend a Christian college in Lynchburg. Honor had wanted to stay close to her sister-in-law.

She'd also wanted to escape the memories that didn't seem to want to let her go.

A cup of tea in hand, she walked into the small mudroom off the kitchen, grabbed her coat from the rack and shoved her bare feet into boots. Cold mist kissed her skin as she stepped outside. A few yards away from the back door, an old swing set stood neglected and worn, its skeletal limbs planted firmly in moist earth. Honor took a seat on a wooden swing, nursing the hot teacup in her hand, the still, quiet morning enveloping her. The silence of it, the beauty, carried her away from the anxiety that had been dogging her for weeks and muffled the wordless demands that had become almost too much for Honor to meet. Here, in the peaceful moments before the day began, she could finally hear the quiet voice of her Creator, whispering that everything would be okay.

A muted sound broke the silence. A branch snapping? Honor tensed, scanning the yard, her gaze finally caught and held by movement at the far end of the property. A line of shrubs separated her yard from the one behind it, and Honor was sure something had moved there. As she watched, a dark figure stepped into view. Tall. Broad-shouldered. Brown hair. Those were the only details she could make out.

All the details she *needed* to make out.

The teacup dropped from her fingers, shattering on the ground as she raced toward the safety of the house.

Grayson Sinclair called himself fifteen kinds of fool as he followed the fleeing figure across Oliver Silverton's overgrown backyard. A squatter, probably. Someone who'd learned that the ramshackle place was empty and had decided to call it home for a night or two.

It wasn't Grayson's business, of course. Oliver had made it clear that he didn't want help taking care of his property. Nor was he open to advice on how best to get the dilapidated house rented out.

After three years of living back to back with the property, Grayson had given up trying to help the old man who owned it. Still, when he'd glimpsed a light shining from a back window, he'd decided to investigate.

More to help himself than to help his neighbor.

The fact was, after two weeks of standing vigil over his brother's hospital bed, wondering if Jude was going to live or die, Grayson needed something else to focus on. A problem he could actually solve.

A brother in New York, facing months of physical therapy and an uncertain future?

That he couldn't fix.

A squatter in Oliver Silverton's house?

Grayson could take care of that problem, and quickly.

He strode to the back door, the anger he felt out of proportion to the squatter's crimes. He knew where his anger was really directed—at the hit-and-run driver who'd slammed into Jude while he'd been out of his car helping a stranded motorist.

Grayson turned the doorknob to the old house, expecting it to open as it had a few months ago when he'd put a stop to a group of kids who'd decided to have a party on the premises. To his surprise, the door was locked. A shadow passed in front of the window and the light spilling from it went out.

Did the squatter really think that would convince him to leave?

Grayson slammed a fist against the door, not worried about the force he was using. Not caring. The person inside the house had better open up and explain himself. Grayson wasn't leaving until he did. "Open up. This is private property and you're trespassing."

There was no response, and Grayson pulled out his cell phone, determined to handle the problem with the same efficient ease with which he pros- ecuted criminals. He couldn't help his brother, but he *could* do this.

And he would.

The phone rang once before Grayson's friend Sheriff Jake Reed picked up. "Reed, here."

"It's Grayson. There's a trespasser in Silverton's place again."

"When'd you get back from New York?"

"Half an hour ago."

"And you're at the Silverton place now?"

"Yeah, trying to kick out the trespasser, but he's locked in and won't budge."

Jake laughed, the sound only adding to Grayson's irritation. "Look, maybe you find it funny, but I've had a rough couple weeks and I'm not in the mood to deal with a vagrant who's decided this is home. So, if you don't mind, I'd appreciate you coming over and dealing with it yourself."

"Hey, sorry, man. I know things have been rough. Tiffany and I have been praying for your brother. Most of the people in Lakeview have. How's Jude doing?"

"He'll be in the hospital for another couple of weeks. Then in a rehab facility. It'll be a while be- fore we know if he'll ever walk again."

"I'm sorry."

"Yeah. Me, too. Now, are you coming over here or not?"

"I was already on my way when you called. Seems the new renter thinks someone is trying to break in."

"Renter?" Surprised, Grayson stepped away from the door.

"Moved in last week. A nurse, her daughter and sister-in-law."

"No husband?"

"Nope. Rumor has it, he's deceased, but I haven't actually met the woman or heard the truth from her."

"She was out in the yard and saw me coming through the shrubs that separate our property. I must have scared her half to death." Grayson's anger fled, and he glanced at the darkened window. He could picture the poor woman cowering just out of sight, a phone clutched to her ear as she prayed the police would arrive before he broke down the door. He had a vivid image in his head—a woman in her forties or fifties. Widowed with a teenage daughter and an older sister-in-law who lived with them. Short. Round. Salt-and-pepper curls.

Terrified.

"You scared her enough that she called nine-one-one. I'll have my dispatcher tell her you're a concerned neighbor and there's nothing to worry about. See you in a few." Jake hung up, and Grayson hesitated. Should he knock again? Walk away? What was the protocol for this kind of thing?

Before he could decide, the door cracked open, an old-fashioned chain pulled tight across the space. "Grayson Sinclair?"

"That's right."

"It appears we're neighbors, then." Her voice held

a touch of Ireland, its husky timbre reminding Grayson of cool fall evenings and warm laughter.

"It appears so. I'm sorry for frightening you. I've been out of town for a couple of weeks and hadn't heard the place had been rented out."

"And I'm sorry for calling the police on you. I get nervous when strangers chase me across the yard. Hold on." She closed the door, and Grayson could hear the chain sliding free. When she opened it again, he caught his breath in surprise.

His new neighbor was not in her forties or fifties.

Not round.

Not sporting salt-and-pepper curls.

Not anything like he'd imagined her to be.

"I'm Honor Malone, Mr. Sinclair. It's good to meet you. Despite the circumstance." Her half smile pulled Grayson's attention to lips that were soft and full.

He jerked his gaze to her eyes, irritated with himself. Obviously, driving all night had left him a few brain cells short of clear thinking. "It's good to meet you, too. Jake didn't say when you'd moved in."

"A week ago. Mr. Silverton mentioned that the place had been empty for a long time. I'm not surprised you were worried about squatters."

"We have had a problem with vagrants a few times over the years. That and kids using the house as a party resort."

"Let's hope that you won't have either problem again. Come in and have a cup of coffee while we wait for the sheriff." She turned and walked through

the tiny mudroom, not bothering to wait for his response.

Grayson followed, intrigued by Honor Malone
despite the voice whispering in his head reminding
him that he'd washed his hands of relationships and
women months ago.

He paused at the threshold of the kitchen, impressed by the changes he saw. Honor had already
begun making the old bungalow into a home. Layers of grime had been scrubbed from the counter-
tops, revealing bright blue vintage tiles. The faded
wood floor had taken on a high shine that must have
taken hours of labor. Cabinets that Grayson would
have been willing to testify under oath were beyond
salvaging, were now a bright white.

"The place looks great." He spoke out loud, and
Honor turned to face him, her cheerful yellow flannel pajamas at odds with the strain he saw in her
face. Despite her smile, she looked worn, her eyes
deeply shadowed.

"Thank you. It's been a labor of love."

"It's a lot of work to put into a rental property."

"Not if you're renting to own." She grabbed coffee
cups from the cupboard, the sleeves of her pajamas
falling back to reveal delicate wrists. Her fingers
were long and slender, her left hand bare.

"You plan to buy this place?" The surprise in his
voice must have been obvious, because Honor stiffened.

"Is there some reason why I shouldn't?"

"It's..." Neglected? Past hope? A money pit? "Going to take a lot of work."

"What doesn't, Mr. Sinclair?"

"It's Grayson, and you've got a point. Most things worth having take hard work to achieve."

"I told myself that a hundred times while I was removing layers of wax from this floor." She smiled, her face going from girl-next-door pretty to stunning in the beat of heart.

More intrigued than ever, Grayson studied her face. Heart-shaped with high cheekbones dusted with freckles. Full lips and wide green eyes tilted at the corners. Not conventionally beautiful. There was something there, though. Something that made him want to keep looking.

"What?" She frowned, her cheeks turning scarlet.

"I was expecting a drifter. Instead, I found a beautiful woman."

"And I was expecting an intruder and instead found a man who knows how to turn a sweet phrase." She busied herself gathering mugs, cream and sugar. Apparently not at all impressed by his flattery.

He supposed that was for the best. He wasn't in the market for a relationship. Even if he were, flattery wasn't the way he'd pursue one. He believed in the direct approach.

A soft knock saved Grayson from having to reply to Honor's comment. Jake. Finally. Grayson could offer another apology to his friend, then be on his way. His life was already complicated enough. He didn't need to add more trouble to the mix.

And something told him that's exactly what Honor Malone would be if he let her—trouble.

Compelling, alluring, distracting trouble.

TWO

Honor hurried through the dining room and living room, sure that she could feel Grayson's steady gaze on her back. His eyes were the bright blue of the flowers that had bloomed in her mother's garden every spring. Looking in them had been like coming home.

Frustrated by her foolish thoughts, she yanked the door open, not sure how she had gone from enjoying a hot cup of tea alone to making coffee for a good-looking, smooth-talking man.

"Next time you might want to ask who it is." A dark-haired stranger stood on the porch, his hard face shadowed by the dim morning light, his sheriff's uniform shouting his identity.

"I knew you were coming, so—"

"You can never be sure who is standing on the other side of the door, ma'am. It may not always be who you're expecting."

"I know. I guess with everything that has happened this morning, I wasn't thinking clearly. You are Sheriff Reed, right?" She knew her face was three shades of red, but Honor tried to smile anyway.

"That's right. And you're Honor Malone."

"Come on in." Honor stepped back, allowing the sheriff to move into the living room. "The dispatcher said you were coming out to make sure everything had been cleared up with my neighbor."

"And to meet you. This is a small town, and I make it a habit to say hello to people when they move in." He didn't even crack a smile when he said it, and Honor wondered if his reasons for meeting new people were altruistic or if he just wanted to add to his list of potential suspects.

She didn't dare ask.

"I've just made a pot of coffee. Would you like a cup?" It seemed like the right thing to say, but Honor couldn't help hoping that the sheriff would refuse her offer. Two men standing in her kitchen drinking coffee was two more than Honor could handle.

"A cup of coffee would be good right about now. Thanks."

Wonderful.

She led the sheriff toward the back of the house, sure he was noticing every detail of the cluttered living and dining rooms—the still-packed moving boxes, the faded furniture and dusty floors. The peeling wallpaper that she planned to pull down as soon as she had a spare minute. Lily's crayons were scattered across the dining room table. Candace's textbooks were piled on a chair.

In the past week, Honor had spent all her time making the kitchen warm and inviting. In her mind, it was the heart of the home, the place where the family gathered to share in each other's lives. The sheriff wouldn't know that, though, and would probably think the chaos was a normal part of Honor's daily life.

"I'm really sorry about the mess, Sheriff Reed. We just moved in a week ago, and I had to start my job two days later. Things have been hectic and…"

Her voice trailed off as she stepped into the kitchen. The room was a lot more crowded than it had been a few minutes ago. Not only was Grayson still there, but Candace and Lily had joined him. The first wore faded jeans and a sweatshirt, her blond hair pulled back into a sleek ponytail. The second wore pink-and-red-striped tights, a pink tutu, an orange sweater and a baseball cap. Both were looking at Grayson as if he were a fairy-tale prince come to life.

Appalled, Honor strode across the room, deciding to deal with the only problem she could. Her daughter's attire. "Lily Mae Malone, what in the world are you wearing?"

"My princess clothes." Lily met Honor's gaze with wide-eyed innocence, her curly brown hair brushing against cheeks still baby-smooth and chubby. At four years old she was only just beginning to lose the baby look, her bright eyes and bowed lips making her look like a mischievous cherub.

"You know better than to entertain guests dressed like that. Now, march back to your room and put on something else."

"But—"

"Go. Now. Before you lose your library privileges." It was the worst threat she could make, and

Lily's eyes widened even more. Precocious and imaginative, Lily had begun reading at three and liked nothing better than to check out books of fairy tales from the library.

"I'll help her find something." Candace spoke quietly. Her eyes—so similar in color and shape to Lily's—were much more somber than her younger counterpart's. She shot a last look in Grayson's direction before taking Lily's hand and hurrying her from the room.

"I'm so sorry if the girls were bothering you, Grayson. We haven't been here long enough for Lily to make friends, and Candace has been busy with her college schedule. They were both probably anxious for a little change in the new routine." Honor grabbed another mug, poured coffee and handed a cup to the sheriff.

"They weren't bothering me. And your sister-in-law isn't really a girl." Grayson stood near the mud-room door, his hip leaning against the counter, a coffee cup in his hand. Light brown hair fell to just below his collar and a hint of stubble shadowed his jaw. He looked rugged and outdoorsy. Exactly the kind of guy Honor would have taken note of years ago.

But this wasn't years ago, and she'd decided after Jay's death that her days of noticing men, of dating them, of falling in love were over. She'd had enough of all three to last a lifetime. "No, she isn't. She'll be nineteen in a few months."

"You said she was a college student. Is she attending Liberty University?"

"Why do you want to know?" Honor's question came out much more abruptly than she'd intended it to. A month ago, Grayson's curiosity wouldn't have seemed odd. Now she was suspicious of everyone.

"Because he can't leave his work at the office," Sheriff Reed answered, a touch of amusement in his voice and a half smile easing the harsh angles of his face.

"His work?"

"He's a prosecuting attorney for the state of Virginia. And he's never met a question he didn't want to ask."

"Guilty as charged." Grayson flashed a dimple Honor hadn't noticed before and shouldn't be noticing now. "Sorry. Sometimes my curiosity gets the best of me. Although this time I had a good reason for asking. We've got several teens in the community who are attending Liberty. I thought Candace might like to meet them if she's attending the same school."

"She is." Feeling foolish, Honor stirred two spoonfuls of sugar into her coffee and topped it off with a dollop of cream. She was suspicious of everyone lately and knew she shouldn't be.

"I'll give the kids a heads-up. Maybe they can stop by one day."

"That's very kind of you."

"It's no problem." He raised an eyebrow as she spooned more sugar into her coffee, but didn't comment.

"And I may be able to hook your daughter up with a playdate or two. How old is she?" The sheriff broke into the conversation, and Honor gladly pulled her attention away from Grayson.

"Four going on forty."

"Mine is three going on thirty. They probably have a lot in common."

"I think they probably do. Would either of you like a biscuit to go with your coffee? I'm sure I've got shortbread." She opened the cupboard closest to her and stretched to reach the box of biscuits on the top shelf.

"Let me." Grayson grabbed it from her hands, his fingers brushing hers. It had been a long time since a man had helped her like that, and Honor's cheeks heated, her heart jumping in silent acknowledgment.

"Thank you. The biscuits are from Ireland. My mother sends them every few months because she knows how much I enjoy them." She opened the box of biscuits, biting her lip to keep from saying more. The last thing she wanted to do was babble on about biscuits when what she should really be doing was hurrying the men through their coffee and out of her house. With Grayson on her left and the sheriff on her right, Honor was boxed in. Outsized and outnumbered by two men who seemed to be taking up more than their fair share of space.

"Ireland, huh? I thought I heard a bit of Irish brogue in your voice." Grayson took a biscuit from the open box she held out to him, smiling his thanks.

And what a smile it was.

Stunningly warm and inviting, begging Honor to relax and enjoy the moment.

"Yes, well, it's faded a lot since I arrived in the States thirteen years ago. Would you like one?" She held the box out to the sheriff, but he shook his head, setting his mug in the sink.

"Actually, I've got to head out. Thanks for the coffee, Mrs. Malone. It was nice meeting you."

"Thank you for coming out for a false alarm. I'll see you out." She set her coffee down, but Sheriff Reed shook his head.

"No need. I can see myself out. Grayson, you take care of yourself. Keep us updated on your brother's progress. Tiffany and I will keep the prayer loop going as long as necessary."

"Thanks. My family and I appreciate that more than you know."

His brother was ill?

Honor wanted to ask, but she was sure that would qualify as getting involved in Grayson's life. And that was something she was certain she didn't want to do.

Of course, she knew she would do it anyway.

As soon as Sheriff Reed walked out the back door, she turned to her visitor, noting the shadows beneath his eyes and the tension bracketing his mouth. Now that she knew something had happened to his brother, she saw the evidence of his worry clearly. Whatever was going on, it had to be big. "You said you were out of town for a couple of weeks? Was that because of your brother?"

If he was bothered by her question, his expression didn't show it. "I'm afraid so. Jude was nearly killed by a hit-and-run driver two weeks ago. Both his legs were crushed, his back was broken and his spinal cord was affected. Add that to head trauma, and you've got injuries that were barely survivable. Jude is stabilized now, but it was touch-and-go for several days."

"I'm so sorry."

"Yeah. Me, too. My brother is a homicide detective in New York City. A good one. That's been his passion for as long as I can remember. Now he isn't sure if he'll ever be able to return to work."

"That's terrible. Is there anything I can do besides pray for him?"

"Unless you can assure him that he'll be up on his own two feet, running and climbing and working like he used to, no."

"I wish I could do that, but the prognoses on spinal cord injuries are as varied as the injuries themselves. That, combined with the injuries to your brother's legs, will give him a long row to hoe, but if the spinal cord wasn't severely damaged then there's every chance your brother will walk again."

"So the doctors said, but it's two weeks after the injury and Jude still has residual paralysis."

"Two weeks out isn't as long as it seems. I've seen people regain nerve function all at once. I've seen others regain it slowly over the course of weeks and even months. Don't let your brother give up hope."

Grayson grabbed another biscuit from the box, eyeing Honor with steady intent. "I'd forgotten that Jake said you were a nurse."

"Should I ask how he knew that since we'd never met?"

"News travels fast here in Lakeview."

"I'll have to keep that in mind."

"Why? Is there something you'd rather people around here not know?" He raised a dark eyebrow, and Honor laughed, hoping he didn't sense the truth. Of course there were things she'd rather keep to herself. Like the fact that she'd been attacked and nearly killed a month ago. Or that the death of the drug user who'd broken into her apartment had been headline news.

"Just that my daughter believes in fairy tales and that she's constantly looking for a prince."

"In that case, your secret is safe with me." He placed his cup in the sink. "I've got to head out. Thanks for the coffee."

"You're welcome."

"Funny, I had the impression you'd much rather I'd declined your invitation."

Honor's cheeks heated, but she refused to look away from his steady gaze. "Entertaining guests wasn't on my agenda for today."

"But you invited Jake and me anyway."

"It seemed like the right thing to do."

"And you always try to do the right thing?"

"Are you back to prosecutor mode?"

"Actually, this time I was just being a curious neighbor." Grayson smiled, his firm lips curving, his eyes crinkling at the corners. Not a man given to sulking and anger, Honor thought. More the kind to find the fun in the most ordinary of circumstances. It was a good attitude to have, though carried too far it could lead to trouble. Honor had seen enough of that in her husband, Jay, to know just how far a happy-go-lucky attitude could take a person—from the height of success to the depth of ruin and back again.

She grimaced as she hurried through the mudroom and opened the door for Grayson, waving goodbye as he strode across a yard bathed in silvery morning light.

It was for the best that he was leaving, and for the best that Honor avoid seeing him again. She'd fallen for an easygoing, fly-by-night kind of guy once. In the six years she and Jay had been married, she'd been passionately in love with him and, at times, just as passionately frustrated with him. No way would she go through that again. Not for love. Not for companionship. Not for anything. Her girls deserved a stable, secure home. That's exactly what Honor planned to provide for them. Nothing would change that. Not circumstances. Not friendships. And certainly not a good-looking prosecutor whose eyes reminded her of home.

THREE

The next few days passed in a blur of work and chores. Honor's supervisor had worked hard to schedule around Candace's classes, allowing Honor to work four ten-hour shifts. Honor appreciated it, but by the end of the fourth night, she was exhausted, dragging herself to the nurse's station to punch out and praying she had the energy to drive home.

"Are you heading straight home, Honor? Or would you like to go have something to eat and a cup of coffee first?" William Gonzalez glanced up from some paperwork he was filing as Honor grabbed her coat and purse. Despite the long shift he'd just worked, Will looked wide-awake and raring to go.

"I'm definitely going straight home. I've got a million things to catch up on this weekend. The sooner I get started, the sooner I'll be done."

"I hear you. Maybe we can hook up another time?" He smiled, flashing straight white teeth. At a little over five foot nine, with dark eyes and a compassionate nature, William was the handsome center of romantic attention at Lakeview Haven, and he knew it.

Unfortunately for Will, Honor was much too busy for light flirtation—or anything else, for that matter. Though she had to admit, since she'd met Grayson Sinclair, she'd spent far too much time wondering what it would be like if she *did* have time. Remembering his dimple, his eyes, the warmth of his fingers when they'd brushed against hers…

Stop it!

You are not some teenage girl mooning over a boy. You're a grown woman who's had enough of love to last her a lifetime.

She forced her attention back where it belonged: on her conversation with Will. "My life is pretty hectic right now. I don't have time for much more than work and the girls."

"Too bad. You and I have a lot in common." He smiled again, but there was a tightness to his expression that hadn't been there before. Had her refusal offended him? Honor hoped not. She and Will worked the same shift and she didn't want there to be tension between them.

"The same thing we have in common with all the other nurses here, I'd say. Our jobs." She tried to make light of things as she put on her coat and buttoned it.

"And that we're both far from home. I grew up in Mexico. My entire family is still there. Makes for a lonely life sometimes."

"Lonely?" Honor smiled and hiked her purse up

onto her shoulder, knowing that Will was anything but that. "The way I hear it, you keep pretty busy with the other nurses around here. I'm not sure how that adds up to being lonely."

Will laughed and shook his head. "I do like to hang out with some of my co-workers, but that doesn't mean I'm not lonely. Especially on the days I work. These ten-hour shifts are killers when it comes to friendship."

"We do get three days off. I'm sure you find plenty of time to go out when you're not here. Rumor has it you've dated every nurse here."

"Except for you."

"Which is exactly how I plan to keep it."

"Why?" He seemed sincerely curious, and Honor answered.

"I was married before, Will, and I have a daughter. At this point in my life, I'm not looking to begin another relationship."

"All right. That's cool. Hey, give me a minute to finish filing this paperwork and I'll walk you out. It's still dark, and you never know what might be hiding in the shadows."

"The parking lot is well lit, I'll be fine. Thanks for offering, though. See you Tuesday?"

"See you then." He waved and turned his attention back to his filing, leaving Honor to walk down the corridor and into the lobby alone.

The front door opened onto a wide veranda that wrapped around the building and provided a covered area for the residents. Colorful chairs and small tables were spaced carefully to allow room for walkers and wheelchairs. During the day, the area had a serene and cheerful air.

In the dark hours before dawn it was anything but cheerful. Bright overhead lights cast long shadows across the cement floor, creating odd shapes that could have been object, creature or person.

Honor shivered as she hurried toward her car, trying to tell herself there was nothing to be afraid of, but unable to shake her fear. She might have left behind the apartment where she'd been attacked, but the memory still haunted her. Wild eyes peering out from a black ski mask. A knife slashing toward her. The quick, hard beat of her heart as she put her hand up to defend herself and fell backward screaming. The crashing thud of the door as her neighbor kicked it in, running to her rescue with his service revolver in hand, shouting for Honor's attacker to put down the knife. The sharp report of the gun as he'd fired. The soft thud of a body hitting the ground.

Blood.

Everywhere.

Honor shuddered. Thank the Lord Lily and Candace had been at the library. If they'd been home…

She shook her head, refusing to put words to what could have happened. She'd been over it all in her mind during the days that followed the incident. After several sleepless nights, she'd known she had two choices—spend her life reliving the horror she'd experienced or thank God for keeping her family safe and move on. She'd chosen the latter.

Sometimes, though, doing that was harder than it should be.

She pulled open the car door and had started to slide inside when she heard the quiet shuffle of feet on pavement. She glanced around, saw nothing and dropped into her seat, pulling the door closed, locking it against whatever might be lurking in the darkness.

A sharp tap sounded on the back window of the car, and Honor screamed, her hands shaking as she tried desperately to get the key in the ignition. Another knock sounded, this one next to her ear, and she screamed again, turning toward the sound, expecting to look into a ski-masked face.

Instead, she met Will's concerned gaze.

She unrolled the window, fear making her angry. "What in the world are you doing?"

"Bringing you a message." If he realized how afraid she was, he didn't show it.

"A message?"

"Yeah. Janice just called and said we've got a staff meeting Tuesday at noon. It's mandatory. She was going to call you at home, but I told her I thought I could catch you."

"Tuesday at noon? Are you kidding? Our shift doesn't begin until two."

"That's what I told her, but she said we've all got to be there."

"All right. I guess I'll have to work it out."

"See you then." Will waved and strode away.

For a moment after his departure, Honor didn't

move. Her hands were too shaky, her legs too weak to drive. She took a deep breath. Then another, forcing oxygen into her lungs, her brain, her limbs. Coming to a small town was supposed to make her feel safer, so why was she jumping at everything?

Frustrated with herself, she put the car into Drive and started toward home, fear still pounding a hollow beat in her throat. "Lord, I need Your help pulling myself together. I can't afford to be afraid all the time. Not when the girls are depending on me. Not when I know You're in control."

She muttered the prayer as she drove along the winding road that led home, the sense of peace she always felt when bringing her problems to God filling her. No matter what her troubles, her faith had always carried her through. These new challenges and new worries would be handled with the same firm trust in God that she'd always had.

And she would get through them.

She would.

She pulled up in front of the bungalow, forcing herself to relax and enjoy the sight of the little house.

A house on a quiet street.

She'd dreamed of it for years, and now she had it. She wouldn't let the past steal the pleasure of achieving what she'd longed for.

The door creaked as she opened it, the light from a small table lamp welcoming her home. Candace's doing, of course. In the five years since the teenager had moved in with Honor, Candace had worked hard to be a productive member of the family. While other teenagers partied and rebelled, Candace studied hard and helped around the house. After Jay's death, when Honor had been at the end of her pregnancy and overwhelmed with the prospect of raising a child alone, Candace had promised to do whatever she could to help out. She'd been true to her word, never once complaining when she'd had to rush home to babysit Lily while Honor worked. Even now, when she could easily exert her independence, insist on living on campus away from her rambunctious niece, she'd chosen to live at home and continue to help out. Honor would miss her when she finally made her step into independent living.

"Mommy?" Lily's loud whisper came from the dark hall, and Honor tensed. She'd been praying for a few hours of sleep before her little girl woke up. Apparently she wasn't going to get them. She shrugged out of her coat and turned to face her daughter.

"Sweetheart, what are you doing up?"

"I have to tell you something."

"At three-thirty in the morning?"

"It's important, Mommy." Lily bounded toward her, the pink nightgown she wore brushing the floor as she moved, her wild curls bouncing.

Honor lifted her, inhaling the sweet smell of innocence and life. "Okay. So tell me. Then we're both getting into bed."

"I've been thinking about something." Lily put her hand on Honor's face and stared into her eyes, the deep blue of her gaze so similar to Jay's it made Honor's throat tighten.

"About what?"

"About the prince."

Honor bit back impatience and answered in a quiet tone. She and her daughter had had this conversation too many times over the past two days. "Lily Mae, what did we decide before I left for work?"

"That there wasn't a prince."

"Then there's nothing to talk about, is there?"

"But, Mommy, there is. There really truly is. He was right here in our house, and he must be a prince because he lives in that big castle."

"That isn't a castle. It's just a big house. And Mr. Sinclair is not prince. He's a man."

"Princes are men."

Honor sighed, setting her daughter down. "Yes, but not every man is a prince. Some are just men. Some are even frogs dressed up as men."

As she'd hoped, the idea caught her imaginative daughter's attention, and Lily laughed. "You're very silly, Mommy."

"And so are you to be thinking we have a prince living in our backyard."

"Not our backyard. In his house. Only I think it isn't a house. I think it's a castle."

"And I think it is not. So that is the last we'll say about it tonight. Come on. Back to bed with you." She took her daughter's hand and began leading her down the hall, but Lily was her father's daughter, and she wasn't willing to give up her dream.

"Can we go there and visit? Maybe we can find his crown. Then we'll know he's really a prince."

"No, we can not. Mr. Sinclair is a busy man. He doesn't have time to entertain us."

"But—"

"Listen, my sweet, don't the princes in fairy tales always ride white horses?"

"Yes."

"And have you seen any white horses around here?"

"No."

"Then there can't be any princes around, either, can there?" It was twisted logic, but if it worked, Honor would use it.

"Maybe—"

"Maybe we should stop talking and go to sleep."

"But I'm not tired."

Honor shook her head and pressed a finger to her daughter's lips. "Maybe you aren't, but I am. I worked for a very long time today, remember?"

"Yes."

"And now it's time for me to sleep so that I can be ready to do lots of fun things with you and Candace later on."

"Like go to the library?"

"Exactly like that." Honor started down the hall again, stopping when Candace peeked out of her room.

"Is everything okay?" Candace's voice was husky from sleep.

"Yes. Lily just needed to talk to me."

"Not about Prince Sinclair, I hope." Candace wrinkled her nose, and shot a disgruntled look in Lily's direction. "Didn't I tell you not to bug your mother about that?"

"I wasn't, Aunt Candy. Really."

"Yeah? So why are we all awake when we should be sleeping?" Candace ruffled Lily's hair and met Honor's gaze. "Sorry about this."

"Why should you be sorry? You weren't the one waiting up for me with dreams in your eyes." Honor smiled at her sister-in-law and pushed open the door to the room she shared with Lily.

"Yeah, but I am the one who keeps bringing books of fairy tales home from the library. Listen, why don't you sleep in a little today? I don't have school, so I can watch Lily until you're ready to get up."

"Candace, you've watched her every night this week. I can't ask you to do more."

"You're not asking. We're family. Helping each other is what we do." She smiled, the shadows in her eyes speaking words she wouldn't say. Words about what real family meant to her. About the time she'd spent without the kind of love every child deserves.

"Maybe I will, then, but the rest of the day will be yours to do with as you please."

"Being here pleases me." She smiled again, stepping back into her room and closing the door before Honor could comment.

Honor resisted the urge to knock on the door, make sure Candace was okay, that the shadows in her eyes were gone. Though she'd tried to broach the subject of Candace's childhood many times over the years, what she knew about it could fit on half a sheet of paper.

Jay's mother had inherited a fortune from her father and the family had lived a high-society life in Houston. Money hadn't bought the family happiness, though. Jay's stories of the abuse he'd suffered as a kid had torn at Honor's heart. When his mother had called to ask if Jay's troubled sister could stay with him for a while, Honor had been quick to agree.

Five years later, she didn't regret the decision. Though she wished Jay had been around to see how much his sister had grown, how mature she'd become.

The melancholy thought brought the sadness that always came when Honor thought of Jay. He might have been a happy-go-lucky dreamer with more ideas than plans for achieving them, but they'd been good friends before they married, and had continued to be friends until the day he'd died. "Come on, Lily-girl, let's lie down until the sun comes up."

"When is that?"

"A few hours." Honor tucked Lily under thick blankets, pulling them up around her chin and leaning down to kiss her daughter's forehead.

"Maybe we should have a snack first so we don't get hungry while we sleep."

"I don't think so. Snacks are for times when the sun is up."

"Later?"

"Yes, later. Good night, sweetheart."

"Good morning, Mommy."

Honor smiled and shook her head. Lily was a funny little girl. Advanced for her age and filled with imagination, she kept Honor and Candace on their toes. For now, though, she seemed to be content to lie in bed quietly. Perhaps she was hoping that would get her an extra snack later on. Whatever the case, Honor was thankful for her daughter's quiet cooperation. Sharing a room with Lily could be difficult. Especially when Honor was tired and her daughter was not. Unfortunately, the bungalow only had two bedrooms, and it had seemed more important for Candace to have her own room than for Honor to have one.

Exhausted, Honor dropped onto her bed, kicking off her rubber-soled shoes and stretching out on top of the quilt. She should get up and change, wash her face, go through her normal before-bed routine, but she was too tired to do anything more than lie there.

A few hours of sleep. That's all she needed.

Then she'd be ready to tackle the chores and the unpacking with the energy and enthusiasm the jobs required. If she worked efficiently, her three days off would be plenty of time to get the house under control and regain the routine she and the girls had thrived on when they were in St. Louis. By the time Honor returned to work on Tuesday, she'd have the last of the moving boxes unpacked, the backyard would be free of debris and the little bungalow she'd rented sight unseen would feel more like home.

FOUR

"Hey! Mister! Hey! Can you hear me?" The muffled voice drifted into Grayson Sinclair's dreams, pulling him toward consciousness. Exactly where he didn't want to be.

He bit back a groan and threw an arm over his eyes, refusing to open them. He'd spent most of the past forty-eight hours catching up on work and calling contractors to try to line up workers who could make his parents' Lynchburg rental property handicap accessible. Jude would be staying there once he was released from the hospital.

It had taken ten phone calls to convince his brother of that. Only by threatening the unthinkable—their mother staying with Jude in his New York apartment while he recovered—had Grayson been able to achieve his goal. He wanted his brother close to family during the long recovery ahead. Eventually his brother might thank him for that.

"Mister?" The little kid's voice intruded again, and this time he couldn't ignore it.

Grayson scowled and dropped his arm, glancing around the sunny solarium, searching for the speaker. He spotted her quickly, the Day-Glo pink coat and bright pink tutu she wore standing out in stark relief against the grays and browns of early winter. Face pressed against the glass, dark hair spilling out in wild ringlets, Honor Malone's daughter looked just as impish as she had two days ago. Not that he'd thought much about the Malone family since then.

Liar.

He'd thought plenty about them. Especially Honor. If he hadn't been so busy, he might have given in to temptation, stepped through the shrubs that separated their property and knocked on the bungalow's door.

"What are you doing out there, Lily?"

"Looking for a horse."

"Well, you're not going to find one here." Grayson strode to the door and pulled it open, the blast of icy cold air nearly stealing his breath.

"Are you sure? Because I was thinking maybe you had one inside your house. It's a big house. Really big enough for a horse to live in." She stared up at him, her eyes a deep shade of blue, her cheeks pink from cold.

"Sorry. I don't keep horses in my house." He grabbed a jacket from one of the fancy coat hooks his ex-fiancée had insisted be installed.

"But Mommy said you had to have one."

"Did she? And did she say you were allowed to come over here to look for it?" He slid on the jacket and put a hand on Lily's shoulder, steering her toward the back of his property as he spoke.

"No."

"Does she even know you're out here?"

"Lily? Lily Mae Malone, you'd better come out from wherever you are. Right now!" Honor's shrill voice carried across the cold backyard and answered Grayson's question. Obviously, she hadn't known her daughter was outside, and obviously Lily was about to catch some major trouble.

He glanced down at the little girl, almost feeling sorry for her. Almost, but not quite. The world was a dangerous place. A kid like Lily should never be wandering around in it alone.

"She's over here," he called out to Honor. They were still fifty yards from the back edge of his property when the thick shrubs parted and she raced into view, dressed in what looked like red nurse's scrubs. Her straight black hair gleaming in the sunlight, her skin glowing pink from exertion or cold, she ran across the yard and pulled Lily up into her arms.

"Thank goodness you're all right. Candace and I were worried sick. What were you thinking leaving the house by yourself?" The words flew out in quick, frantic pants of breath, fear flashing in her eyes as she met Grayson's gaze.

Green eyes. Much brighter than he'd remembered. Flecked with blue and gold. Rimmed with black lashes that were striking against Honor's creamy skin. For a moment, Grayson felt caught in her gaze, pulled deep into a world he'd stayed away from for months. When he looked in Honor's eyes, he forgot why.

"I'm so sorry, Grayson. I hope Lily wasn't bothering you." Honor's voice shook slightly as she spoke and her arms were tight around her daughter as if she planned to hold the little girl close forever, keeping her safe from the ugliness that existed in the world.

If only life were that simple.

If only a person really could keep a loved one safe by sheer force of will. "She wasn't."

"I'm not sure I believe you. Lily has a one-track mind about certain things. Though I have to say, she's never pulled a stunt like this before." She paused, looking her daughter in the eyes. "And she never will again. Will you, Lily Mae?"

"I just wanted to see if he had a horse, Mommy. A white one. Like you said. Remember?"

Honor's brow furrowed and she frowned. "I remember. Just as I'm sure *you* remember our rules about going outside without permission. Don't you?"

"Yes." Lily lisped the response, her face a mirror of Honor's. Both were pink-cheeked with freckles dotting their noses. Lily's hair was a few shades lighter than her mother's, her eyes blue rather than green, but she possessed the same heart-shaped face and high cheekbones. And the same indefinable quality that would make people want to take a second look.

They made a pretty picture as they frowned into each other's eyes, barely aware of Grayson. If he'd had a camera with him, Grayson would have snapped a picture. It was the kind of moment he'd thought he'd see a lot of as he watched his wife and children blossom in the large house his ex-fiancée, Maria, had insisted on…before she'd informed him that kids weren't in her plans for at least another five years.

He frowned, wondering why he was thinking about something he'd decided months ago to put out of his mind.

"If you knew the rules, then why did you break them? You could have been hurt, or gotten lost. Anything could have happened. We've talked about this before. You know how important it is never to go out alone." Honor's words broke into his thoughts, and he was glad for the distraction.

"I'm sorry, Mommy. I just needed to know." There were tears in Lily's eyes, and Grayson felt his heart melting.

"What did you need to know?"

"If he was a prince. A real one with a white horse. Because if he is, he can slay the dragon. And then everything will be okay."

"Sweetheart, we've been over this a hundred times before. There are no princes in Lakeview. And there are no dragons, either." Honor spoke with weary resignation, and Grayson wondered how many times and in how many ways she'd said the same thing.

"But, Mommy—"

"Lily, enough! Just for a while, let's stop talking about it." Honor brushed a hand over Lily's cheek, shivering a little as she set her daughter on the ground. The nurse's scrubs she wore were short-sleeved and her feet were bare. She must have run from the house without thinking of anything but finding Lily. That kind of desperation, that kind of fear was something Grayson understood only too well. When he'd received the call about Jude, he'd left the house unlocked, left the lights blazing, left cases that were going to trial. He'd driven to New York with nothing but his wallet and the clothes he was wearing. And he'd stayed there until his brother was on his way to recovery.

"Here." He shrugged out of his jacket and dropped it around Honor's shoulders. For a moment she met his eyes again, the worry and fear in her gaze making him want to tell her that everything would be okay. That her imaginative little girl would stay safe. That the world would be as kind to Lily as it should be.

Then she looked away, the contact between them gone, the moment spent. "Thank you, but now you'll be cold."

"I'm wearing a sweater. I'll be warm enough."

"My mother would call you a true gentleman."

"Yeah? And what would you call me?"

She eyed him carefully, her gaze touching hair he knew needed a trim, the beard that he hadn't taken time to shave, the thick sweater his sister Piper had bought at a county craft fair a few months ago and given to him because, she'd said, it matched his eyes. "Trouble."

Her answer surprised him, and Grayson laughed. The first honest-to-goodness laugh he'd had in weeks. Maybe longer. "I guess you get points for honesty."

"And I guess you get points for not denying the truth." Honor took her daughter's hand. "We've got to get back home, Lily Mae, or Candace will have the police out here looking for you."

"But, what about the dragon? We need to find a prince to slay him before he gets us."

"There is no dragon, so there's no way he could get us."

Really, Grayson should stay out of it. Go back inside the house, close the door and let Honor and her daughter work things out without an audience. Unfortunately, staying out of things wasn't something Grayson had ever been good at. "Listen, Lily, I don't have a white horse. I don't have a horse at all, but if a dragon does show up, I'll do my best to slay it. I promise."

Honor stiffened, shooting Grayson a censorious look. "Promises are a dime a dozen, Grayson. As easily broken as they are made. Besides, there *are no dragons*. And if there were, I would figure out a way to slay them myself." Obviously, he'd touched on a sore point, but Grayson didn't plan to apologize.

"I'm sure you would, but a little help wouldn't be amiss in a situation like that."

"Besides, Mommy, the princess never slays the dragon. Only a prince can do that." Lily had broken away from her mother and was spinning around in circles, her tutu as bright as the flowers that had bloomed last spring.

"Who says princesses never slay dragons?" Honor continued walking across the yard, Grayson's coat falling past her thighs. She looked smaller than he'd remembered. More delicate.

"All the books, Mommy. Every single one."

"And we know how true those books are, don't we?" There was amusement in her words and in the fond gaze she settled on her daughter.

"They are true. They really are."

"Oh, Lily, what am I going to do with you?" Honor spoke so quietly, Grayson almost didn't hear.

"You're going to keep doing what you've been doing—loving her unconditionally." He bent close to whisper the words in Honor's ear and caught the heady aroma of summer sunshine and wild flowers.

"You're right. That's exactly what I'll do. That, and worry every day that her dreams will take her away from me." She smiled, but the sadness behind her eyes was unmistakable. "For now, I'm just enjoying her. She's such a funny little girl."

"And a special one."

"That, too." Honor called to Lily and pushed through the heavy shrubs.

Grayson knew he should probably stay on his side of the barrier, but knowing that didn't stop him.

He followed the two Malones through the shrubs and into Honor's backyard, pausing as the two went up the back steps, not sure how he'd even ended up there. Honor was pretty. Intelligent. Compassionate. He'd known other women like her. What was it about Honor that made him want to know more?

That made him want to talk to her about everything and about nothing?

She turned before she opened the door, the morning sunlight reflected in her blue-black hair and shimmering in her forest-green eyes. The sight made the breath catch in Grayson's throat, made his heart leap in acknowledgment of her simple beauty.

"I'm putting on a pot of coffee if you'd like a cup."

Being pulled into Honor and Lily's lives probably wasn't the best idea. Then again, sharing a pot of coffee with a neighbor seemed a lot more appealing than reading the deposition he'd left sitting on the table in the solarium. And, quite honestly, he wasn't ready to say goodbye yet. "That would be great. Thanks."

"Come in then, but just remember, I've been working long shifts. The house is still a bit cluttered."

"Why would I notice clutter when I have two beautiful ladies nearby?"

Lily must have been listening, because she giggled.

Honor, on the other hand, didn't look amused. "There you go again with your flattery."

"Is it flattery when it's the truth?"

"Grayson Sinclair, you are more trouble than I have time to deal with." Honor shook her head and pushed open the back door, ushering Lily into the house. "Come in anyway. We'll discuss what flattery is after I start a pot of coffee. And Lily, we'll discuss the consequences of your behavior after Mr. Sinclair leaves. Off to your room, now."

"But, Mommy—"

"Lily Mae, is that you I hear?" Candace's voice rang out from the kitchen, cutting off whatever argument Lily might have made. Too bad. The kid was a good negotiator. A lawyer in the making. And Grayson enjoyed seeing her in action.

"Yes."

"Where have you been? Do you realize how worried I've been? I was just getting ready to call the police."

"I'm sorry, Aunt Candy."

"Sorry? Sorry doesn't help. You should never have disobeyed me. Do you realize…" Candace's voice trailed off as she stepped into the mudroom and saw Grayson. "Oh, sorry. I didn't realize we had company."

"Mr. Sinclair is here for a cup of coffee. It's a thank-you for keeping Lily safe until I found her."

Honor seemed to want to qualify the invitation. Grayson told himself that that was fine with him. Whatever it was about her that attracted him, he didn't have time to act on it. He had work to catch up on, a brother to worry about. He didn't need to add more complications to his already complicated life.

Whether or not he wanted to, that was a different story altogether.

"You were in the neighbor's yard? Lily, how could you?" Candace brushed thick blond bangs from her eyes and sighed, taking the little girl's hand and leading her from the room. Lily sent a beseeching look in Grayson's direction, and he did his best not to smile at the dramatics. Honor had quite a kid.

"She's quite a drama queen, my daughter." Honor spoke as she started the coffeemaker, her voice lilting and exotic.

Maybe it was the accent Grayson found so appealing.

Or maybe it was simply the woman herself. "She's definitely got an acting career ahead of her if she wants one."

"Funny you should say that. Her father always dreamed of being a film star." Honor smiled, but it didn't hide the sadness in her eyes.

"And did you always dream about being a nurse?"

"I always dreamed about being married and having kids."

"Then I guess you achieved your dream."

"I guess. Sometimes, though, the reality of a dream isn't nearly as beautiful as the dream itself." She poured coffee and offered him a cup, her expression filled with a yearning that made Grayson's chest tighten.

"You didn't have a happy marriage."

"Everyone's definition of happy is different, Grayson. I was content enough. How about you? Did you always want to be a prosecutor?"

"For as long as I can remember."

"Then you've achieved your dream, as well."

"Yes, but it's like you said. Sometimes the reality doesn't quite live up to the dream."

"You're not happy?"

"I'm happy." But he wasn't content. And until this minute, standing in Honor's warm kitchen, sipping coffee and listening to the lyrical sound of her voice, he hadn't realized it.

"Then you've got nothing to complain about." She reached into the cupboard and pulled out the box of cookies she'd offered the previous day. "Biscuit?"

"Thanks." He took one, watching Honor's face as she bit into one of the rich shortbread rounds. "I'll have to remember how much you love these cookies if I ever visit Ireland."

"No worries. Mum keeps me well stocked."

"Yes, but I'd still want to bring back a gift for a friend."

"Is that what we're going to be, Grayson?"

"Maybe."

"Unless my daughter comes in your yard and bothers you again?" She grinned, all the sadness and longing that had been so clear in her face gone.

"Actually, I was thinking we would become friends unless we became something more than that." The words slipped out, surprising him.

Honor froze at his words, her expression closing off, her bright gaze dimming. "I'm afraid that is an impossibility."

"I don't believe in impossibilities." He set his cup in the sink, took another cookie from the box. Honor might think that a relationship between them was out the question, but he didn't have to agree.

"And I don't believe in more than friendship."

"Then for now, I guess friendship will be enough."

"For now?" The wariness in her eyes was unmistakable, and Grayson wondered what her marriage had been like. Obviously much more disappointing than she'd let on.

"You never know what time will do. It can fade memories and it can change minds. I've got to run. I'm meeting contractors in Lynchburg. We've got to have my parents' rental property ready when my brother is finally released from the hospital."

He purposely shifted the conversation, and Honor seemed relieved. Her shoulders relaxed as she walked him to the back door. "Let me know if I can help your brother in any way."

"I will."

"Thanks again for looking after Lily when she wandered away. Goodbye, Grayson." The way she said it, Grayson was certain she'd meant it to sound permanent.

Too bad.

Because suddenly Grayson's decision to avoid relationships seemed premature. Suddenly the idea of getting to know a woman, of courting her, of inviting her into his life seemed much more appealing than it had a few hours ago.

FIVE

Obviously, Honor was even more tired than she'd thought. Why else would she have invited Grayson Sinclair in for coffee? There were unpacked boxes awaiting her attention, dishes piled up in the sink and a load of laundry in a basket on the coffee table waiting to be folded. She had more than enough to do without adding entertaining a neighbor.

And not just any neighbor.

Grayson Sinclair.

Handsome, charming, Grayson Sinclair.

She shook her head and drained the last dregs of coffee from her cup, hoping the caffeine would work its way into her system and clear her thinking. The shock of being woken up from a sound sleep and told that her daughter was missing must have scrambled her brains and affected her judgment.

Grayson wasn't all that handsome or charming.

Okay. He was. But that didn't mean Honor found him attractive. She'd learned her lesson about men like that when she'd married Jay. They could be loved, but they couldn't be counted on and they couldn't be trusted. She'd do well to keep that in mind.

Honor sighed, rinsing her cup, and then walked down the hall. She needed to put Grayson out of her mind and deal with her daughter. She had to make it very clear that there would be no more wandering outside without supervision.

A quick, hard rap on the front door made Honor jump. She turned toward the sound, her heart racing in her chest. The neighbors had stopped by on moving day, but since then there had been no unexpected visitors. Unless she counted Grayson.

She frowned.

There he was again.

Right in the center of her thoughts.

The visitor knocked again, the sound echoing through the cozy living room. Honor knew she shouldn't feel alarmed. There was nothing frightening about someone knocking on the door during daylight hours, but adrenaline coursed through her as she approached the door, telling her she should run and hide rather than see who it was. "Who is it?"

"Flower delivery for Honor Malone." The speaker was female, and Honor relaxed.

Surprised, she peered out the peephole in the door to see a bouquet of bloodred roses.

"Who are they from?"

"I don't know. There's a card though. Want me to open it?"

"No. That's okay. Thanks." She pulled the door

open and accepted the flowers from a fresh-faced blonde who looked to be about Candace's age.

"They're beautiful."

"Yeah, they are. Enjoy them. Have a good day." Before Honor could ask any more questions, the young lady hurried back to the driveway, climbed into a bright pink delivery van with the name "Blooming Baskets" emblazoned on the side and drove away.

Honor carried the roses into the house, touching a smooth petal as she set the vase on the coffee table in the living room. Someone had sent her roses.

How long had it been since that had last happened?

Five years ago. She could remember it as vividly as if it were yesterday. Jay had been deployed to Iraq the previous month and Honor had realized she was pregnant soon after. She'd called him with the news and a day later he'd managed to have four dozen roses delivered to the apartment. One dozen for each member of their family. Four dozen more than they could afford on his soldier salary.

Honor blinked away the memory, reaching for the note attached to the vase.

I've missed you.

Three words that meant absolutely nothing to Honor. She turned the card over, searching for a name, but there wasn't one. No signature. Nothing indicating who had sent the flowers.

Curious and slightly uneasy, Honor grabbed the phone and called information, then dialed the num-

ber of the florist. The owner tried to be helpful, but
the information she had was vague. A dark-haired
man wearing a suit had ordered the flowers. He'd
paid cash and hadn't given a name.

Honor found the news oddly disturbing.

She touched a petal again, frowning as she stared
down at the flowers.

I've missed you?

She didn't know anyone in Lakeview well enough
to be missed by them, and she couldn't believe someone from St. Louis had come all the way to Lakeview to send her a bouquet. If someone in the city
had missed her enough to come to town, surely he
would have stopped in to visit before going home.

"Oh, flowers!" Candace walked into the room,
her eyes bright with excitement as she caught sight
of the roses. "They're gorgeous."

"They are, aren't they?"

"So why do you sound less than happy about getting them?" As usual, Candace picked up on Hon-
or's worry.

"I'm just not sure who sent them."

"Is there a card?"

"Yes, but no name." As she spoke, she slid the
card into her pocket. There was no sense in sharing
her worry with Candace.

"If you really want to know who sent them—"

"I already called the florist. They weren't able to
tell me who the flowers are from."

"Of course you called the florist." Candace smiled

and shook her head, her sleek ponytail sliding over her shoulder.

"What is that supposed to mean?"

"It means, you don't have an impractical bone in your body. Everything has got to be planned out and scheduled and perfectly in line. Unless it is, you just can't enjoy yourself."

"And is it so wrong to want things to go smoothly?" Stung by her sister-in-law's assessment, Honor turned and grabbed a box from the floor, pulling out a few framed photographs that were wrapped in brown paper and setting them on the end table.

"No, but sometimes it's okay to not have all the answers. Sometimes it's good to just go with the flow."

"'Going with the flow' often means being dragged by a current carrying you where you don't want to go." Jay had been a prime example of that. His laid-back attitude had resulted in more trouble than Honor cared to remember. Unpaid bills, missed appointments, paychecks spent before they ever made it to the bank. That had been Jay's life. It would never again be Honor's.

"Probably, but in this case, it just means accepting a gift from a secret admirer. A secret admirer! How cool is that?"

Not cool, creepy, but Honor decided not to say that to Candace. "Really cool. Is Lily still in her room?"

"She was sitting on her bed looking dejected when I checked on her." Candace didn't seem to care that Honor had changed the subject. Her gaze was on the flowers, a soft smile playing at her lips. Did she dream of finding a handsome prince to carry her away? In all the years she'd been living with Honor, Candace had never mentioned wanting to date, get married or have children.

And Honor knew better than to ask. Candace was as closemouthed about her dreams as Jay had been verbal. "I guess I'd better go deal with our little escape artist."

"I'll put the flowers on the dining room table. They'll look nice there."

For some reason, the thought of having the flowers sitting in the middle of the table while she enjoyed a meal with the girls didn't sit well with Honor. "No. Just leave them here. They're too pretty to put in the dining room. We'll keep them out here where visitors can see them."

Candace looked doubtful, but shrugged. "If we had any visitors that would make sense."

"We've had a few visitors recently."

"A sheriff and our neighbor." Candace paused. "You know, maybe that's who sent the flowers."

"Who?" Honor headed toward her bedroom, anxious to put the conversation behind her, but not wanting to cut Candace off. Despite her harsh upbringing, Candace was a sensitive soul. Sometimes too sensitive.

"Grayson Sinclair."

"You're kidding, right?" Honor laughed at the thought of her good-looking neighbor sending flowers and a note that said he missed her. Sure, he'd hinted that he might like to pursue something with her. Friendship. More. But Honor knew enough about men like him to know his words were as meaningless as thunder in the desert.

"Why not? He's handsome, rich and has a house to die for."

"If I were looking for someone to date, which I'm not, those wouldn't be the most important qualities on my list."

"Then what would?"

"I don't know. I've not spent much time thinking about it."

"Maybe you should, Honor."

"No. I shouldn't. Now, I'm going to deal with our Lily before she completely forgets she's in her room because she's in trouble."

"And I'm going out. I'm meeting a few friends in town."

"Friends from college?"

"Yeah. A couple of kids from my English class. We're going to study together, then they're going to bring me to the mall in Lynchburg. I'll be home for dinner."

"Have fun."

"I will." Candace walked back down the hall, and Honor pushed open the bedroom door. It was time to deal with Lily. After that, she'd tackle the chores. What she wouldn't do was spend one more minute thinking about the roses or wondering who sent them. Nor would she think about Grayson and his blue eyes that reminded her so much of home. God was in control. Of her life. Of her daughter. Of Candace. There was no reason to worry and fret. No reason to think beyond this moment.

The future would come soon enough, bringing whatever the Lord had in store. For now, Honor had a house to organize and a child to discipline. That was quite enough for one day.

SIX

The hard day's work had paid off, and by midnight Honor had finished turning chaos into order. Every box was unpacked and ready to be recycled, all the laundry was washed, dried and put away and the dishes were sitting in cupboards, scrubbed free of grime and grease. All in all, it was a good effort toward turning the ramshackle little bungalow into something more. Something worthy of creating memories.

Considering the fact that Honor had signed the rental paperwork before she'd ever stepped foot in the house, she couldn't complain. Renting to own had always been her goal, and Mr. Silverton had been as anxious to find someone willing to take on the run-down place as Honor had been to plant roots. If she stayed long enough, she'd own the little bungalow and the half acre of land it sat on. Close to the lake, in a quiet community set apart from the more commercial areas around Smith Mountain Lake, the 1920s-style house had the potential to be a forever kind of place. After years of apartment living, that had appealed to Honor as much as the price. She made decent money as a nurse, but had taken a pay cut to be closer to Candace. The fact that she'd spent the past several years paying off the debt Jay had accrued, hadn't helped Honor's financial situation. There had been no money for a down payment on a house, no way to come up with closing costs. She'd been sure she'd have to rent an apartment in Lakeview and had been on-line comparing places when she'd spotted Mr. Silverton's lonely little house. She'd known immediately that she and the girls would fit there perfectly.

She glanced around the living room, satisfied with the time-nicked but gleaming hardwood floor, the newly polished art deco mantel. Next weekend, she'd buy paint and put some color on the walls. Maybe a creamy yellow or cool sage. In the meantime, she'd simply enjoy the fact that the place was clean and neat and organized.

Not that everything *had* to be organized for Honor to be happy.

She frowned, thinking over her earlier conversation with Candace and wanting to deny the truth of her sister-in-law's words. Honor was open to a little spontaneity in life. She wasn't completely sold on plans and structure.

Of course she was.

Since Jay had been killed by a roadside bomb in Iraq, she'd kept a tight rein on her little world. Her daughter might not have a father, her sister-in-law might not have a brother, but they would have security. There was nothing to be ashamed of in wanting that for her girls, was there?

No. Of course there wasn't.

And liking things orderly and predictable did not make a person boring.

She circled the room, checking the windows and the front door to make sure they were locked. She studiously avoided looking at the roses. They'd been sitting on the coffee table all day, and if it wasn't for the fact that the girls would demand an explanation, she probably would have given the flowers a new home in the trash can outside.

Bloodred roses from someone who missed her.

She shuddered, turning off the light and leaving the room. Everything was locked up tight. The girls were safe in their beds. Still, she couldn't shake the unease that shivered along her spine as she changed into thick flannel pajamas.

The wood floor was cold under her feet, the house silent as she crossed the room and stood over her daughter's bed. Lily slept soundly, her face turned toward the wall, a stuffed bear clutched in her arms. Even in sleep she looked restless, her brow furrowed with whatever images filled her dreams, her body tense as if she were ready to leap from the bed.

"Lily-girl, you're going to be the kind to put gray hair on your mother's head, aren't you?" Honor whispered as she brushed strands of baby-fine hair from Lily's cheek. "It'll be worth it, though, to see you grow into the woman God plans for you to be."

She let her hand drop away from her daughter's cheek, and moved to the window that looked out over the backyard. In St. Louis, they'd lived on the third floor of an apartment building in a decent part of the city. There'd been no worry that someone might knock out a pane of glass and get inside. Now that they lived in a one-story house, Honor realized just how little protection a window offered. A brick could easily shatter the glass. Then, as quick as a wink, danger could enter their sanctuary.

She scowled, leaning her head against the cold glass and staring into the darkness. At times like this, she missed Jay desperately. Despite all the disappointments and heartache he'd caused, his solid presence had always made Honor feel safe. Alone with the girls, she felt vulnerable. It was a feeling she didn't like at all.

Darkness pressed against the glass, the shadowy world beyond the window cast in shades of black and gray. Honor had never been afraid of the dark, but suddenly she was sure a million eyes were watching her from the gloom.

What she needed to do was climb into bed, close her eyes and sleep. When the sun rose, she'd feel more herself and less—

A face appeared at the window. Pale against the darkness. Hollow eyes. Blurred features.

A mask?

Honor screamed, stumbling back, her heart slamming against her ribs, her body cold with horror. She grabbed the phone, lifted Lily and raced from the room, sure that at any moment she'd hear the sound of shattering glass.

Call 911. Get the police here.

Frantic, she dialed the number as she skidded into Candace's room, praying the Lakeview police would arrive before whoever was standing outside her window realized just how easy it would be to get inside the house.

Something was going on at Honor's house. Grayson watched with mounting concern as the formerly dark bungalow lit up one room at a time. There were plenty of reasons he could think of for Honor to be walking through her house flipping on lights, but none of them were good. The one that was the most worrisome involved Lily wandering outside again.

Grayson rubbed the back of his neck and watched as the outside light beside Honor's back door went on. Midnight wasn't the best time to be awake, but since he and his neighbor both were, maybe he should take a quick walk across the yard and find out exactly why every light in Honor's house was blazing.

In a matter of moments, he was stepping out his back door and starting across the yard. Still and silent, the night seemed hushed with anticipation, the sky deep azure and speckled with stars. Nothing moved. Dry grass crackled beneath Grayson's feet, the thick scent of pine needles and wood smoke wafting on the frigid air.

Somewhere in the distance a siren blared, the sound a discordant note that jarred Grayson's nerves and made the hair on the back of his neck stand on end. Lakeview was a quiet town not given to sirens in the middle of the night. Something was going on, and he prayed it wasn't what he'd first suspected. It was too cold for a little girl like Lily to be outside. Too dark. Too dangerous. Sure, Lakeview was safe, but no matter how safe a neighborhood was there were always predators just waiting for an opportunity to strike.

He pushed through the shrubs that separated his yard from Honor's and hurried to the back door. Despite the bright lights, the bungalow was silent, the windows empty of life. Grayson could see into the kitchen, but none of the Malones were there. He knocked on the door, anxious to make sure Lily was okay. The kid had a wild imagination and the kind of gumption that could get her into all kinds of trouble.

It would kill Honor if anything happened to her little girl. Images flashed through Grayson's mind. Family members sitting in the courtroom, listening as the criminals who had stolen their loved ones were tried. So many tears. So much heartache. It was what drove Grayson to continue as a prosecutor, and what drove him now. If Lily had wandered away, they needed to call in tracking dogs, gather the teams who would make finding her a possibility.

Grayson knocked on the door again. This time with more force.

"Who is it?" Honor's voice was thick with fear.

"Grayson."

"It's late for a visit, isn't it?" She didn't open the

door, and Grayson didn't ask her to. Whatever was going on had frightened her enough to make her hesitant. That was good. Smart. As far as he was concerned, a little caution went a long way toward keeping people safe.

"I saw all the lights on, and I wanted to make sure everything was okay."

"We're fine. Thank you."

"Lily hasn't escaped again?"

"No."

"So she's with you?" Grayson knew there was a problem. Whether it was big or small remained to be seen, but he did intend to find out what it was.

"Yes, where else would she be?"

"Looking for horses and princes?"

"Not this time."

"Then I guess there's another reason that all the lights in your house are on?"

"We've had…" She paused as if trying to decide what to say. "An incident."

"What kind of incident?" The sirens were screaming closer, the throbbing pulse of them pounding in Grayson's ears.

"The kind that requires police help." The door cracked open, and Honor peeked out, her face pale, silky strands of hair falling across her cheeks. Just seeing her made Grayson's heart trip and his pulse race. It was as if he'd been waiting his entire life to meet her and as if he had known her forever.

"Do you want me to wait while you speak to the police?"

She hesitated, and Grayson was sure she was torn between needing another adult around and wanting to take care of her family herself.

Finally, she pulled the door open farther, her gaze darting to the yard behind him. "You didn't see anyone out there, did you?"

"No."

"Good. Maybe that means he's long gone."

"Who? What happened, Honor?" He put his hands on her shoulders, looking down into her face and trying to will some of his calmness into her trembling body.

"Someone was at the window staring in at me. I only saw him for a second, but it was enough." She shuddered, turning as a loud knock echoed through the house. "That must be the police."

He followed her through the kitchen and dining room and into the living room. A bouquet of roses sat on the coffee table, bloodred and velvety. A gift from a friend? An admirer?

Honor fumbled with the chain that hung across the front door, her hands shaking so hard she couldn't seem to maneuver it open.

"Let me help." Grayson covered her hand with his, sliding the chain off in one easy movement. For a moment, he let his palm rest against her knuckles, letting the warmth of his skin heat the coolness of hers. Then he let his hand drop away, gently nudging her aside so that he could open the door.

Sheriff Reed stood on the other side of it, a scowl

darkening his face as he met Grayson's eyes. "I hear there's been some trouble out here."

"So Honor was saying."

"You were here when the incident occurred?"

"No. I came over when I saw all the lights being turned on. I wanted to make sure everything was okay."

"But you didn't see anything?"

"I'm afraid not."

"According to the dispatcher, someone was looking in your window." Jake addressed the comment to Honor, his gaze searching the room as if a clue as to what had happened might be there.

"Yes, the bedroom window."

"It looks out over the backyard?"

"Yes."

"Why don't you show me which one?"

"The bedroom is right this way." Honor led Jake down the hall, and Grayson stayed put, walking to the windows and checking the locks on each. They were old. Not much protection if someone wanted to break in. He needed to replace them. Make sure that no one could harm Honor or her girls.

But would she let him? Honor seemed so determined to do everything herself—and to keep him at a distance. Grayson had a feeling that if he insisted on stepping in, she'd push him away completely. Better to step back than risk that.

If Honor wanted help, he'd give it, but forcing his ideas on a woman who'd obviously had her fill of men, a woman he was determined to get to know better, wasn't a good idea.

He'd find another way to make sure she was safe. Maybe a few subtle hints about the condition of her window and door locks?

It only took a few minutes for Honor and Jake to return, but it seemed like a lifetime.

He walked toward them as they reentered the room. "What did you find?"

"Nothing yet. I'm going outside to look around." Jake started toward the kitchen, and Grayson followed.

"I'll come with you. Two people looking will make finding something more likely."

"You know better than that, Grayson. If there's evidence out there, I don't want it contaminated. I'll be back in a few minutes." Jake walked outside, and Grayson stared after him, frustrated and not sure why. Jake was right. Of course he was. But Grayson wanted to be out there with him, searching for the guy who'd frightened Honor so badly.

"Come back in the kitchen. I'll make some coffee." Honor touched his bicep, her fingers barely grazing his arm before dropping away. Even that was enough to send Grayson's pulse racing.

"I'd rather be out there with Jake."

"I can see that. You look like you're ready to knock someone's head off."

"And you look ready to collapse from exhaustion." He studied her face, wondering if the dark circles beneath her eyes had been there earlier in the day.

Raising a child alone had to be a challenge. No matter how much you loved her. And then to have this would-be intruder? No wonder she looked so tired.

"It's been a long day."

"Things will be better tomorrow." He reached out and tucked a strand of hair behind her ear, surprised when she didn't move away.

"Funny, that's what my dad always says when I'm having a tough time."

"It sounds like your dad is a smart man."

"I guess that makes you one, too. I'm sorry you keep getting pulled into my troubles, Grayson."

"I haven't been pulled into anything."

"Yet here you are."

"We're neighbors, Honor. Working our way up to friends." And maybe something more, but Grayson decided Honor would rather not hear that again. "Should I have ignored all the lights going on in your house at midnight?"

"Plenty of other people would have."

"I'm not any of them, Honor. And I won't stand back and watch you deal with this trouble by yourself."

"Maybe that's what I want you to do." She sounded more uncertain than confident, and Grayson took her hand, squeezing it gently.

"It's what you think you should want me to do, but it's not what you want. For tonight, why don't you let that be okay?"

She studied his face for a moment, seeming to take in everything about him. Not just his appearance, but his soul. Finally, she nodded and squeezed his hand. "Okay. Just for tonight."

"For tonight."

When she pulled away from his hold, he let her, following as she leaned out the open mudroom door.

"Do you think the sheriff has found anything?" Her voice was calm, her words free of the anxiety he'd seen in her eyes.

"If he has, he'll let us know."

"Hopefully it will be soon. The girls are scared, and I want to be able to tell them everything will be okay."

"And who will tell you that, Honor?"

She glanced over her shoulder, meeting his eyes, her expression guarded. "I'm an adult. I don't need anyone to. I hear the sheriff coming back. Hopefully he has some news." She stepped out in the cold, cutting off their conversation.

Grayson followed, tensing when he saw Jake's grim expression. He'd found something.

SEVEN

"Ms. Malone, can you come with me, please? I have something I'd like to show you."

Honor didn't like the sound of that, but she stepped toward the sheriff anyway, aware of Grayson's gaze as she did so. His intense focus was as warm as a physical caress, tempting her to reach back, take his hand, permit herself to accept the support he'd offered.

Of course she wouldn't.

Not even for tonight.

She'd allow him to be here, allow herself to face whatever the sheriff had found with Grayson by her side, but she wouldn't allow herself to depend on him. That could only lead to heartache.

"What is it?" A dead animal? A bloody note? A *body part?* Something horrible. She was sure of it.

"Nothing terrible. Just something I want your thoughts on."

Okay. So it wasn't a body or a piece of one. At least Honor could take comfort in that. "Where is it?"

"On the slide. I'd like to know if it was there earlier."

"As far as I know, there hasn't been anything left on the slide today." She hurried after him, acutely aware of Grayson following close on her heels. Two days ago, she hadn't known he existed. Now it seemed as if he'd become a fixture in her life.

How that had happened, she didn't know. She only knew it was troubling. And that now wasn't the time to think about it. She needed to focus on the task at hand, find out what the sheriff had found and figure out how she was going to deal with it.

Up ahead, the sheriff had stopped near the old swing set, and Honor hurried to catch up with him, her feet catching in tangled weeds. She tripped, arms windmilling as she searched for balance. Grayson grabbed her elbow, holding her steady while she regained her footing, his palm warm through the thick flannel of her pajama top, his breath whispering against her cheek as he leaned down to look into her eyes.

"Arc you okay?"

"Fine. Thank you."

"Are you sure? You don't have to look at what Jake has found. I can check it out for you, and we can discuss it in the house."

"No. This is my problem. I need to deal with it."

If he'd insisted, she might have been able to pull from his grasp, walk toward the sheriff and let Grayson trail along behind her.

He simply nodded, his expression so filled with

understanding that tears burned behind her eyes. Had Jay ever looked at her like that? So intently? So filled with compassion?

Honor couldn't remember.

And for reasons she'd rather not examine, she let Grayson escort her the last few feet to the sheriff.

"What did you want me to see?"

"There." The sheriff aimed his flashlight beam at the slide, and Honor's heart sank when she saw what lay on it. No body parts. No frightening notes. Nothing overtly terrifying. Just a rose. Lying by itself, a single thorn visible on the stem. The light cast long shadows that hid the flower's true color, but Honor knew it was deep bloodred, the petals delicate and velvety. Just like the flowers that were sitting on her coffee table.

Honor took a deep breath, trying to control the terror that thrummed along her nerves. "A rose. How did it get there?"

"I was going to ask you the same thing." Sheriff Reed leaned closer to the slide, but didn't touch the rose.

"I have no idea."

"You do have a vase of roses on your coffee table."

"Yes."

"Is it possible your daughter brought one out here to play with?"

"No. Lily was by my side all day, and we never came outside. A dozen roses were delivered. If we count, I'm sure a dozen will still be in the vase." Her words were sharper than she'd intended, the fear rising inside of her making her stomach churn and her heart race.

"Then apparently the person who was looking in your window left you a gift."

"Not just this one." Honor spoke her fear out loud, sure that the person who'd sent the flowers had been the one looking in the window at her.

"What do you mean?" Grayson's grip tightened on her elbow as he leaned past her to look at the rose.

"The flowers on my table. They were delivered today."

"From?" Sheriff Reed turned to face her, the beam of light jumping away from the rose and landing at Honor's feet.

"I don't know. There was a card, but no name. I called the florist, but the flowers were paid for in cash, and she couldn't tell me the purchaser's name."

"Did you keep the card?"

Had she? Honor remembered shoving it in her pocket when Candace came into the room. Was it still there? "I think so."

"You moved here less than two weeks ago."

It wasn't a question, but Honor answered anyway. "That's right. We moved from St. Louis."

"Was there a reason for that?"

"My sister-in-law is attending Liberty University in Lynchburg. I wanted to be close to her."

"So nothing happened? Nothing that made you feel you had to leave the city?" Sheriff Reed jotted down notes as he spoke, and Honor wondered if he'd noticed her sudden tension.

Grayson must have, because his fingers tightened on her arm, and he looked down into her face. "Something happened. What?"

"A month ago, I was attacked by an intruder in my apartment."

The sheriff stopped writing and looked up from his notebook. "Was it someone you knew?"

"No. He was a drug user, looking for easy cash. I guess he managed to jimmy my lock and get inside the apartment. I surprised him, and he came after me with a knife." Her words came out in a rush, and Honor tried to slow them. "My neighbor was an off-duty police officer. He heard me scream and ran into the apartment with his service weapon."

"What happened to the perpetrator?" Jake was writing again, his hand flying across the page.

"He wouldn't put down the knife. My neighbor had to shoot him." The blood had sprayed everywhere, splattering the walls and ceiling. Honor shuddered at the memory.

"Did he live?"

"No. He died at the scene." She took a deep breath, trying to calm her racing heart. "So, I don't see how it could be related to what's happening here."

"You never know if you'll find connections unless you look. I guarantee I'll be looking." Sheriff Reed tucked the notebook in his pocket. "I'm going to get an evidence bag for the rose. I'll join you inside the house once I'm done. I've got a few more questions I want to ask."

"All right."

"I'm sorry about what happened to you, Honor," Grayson said quietly as the sheriff walked away.

"You don't have to be. I survived. That's more than a lot of people get."

"I know. I've seen what drugs can do. It's never pretty."

"No. It isn't. As frightening as the experience was, I can't help mourning the life that was lost." She glanced at the house. "I'd better get back inside."

"Do you want me to come with you?"

For a moment, she was tempted to say yes. For a heartbeat or two, she wanted desperately to have another adult to lean on. Someone who could take the burden of responsibility—for the situation, for the girls, for their well-being—from her shoulders.

She'd tried that before, though, and all the love that Jay had brought her, all the promises he'd made and dreams he'd shared with her hadn't been able to balance out the promises he'd broken, or the dreams that he'd pursued with more passion than he'd ever pursued Honor.

The thought was sobering, and she shook her head, denying what she wanted in favor of what was safer. "You can go home. Thanks for coming to check on us."

"You know where to find me if you need me, Honor. I'll come. No matter the time or the reason. You know that, right?"

The only thing she knew for sure was that she'd been hurt before, and she didn't want to be hurt again. "I know where to find you if I need you."

His jaw clenched, but he didn't argue, just ran a finger down her cheek, the touch as soft as a baby's breath. "Good night."

He walked away before she could respond.

She knew that was for the best. Grayson Sinclair was a charming and very handsome man. The kind of man she'd do well to avoid having any more contact with.

She had enough problems without adding a man to them. Someone had sent her a dozen roses and had left one on the slide. Had peered in the window at her, his face covered with what could only have been a sheer stocking.

Who? Why?

They were questions she needed answers to, and she could only pray the sheriff would be able to find those answers quickly.

It took less than a half hour for her to realize that the answers wouldn't be forthcoming. She'd tucked Lily back into bed, sent Candace to her room and then answered every question the sheriff issued. In the end, he'd been able to tell her only one thing and it wasn't comforting. According to the sheriff, someone might be stalking Honor. A friend. An acquaintance. A co-worker. A stranger. He'd jotted down names, taken the card that had come with the flowers as evidence, assured her that he'd do everything he could to find the person who'd been looking in her window and then he'd left.

Tired, but unable to sleep, Honor paced the living room, her gaze going to the empty coffee table again and again. She'd asked the sheriff to take the vase and flowers with him even though he hadn't needed them for evidence. Knowing they were still in the house would have kept her awake all night.

She grimaced at the thought. If she didn't stop pacing the living room she *would* be awake all night. A cup of chamomile tea might help her relax.

She stepped into the kitchen, put the teakettle on to boil and stared out the kitchen window into the backyard. Maybe she should be afraid that her Peeping Tom would appear again, but she doubted he'd be back so soon.

What she didn't doubt was that he'd be back.

The phone rang as she pulled a tea bag from the canister, and Honor jumped, her heart crashing against her ribs. Did the stalker have her number? She grabbed the phone, glancing at the caller ID and relaxing as she saw the name. Grayson.

She smiled as she answered, her heart feeling lighter than it had in hours. "Shouldn't you be asleep?"

"Shouldn't you?"

"How did you know I wasn't?"

"I can see the light on in your kitchen. Look outside."

Honor did, and saw a light glowing in one of Grayson's upstairs windows. "I can see yours, too."

"Good. It'll remind you that you're not alone. Now go to sleep. You need your energy to deal with that daughter of yours." The phone clicked and Grayson was gone, but the light in his window continued to glow as Honor sipped her tea, a warm reminder that someone who cared was close by.

EIGHT

Honor was running late the next morning, her frustration only adding to the anxiety that had haunted her dreams and made sleep nearly impossible. Both girls seemed out of sorts, their grumpiness matching Honor's. She liked Sunday mornings to be calm, easy and filled with family time. Not rushed, hectic and filled with grumbling. Honor passed a church called Grace Christian on the way to work every day and had been looking forward to visiting, but in the wake of the morning's frustrations, the idea had lost some of its appeal.

She'd go anyway.

With her parents across the ocean, church family was important to her, and she'd been praying all week that she'd meet people she could grow to care about when she visited Grace Christian.

"Mommy? I want to change into another dress." Lily hovered in the bathroom doorway as Honor put on her makeup. The little girl's eyes were wide and filled with worry, the front of the pink dress she wore clutched in her fists.

"Why is that, sweetie? Did you get something on that one?"

"No, but I need to wear my yellow dress."

"Your yellow dress is a summer dress. You can't wear it when it's so cold outside."

"But it's pretty and cheerful."

"It certainly is, but it's also a sundress. The little strap sleeves on it won't keep your arms warm."

"But I really need to wear it."

"Need to? Why?" This was going to be good. Or bad. Depending on her perspective. Honor decided that after such a difficult night she should try to maintain a sense of humor about whatever Lily said.

"Because it's my only yellow dress."

"Honey, the dress you've got on is beautiful. And pink is your favorite color. I don't see any need to change."

"But, Mommy, I have to change because dragons don't like yellow."

Here they went again. Honor grimaced and tried to hold back her irritation, her sense of humor slipping rapidly. "I thought we decided there were no dragons."

"Just in case there are, we should both wear yellow."

"And who's been telling you that dragons don't like yellow?"

"Aunt Candy. She said if I had a yellow blanket, the dragon wouldn't come into the room. And guess what? I do have a yellow blanket!" Lily's eyes were wide with wonder.

"When did your aunt tell you this?"

"Last night. While you were talking to the police."

"I see." What she saw was that Candace had probably been desperate to get Lily settled back into bed and had said the only thing she thought would get the little girl to sleep. It had worked. Unfortunately, it had caused a whole new set of problems.

"She's right, isn't she, Mommy? Dragons don't like yellow."

"Listen, my darling," Honor pulled Lily into her arms. "There are no dragons. I keep telling you that, and you know that I would never lie to you, right?"

"Yes."

"Good. So believe me when I say there are no dragons."

"Not even one?"

"No. Not even one. Now, let me finish putting on my makeup or we'll be very late for church."

"Okay, Mommy. But maybe I could wear my yellow ball cap?"

Honor sighed. Obviously, Lily wasn't buying the idea that there were no dragons. More than likely what she really feared was something she couldn't verbalize. The past few weeks had been unsettling and obviously Lily had been affected by them. Honor could only pray that the ones that followed would be better. "Go get my purse, sweetie. There's some ChapStick in there. I think you need to put some on your lips."

"Really?"

"Yes. Hurry, we've got to leave in a minute." The distraction worked, and Lily rushed away. Content. For now. No doubt the conversation would come up again. Honor would just have to keep her cool and continue to reassure her daughter that they were safe. Eventually, Lily would settle down and stop worrying.

In the meantime, Honor would have to talk to Candace and let her know that there were some subjects that shouldn't be entertained in the house. Dragons, for one. Princes, for another. Lily had a big enough imagination without having the adults in her life playing into it.

Honor shook her head and lifted a mascara wand, staring at herself in the mirror as she applied it to her lashes. At thirty, she should still look young and fresh, alive and excited to see what the world had to offer. Instead she looked tired and worn, her dark hair lackluster and lank, her skin pasty, her freckles standing out in stark contrast. She supposed she shouldn't care. After all, she wasn't in the market for a relationship, and what she looked like really didn't matter much to Lily or Candace.

For a moment her mind flashed back to the previous night. To Grayson's bright blue gaze. The way he'd studied her face with such intensity. As if everything about her was fascinating. What had he seen? Surely not the worn mother staring out of the mirror.

Honor frowned. Grayson seemed to be taking up

too much of her thoughts. She needed to put him out of her mind, focus on getting her life in order.

"Honor?" Candace appeared at the doorway, dressed in a knee-length skirt and blue sweater, her hair pulled back in a sleek ponytail.

"You look like you're all ready to go. Do you want to drive, or shall I?"

"Actually, I was thinking of driving into Lynchburg and going to church on campus. A lot of my new friends live in the dorms and go to church there."

"That sounds great." Honor hoped her bright tone would hide the disappointment she felt at Candace's words. She knew it was time for her sister-in-law to forge her own path and go her own way, but that didn't make it any easier to watch. Candace had been a scared teenager with pitch-black lipstick and matching hair when she'd stepped into the little house Honor had shared with Jay. It hadn't taken long for the young teen to settle in and settle down. A little love and a lot of understanding had done wonders for the kid whom everyone else had given up on.

And now Candace wasn't a kid, she was an adult with goals and dreams that included Honor in only a peripheral way. The knowledge was bittersweet.

"If you want, I can come to church with you and Lily this week." Candace must have sensed her thoughts. Her eyes were the same deep blue as Lily's, the same as Jay's, but filled with more anxiety than Honor had ever seen in the other two.

"What I want is for you to go and have fun with

your friends. Tell me about the church later. Who knows, maybe Lily and I will visit next week."

"Are you sure? Because I really don't mind coming with you."

"Of course, I'm sure."

"Thanks. You're the best." Candace hugged Honor, holding her tight for a moment before she disappeared back in her room and closed the door. Not Honor's daughter or sister, but as much a part of her life as any blood relation could ever be. Honor really would miss her when she finally moved out of the house.

Of course Honor had always known that Candace would eventually grow up and grow away. That was part of life, as natural as heat in the summer and as predictable as the tide. Honor didn't expect or want it to be any different. When the time came for Lily to have a life on her own, Honor hoped she would accept it just as pragmatically. The house would be empty, then. And Honor would be alone.

The thought wasn't comforting, and for the first time since Jay's death, Honor wondered if her decision to stay single was the best one. If maybe finding someone to spend her life with wouldn't be such a bad thing.

She pushed the thought aside, refusing to dwell on it. No matter what the future brought, Honor wouldn't be alone. God was always with her, His presence true and sure. That was enough.

It had to be.

NINE

The phone rang as Grayson was taking a sip of his second cup of coffee. He answered quickly, knowing the only people that would call him early Sunday morning were family. Or Honor.

Had something else happened at the Malone house?

"Hello?"

"Gray? It's Dad."

Grayson tensed at his father's voice, worried that he might be calling with bad news about Jude's progress. "Hey, Dad. Is everything okay?"

"As good as can be expected. The doctors are saying Jude will be here another two weeks at least."

"That's not good news."

"No, but it's better than the alternative."

"Very true. How's Jude taking things?"

"You know your brother. He's fighting everyone and everything."

"Good for him."

"Yeah. As long as he's fighting, I figure he'll be okay."

"Listen, do you guys need me to come back up there? If you do, I'm on my way." As he spoke, his gaze was drawn to the window above his sink. From there he could see the roof of Honor's house. The thought of leaving before Jake caught the person who'd been peeking in her window last night filled Grayson with a sick sense of helplessness. The same way he'd felt when he'd been told about his brother's accident.

"Right now, we need you there more. The rental has got to be ready when Jude is released. We've got a rehab set up in Lynchburg, doctors, everything he'll need."

"I'll keep things moving along here, then. Just keep me posted on his progress." Relieved, Grayson rinsed his coffee cup and put it in the dishwasher.

"I will. Listen, I've got to go. We're heading out to church in a bit. Mom wants to get as many people praying as we can."

"Good idea."

"Yeah. We've already contacted our church in Forest. Make sure you ask your church to pray, too."

"I will, Dad." Though he hadn't actually planned to go to church.

"Thanks, Gray. I'll call you again soon."

Grayson hung up the phone, and ran a hand down his jaw. He'd have to shave if he went to church, and he'd have to dig out his Bible. He frowned at the realization. It had been too long since he'd immersed himself in God's word and too long since he'd taken the time to attend services. A month at least.

Where had the time gone?

His church his father had called it, but even years ago, when Grayson had been attending regularly, it hadn't felt like that. That probably had more to do with Grayson than with the people at Grace Christian. It wasn't that they hadn't tried to make him part of the church family. It was more that he'd been too busy pursuing other goals to participate in the men's Bible studies, men's breakfasts and the many other activities he'd been invited to.

Guilt reared its ugly head, and Grayson had no choice but to acknowledge it. Church hadn't been important to Maria, and Grayson hadn't pushed the point. During the years they'd dated, he'd gotten out of the habit of regular attendance. Seven months after breaking up with her, he still hadn't gotten back into the routine.

He needed to. He knew it and glanced at the clock, calculating the time it would take him to shower, shave and get ready for church. If he hurried, he might just make it there before the service began.

Grayson pulled into the parking lot of Grace Christian Church with five minutes to spare. Organ music drifted into the corridor and mixed with the sound of happy conversation as he hurried down the hall and pushed open the sanctuary door. The room was packed, most of the pews filled, people talking and laughing as they waited for the service to begin. Grayson searched for his brother Tristan and

Tristan's wife, Martha. He didn't see either of them. A few pews near the front looked like they might have room for one more, and Grayson moved toward them, pausing when he caught a glimpse of deep black hair and rosy skin.

Honor.

Her name filled his head and lodged in his heart.

She looked lovely, her hair down and spilling around her shoulders in a silky curtain of black.

She glanced his way as he approached, her eyes widening, her lips turning down in a slight frown. "Grayson. I wasn't expecting to see you today."

"Does that mean you'd rather I not sit with you?"

She was too polite to say yes, and Grayson knew it.

"It just means I'm surprised."

"Why are you surprised?"

"Because you seem like the kind of person who is too busy to bother with church."

Ouch! She'd hit the nail on the head with that one, and Grayson wasn't afraid to admit it. "I've had a lapse in attendance, but realized this morning it was time to come back."

"Because of your brother?"

"Partly, but mostly because of me. There are more important things than work. I think it's past time I started paying attention to them."

She looked up at him, her gaze intense, as if she were weighing the truth of his response.

Finally, she smiled. "You're serious."

"Why wouldn't I be?"

"I thought maybe you had found out I was coming, and decided to do the same." Her cheeks turned pink as she said it, and Grayson laughed softly.

"I had no idea you'd be here. If I had, I would have arrived sooner."

Honor smiled and shook her head. "You're incorrigible."

"I try. So—" he paused and gestured to the pew "—are you going to let me sit?"

Her cheeks grew even redder, and she scooted over, making room for him. The clean fragrant scent of her perfume drifted in the air as he sat beside her. Summery and light, it tugged at Grayson's senses, tempting him to move closer.

He didn't, but only because he thought doing so might send Honor running.

The pastor's sermon on faith during trials touched Grayson's soul, and he prayed fervently during the benediction. For himself and his weakened faith. For his brother's recovery. For Honor. When the last strains of the final hymn faded away, he stepped into the aisle, waiting for Honor and walking out of the sanctuary with her.

"That was a wonderful sermon, wasn't it?" Honor's eyes glowed, and she looked more relaxed than Grayson had ever seen her.

"It was definitely something I needed to hear."

"Me, too. Sometimes it's so hard to understand why things happen. Knowing that God is in control of it all makes it much easier to bear." That she could say that after all she'd been through touched Grayson's heart as few things had. This was real faith. This was true relationship with God. Something alive and vital and real.

"You're a special woman, Honor."

"No more special than anyone else." She brushed a hand over her hair, and he knew his comment had made her uncomfortable. "I need to go get Lily."

"And Candace?"

"She went to a church at the university." Honor smiled, but Grayson couldn't miss the sadness in her eyes.

"You miss having her with you."

"Of course, but she's an adult. It's time for her to step out on her own. Now, I really do have to get Lily. Who knows what kind of trouble she's caused this morning."

She hurried away.

Grayson started to follow her, but was pulled up short by an elderly woman who wanted to discuss suing the county for not maintaining her yard. Grayson spent the next five minutes explaining that it wasn't the county's responsibility, then walked outside.

The air was bitter and cold, whipping against his cheeks and stealing his breath. He could go home and work, but the thought didn't appeal to him. He could drive to Lynchburg and check on the rental property that his brother would be using, but the contractors weren't scheduled to begin work until Monday.

Which left him with plenty to do but no desire to do any of it.

"Mister. Hey, Mister Prince!"

Grayson recognized Lily's voice immediately, and he scanned the parking lot until he spotted her a few yards away.

Dressed in a fluffy pink coat and hat, her cheeks red from the cold, she was pulling against Honor's hold and trying desperately to move toward him.

"Hello, Princess Lily." He smiled and walked toward her, ignoring Honor's uneasy expression.

"I'm not a princess."

"No?"

"Mommy is. And she needs a prince to save her from the dragon."

"I see." He met Honor's eyes, and smiled as she blushed.

"I do not need a prince, young lady. What I need is some Tylenol." Honor shook her head, and tugged Lily toward an old Ford. "This child just does not know when to quit."

"I don't have any Tylenol, but I could offer lunch. That might do just as much to get rid of your headache."

"Headache? I've got an entire body ache." She opened the car door and motioned for Lily to get into her booster.

"Food will help."

"Don't tell me that you actually believe that."

"What I believe is that good food and interesting conversation can solve a multitude of problems."

"I appreciate the offer, Grayson, but I'm not hungry."

"Big breakfast?"

"Mommy didn't eat breakfast." Lily peeked out the open car door.

"Lily, I said to get in your booster." Honor's exasperation was obvious, and Grayson bit back a smile.

"It seems to me that hunger can cause headaches. But you're the nurse. Maybe you've heard something different."

"We're both busy—"

"And we both need to eat." He linked his fingers with hers, tugging her a step closer so that he could see the flecks of gold in her eyes, feel her quick intake of breath.

"Grayson—"

"It's just lunch, Honor."

"Why does it feel like more?"

"Because that's where we're heading. For now, though, it's just a meal between friends."

She hesitated, and he was sure she'd say no. Then she glanced at her daughter, frowning slightly. "It will make Lily's day if we go to lunch with you."

"Then come."

"All right. But I'm taking my own car and I'm paying for my meal and Lily's."

"Taking your own car makes sense. We'll discuss who's paying the bill after we eat."

"We'll discuss it now, or we won't go at all." Her lips were set in a tight line, her eyes flashing.

"You're beautiful when you're irritated, you know that?"

"And you're a man who knows exactly what to say to get what he wants."

"Compliments make you uncomfortable, don't they?"

"I've learned that the sweeter the compliment the more bitter the deception that follows."

"Deception? What kind of men have you been dating?" The question slipped out before Grayson could stop it, and Honor stiffened, reaching into the car to buckle her daughter's straps, then shutting the door before responding.

"I don't date. I don't have time for it. But I was married to a man whose words were sweet cream and warm sunshine. He used them to convince anyone of anything." She spoke quietly, her words devoid of emotion.

"He doesn't sound like a very nice guy." And not the kind of man Grayson thought a woman like Honor would be attracted to.

"Jay was a wonderful guy. Sweet, funny, imaginative."

"And a deceiver."

"Not in his mind. In his mind, he was painting prettier pictures of the way things were and making his life better in the process."

"Deception is deception, regardless of the reasons."

"You don't have to tell me that, Grayson. I know it. And I know the damage it can do." She smiled sadly. "Jay wasn't a bad person. He was just Jay… It looks like my daughter is getting restless. We'd better get to lunch. Where were you planning to eat?"

"Becky's Diner. Do you know it?"

"Know it? We ate there once, and Lily has been begging me to bring her back ever since."

"Then she should be very happy. See you there?"

"Yes." She got into her car, closing the door and pulling away, Lily strapped into her car seat in the back, waving wildly.

Seeing the little girl there, her cheeks still chubby with baby fat, her eyes wide and filled with happiness, made Grayson's heart clench. Innocence and life wrapped up in a tiny package, Lily was the kind of child who went through life with pure excitement and enthusiasm. The kind of child who could easily be hurt by one of the many predators who wandered through the world looking for victims.

He walked back to his car, more determined than ever to make sure Honor and her family stayed safe.

TEN

Honor hurried Lily across the nearly full parking lot of Becky's Diner, irritated with herself for falling into Grayson's plans. Lunch with him was a bad idea. A really bad one. Yet here she was, doing exactly what she knew she shouldn't.

"Mommy, are you sure Mister Prince is having lunch with us?" Lily bounced next to her, her cheeks glowing pink from the cold.

"Mr. *Sinclair* is having lunch with us. And that is what I would like you to call him."

"I will."

"And no more talk about him being a prince, or slaying dragons or having a horse. Okay?" Honor looked down into Lily's face and tried to force sternness into her voice. Despite the trouble it often caused, Honor loved the quirky side of her daughter's personality. It was so much like Jay's. So much a part of what had attracted Honor to him.

"All right, Mommy."

"And no calling me a princess, either. Because

we both know I'm not one. If I were, I'd have ball gowns in my closet instead of work uniforms, and I'd wear glass slippers on my feet instead of sneakers."

"We could get you ball gowns and glass slippers."

"No, we couldn't. But we can get a nice sandwich and a cup of soup for me and something yummy for you."

"Chicken nuggets and fries?"

"Sure." They stepped into the diner and were seated in a booth near the front window of the busy restaurant. From there, Honor had a view of the parking lot and the people walking and driving through it. She imagined Grayson would drive up in something fancy. Maybe a shiny new sports car. A Jaguar. A Corvette. Something showy, like his house.

When a midsized charcoal sedan pulled into a parking space, Honor ignored it, turning her attention to the red Corvette that zipped into another space farther away. She was so sure Grayson was going to get out of it, she had to look twice when a short, balding man emerged.

"Look, Mommy. It's Mr. Sinclair." Lily bounced in her seat, poking a chubby finger against the glass.

"Where?"

"Right there. Near the black car."

Honor looked in the direction her daughter was pointing. Sure enough, Grayson was closing the door to the charcoal sedan she'd noticed. "So he is. Now, remember what we talked about, Lil. No going on about your fantasy worlds while Mr. Sinclair is with us."

"I won't." Lily stood up on the bench seat and waved her arms. "Mr. Sinclair, we're over here."

"Lily Malone, you know better than to stand on a chair. And use your inside voice." Honor's cheeks heated as the diner's guests turned to look at Lily.

"Sorry, Mommy." But it was obvious Lily wasn't all that concerned about being chastised. She grinned from ear to ear as Grayson approached, her deep blue eyes shining with excitement. "You finally came."

"We've only been here a couple of minutes, Lily." Honor tried to reel in her daughter's enthusiasm, but she knew it was a lost cause. Life was an adventure to Lily. One that she experienced with pure zeal.

"Is that black car yours, Mr. Sinclair? Because I thought you'd have a special car. Like a gold one. Or a silver one. Or a really fast one." Lily's dark curls were brushing against her cheeks, and despite Honor's reservations about having lunch with Grayson, she couldn't help smiling.

"I used to have a silver car and it was really fast. I traded it in for this one a few months ago." Grayson smiled, and took a menu the waitress was handing him. If he noticed the fact that the platinum blonde was sending him signals about her interest, he didn't show it. His attention seemed to be completely focused on Lily.

"Why did you trade in your car?"

"Because it was too silver and too fast."

"And you got too many tickets while you were driving it?" Honor asked the question before she thought it through, and heat spread along her cheeks. "Sorry. That wasn't a very tactful question."

"There's no need to apologize. I'm known for asking tactless questions. I can't fault other people for doing the same."

"Yes, but asking questions is part of your job."

"Who said I only ask them when I'm doing my job?" Grayson grinned, flashing his dimple, his straight white teeth.

His charm.

That charismatic something that begged Honor to drop her guard and let him in.

She lowered her gaze, staring at the menu and doing her best not to let Grayson see just how much he affected her. Jay had always known how she melted when she looked into his eyes, and he'd used that knowledge to his own benefit too many times. "Our waitress will be back in a minute. We'd better decide what to order."

He didn't respond, and Honor met his eyes. There was curiosity in the depth of his gaze. Interest. Concern. What did he see that made him feel that way? A single mother doing her best to raise a little girl? An overwhelmed widow who hadn't managed to settle into her new life? The victim of a stalker?

"You don't have to worry, Honor. I don't bite." He reached across the table, covering her hand with his, the contact as familiar as it was new.

"I'm sure you don't."

"Then why do you look so scared?"

Because she'd been hurt before. Because she

didn't want to be hurt again. "I'm not scared. I'm hungry. Are you ready to order?"

"Sure."

"Without even looking at the menu?"

"There are more interesting things to look at, I think." He smiled again, and Honor's cheeks burned.

"You really are full of flattery, aren't you?" But Honor wasn't flattered. Grayson's words were just a means to an end. Though what end he had in mind, she didn't know.

"Like I've said before, it's not flattery when it's the truth." Grayson glanced at the menu. "What are you two having today?"

Flustered, Honor looked at Lily. "You want chicken nuggets and fries, right?"

"And ketchup."

"Of course, ketchup. Fries aren't any good without it." Grayson said, and smiled at Lily. Honor's heart skipped a beat. There was just something about a man who liked kids.

There was just something about Grayson.

She shoved the thought aside and turned her attention to the waitress who was winding her way back to their table. All Honor needed to do was order, eat and get Lily out of the diner. Then she'd forget that she'd spent an hour sitting beside Grayson at church. She'd forget that his smile made her want to let her guard down. And she'd forget that even with the girls around, her life had become more lonely than she wanted to admit.

She ordered for herself and Lily, doing her best

to ignore the way the waitress flirted with Grayson. It seemed to Honor that the woman should be a little more subtle considering that Grayson wasn't at the table alone.

"You're lost in thought," Grayson said as the waitress walked away, an unspoken question hovering behind his words. He wanted to know what she was thinking about, but Honor wasn't willing to share. There was too much on her mind. And too much of that had to do with Grayson.

"I'm just wondering if the sheriff has found anything new regarding those flowers I received." She *had* been wondering that. Just not at the exact moment Grayson had asked.

"You haven't spoken to him?"

"Not since yesterday."

"You could call him now."

"I'm sure if he had something to tell me, he'd have let me know already."

"True, but if talking to him will give you peace of mind..." Grayson shrugged, accepting a refill of water from the overly solicitous waitress.

"The only thing that can do that is finding out who put the rose in my backyard and why."

"Someone wants your attention. It was his way of getting it."

"Who? Why? I keep going back to those two questions, and I keep not finding the answers."

"I can think of a few reasons why off the top of my head." Grayson frowned, then glanced at Lily who was busy coloring on the paper placemat the waitress had given her. "But now is probably not the best time to mention them. As far as who left it, I think it was left by someone in your past. Someone who doesn't want to be forgotten."

"Then he's going to be disappointed, because I already have forgotten him."

"He could be an acquaintance. Someone you've only met briefly. An email contact."

"Or a dragon. A dragon could leave flowers, Mommy. And then maybe he could blow fire on our house." Lily stopped coloring and looked up, her brow furrowed with worry.

"No need to worry about that, Lily. I told you that I'd slay any dragons that came around." Grayson spoke before Honor could, his words firm and filled with conviction. As if he really believed that he could solve whatever problems Honor and her family had.

But without action, words meant nothing. And even if Grayson planned to act on his promise, Honor wasn't sure she wanted him to. She'd been slaying all kinds of dragons on her own for years, even before she lost Jay. Missed mortgage payments, credit collectors, angry people who'd been promised the moon and received nothing. Jay had been as good at breaking promises as he had been at making them.

"Are you okay?" Grayson's voice broke into her thoughts, and Honor blinked, trying to pull herself firmly back into the present.

"Of course." Her tone was brittle. Even she could hear it. Grayson's steady gaze bore into hers, demanding answers she had no intention of giving.

"And yet you're frowning and shredding napkins." He reached across the table, stilling her hands. His fingers caressed her knuckles, soothing tension Honor hadn't even realized she was feeling.

She dropped the napkin, frowning at the small pile of white sitting in front of her.

"I wasn't shredding. I was tearing."

"And that makes it different?"

"It looks like our food is coming. Elbows off the table, Lily." Honor swept the pieces of napkin into her hand, determined to change the subject. She never talked about the problems she'd faced during her marriage. Not with her parents. Not with her friends. And certainly not with men she barely knew.

"Chicken nuggets and fries!" Lily squealed with delight as the preening waitress set a plate in front of her.

Honor did her best to smile at her daughter's enthusiasm. Her stomach was tied in knots, and the thought of eating only made it worse. The sooner she got out of the diner and away from Grayson, the better she'd feel. Talking to him only served to remind her of all the things she used to dream of. All the things she now knew she'd never have.

"Let's say the blessing so we can eat." She linked hands with her daughter and was surprised when Grayson reached across the table to grab Lily's free hand. When his other hand covered hers, Honor couldn't make herself pull away. Couldn't force herself to break the circle of faith that they had formed.

"Would you like me to pray? Or do you want to?"

Grayson's tone was as warm as his palm, his hard face softened by whatever he was thinking.

"You can." Honor's throat was tight with emotions she shouldn't be feeling, and with a longing she didn't want to acknowledge.

"Lord, thank You for the bountiful gifts You've given to us, for this wonderful meal that we can share together, and for the gift of new friendships. Amen."

The prayer was simple and sweet without the frills and showiness of someone who wanted to make an impression. That intrigued Honor, and she looked into Grayson's eyes. Really looked. He didn't glance away. He just met her gaze, letting her search for a truth she didn't expect to find, for sincerity she presumed she wouldn't see, but did.

Honor's pulse jumped in acknowledgment, her heart shuddering with feelings that had died long ago. Feelings that she'd believed were better off dead.

Grayson's eyes darkened, his gaze dropping to Honor's lips, his thumb caressing the back of her hand, and for a moment it was as if Lily weren't sitting at the table chatting about the ketchup she was pouring on her fries. As if there wasn't a restaurant filled with people surrounding them.

Honor's breath caught, her mind went blank and suddenly she couldn't remember all the reasons why she needed to guard her heart. Suddenly the past was nothing but a distant memory, and the present was all that mattered. Grayson's vivid blue eyes, his somber expression, his palm still pressed against her hand. The newness of it all. The simple pleasure of having a man look at her as if she were as beautiful as a flower blooming in the desert.

Shocked, she pulled her hand away and turned her attention to the salad that had been set in front of her. "We'd better eat. I'm sure you have a lot to do this afternoon."

"Nothing that can't wait a while." He didn't smile when he said it, and Honor had the impression that he was as surprised at what had just happened as she was.

She wanted to say something that would change things back to how they'd been before, but the words caught in her throat and she remained silent, picking at lettuce and tomatoes and praying that Lily would eat quickly so they could be on their way.

"Relax, Honor. We're just two friends sharing a meal." Grayson spoke quietly, and Honor nodded her agreement. Anything to avoid discussing what she'd felt.

"Friends sharing a meal?"

"Sure. People do it all the time."

She looked up, got caught in Grayson's smile and found herself returning it and relaxing. He was right, of course. They were having lunch together. It wasn't a big deal unless she made it one. "They do, but *we* won't be if we don't spend a little more time chewing and a little less time chatting. Lily will be done before we even begin."

"Practical as always."

"There's nothing wrong with that."

"You're right. It's a quality I've always admired."

Honor frowned, sure the conversation was heading back into dangerous territory. "Look, Grayson, I think I need to be clear on—"

Her cell phone rang, cutting off Honor's words. She grabbed it, glad for the reprieve. "Hello?"

"Honor? It's Candace." There was a tremor in Candace's voice, and Honor tensed.

"Is everything okay?"

"I don't know. I decided to come home after church so we could all have lunch together."

"I wish I'd known what you'd planned. Lily and I stopped for lunch at the diner." She didn't mention that Grayson was with them.

"It's okay, Honor. No big deal. The thing is, when I got home, there was a package sitting on the porch."

"A package?"

"Yes. It's wrapped in brown paper and has your name on it."

"And this is worrying you?"

"No. Yes. Maybe." Candace's laugh was tight and filled with nervous energy. "I mean, after what happened with that guy in the yard and the flower and everything, the package is just kind of freaking me out. I keep wondering if someone is outside. You know, watching the house. Maybe even watching me. That's silly, I know. And stupid. Just forget I called, okay?"

"I'm not going to do any such thing. How about I just come home and take a look?" Honor glanced at Lily who was dipping a chicken nugget into ketchup. She'd be disappointed to have to leave, but it couldn't be helped. For as long as Candace needed her, Honor planned to be there for her.

"No, really. It's okay. I'm fine. I was just letting my imagination get the better of me—"

"Better to be cautious than to be sorry. I'll be home in about ten minutes." She cut off Candace's protest and hung up the phone, knowing that her sister-in-law must be really scared if she'd called. Asking for help wasn't something the eighteen-year-old liked to do. Honor shoved the phone into her purse and placed a twenty on the table. "I'm sorry, Grayson, but Lily and I need to go home."

"We can't go, Mommy. We're not done eating."

"We're going to have to be done. Candace needs us to come home."

"What's going on?" Grayson stood and threw some money on the table, his brow furrowed with concern.

"Nothing terrible." Honor took Lily's hand and headed for the diner's door.

"But something. Why not tell me what it is? You know I'll just keep asking until you do." Grayson pushed the door open and held it while she and Lily stepped outside.

"Candace found a package on the front porch when she came home. She's a little worried after what happened with the flowers. I told her I'd come home and check things out."

"Did she bring it inside the house with her?"

"I didn't ask."

"Call her and find out. If she hasn't touched it,

she needs to leave it where it is. I'll call the sheriff and have him meet you at your place."

"But—"

"Look, I know what you're going to say. 'It's probably nothing. There's no sense in calling the sheriff.' Right?"

"That's kind of what I was hoping *you'd* say."

"There are a lot of things I will do for you, Honor. Lying to make you feel safe isn't one of them. After what happened last night, we've got every reason to be worried about that package."

"That's what I thought, too. I was just hoping that you'd have a different perspective on things."

"Sorry, but my opinion stands. We've got to call Jake."

"Of course, you're right."

"We finally see eye to eye on something." He smiled, but there was no humor in his expression.

"I've got to get home. Candace is waiting."

"Make sure you call her and let her know that the package shouldn't be touched."

"I will."

"Good." Grayson seemed to relax at her words, his warm gaze caressing her face and touching her lips as it had in the diner. Her cheeks heated, and she looked away, unwilling to accept what she was seeing in his eyes.

The kindness. The concern.

The attraction.

She most definitely didn't want to acknowledge that.

There could be nothing between Grayson and Honor.

The sooner she got that into her head, the better off she'd be.

She strapped Lily into her booster seat, got into the car and drove away, telling herself that her racing pulse had more to do with fear than it had to do with Grayson, and knowing she was lying to herself.

ELEVEN

Grayson called Jake before he got in his car, relaying the information and disconnecting as he climbed into the Saturn. He was going over to Honor's, of course. No way did he plan to head home until he knew everything was okay at her house.

He turned the key and started the engine, smiling as he remembered Lily's comments about his vehicle. She'd been expecting something flashy and bold, like the car he'd let Maria talk him into buying two years ago. A silver Jaguar. A smooth ride, but not something Grayson had cared much about one way or another.

He needed something practical, not fancy, and he'd traded in the Jaguar days after saying goodbye to Maria. He didn't regret it. Nor did he regret ending a relationship that had become more a habit than anything else. Maybe if he'd thought about that a little more during the time he and Maria had dated, he wouldn't have asked her to marry him. And maybe if he'd spent more time going to church and reading his Bible and less time pursuing his career, he wouldn't have dated her in the first place.

Looking back, he realized their relationship had been based more on convenience than anything else. He'd wanted marriage. Family. All the things a successful person had. He just hadn't wanted to put much time or effort into building them. Maria had been no different. The fact that neither of them had been brokenhearted when he'd called off the engagement had reaffirmed what it had taken him too long to realize—they weren't meant to spend their lives together.

Until a few days ago, Grayson had been convinced he wasn't meant to spend his life with anyone but himself. Funny how such a short amount of time could change a person's perspective on things.

Funny how willing he was to accept that change.

Now if he could just convince Honor to trust him, things might turn out better than Grayson had ever imagined.

Jake's cruiser was already parked in Honor's driveway as Grayson pulled up in front of her house. He knocked on the front door anyway, waiting impatiently until it cracked open.

"Grayson. Come on in." Honor stepped back, letting him into the living room.

"I see that Jake has already arrived."

"He's in the kitchen."

"Did he open the package?"

"Yes. It seems I've received another anonymous delivery."

"What was it?"

"Come and see." She led him through the dining room, her hair a silky curtain falling straight past her shoulders. No highlights. No forced curls or stiff styling. Just smooth and natural.

He wanted to run his hand over it, let the silky strands slide through his fingers. Instead, he shoved his hands into his pockets and pretended that Honor was any other woman. Or at least, he tried to. "I guess Candace was right to be concerned."

"Yes. Thank you for insisting I call the sheriff. If you hadn't, I may have convinced myself the package was nothing to worry about and decided not to bother anyone." She glanced over her shoulder as she said it, and Grayson could see the anxiety in her eyes, the tightness around her mouth. Whatever Jake had found was bothering Honor more than she wanted to let on.

"It's never a bother to investigate suspicious activity." Jake spoke as Grayson entered the kitchen behind Honor, but he didn't look up from the box sitting open on the table.

"What's in it?" Grayson stepped forward, his muscles tense, his mind filling with a million possibilities. Years of working as a prosecutor for the state of Virginia had taught him more than he needed to know about the depth of depravity that could live inside a human being.

"Not much, but more than enough to have me worried." Jake reached into the box with a gloved hand and lifted out a piece of paper. "Take a look."

Are you dreaming of me?

The words were black and bold, typed on plain white paper. Generic. Nothing noteworthy about any of it. Still, the message made the hair on the back of Grayson's neck stand on end. How many times had seemingly innocuous things led to dangerous situations? To crime? To death?

"This was with it." Jake lifted a photograph by the corner. It had been taken at night, but Honor's face was clearly visible, her dark hair covered by a knit cap, her coat unbuttoned to reveal what looked like a nurse's uniform. Even in the poor lighting, her skin had a creamy tone, her eyes deep green and filled with worry. Had she sensed the voyeur who'd been watching? Had that been the photographer's goal? To capture her fear and anxiety so that he could replay the moment over and over again?

Anger bubbled up, but Grayson tamped it down again. Getting angry wouldn't help anything. No matter what the crime or who the victim, keeping a cool head went a lot further in making sure the perpetrator was brought to justice. "Do we know when that was taken?"

"Within the last few days. I think after I finished my night shift. I must have been heading to my car. See the building in the background? That's Lakeview Haven." Honor spoke quietly as she pressed in close to Grayson, the subtle scent of flowers and sunshine drifting around her. He knew she only meant to get a better look at the photo, but warmth spread through him at the contact, his heart beating a slow heavy rhythm. The need to protect her, to make sure that the person stalking her didn't ever get close enough to hurt her, made his muscles tighten and his hands fist.

Honor might be strong and determined. She might be independent and capable. But she was no match for evil. No match for the kind of predator that hunted her. "Do you walk to your car by yourself every night?"

"I hadn't had a reason not to." *Until now.* The words were left unsaid, but Grayson heard them clearly enough. They held the kind of fear no person should feel. The insidious kind that left a person awake at night. That made her jump at every creak and groan of floorboards. That left her exposed, vulnerable and helpless.

Grayson had heard the stories over and over again. Each time he'd been filled with anger, but this time was different. This time the victim was a woman he knew. A woman he admired. "Are there people who can walk you to your car?"

"I'm sure someone can." She pressed in closer to his arm, leaning past him to stare down at the picture. Tension radiated from her, and Grayson fought the urge to put an arm around her shoulder, offer comfort that he knew she wouldn't accept.

"If there's no one there who can walk you to your car, call my office. I'll make sure you have an escort. We're not going to take any chances with this. Whoever this guy is, he wants you to know he's around. That means he's getting bold. Boldness can lead to anything." Jake's words were grim. "I'm going to send the box and its contents to the state CSI. They'll be able to search for evidence my team here can't."

"How long will it take for the results to come in?"

"Not long, but sending it out doesn't guarantee we'll be any closer to finding the guy who's doing this." Jake lifted the box and slid it into a large plastic bag. "In the meantime, you need to be careful, Honor. Don't go out alone. Be aware of your surroundings. If you feel nervous about something, don't hesitate to call for help."

"I won't."

"This is a small town. It's hard for a stranger to hide in it. If our guy is someone unfamiliar to people around here, we'll hear about him soon enough." Jake sounded confident, but Grayson wasn't so sure things would play out that way. Stalkers were notorious for staying hidden until they were ready to show themselves.

Their time. Their place. Their agenda.

"Are there security cameras at Lakeview Haven?" Grayson followed Jake as he walked out the front door. "If there are, you might catch a glimpse of our guy."

Jake speared him with a look that said exactly what he thought about being told how to do his job. To his credit he didn't say what he was thinking. "I'm already on it. There are security cameras in the parking area. I'm going over there now to view them."

"I think I'll come along with you and—"

"I don't think so, friend. This is a police investigation. You're a prosecuting attorney. When I have enough evidence to bring someone in, I'll let you know. Until then, it's best if you steer clear and let me do what I've been trained to do." There wasn't any heat to Jake's words, but Grayson felt his own anger flaring up.

"How much information are you going to be willing to share, Jake? Because I want it all. I want to know who's responsible as soon as you do. And I want to know exactly what steps you're taking to bring him in."

"No need to get up in arms about it, Gray. You know I'll keep you and Honor informed." He glanced over Grayson's shoulder, making his point without saying it. Honor was the victim. *She* was the one who needed to be kept abreast of the investigation.

"Thank you for your help, Sheriff Reed." Honor moved past Grayson and stood on the porch steps, her posture stiff as if she hadn't liked the direction of his conversation with Jake. Too bad. Having him concerned and involved might not sit well with her, but Grayson had no intention of backing off.

"I'll be in touch." Jake put the box into the trunk of his cruiser and got into the car, waving before he drove away.

The car was barely out of the driveway before Honor turned on Grayson and said exactly what he knew she'd been thinking. "I appreciate your concern, Grayson, but I can handle the situation. You really don't need to get involved."

"Sorry, but I already am involved."

"Why?"

"Because we're neighbors. Because your daughter seems to think I can protect you. Because I don't want to let her down. And because no matter how much you might want to deny it, there's something between us."

"I'm not denying it. I'm just refusing to allow it."

"Do you think it's that easy? You just decide you're not going to get involved and you don't? Because it's not that easy for me, and I don't think I want it to be." There was heat in his voice, but Grayson didn't care. This wasn't just about friendship. It wasn't just about building a relationship. This was about Honor's safety, and he wouldn't back off until he knew they'd achieved that.

"Maybe that's because you've never known what it's like to have your heart broken again and again and again. Maybe it's because you've never loved someone who loved himself more than he loved you."

"You're right, I haven't "

"Then for you, I can see why stepping into a relationship is easy. For me, it's impossible."

"Nothing is impossible." Grayson took a step closer, inhaling sweet summer and flowers.

"Lots of things are, Grayson." She smiled, the expression filled with sadness. "I put my dreams into someone before. I don't regret it, but I won't do it again. I won't be that vulnerable, that needy. And it wouldn't be fair to let you think I might."

"You don't have to worry about me, Honor. I'm a big boy, and I can take care of myself."

"And you don't have to worry about me. I'm a big girl and can take care of *myself.* I'm going to take precautions until Sheriff Reed finds the person who is stalking me. I'm going to make sure the girls and I are safe."

"Precautions aren't always enough, Honor. I've seen cases like this before. I've tried men who've stalked their prey for weeks, months, even years. Even with the police searching for the person responsible, it can take time to put him behind bars."

"You're not telling me anything I don't know, but what choice do I have but to believe that everything will work out? I've got two girls depending on me, Grayson. My closest family is in Ireland. Even if I could afford to fly there with the girls, I wouldn't pull Candace out of school to do it. Not unless I was absolutely convinced that that was the only way to keep my girls safe."

"What about keeping yourself safe?"

She stiffened at the question. "One thing I've learned is that anything can happen in life. We can live in fear, worrying about the trouble that may be heading our way, or we can trust that God is in control and that anything that happens is part of His plan."

"Everything?"

"Everything. Good and bad."

"You've got a lot of faith, Honor, but faith doesn't preclude caution." Although it helped. Grayson had seen the evidence of it over and over again in his work. Those with strong faith healed more quickly, faced trials with more grace and less anger and were able to move on with their lives in a way that others often couldn't.

"I know that. I also know that when faith is all a person has, she learns that it's enough." She shivered and rubbed her hands up and down her arms. "It's cold. I'd better head back inside."

Grayson knew she wanted him to go.

But for him, walking away wasn't an option.

He cupped her elbow, holding her in place when she would have walked away. Her bones were delicate beneath his hand, her muscles sinewy and strong beneath her silky dress. "You work nights, don't you?"

"Yes." She didn't try to pull away, but he could feel the tightness of her muscles and the subtle shift of awareness between them. They weren't just two people having a discussion anymore. They were a man and a woman alone together on a porch, chilly winter air urging them closer to each other.

"Can you switch to days?"

"No. Candace is in school during the day. I've got to be here for Lily."

"You could find a day-care provider for a few weeks."

"I looked into it before we came. We can't afford it. Not with Candace's tuition, books, gas for her car." She shrugged. "Besides, the schedule at Lakeview Haven was shifted to accommodate my availability. Even if I could afford day care, I couldn't ask them to rework things again."

"Not even for your own safety?"

"I'll make sure I have an escort." She eased her arm from his, her cheeks flushed with cold, her hair black silk against alabaster skin. It was no wonder Lily imagined her to be a princess. Honor looked like a fairy tale come to life.

"And you'll call Jake if you don't?"

"Of course."

"If you can't reach him, or he can't send someone out for you, give me a ring. I'll make sure you get to your car safely."

"I couldn't ask you to go to all that trouble."

"You haven't asked anything. I'm offering. I've got to make sure I'm around if a dragon shows up and needs slaying. I promised Lily, after all." He smiled, but Honor's expression remained sober.

"I appreciate your concern, Grayson, but we really aren't your responsibility. No matter what promises you made my daughter."

"I guess we have a difference of opinion, then. I don't make promises I don't intend to keep."

She looked like she might argue, but shook her head instead. "I really do need to get back to the girls. Candace has a lot of studying to do, and she'll never get it done with Lily under her feet."

"Take care. Call me if you need anything."

"I'll keep that in mind." She shut the door, the old wood clicking into place with a finality that bothered Grayson more than it should.

What was it about Honor that got under his skin? She was beautiful, but he'd dated women even more stunning. She had a deep abiding faith that he admired, but he'd known other women who had been just as strong in their beliefs. So what was it about her that made him want to knock on her door, tell her again that he was nearby if anything happened? That made him want to stand on the porch with her in the bitter cold, made him want to think about impossibilities becoming possible? A wife. Children. The kind of family his parents had created.

Whatever it was, Grayson couldn't ignore it and he couldn't walk away from it. Only time would tell if he could convince Honor to feel the same.

The sobering thought followed him into the car and home to the empty house that only seemed emptier since he'd met Honor.

TWELVE

The next two days passed without incident. Honor spent her time at home playing board games with Lily, proofing a paper for Candace, making lists of items she needed to buy at the grocery store. Grayson stopped by twice. Once to borrow a cup of sugar. Once to return the bowl he'd taken with him. Honor didn't believe for a minute he'd needed sugar. She couldn't imagine him baking anything, or needing sugar for his coffee. What had drawn him to her house was the same thing that drew Honor's attention again and again—worry.

Grayson didn't say it. He didn't push for personal conversation, didn't ask to be included in the family's daily life, but Honor knew he wanted to keep close. Make sure she and the girls were okay.

And somehow that knowledge warmed her as she went about her day.

A stalker was watching her, taking pictures of her, biding his time. Waiting for an opportunity to follow through on whatever insane plans he was making.

But Grayson was watching, too. And Honor was certain if she needed him, he'd be there for her.

She scowled at her reflection in the mirror, wishing she could turn her thoughts off for a while. She seemed to have two pet subjects—Grayson and the stalker. The first was pleasant, but worrisome. The second was terrifying. Both were wreaking havoc on her sleep. At night, she tossed and turned, her dreams filled with masked intruders and demonic figures. The lack of sleep showed on her face. The dark circles under her eyes. The pale skin.

She'd thought coming to Lakeview would make life easier for herself and for the girls. Instead, it just seemed to have complicated things. "But I know You're in control of it, Lord. I know that You are going to make sure it all works out okay. I just have to keep believing." She whispered the prayer as she applied the last of her makeup. She had to be at work in twenty minutes, but the thought of leaving the house had her feeling vulnerable and afraid. She had to drive the ten miles to Lakeview Haven alone. Get out of the car alone. Walk to the building. Alone.

"Enough. It's broad daylight. There will be plenty of people in the parking lot. Plenty of people on the porch. You've got nothing to worry about."

"Mommy, who are you talking to?" Lily peeked around the open bathroom door, her blue eyes filled with curiosity.

"Myself."

"Why?"

Why, indeed. Honor crouched down so she was

on eye level with her daughter and looked into her eyes. "Because it's better than talking to no one."

"You don't have to talk to no one, Mommy. You can talk to me."

"Very true, my sweet, but you weren't here. I was all alone."

"No you weren't. God was with you. Just like you always tell me. We're never alone."

Out of the mouth of babes.

Honor smiled and hugged Lily close. "I do say that, don't I?"

"Yes."

"Then I guess you're right, and I've got no reason to talk to myself. Now, you be good for Candace tonight, you hear?"

"I will."

"Go to bed on time. No arguing."

"Okay."

"I love you, Lily Mae." She kissed her daughter's cheek, and stepped out of the bathroom. "I'm leaving, Candace."

"Already? I thought you didn't have to be there until two." Candace came to the threshold of her bedroom, her face pale and drawn.

"We've got a mandatory meeting before my shift. I doubt I'll have time to swing back home afterward. I'll probably just stay at the Haven and get some paperwork done. I thought I'd mentioned this to you."

"You didn't. I would have remembered." Candace frowned, and Honor's anxiety ratcheted up a notch.

"I'm sorry. I guess with everything that's happened the past few days, I forgot. Do you have plans? If so, I can probably skip the meeting." Though she doubted her supervisor would be happy about it.

"No, that's okay. I don't have any plans. I just was expecting you to be home a while longer."

"Is something wrong? Do you need me to stay? I will. I'm sure my supervisor will understand." She wasn't sure of any such thing, but her family came first, and if Candace needed her home, home was exactly where she would be.

"No. That's okay. I was just surprised." Candace's gaze dropped to Lily, then met Honor's again. "Just make sure you're careful, okay?"

"You know I will be. Call my cell phone if you need me."

"We'll be fine." *Please, please make sure* you *are.*

The words were unspoken, but seemed to shine from Candace's eyes, begging for reassurance. Her parents had shown no interest in her during the past years, and Honor knew that she was all the young woman had.

Honor wanted to pull Candace into a hug, but knew her sister-in-law well enough to refrain. Malones didn't admit to weakness. Jay had told Honor that often enough during their marriage. Candace might not verbalize the sentiment, but from the day she'd entered Honor's life, it had been obvious that was how she felt. Tough, independent, but with a soft spirit that could so easily be bruised and broken.

"I'll be okay, too, Candace." Honor whispered so

that Lily couldn't hear, hoping her words would be enough to ease Candace's worry.

"You'd better be." Candace spoke just as quietly, but Honor could still hear the fear in her voice.

Guilt at having to leave followed Honor out the door and into the car. It stayed with her as she drove along the winding road that led out of town. Past pastures steeped in golden sun, across a bridge that spanned a tributary of Smith Mountain Lake, then along the lengthy driveway that led to Lakeview Haven. Guilt that she couldn't do more to make the girls feel secure. Guilt that she'd somehow brought danger into their lives.

"Lord, please help Sheriff Reed find the person stalking me soon. Please keep the girls safe. Keep me safe. Help us to put this behind us and to build wonderful memories here in Lakeview," she prayed. And as she pulled into a parking spot close to the front entrance of the building, a sense of peace filled her.

There was nothing to be afraid of when God was in control. Nothing to worry about. She just needed to cling to her faith, trust that God would work things out according to His will and His way. Everything else would fall into place.

She stepped out of the car and started toward the building, aware of the emptiness of the parking lot and the porch. Obviously, the cold weather was keeping everyone inside. Hopefully it was keeping her stalker inside, too. The thought of him watching as she made her way up the wide steps to the front door made her shiver from something other than freezing temperatures.

"Honor! Wait!" The masculine voice calling from somewhere behind Honor sent her heart tripping. She lunged for the door, pushing it open and racing into the lobby, visions of a masked pursuer filling her mind.

Safe inside, Honor nearly sagged with relief, her heart slowly settling into a normal rhythm. She was halfway across the wide lobby when the door swung open, the sound sending her pulse racing again. She whirled around, expecting to see a stranger highlighted in the afternoon light. Instead, she saw Will walking toward her, his deeply tanned face set in a scowl. "Hey, didn't you hear me calling you?"

"Sorry, it was so cold outside, I couldn't wait to get in where it was warmer."

"Yeah?" His dark gaze raked her from head to toe. "Because the way you were running, anyone would have thought Jack the Ripper was after you."

Jack the Ripper?

Not a good image.

Honor tried to relax and smile. Act like she hadn't been scared out of her wits over nothing. "If Jack the Ripper had been after me, I wouldn't have just been running. I would have been screaming."

"And risk waking Mr. Erickson? I think I'd rather face the Ripper." Will smiled, the irritation in his face easing as they moved toward the nurse's station together.

"True. Mr. Erickson can be a challenge, can't he?"

"A challenge? I got called in this morning because he insisted I stole five dollars in quarters off his dresser."

"You're kidding." No wonder Will looked on edge.

"Do I look like I'm kidding? The old guy asked me to put the change in a sock in the bottom drawer of his dresser. Said he wanted to make sure no stinking thief got his hands on it. Next thing I know, I'm being accused of being a stinking thief." Will nearly spit the words.

"I'm so sorry."

"Yeah. Me, too. Fortunately, this isn't the first time Erickson has pulled something like this. He accused an orderly of stealing his iPod last month. We found that under Erickson's mattress. Once I showed Janice where the quarters were, the matter was dropped."

"It sounds like Mr. Erickson is in desperate need of attention."

"You're probably right about that. I just wish he'd go about getting it in a different way." Will smiled, his gaze searching Honor's. "How about you? Did you have a relaxing weekend?"

"As relaxing as any weekend can be when you've got a four-year-old in the house." That was as much as she planned to say on the matter. Her problems weren't something she wanted her co-workers to know about. Not yet, anyway.

"So, nothing exciting happened? No hot dates or secret assignations?"

Surprised, Honor took a harder look at Will. Was he asking for a reason other than simple curiosity? Did he know what had happened? Had he somehow heard about the package Honor had received? Or did he know because he'd been the one to deliver it? "No. Why do you ask?"

"Because I'd like to believe you have a more exciting life than I do." Will grinned, flashing straight white teeth.

He was young, brash and too handsome for his own good, but that didn't make him a stalker. Honor really did need to gain control of her imagination. "I'm sorry to tell you, I don't."

"Yeah, well, both of our lives are about to get a little more boring. These meetings tend to drag on. Lots of talk. Little change."

"It can't drag on too long. Our shifts begin in two hours."

"Two hours can feel like an eternity when Janice is talking." Will winked and pushed open the door to the conference room, gesturing for Honor to step in ahead of him.

She did, walking into warmth and soft conversation. The sharp scent of coffee and the sweeter aroma of doughnuts. The easy rhythm of men and women who worked together.

Honor took a seat next a gray-haired RN she'd never met before and introduced herself, relaxing for the first time in what seemed like days. Here, in a room filled with people, she felt safe. Any length of boredom would be worth it for that.

* * *

Honor's shift proved to be busy enough to keep her mind off her troubles. Several patients were sick with a flu that seemed to be running rampant through the facility. Another had difficulty breathing and had to be taken by ambulance to a local hospital. Between administering medicine, lending an ear to some of the lonelier residents and making her rounds, she had little time to worry about who might be waiting for her when she left the safety of Lakeview Haven.

By the time she punched out, her back ached and her head throbbed, but at least she wasn't as scared as she'd been when she left home. She waited until Will came to the nurse's station, unwilling to walk out to her car by herself.

"Waiting for me?" He grinned, his boyish charm meant to melt hearts, but doing nothing for Honor. She preferred a little more maturity, a little more experience.

A picture of Grayson Sinclair flashed through her mind, and she shoved it away.

What she preferred was going it alone.

And if she told herself that enough she just might believe it.

"I'm waiting for someone to walk out with."

"Ah, so it's not me specifically you were waiting for. Too bad." His smile faded, but he seemed happy enough to walk to the lobby with her.

"Actually, I *was* waiting specifically for you. We *are* the only two nurses working this shift, after all."

Will laughed and pushed open the door. "That makes me feel so much better."

"What would make *me* feel better is a little warmth." Honor shoved her hands into her coat pockets, wishing she'd brought her gloves to work. Wishing even more that she didn't have to drive home and get out of her car with the night hiding anyone who might be watching.

"We've got a few more months before that happens. Of course, I can think of plenty of other ways to warm up, if you're interested."

"You never give up, do you?" Honor would have laughed if she weren't so anxious to get in her car, get back to her house and hide inside again. She felt exposed, vulnerable and very aware of how easy it would be for someone to watch undetected.

It had been done before.

It was possible it was being done that very moment.

She shuddered at the thought, hurrying down the stairs next to Will. "I guess I'll see you tomorrow."

"See you then." Will continued through the parking lot while Honor half jogged to her own car. Fear made her pulse race and her hands tremble as she shoved the key into the lock. She really needed to get herself under control. Getting panicky wasn't going to keep her safe.

Headlights flashed as Honor opened her car door, and she looked up at the vehicle driving toward her. Not Will's car. He drove a Jeep. Someone else. Heading right toward her and flashing his high beams.

Honor yanked open her car door, her heart slamming against her ribs as she slid into the driver's seat. Her cell phone was in her pocket, and she pulled it out, her hand shaking so badly that she nearly dropped it on the floor. She needed to call the police. Though what good calling for help would do if the person in the car was carrying a gun, Honor didn't know.

The car pulled into the space beside hers, and Honor tensed, her fingers poised and ready to dial. As she watched, the interior light turned on, revealing sandy hair, strong features, eyes she knew were the same vivid blue as the flowers that bloomed in her mother's garden. Grayson.

She unrolled her window, relieved and frustrated at the same time. He'd scared five years off her life. "And just what are you doing out at this time of night, Grayson Sinclair? Besides scaring me to death, that is."

"Same thing as you. I just got finished working."

"Maybe so, but you weren't working here, so how did you end up in Lakeview Haven's parking lot?"

"It was on my way home from Lynchburg." The yellow interior light cast shadows beneath his eyes and added hollows under his cheeks. He looked hard and tough, and so appealing Honor almost had to look away.

"It was on your way home, so you thought you'd stop by? And you just happened to arrive as I was getting done?"

"The timing wasn't quite that perfect." He grinned, and Honor's heart jumped in response.

"No? Exactly how long have you been waiting?"

"One hour and fifteen minutes."

"Are you crazy?"

"That's up for debate."

"Really, Grayson, you should be home sleeping. Why wait out in a cold parking lot?"

"Why do you think? I wanted to make sure you got home in one piece."

"Grayson—"

"Look, I'm here. You're here. We're both heading home. Let's save the discussion of the reasons I shouldn't have done this for a time when we're not so tired." There was a weary edge to Grayson's voice that made Honor want to ask questions. Questions about his life, his work, his brother. Questions that shouldn't be asked by someone who wasn't interested.

And she wasn't interested.

No matter how much her heart might be saying otherwise.

"I guess I *am* tired. Let's go." She rolled her window up and pulled out of the parking lot, the headlights from Grayson's car reminding her of just how nice it was to not have to go it alone. Of just how comforting it was to have someone in her corner.

She closed her mind to the thought.

God was in her corner. She didn't need any more than that.

But maybe she wanted more.

Maybe she wanted to know what it would be like to let a man like Grayson into her life.

And maybe she was too tired and too scared to think straight.

Determined to change the direction of her thoughts, she turned on the radio, letting the soft classical music fill her mind and chase away the longings she didn't want to feel, but did.

THIRTEEN

Grayson's day hadn't gone well. Aside from the normal hectic pace of work and the hassle of trying to get several crews to work simultaneously on his parent's rental, he'd received a call from his father. Jude's condition had worsened, his weakened body attacked by a bacterial infection. According to his attending physician, the infection had been caught early and was under control, but Grayson still felt uneasy. He was worried about his brother, frustrated to be so far from him. He had wanted to take the next flight up to New York, but Jude had called before Grayson could buy the ticket and insisted that he didn't need another person hovering over his hospital bed.

Grayson knew his brother well enough to believe him. Jude had always been independent to a fault. Going his own way, forging his own path, determined to make decisions apart from the family. There was nothing wrong with that, but it had led him farther away from home than the rest of the Sinclair siblings. If Jude said he wanted Grayson to stay away, there was no doubt that he meant it.

Of course, there were other reasons Grayson hadn't flown to New York. Three of them. Honor, Lily and Candace Malone. As long as Jude was holding his own and insisting he didn't need his brother at his bedside, Grayson would keep doing what he had been doing—keeping his eyes on the Malone women.

He rubbed the back of his neck, trying to ease the tension there as he followed Honor home. He hadn't meant to stop by Lakeview Haven, but he'd seen the sign for it on his way back from Lynchburg and had found himself traveling down the back road that led there. Compelled. Intent. Determined to help.

The night was silvery gray and silent, the moon pale gold as Grayson pulled into Honor's driveway and got out of his car. Honor's house was dark but for the light that illuminated the porch and cast shadows across the yard. Grayson surveyed the area as he approached her car, looking for signs that they weren't alone, that someone was watching from the darkness. There didn't seem to be anyone, but someone could be hiding out of sight, snapping pictures, getting ready to send another "gift" to the object of his affection.

The thought filled Grayson with rage, but he forced it down as Honor's car door opened. She had enough on her plate. The last thing she needed was to deal with his emotions.

He offered her a hand out of the car, and she hesitated before accepting, as if she were afraid letting him help would give Grayson an inroad into her life.

He didn't bother telling her that it was too late. That he was already too deep in to ever back out. She didn't need to deal with that, either. Eventually, there would be time for a discussion about their relationship, but that time wasn't now.

His hand tightened around hers as he pulled her from the car, and she smiled into his eyes. "Thanks."

"For what?"

"For following me home, though you really didn't have to."

"Sure, I did. Otherwise, I would have been lying in bed wondering if you'd made it into your house safely. Eventually, I would have given in and called to check on you. This saved us both some time."

"Well, now you know I'm home. Safe and sound. You can go back to your place and sleep peacefully. Good night, Grayson." Honor smiled at him, gently pulling her hand from his grip, her dismissal hinting that he was welcome to leave before she was inside.

"Not until I walk you to your door and make sure you're locked in tight."

"So, you really are a true gentleman?" There was laughter in Honor's eyes, and Grayson wondered what it would be like to know her under different circumstances. Wondered how she'd be acting, what she'd be saying if she hadn't been hurt before.

"I like to think so."

"Ah, but what *you* think in that regard doesn't matter. What matters is what others think."

"Then I guess I should be asking you."

"Whether or not you're a true gentleman? Right now it seems you might be." She smiled again as they moved up the porch stairs. "But it takes time to know the truth about someone."

"Then I guess we need to spend more time together so you can figure it out."

"I'm sure my opinion about you doesn't matter so much that I need to spend time figuring anything out. Or that you need to spend time worrying about what it is." She put her hand on the doorknob, and Grayson expected her to go inside. Instead she turned to him, her eyes scanning his face, her brow furrowing. "I've been thinking about you today."

"Have you? Then maybe there's hope for us after all."

"Actually, my thoughts were centered more around your brother. How is he doing?"

Her question sobered Grayson, and he shook his head. "Not as good as I'd like. He's got a bacterial infection. The doctor is treating it aggressively, but Jude is pretty weak. It's hard to know what's going to happen."

"I'm sorry. I know how frustrating it can be when someone you love is sick." She touched his hand, her fingers lingering for a moment on his knuckles, their warmth searing into his skin, comforting him.

Grayson's pulse raced in acknowledgment. "What's more frustrating is that he doesn't want me up there with him."

"He's alone?"

"My parents are there. My sister and her husband are, too. And my brother and his wife. I've got another brother in Egypt who calls the hospital every day."

"No wonder he doesn't want you up there. He's being smothered by well-meaning loved ones." She leaned against the door, her dark hair falling over her shoulders, her eyes filled with compassion.

"I'm sure that's the way Jude sees it, but it's not the way we do."

"Of course not. You love him. You're not thinking how frustrating it is for your brother to have his independence taken away, or how demeaning it is for him to have his dignity lost to hospital gowns and catheters. And you're certainly not thinking about how hard it is for your brother to let all the people he loves see him weak and diminished."

"He's not diminished."

"Not in your eyes, but he is in his."

She was right, of course. Jude *would* feel diminished by his injuries. The hallmark of his personality was his independent spirit. "The fact that you're right doesn't make me feel better about being hundreds of miles away from him."

"I understand. I've spent a lot of time working with people who are going through similar things. Physical trauma doesn't only affect the person who's been hurt. The entire family suffers." She shivered and rubbed her arms. "It's cold and it's late. I'd better go in."

"Too bad. Talking to you is the best thing that has happened to me today."

She smiled and shook her head. "You really need to work on some better lines, Grayson."

"Who said it was a line?"

"I can't believe it's the truth. A man like you must have plenty of wonderful things happen every day."

"A man like me? What kind of man would that be?"

"Successful. Charming. Handsome."

"Somehow, coming from you, those don't seem like compliments."

"What else would they be?"

"Accusations."

"Why would they be that?"

"Because you've made it clear that charm and flattery go hand in hand and that neither are qualities worth admiring."

"What I admire or don't doesn't matter. You can't help what you are anymore than I can help what I am." She unlocked the front door. "Besides, I can think of much worse things to be than successful, charming and handsome."

"And much better ones?"

"I don't know about that. I suppose what someone finds admirable depends on what she's looking for." She stepped into the house, but Grayson put a hand on her arm before she could close the door.

"What is it *you're* looking for, Honor?"

"Nothing. Everything I need, I have. Now, I really do need to go. Lily gets up early, and I need to get some sleep before I begin another day."

"Good night, then."

"Good night to you, too, Grayson. And thanks again for escorting me home."

"Even though you really didn't need me to?"

"Maybe I did need you to, and I just didn't want to admit it." She started to close the door, but froze as the sound of a car engine filled the night.

Three houses up, headlights flared and a car pulled slowly into the street, easing toward Honor and Grayson with a deliberateness that made Grayson's muscles tighten. "Shut the door and call Jake."

"But—"

"Shut the door." He growled the words as he jogged down the porch stairs. The driver of the other vehicle paused in front of Honor's place, flaunting his presence with the kind of casual arrogance that was often the downfall of stalkers. Darkness hid the driver from view, but Grayson had every intention of putting a face and a name to the person behind the wheel.

He got in his car and started the engine, scowling and unrolling the window as Honor knocked on the passenger-side door. "Get inside the house."

"This isn't your battle to fight, Grayson. And I'd never forgive myself if something happened to you while you were chasing after that lunatic."

"Would you forgive yourself if Lily or Candace were hurt because of him?"

She blanched, but didn't step away from the car. "I won't let that happen."

"How will you stop it?"

"By coming with you to make sure you find him." She pulled the door open, slid into the seat.

Arguing would waste time they didn't have, so Grayson threw the sedan into Reverse and backed out onto the street.

The car they were following accelerated, taking a left turn and disappearing from view. If Grayson didn't hurry, he'd lose the guy. He stepped on the accelerator, adrenaline racing through his veins as he tried to close the gap between his car and the one he was following. For the first time since trading in the Jaguar, he missed it.

"Use my cell phone and call nine-one-one. Maybe the sheriff's department can cut this guy off before he gets to the highway. Tell them he's heading toward the Blue Ridge Parkway in a black sports car. No license plate."

Honor's fingers slipped as she tried to call the sheriff, her racing pulse and shaking muscles doing little to help the situation. She knew she sounded frantic as she relayed information to the 911 operator, but she didn't care. She should have listened to Grayson and gone back inside the house. Traveling at an excess of ninety miles an hour wasn't her idea of fun. Nor did she much like the idea of coming face-to-face with the man who was stalking her.

Up ahead, the car rounded a curve in the road,

disappearing from view. Grayson followed, taking the curve a little too quickly. Honor expected to see taillights again, but the road was empty. "Where did he go?"

"He may have turned off his lights and gotten off the road. Or he might have pulled over to the side of the road to wait for us. We're outside of town in a rural area. In his mind, this might be a great place for a confrontation."

"Confrontation? I'm not sure I like that idea." As a matter of fact, she was confident she didn't.

"I do. I'm looking forward to having a little chat with the guy."

"Shouldn't you leave that to the police?"

"Only if they get to him before I do." Grayson's smile was hard and feral, and for the first time since she'd met him, Honor saw the iron will beneath the charm. The power. The ruthlessness. The determination.

He wouldn't give up on a goal. Wouldn't back away from a fight. He was the kind of man who could be a great friend or a bitter adversary. The kind of man Honor wouldn't ever want to cross. The kind she just might want to have on her side.

She shook her head, refusing to acknowledge the thought. Grayson was trouble. In more ways than one. As long as she kept that in mind, she'd be fine. "Maybe we should go home and let the police handle things."

"If we have a chance to stop this guy, we've got to take it. Men like him are unpredictable. First he sends anonymous gifts and now he's following you around. What will he be doing in a week? A month?"

"Sheriff Reed will find him before then." She hoped. She prayed.

"I've worked too many cases where that hasn't happened." Grayson eased up on the accelerator, and the speedometer dropped from ninety to forty-five. "If our guy was waiting for us, we'd have seen him by now. He must have turned off. Let's backtrack. There's got to be a side road or driveway here somewhere."

"Grayson—"

"We're doing what we have to do to keep you and your family safe, Honor. There is no other option. You know that, don't you?" He met her eyes briefly before he turned his attention back to the road, and Honor saw the truth in his gaze. His need to protect, his concern. His integrity and honor. So many things she'd thought were impossibilities. There for the taking. If only she could believe they were real.

Her hands tightened into fists, her heart racing in her chest. Fear did funny things to people. It made them imagine things that weren't there. That's obviously what was making her see all the things she'd longed for written boldly in Grayson's eyes.

She continued to tell herself that as Grayson backtracked along the country road, found an old gravel driveway and turned onto it.

FOURTEEN

The gravel drive meandered through thick trees and ended abruptly at an overgrown clearing, a decrepit house standing forlorn and abandoned in its center. A sporty black car sat in front of it, shiny and out of place in the neglected clearing.

"Is that the car?" Honor whispered. Though why she felt the need to keep her voice down she didn't know. If the driver was still in the car, he'd seen them coming and knew they were there. Talking quietly wouldn't change that.

"Yeah. That's it, but it doesn't look like the driver is still in it."

"What do we do now?"

"We call for backup." He took the cell phone she was still clutching in her hand and dialed, speaking rapidly to the person who answered. Giving their location. Their situation. A description of the car.

And all the while, the clearing remained lifeless and black, the stalker's car a glaring reminder that a criminal lurked somewhere in the darkness.

By the time Grayson hung up the phone, Honor's nerves were taut, her stomach tight with fear. She definitely should have done what he'd asked and gone back inside her house, locked herself inside and let other people deal with her troubles.

Should have.

Hadn't.

Now she was regretting it in a big way and praying that she'd get home to Lily and Candace in one piece.

"It's going to be okay. We're safe enough here." Grayson spoke quietly, his tone soothing.

"How can you say that? We're sitting in a car a hundred yards away from a lunatic's vehicle."

"He's not in it."

"That just makes it worse. He could be anywhere."

"He's as far away as his legs have been able to carry him."

"You don't know that." She crossed her arms over her chest, feeling vulnerable and scared in a way she hadn't since the days following Jay's death when she'd realized just how deep in debt he'd left her, and just how much her life was going to change.

"Sure I do. The guy is a coward. He skulks around in the dark shooting pictures of someone who doesn't know he's watching. Then he runs and hides. There's no way he's going to come out from wherever he's gone."

"He was brazen enough to drive by us while we were talking."

"Because he knew we couldn't see him. Men like

him have agendas. They have plans. They don't veer from them. This guy has already chosen a time and day to meet you face-to-face. He's not going to want me around when that happens."

"That doesn't make me feel better."

"I didn't mean it to." Grayson shifted in his seat so that he was facing Honor, his eyes gleaming in the darkness, his face sharp angles and hard planes. "I've prosecuted men like this before, Honor. I know how they think. I know how they act. And I'll do anything I can to make you view the danger you're in as real."

"I do view it as real." More real by the minute.

"You don't. If you did, you'd have done exactly what I said and gone inside your house, locked the door and called the police."

"I couldn't let you come out here by yourself."

"You *should* have let me come out here by my-self."

"I've told you before, Grayson. My problems aren't yours."

"And I've told you that I don't make promises I can't keep."

"Look—"

Grayson pressed a finger against her lips, sealing in her protest. "I hear sirens. Jake and his crew must be close."

"Do you always have to have the last word on a matter, Grayson Sinclair?" She huffed the words, her frustration with the man beside her spilling into her tone.

"Only when it serves a purpose."

"And exactly what purpose did it serve this time, I'd like to know?"

"You're not scared anymore, are you?" He got out of the car and closed the door before the words registered.

When they did, Honor wasn't sure if she should be angry or amused.

Or both.

She followed Grayson out of the car, relieved to see several police cruisers speeding into the clearing. Within seconds the once-dark yard was lit by spotlights, and uniformed officers were surrounding the stalker's car.

Not sure if she should get back in the car or stay put, Honor glanced around, searching for Grayson.

"Where's Gray?" Sheriff Reed strode toward her, his gaze probing the shadows at the far edge of the clearing before meeting Honor's.

"I don't know. He was here a second ago."

"Hopefully, he didn't go chasing after our perp alone."

"I don't think Grayson would do something like that." At least she hoped he wouldn't.

"He followed the guy here, didn't he?"

"Yes, but we waited in the car until we heard your sirens."

"*He* waited until he knew you'd be in good hands before he took off searching." The sheriff scowled, and Honor's stomach twisted with anxiety. Obviously, that was exactly what Grayson had done—

waited until help arrived and then gone looking for the confrontation he'd talked about earlier.

"He's only been gone for a couple of minutes."

"Then maybe I can catch up to him. Get in the car and stay in the car until one of us comes back for you. Okay?"

She didn't think she had a choice, so Honor nodded and did as the sheriff asked.

Minutes ticked by as the activity in the clearing intensified. More police cars arrived. More people. More lights. The house lit up room by room, flashlights illuminating the dark interior. A van pulled up behind the car and a team of people began searching the sports car. From what Honor could see, they didn't find much.

A half hour passed. Then another.

Where were Grayson and Sheriff Reed? What was taking them so long? Had they found a trail to follow? Some sign that indicated which way the stalker had run? Or had something happened? A run-in they hadn't been expecting? An ambush? Were they hurt? Did they need help?

The questions circled around in her mind until she wanted to scream with frustration. She was too used to doing things on her own. She wanted to be outside the car, in the thick of things.

And she wanted to be home.

Safe.

Checking on Lily and Candace. Going on with her life the way it had been for so many years.

But she didn't think that would happen.

She didn't think things would ever be the same again. The tide had turned and she'd been turned with it. Struggle as she might, she'd never be able to free herself from its grip.

She shuddered at the thought, pulling her coat tighter and hugging her arms against her chest.

Where *were* they?

As if her question had conjured him, Grayson pulled open the driver's side door and got in the car, his expression dark and unreadable.

Relieved, Honor grabbed his arm, wanting to hold on tight so that he wouldn't leave again. "Thank goodness you're back. I was beginning to think something terrible had happened."

"Nothing terrible. Nothing good. Nothing, period." Grayson ground the words out, and then sighed, running a hand down his face. "Sorry. It's not your fault we came up empty."

"No apology needed. I'm just happy you're okay."

"Yeah?" He squeezed her hand and offered a smile that didn't reach his eyes. "I won't be happy until we find our guy."

"There was no sign of him?"

"I found some tracks and followed them to Summer Creek Road. It's a mile through the trees. After that, nothing. No tracks. No clue as to which direction he went."

"Could he have gotten a ride?"

"Anything is possible. Jake is going to call in a search team. They'll bring in their dogs, try to get a scent from the car and then see if they can catch his trail."

"And the car?"

"The state sent in their CSI unit. They've recovered a camera, but that's it. No papers. No old cups. Not even a fingerprint. The car is clean as a whistle and looks brand new."

"So we're at a dead end?"

"I'd say it's too soon to tell. I'd also say it's past time to get you home." He shoved the keys into the ignition and started the car.

"Should we tell the sheriff we're leaving?" Honor glanced out the window, searching for Sheriff Reed and finding him easily enough. He was standing near the crime scene van, talking to a tall, rail-thin woman.

"He already knows. He followed me to Summer Creek and read me the riot act for going it alone."

"And well he should have. You're a lawyer. Not a police officer."

"I'm a man before I'm a lawyer, and when a person I care about is in trouble, I don't wait around for someone to help me solve the problem." Grayson's sharp retort surprised Honor, and she put a hand on his arm, feeling the tension through his wool coat and wishing she could do something to ease it.

"I know. I didn't mean to imply otherwise."

"You didn't. I'm just frustrated that this guy slipped through my fingers. I can't believe I let him escape."

"You didn't let him do anything. I did. If I hadn't

insisted on coming along, you would have gone after him sooner and found him."

"So, I can blame it on you, huh?" He glanced at Honor, and she saw the darkness in his eyes, the fury he was hiding beneath his smile. Despite his statement, she knew where his anger was directed—not at her for insisting she be included in the hunt, but at himself. He'd wanted to rescue Honor and her family, and he blamed himself for not being able to.

Something inside Honor shifted as she read the truth in his eyes. Some icy part that had grown around her heart in the years after she'd married Jay, when she'd realized that the one person she most wanted to trust couldn't be depended on.

She took a deep, steadying breath, refusing to believe what she knew was true—that Grayson was the kind of man she could trust. "I guess you can blame me, since I'm the one who slowed you down."

"I can't blame you for what you didn't intend." Grayson pulled up in front of Honor's house and turned off the car. "Besides, Jake was right. Rushing blind after someone who could have been carrying a weapon wasn't the smartest thing I've ever done."

"And insisting I come with you wasn't the smartest thing *I've* ever done."

"It seems neither of us are at our brightest tonight." Grayson's fingers brushed Honor's arm, coming to rest on her shoulder. His hand smelled of spicy cologne and cold winter nights, the scent masculine and compelling.

"Fatigue does funny things to people. Stealing

their reasoning skills is just one of them." Honor knew she should get out of the car, go in the house and put the night behind her. Grayson's touch was light enough that she could move away, yet so comforting that she didn't want to.

"And can it make them imagine things?" He stared into her face, his expression unreadable, his eyes dark and somber.

"Like what?" She took a deep breath, trying to clear her thoughts and only succeeding in inhaling more of Grayson's scent. Her pulse throbbed in response, her skin heating.

"Like how soft your skin would be if I touched it?" His fingers skimmed down her cheek. "Because I've been imagining it all the way home. And you know, my imaginings didn't even come close to the reality of it. Your skin is soft as silk and warm as morning light."

"Grayson..." Her voice trailed off as his hand slipped beneath the hair at the nape of her neck, his fingers kneading the tender flesh there.

"Like you said, Honor, fatigue can do funny things to people. Maybe that's what's going on here. Or maybe something else is. And maybe that something needs to be explored." His lips barely grazed hers, and Honor's heart jumped, her pulse racing in acknowledgment. She'd forgotten the feel of a man's touch. The firmness of a man's lips pressed against hers. She'd forgotten how rational thoughts could fly away. How easily her defenses could be breached.

She backed away from Grayson, fumbling for

the door handle. "I need to get inside. Good night, Grayson."

She hopped out of the car, racing up the porch stairs and into the house, running from things she didn't want to feel, from disappointments she didn't want to remember and from the man who seemed intent on dragging her back into the kind of relationship that could only lead to a broken heart.

FIFTEEN

The sun rose in fits and starts, first hidden by clouds, then revealed in golden beauty only to be hidden again. It reminded Honor of her life. The good and bad of it. The difficulties that were always followed by something wonderful. She stood on the back stoop, sipping a steaming cup of coffee and staring over the backyard, letting the cold autumn air swirl around her and watching as the sunlight peeked from the clouds and retreated again. Gold. Pink. Gray. Blue. There was no better place to be at dawn than outside. The silence, the peace, always made Honor feel closer to her Creator.

And right now, she desperately needed to feel that He was near.

She'd slept poorly again. Thoughts of the stalker had made it difficult to close her eyes. Thoughts of Grayson had made it difficult to keep them closed. She'd come to Lakeview with hopes of the kind of life she'd been dreaming of for years. What she'd gotten was something else entirely.

But maybe that was the point. Maybe her plan hadn't been God's. Maybe this was His way of showing her that. She could move back to St. Louis. There were plenty of nursing jobs there.

"But I don't want to, Lord. This place feels like home, and it's been a long time since anything has felt that way."

"Mommy?" Lily peered out from the open back door, her cheeks still flushed from sleep, her dark ringlets bouncing around her cheeks.

"What are you doing awake, my sweet?"

"Looking for you. I needed to tell you something."

"Something good?" Honor walked the few steps back to the house and shrugged out of her coat, letting it drop around her daughter's shoulders.

"No. Something scary." Lily's eyes filled with tears, and Honor pulled her into her arms.

"What is it, Lily Mae?" Fear made Honor's heart slam against her ribs and her arms tighten around her daughter.

"I saw the dragon last night."

Honor almost sagged with relief at the words. "Did you?"

"Yes. He was looking in the window while I was sleeping."

"If you were sleeping, how do you know he was looking in the window?"

"Maybe I wasn't sleeping. Maybe I was looking out the window."

"And why would you be doing that?"

"I wanted to see if Mr. Prince was home."

"You mean Mr. Sinclair."

Lily nodded, her blue gaze darting to Grayson's house.

"And this was after Candace put you in bed?"

"Yes."

"Lily, you know the rule. No getting out of bed after you've been put in it."

"I know, Mommy." She paused, placing her hand against Honor's cheek, her palm small and warm and too sweet for words. "But I was missing you, and I just wanted to see if Mr. Sinclair was home because that would make me less lonely."

"Candace was home with you. There was no need to be lonely."

"But Candace can't fight dragons." Lily said it as if it made perfect sense. To her it probably did.

"So you looked out the window and saw a dragon. Where was it? Near the swing set?"

"No. He was right there. Right near the window." Lily pointed toward the window, and a chill raced up Honor's spine. Had the stalker been outside her window again?

"What did he look like?"

"Black. And he breathed red fire."

"Fire?"

"Yes. Right at me."

"Oh my. That does sound scary." The more she heard, the less Honor believed that her daughter had actually seen something, but she set Lily down in the mudroom and retrieved her coat anyway. "Tell you what. You go get a juice box from the fridge while I go look for dragon prints."

"I want to come with you." Lily grabbed the hem of Honor's coat and seemed determined to hold on. Usually, Honor would have ignored her daughter's antics, but there was a frantic quality to them today that she couldn't disregard.

"All right. Put your coat and boots on and we'll go out together." She waited while Lily tugged on the fluffy pink coat she loved so much and shoved her sockless feet into snow boots. Her pink flannel nightgown fell to the floor, and Honor decided it would keep her warm enough for the few minutes it would take to check for footprints beneath the window. "Ready?"

"Yes."

"So, let's go exploring."

Clouds were covering the sun again as Honor led her daughter to the area beneath the window, the gray morning chill suddenly seeming more sinister than peaceful. Beneath the window, dry grass and weeds were matted down, but the entire yard was like that and Honor found nothing alarming at the sight. Frozen earth revealed no sign that someone had stood there, but Honor leaned close anyway, searching for some sign that what Lily had seen was more than imagination.

"Do you see any, Mommy? Do you see dragon prints?" Lily's whispered question was loud enough to send a squirrel racing up a tree, and despite her worry, Honor smiled.

"All I see is brown grass and weeds and dirt."

"That's because dragons fly. Maybe the dragon last night was flying. Maybe he didn't put his feet on the ground."

"Lily, I don't think you saw a dragon last night. At least not one that was breathing fire and flying."

"I did see him, Mommy. I really did."

Honor bit back a sigh of frustration. Whatever Lily had or hadn't seen, there had not been a dragon in the yard. "Maybe you saw something else."

"I saw a dragon. So tonight I want you to stay home. Okay? That way you can call Mr. Sinclair to come slay it if it comes back."

"You know I can't stay home tonight. People at work depend on me to be there."

"I depend on you, too, Mommy." Lily stared up into her eyes, her heart-shaped face and chubby cheeks making her look like a dark-haired cherub. Innocent. Sweet.

A child who needed her mother more than she needed anything else.

Honor rubbed the back of her neck, trying to ease the tension there. It was hard enough to leave her daughter every night. Having Lily beg her to stay just made it that much more difficult.

"Come here and sit on the swing with me." She lifted her daughter, ignoring the pain that speared through her lower back from too much time on her feet and too much tension.

She eased down onto one of the old swings, wincing a little as her muscles protested. Lily snuggled close, her head under Honor's chin, her arms wrapped around her neck. It wouldn't be long before Lily was too big to be held like this. A few years. A few inches. A few pounds. The little girl would be big. She wouldn't need Honor as much. And just like Candace, she'd begin to grow away. When that happened, Honor would be truly alone.

That was the way life was, and Honor knew it shouldn't hurt so much to think about. She pressed a kiss onto Lily's head, breathing in baby shampoo and innocence. "Did I ever tell you that when I was a little girl, I thought a troll lived under my bed?"

Lily shook her head, but seemed content not to speak. It was possible her fears had made her night as rocky as Honor's.

"Well, I really thought one did. Every night I'd climb into bed and hide my head under the covers because I was so afraid that the troll would come out. One day, I told Grandmom about the troll, and do you know what she said?"

"What?"

"She said there were no such things as trolls, but if there were, God's love was so big that when it was in a room, it chased everything else away. She said that since God loved me and was always with me, I never had to worry about trolls or anything else hiding in my room."

"But the dragon wasn't in my room. It was outside."

"There was no dragon outside, Lily. But sometimes there are scary things in the world. And you know what? God's love is so big that it can chase all those things away. Which does *not* mean that you should wander outside alone like you did the other day." She tickled Lily's belly, smiling as her daughter giggled.

When her giggles died away, Lily shifted in Honor's lap and stared into her eyes. "But God's love can't chase you away. Right, Mommy?"

"God's love only chases bad things away. When something is good, His love adds to it. And my love for you is very, very good. His love only makes mine stronger."

"And Candace's?"

"Of course."

"And Mr. Sinclair's?"

"Well, he doesn't know you very well yet, but if he did, I'm sure he'd love you, too."

"Of course I would. Lily is a very lovable little girl."

At the sound of Grayson's voice, Honor's heart skipped a beat. She whirled toward him, releasing her hold on Lily who was frantically trying to escape. Grayson stood a few feet away, near the shrubs that separated their property. Dressed in dark slacks, a white button-down shirt, a tie and a sports coat, he was immaculate, masculine and ready to face whatever the day brought.

Honor resisted the urge to smooth her flyaway hair or pull her coat tighter over her old cable-knit sweater and soft, faded jeans. "Grayson, I didn't hear you coming."

"Yeah. We'll have to talk about that another time." He met her eyes, and she knew what he was thinking—that she'd been foolish to come outside alone when a stalker was on the loose. She didn't agree. She'd been safe enough.

Until now.

Grayson's eyes narrowed as if he knew what she was thinking, and then he smiled. Full-out and charming, his teeth gleaming white, before turning his attention to Lily who was staring up at him as if Prince Charming had walked out of one of her fairy-tale books.

"Mr. Sinclair! Guess what?"

"What?"

"I saw a dragon last night. And he breathed fire and everything." Lily told her story in a voice loud enough to scare birds from the trees, but Grayson didn't seem to mind. He waited until she finished, then crouched in front of her and took both her hands in his. "I have a friend who might want to hear your story. Will you share it with him if your mom says it's okay?"

"Is he a prince?"

"No, but he loves stories."

"Okay." Lily bounced away, twirling in the gray morning light, her coat the only bright spot in the dreary yard.

"She's a cute little girl." Grayson lowered himself onto the swing next to Honor's.

"With a wild imagination."

"It may not have been her imagination."

"I know." Honor's throat tightened around the words, the fear she'd been trying to hold at bay rearing up and pulling her in.

"I want to bring Jake out here later. Let him listen to Lily's story. He's got a little girl. He might get kid-speak better than I do."

"All right."

"And I want you to stay in the house unless someone is with you." He glanced at Lily who was hopping up and down the back stairs. "And I don't mean a four-year-old."

"You're not going to tell me I shouldn't have come out here this morning, are you?"

"What good would that do? You're already out here. Besides—" he leaned over and brushed hair from Honor's eyes, his gaze pulling her in, making her forget for a moment just how dangerous he was "—when I saw you and Lily out here it gave me an excuse."

"For what?" She asked even though she knew his answer was one she didn't want to hear.

"To see you again." The words hung in the air between them. Huge. Impossible to ignore.

But Honor *would* ignore them, because if she didn't, she'd have to admit that she'd been just as interested in seeing Grayson again. "And do you often go see neighbors at seven in the morning?"

"Only when they're already out in their yards. Though, I've got to say, it's a little cold out for visiting this morning."

Don't invite him in for coffee.

Do. Not. Invite. Him in.

Even as her mind shouted the words, Honor's mouth was opening and she found herself saying, "I've got a pot of coffee on. Would you like a cup?"

Grayson glanced at his watch and frowned. "I'd love to, but I've got a meeting at nine. I've got to grab some breakfast and get over to my parents' rental before then."

"I've got biscuits ready for the oven, and I'm making omelets. Why don't you join us for breakfast?"

What?

Had she lost her mind? Not only had she invited him for coffee, but now she was offering breakfast.

He wouldn't accept, of course. He'd already said he was busy. He'd head back to his house and Honor would go inside with Lily, and she'd never, ever do something so foolish again.

"Biscuits and an omelet sound great. I haven't had a home-cooked meal in weeks, but I don't want to impose."

"Pardon me?" Honor pulled her thoughts back to the conversation, not sure how the morning had gotten so completely out of her control. All she'd wanted was a few minutes of peace as the sun rose. What she was getting was trouble with a capital *T*.

"I said that I'd love to accept your offer, but I don't want to impose."

"If it was an imposition, I wouldn't have offered." She blurted out the words, knowing she sounded ungracious.

Grayson didn't seem to care. He stood, his light

brown hair falling over his forehead, his eyes such a clear blue that it almost hurt to look in them. Clean-shaven, dressed for his meeting, he looked like exactly what he was—a successful, confident man. A man most women would be happy to invite for a meal.

Honor wasn't as enthusiastic, and it wasn't because she didn't see all the qualities in Grayson that other women would. It was because she *did* see them, and the more she saw, the deeper she fell. Soon, she'd be so deep that there'd be no climbing out.

"Then I guess I'll accept and not feel bad about it." He offered a hand, and Honor accepted, allowing him to tug her to her feet. She expected him to release his hold, but he just shifted his grip, linking fingers with hers as they walked to the back door.

She knew she should pull away, but somehow she found herself walking along with Grayson, enjoying the feeling of companionship his presence brought.

"Come on, Lily Mae. We're going to have some breakfast."

"With Mr. Sinclair?" Lily skipped up beside them, and grabbed Honor's other hand. Linked together, they walked up the back stairs and into the mudroom. To an outsider, they'd look like a family. Mother, father, child, heading back into the house after enjoying the sunrise together.

Of course, they weren't and just thinking in that direction made Honor uncomfortable.

She tugged away from Grayson's hold and stepped into the kitchen. "Go ahead and have a seat, Grayson.

Everything will be on the table in ten minutes. Lily, go wash your hands and put on the clothes I laid out for you. But do it quietly. Candace is still asleep." She grabbed the apron her mother had always worn when she was cooking, the bright green one that had been handed to Honor the day she married Jay, and tied it around her waist, ignoring Grayson's raised eyebrows.

"What kind of omelet would you like?"

"What kind were you planning on making?"

"Vegetable. Peppers, onions and mushrooms." She pulled ingredients from the refrigerator and set them on the small counter.

"Sounds perfect to me. Can I help?" Instead of sitting at the table, he moved close, his chest brushing against her back as he leaned over to see what she was doing.

Honor's cheeks heated, her mind jumping back to the years when Jay had been alive. He'd always been content to read the paper while she cooked and had teased her good-naturedly when she wore her apron. It had been easy to have him in the kitchen, but Grayson was another story altogether.

He was a distraction, his scent and his warmth surrounding Honor as she diced onions. "You can put the biscuits in the oven for me. They're on the counter under that cloth. The oven is already preheated."

Any other day, Honor would have brushed melted butter over the biscuits before putting them in the oven, but today she didn't care about butter. She cared about putting some distance between herself and Grayson.

Grayson moved away, and Honor hurried to finish the onions. The sooner she finished, the sooner she could get Grayson fed and out of her kitchen. A kitchen that had seemed plenty big enough until he'd walked into it.

"All set. How long do you want me to set the timer for?" He spoke over his shoulder, and Honor had the feeling he wasn't nearly as affected by her as she was by him.

And why would he be? He probably dated all the time. Saw a different woman every week. Whereas Honor hadn't been on a date in years.

"Ten minutes is fine." She grabbed eggs, whisked them and poured them into a large skillet, working by rote, doing what she'd done hundreds of times over the years. It felt different, though. As if the gray world she'd been living in had bloomed into full color. Her senses were alive, her body humming with awareness.

Had it been like this with Jay?

She'd wondered that a lot lately, but she couldn't remember. The hard years, the years when Jay had spent money they didn't have on dreams that never panned out, the years when he'd made promises that he hadn't been able to keep—those years had wiped out the sweeter things. The gentle comfort that came from being together. The soft beauty of mornings spent sharing coffee and conversation.

Honor blinked back tears, refusing the sadness

she knew she shouldn't feel. Jay had loved her. She had loved him. If they'd had time, they might have been able to forge something strong and unbreakable. They hadn't, and Honor couldn't spend her life regretting the things she'd never had with him.

"You look sad." Grayson moved up beside her, grabbing a knife from the cutting board and chopping a green pepper. He'd taken off his coat and rolled up his sleeves, revealing forearms that were tan and muscular. His hands were broad, his fingers long, and Honor vividly remembered the feel of them on her neck—warm and gentle.

She averted her gaze, concentrating on the mushrooms she was cleaning. "What do I have to be sad about? Any day my family is healthy and safe is a good one."

"Having a good day doesn't mean that we can't also feel sadness." Grayson dropped peppers onto the omelet, then stepped aside while Honor added mushrooms and onions. "So, what's on your mind that's making your eyes so dark and shadowed?"

"I don't think I'd like to be on the stand with you questioning me," Honor muttered as she folded the omelet and slid it onto a plate.

"Why's that?"

"You never give up. One question is always followed by another and another and another."

"How else can I find the truth?"

"It isn't always your job to do that." She poured more egg into the pan, starting another omelet and refusing to meet Grayson's steady gaze. He read her too easily, saw more in her than she wanted to show.

"Just so we're clear—" he used his forefinger to tilt her chin, his eyes searching her face "—I don't think of you as a job."

Honor's heart stuttered as she remembered the warmth of his lips against hers. The brief, barely there contact that had left her longing for more.

It was definitely time to feed Grayson and send him on his way.

"Can you check on the biscuits? I think they may be done."

He looked as if he was going to refuse, but then he nodded, his finger dropping away from her chin as he turned and opened the oven.

She took a deep, steadying breath, trying her best to calm her pulse and her thoughts. What was wrong with her? Why was she so affected by Grayson? Had Candace's high school graduation and acceptance to college sparked an early midlife crisis?

Whatever the case, Honor needed to regain control and she needed to do it quickly.

The phone rang, the sound so surprising that Honor jumped and swung toward it. "Now who could that be at this time of the morning?"

"Want me to get it?" Grayson reached for the phone, but Honor shook her head.

"No. I will. Thanks." She lifted the receiver, half expecting to hear someone from work asking her to fill in for a shift. "Hello?"

"Tell your friend he'd better watch it. I don't like

people moving in on my territory. If he doesn't back off, he's going to wind up as dead as that lying, cheating husband of yours." The words were followed by a click, the line going silent as Honor's heart beat louder and harder in her ears.

"Is everything okay?" Grayson took the phone from her hand and placed it back on the receiver, studying her face as if he could read the answer to his question there.

Was everything okay?

No.

No, it wasn't okay.

A man, someone she didn't know, knew more about her than anyone should.

Your lying, cheating husband?

No one but Honor knew the truth of Jay's infidelity. She hadn't told her parents. Hadn't told her friends. Finding out at his funeral had only compounded Honor's grief, but she had felt no need to rehash the information. No desire to let other people know just how foolhardy her husband had been. And how naive she'd been.

Lying.

Cheating.

Jay.

She shook her head, trying to stop the words from echoing through her mind. But as soon as they stopped, others were there.

Tell your friend he'd better watch it.

He's going to wind up as dead as your lying, cheating husband.

Grayson. Her neighbor. Her friend.

More?

She reached for the phone, meeting Grayson's eyes, seeing his strength, his determination, his integrity. All the things that had brought him into her life, and had kept him there. Had put him in danger. "No, everything isn't okay. I need to call the sheriff."

SIXTEEN

"You're absolutely sure that you never mentioned your husband's affair to anyone?" Jake Reed asked Honor the question for the fourth time in as many minutes, and Grayson ground his teeth to keep from telling his friend to stop beating a dead horse.

"I'd think I'd remember revealing something so personal." Honor's gaze jumped to Grayson, then dropped away again, her cheeks deep pink with embarrassment. Though what she had to be embarrassed about, he didn't know. Her husband had been a fool. Pure and simple. That was his sin, not Honor's.

Maybe she was embarrassed that Grayson had heard the truth? He was sure she would have been more comfortable if he'd left her alone while Jake questioned her.

He'd known it, but he'd stayed anyway.

There was something off about Honor's stalker. Something that didn't ring true. Grayson had been thinking about it most of the night...when he hadn't been thinking about Honor and the soft, sweet feel of her lips against his. The whisper of her breath as she'd allowed the contact between them.

He pulled his thoughts up short.

That was not something he should be dwelling on. Not now, at any rate.

What he *should* be concentrating on was putting the pieces of the puzzle together. Honor had lived in St. Louis for years. In all that time, she'd never had any indication that someone had taken undue interest in her. No flowers. No gifts. No notes left for her to find.

Nothing.

Then, in the course of a month, she'd been attacked in her apartment by a drug addict, moved to Lakeview and started receiving anonymous gifts and phone calls.

Had her picture been in the newspaper after the attack? If so, it was possible she'd been seen by someone who had created a fantasy relationship with her and had then followed her to Lakeview.

Stranger things had happened.

But the information the stalker had about Honor's husband put a crimp in that theory, and Grayson was growing more and more uneasy with the assumptions they were making about Honor's troubles.

Something was definitely off.

Honor had repeated the same information over and over again in answer to Jake's query—she'd told no one about her husband's affair.

Yet someone knew.

"What about your husband's military friends?

Would they have been privy to the information?" Jake had a small notebook and was writing in it, but as he spoke he shot a questioning look in Grayson's direction.

More than likely, he was wondering why Grayson hadn't left. It was a good question, but one Grayson wouldn't answer. Not unless Honor asked, and he knew she wouldn't. She preferred to pretend that their relationship was as simple as two neighbors getting to know each other.

"I'm sure they were. Jay was well liked. He had many friends. He wrote me several times after he went to Iraq, and he often included names of people he spent time with. It's possible some of them knew he was having an affair."

"Would it have been in character for your husband to share something so personal with people he knew?"

"If he thought they would keep the information from me, yes."

"Do you have the letters he wrote you?"

The color in Honor's cheeks deepened, and she shook her head. "I'm afraid I shredded them after the funeral."

"I can't say I blame you, but it would sure help if any of the names came to mind."

"I wish I could help you, but I can't remember much about the months before my husband died. I was quite pregnant and very caught up in getting ready for Lily's birth. After he died, I was just trying to put my life back together."

"You said Jay's girlfriend was at the funeral, and she made it very clear that she'd loved Jay and that he'd loved her." Grayson broke into the conversation, knowing neither Jake nor Honor would appreciate it, but not caring. He had questions, and he wanted answers. Asking was the only way to get them.

Honor glanced down the hall to the room where she'd sent Lily after the little girl had told Jake her dragon story. No doubt Honor was worried that her daughter would hear secrets that were better left hidden. "That's right."

"Who was there when she confronted you?"

"I don't know. It's been over four years."

"I know you'd rather not think about it, but any details you can give will help." Jake spoke with quiet authority, shooting Grayson more than a questioning look. This time he was clearly saying "back off."

Honor didn't seem to notice. She cocked her head to the side, her dark hair falling in a silky line over her shoulder as she stared into the past. "They'd already lowered the coffin into the ground. We'd thrown dirt on top of it. I was holding the flag I'd been given and staring down at my husband's coffin while everyone else began to wander back to their cars. That's when she approached me."

"No one else was around?"

"A few people were. Mostly military people. And Jay's mother and father, I think. They were there. I remember that very clearly because Candace had gotten in the car to avoid being near them, and I was relieved she hadn't been there to hear what was said."

"So maybe a half dozen people heard?"

"Maybe."

"Do you have the name of the girlfriend?" Jake wrote something in his notepad, and Grayson knew he'd be contacting Honor's in-laws before the end of the day. The answer could lie in that direction. It was possible they remembered something Honor didn't. There was no way Jake would let that possibility go unexplored.

"I'm afraid not. She never introduced herself, and I didn't ask. Not her. Not any of Jay's friends. Once the funeral was over, I tried to put it all behind me. Jay was gone. There was no sense in holding on to anger over what he'd done."

"You're right about that, Ms. Malone. Although I've met plenty of people who don't subscribe to the same idea." Jake closed his notepad and tucked it in his pocket.

"Forgiveness is something we're told to do. For others. For ourselves. For our relationship with God. I really didn't have a choice in the matter." Honor smiled, but the sadness Grayson had seen her eyes earlier was still there. Only now he understood it. And understanding made it all the harder to bear seeing.

He wanted to smooth the soft strands of her hair, wanted to tell her how much he admired what she was trying to do for her daughter and her sister-in-law. Wanted to say that protecting them by forgiving and moving on showed true courage and grace.

And he wanted to tell her that her husband had been pond scum.

But he didn't think she'd want to hear any of those things, so he remained silent as Jake asked a few more questions, issued a few warnings about staying safe and then headed for the front door. "I'm putting a patrol car at the end of your street until we find the guy who is stalking you. If something happens, we'll be close by."

The budget wasn't there for that, and Grayson wondered what Jake would offer his men to get them to volunteer for twenty-four-hour guard duty. Knowing Jake, it would be something good. Maybe a week's worth of vacation while Jake covered shifts. Grayson would ask his friend when Honor wasn't around, and then offer to help pay for whatever it was. Honor wouldn't be happy to know either of them had gone to the trouble, but in this case, what she didn't know wouldn't hurt her.

"I appreciate that, Sheriff."

"Jake. We've been seeing plenty of each other, so I'm thinking it may be best if we're on a first-name basis. I'm going to check into some of the things you've told me. Contact your in-laws. Maybe see if I can get the name of your husband's girlfriend. Is that okay with you?"

"Sure, but I don't know what good it will do."

"I want to find the person who's stalking you. Any information anyone can give me about who might have known about your husband's affair will help with that."

"It's just been so long. I can't believe it's suddenly being dragged out and examined. If I'd known…" She paused, then shrugged. "But hindsight is always twenty-twenty, isn't it?"

"It is. And, for what it's worth, I think you made the right choice. Having a name wouldn't have changed what happened. I'm going to try to get a trace on your caller, but I'm thinking our perp made the call from a pay phone. Either that or he stole someone's phone and used it. No way would he be stupid enough to use his own."

"If he did, it would make your job easier." And make Grayson a whole lot happier.

"So far he hasn't done much to give himself away. But eventually he'll slip up. That's when we'll get him."

"What about the car he was in last night?" Honor's face was pale and tightly drawn, and Grayson briefly wondered how many more days of this she could take.

The answer was obvious—as many as it took. That was Honor's personality. It was her gift. To work toward a goal with determination and drive, but with her gaze always focused on others, her purpose always to serve rather than be served.

"Nothing from CSI yet, but we're trying to trace the car to its dealer. If we're able to, we may find out who purchased it." Jake stepped outside, letting bitterly cold air into the house. In the distance, dark clouds pressed low against the Blue Ridge Mountains. "On a lighter note, my wife and I are having a birthday party for my daughter next month. She's turning four. My wife would love for you to bring Lily."

"That's very sweet of her. I know Lily would love to come."

"You can bring your sister-in-law, too. We've got a dozen college students in our young-adult class at church. It might be nice for Candace to meet them. I'll tell Tiffany to go ahead and send the invitation." Jake paused with his hand on the cruiser's door. "Grayson, I think we need to talk later."

"Do you?" Grayson leaned against the doorjamb, not nearly as anxious to have a discussion with Jake as his friend seemed to be to have one with him.

"Yeah. Your life has been threatened. I don't take that lightly."

"Neither do I, but I think Honor is in a lot more danger than I am."

"How about we meet for lunch anyway? We'll discuss measures I want you to take to stay safe."

"Sure, but if those measures include staying away from Honor, forget it."

"I'm due for some time off. I'll drive out to your office. We can go from there."

"See you then." Grayson waited until Jake pulled away before turning to Honor. She was watching him, her eyes filled with fear.

"He's right, you know. You *are* in danger. Because of me. I think it would be best if—"

"I'm not going to stay away, Honor. Nothing you

or Jake or your stalker say will convince me to do that."

"If something happens to you because of me…" She shook her head. "I couldn't live with that, Grayson."

"You won't have to. Your stalker isn't the first criminal I've angered. He won't be the last."

"Just be careful, okay?" She grabbed his hand, her touch sending heat through him.

"You don't need to worry about that, Honor." He brushed hair from her cheek, his palm resting against silky flesh. "I'll be as careful as you are going to be."

"Then I guess I'll be very, very careful." She stepped away from his touch, putting distance between them that Grayson didn't want. "Do you think any of the information I've given the sheriff will help him find the stalker?"

"If anyone can find answers, it's Jake. He's like a dog with a bone. He'll never give up. Not until he gets what he wants."

"I hope you're right. That phone call this morning…" She shook her head.

"What?"

"It was like a stranger had stepped into my life and stolen something sacred to me. The secrets closest to my heart." She frowned, her gaze on the distant mountains and the darkening clouds.

"You've been through a lot in the past few years, Honor. You deserve to keep whatever secrets you choose."

"Maybe. Maybe not. But I'd at least like to have a

choice about whom I share them with." She rubbed her arms and Grayson pulled her close, wrapping her in his coat.

For a moment, her hands rested on his shoulders, and he was sure she planned to push him away. Instead, her palms settled tentatively, her touch so light it was barely there.

Like the kiss they'd shared.

Like the longing that seemed to have settled into Grayson's soul. A quiet whisper that said that this was the right place, the right woman, the right time and he'd be a fool to walk away.

Honor sighed, settling more deeply into his arms, her hair soft as silk against his chin, her warmth seeping through his shirt, heating his skin, the scent of summer drifting around them.

"Honor?" Candace's spoke quietly, but Honor jumped as if she'd shouted, pushing against Grayson's arms and turning to the open front door, her cheeks cherry red.

"Yes?"

"I hate to interrupt, but I've really got to get going or I'll be late for class." Candace's words were directed to Honor, but it was Grayson she was eyeing with curiosity he didn't miss.

"And I've still got to feed Lily. Breakfast got interrupted by the sheriff's arrival. Have a good day, Candace. It looks like a storm is coming in, so drive carefully." The words spilled out in a breathless rush, and then Honor was running into the house, carrying the scent of summer with her.

"Well, that was awkward." Candace smiled at Grayson, a hint of amusement in her eyes as she looked him up and down, searching, Grayson thought, for flaws.

"Why?"

"Because it's Honor. She doesn't 'do' men." Candace hitched a backpack onto her shoulder and started down the porch steps.

"She married your brother."

"Yeah. Poor thing. Not only did she get stuck with a lying, cheating rat, but she ended up with me." Candace smiled again, but there was no mistaking the truth in her words.

"She loves you."

"She loved my brother, too. That didn't make living with him easy. He was like my dad. All polished and pretty on the outside, but stuffed with rotting, fetid things. Both were parasites who lived off the people around them. My mom had money my dad fed off. Jay fed off Honor's love. Taking and taking and never giving back. If he hadn't died, Honor would have found out the truth and it would have ruined her. At least this way, she's been able to make a life for herself." She shrugged too-slender shoulders, the gesture so much like Honor that Grayson could almost believe the two were related by more than name.

"She would have tried to make it work. You might have all ended up a happy family."

"Please, Mr. Sinclair, you don't know my family. We're cursed. The men are always brutes and the women are always doormats. No one is ever normal. And no one even knows the meaning of the word 'happy.'"

"I'm sorry things were so tough for you, Candace."

"It's water under the bridge now. I just pray every day that I won't end up like my biological family."

"You won't."

"No? I'm sure my brother thought the same thing before he cheated on the only woman who ever loved him." Candace climbed into an old Chevy and drove away before Grayson could ask her for more information.

What he'd gotten wasn't nearly enough.

Candace knew that Jay had cheated on Honor.

Had she just found out, or was it something she'd known about for years?

And if it was, had she told anyone else?

The answer would have to wait until later. Grayson had a meeting in—he glanced at his watch—forty minutes. If he didn't hurry, he'd be late.

And if he stayed on Honor's front porch any longer, he might just decide he didn't care.

He chose not to knock on the door and walk back through Honor's house. Instead, he walked around to the back and crossed the tangled mess that passed for a yard. He had a lot on his plate today. Plenty that needed to be dealt with. Not the least of which were his brother's accommodations. The bacterial infection was clearing; Jude was getting better. According to Grayson's parents, that only made their police veteran son more difficult to deal with. A week, two at the most, and then Jude would arrive in Lynchburg. Making sure everything was ready was Grayson's priority.

Or one of them.

Honor had become a priority, too.

And just like the previous night, Grayson planned to be waiting for her when she got off work, planned on making sure she got home safely. Honor might not "do" men, but she needed Grayson. Whether she wanted to admit it or not.

And Grayson was beginning to believe he needed her, too.

A woman like Honor could ground him. In faith. In family. In all the things he'd always known were important, but that had somehow gotten lost in his rush to get ahead.

God's plan?

Grayson was starting to think so, and he was beginning to believe that the path he'd taken, the one he'd thought had brought him too far away from God to ever lead him back, had come full circle. That the things he'd once valued, the things he'd been so sure he'd never have, were within his grasp. All he had to do was have the faith to go after them.

SEVENTEEN

Rain poured from the sky as Honor hurried to her car. The night shift had been brutal, with one of Honor's Alzheimer's patients going into cardiac arrest. Despite every effort, the seventy-year-old had passed away en route to the hospital. Death was as much a part of her job as life, but Honor never got used to it, and the cold rain and deep black night only reminded her of how sad the night had been.

She waved goodbye to William and slid into her car, anxious to get home. Lily hadn't wanted her to leave, and there had been tears. That was unusual enough to worry Honor. Her daughter wasn't one to cry and whine. Like her father, she was quite good at taking life in stride.

Jay.

He'd been on her mind way too much lately. She knew why. Being with Grayson reminded her of what she'd thought she would have when she'd married her husband—a shoulder to lean on; someone to depend on.

It also reminded her of betrayals she'd rather forget.

Sharing the story of Jay's infidelity had been painful. Sharing it in front of Grayson had made her want to climb into bed, curl up under her covers and hide her head in shame. The rational part of her told Honor that Jay's sin had been his own. The other part whispered that if she'd been a better wife he never would have strayed.

Foolishness, she knew, but painful anyway.

She pulled out of the parking lot and started toward home, tensing when a car pulled out behind her. Headlights flashed. Once. Then again. Some kind of signal that she couldn't even begin to understand. Whoever was following her had been waiting in the parking lot, biding his time until Honor was alone.

Her pulse raced and she pressed on the accelerator as she fumbled in her purse and pulled out her cell phone. It rang before she could flip it open, and Honor screamed, nearly dropping it in her surprise.

Could the stalker have gotten her cell phone number? Was it possible he was behind her, calling to taunt her before making his move? "Hello?"

"Ms. Malone?" The female voice surprised Honor, and her fear was replaced by anxiety. Phone calls didn't come at three in the morning. Not good ones, anyway.

"Yes?"

"This is Deputy Raintree. I'm with the Lakeview sheriff's department."

"Is everything okay? Are the girls okay?" Honor's heart beat a terrible rhythm, hard and harsh and uneven. There were things she never let herself think about. Things that were too horrible to even contemplate. Losing the girls was one of them.

"I'm sure they're fine, Ms. Malone. I'm calling about the car that is following you."

"What?" Honor glanced in the rearview mirror and eased up on the accelerator.

"The car that's behind you. Mr. Grayson Sinclair is driving. He asked me to call and let you know that he's providing an escort home."

"He could have called me himself."

"He didn't have your cell phone number. We had it on file here." Was this woman for real? Or was this an elaborate scheme to get her to let down her guard? Honor glanced at the caller ID on the cell phone, saw the sheriff's department listed as the caller.

Okay.

Maybe she had let her imagination get the best of her. Obviously, the police weren't in on the stalker's scheme.

"Are you sure it was Grayson you spoke with?" Honor glanced in the rearview mirror again. "Anyone could have called and asked you to contact me."

"Ma'am, I've known Grayson Sinclair for six years. It was definitely him. As a matter of fact, he promised me a box of Godiva chocolate if I did this favor for him. You tell him, I'm holding him to that."

"Right. I'll do that."

"And give him your cell phone number, will you? Sheriff Reed doesn't pay me to make personal phone calls." The deputy was laughing as she hung up the phone.

Honor wasn't quite as amused.

Grayson had taken years off her life. Worse, in the short time she'd known him, he'd already become an expected part of her day. Sure, she'd been surprised to hear he was the one in the car behind her, but a small part of her had almost expected it. Like being told the golden light on the horizon was the sun, the deputy's news had made perfect sense.

She drove home slowly, mindful of the slick road and the pouring rain, and just as mindful of Grayson following behind. Not too close. Not too far away. The fact that he'd come to Lakeview Haven again, had waited until her shift was over and followed her home, these were the kind of things she'd once longed for from Jay. Her husband had seen her as a strong, capable woman. That had been both a blessing and a curse. While he'd trusted her to handle whatever problems came their way, he'd also counted on her to do so. The responsibility for the well-being of their family had always rested squarely on her shoulders. She'd told herself that it was okay, had tried to convince herself that Jay's willingness to let her handle things was a compliment. Often, though, it had felt more like a burden.

More thoughts about Jay.

More memories she'd wanted to keep buried.

She'd thought she'd forgiven him and let go of the anger that had filled her when she'd learned of his betrayal, the anger that had eaten at her soul when she'd realized the debt he'd left her. Realized she'd have to move out of her house and rent an apartment in order to pay the bills he'd accrued.

Maybe she hadn't, because when she thought of him now, she could only think of the bad memories. Never of the good times. But, then, there had been so few of those.

She passed a marked police car parked at the end of her street and pulled into her driveway, exhausted and frustrated by her thoughts. In the past month, her life had gotten completely off track and she wasn't sure how to get it back on again. She wasn't even sure she knew what the "right" track was. Moving, getting a new job, providing for her girls. Those things were givens. They were already done and nothing could change them.

But what now?

That was the question she couldn't answer until the predator who was hunting her was found. Things were too confusing. Too unbalanced.

She opened the car door, icy pellets of rain sliding down her hair and into her coat collar. Winter gloom had ruled the day and had given the night an arctic chill. Honor hurried onto the porch, waiting beneath its sheltering roof as Grayson got out of his car and followed. His hair was mussed, his shirt open at the collar, his tie hanging loose around his neck. He looked tired.

And much more handsome than any man had a right to be.

Every woman in the courtroom must dream of

romance and love when Grayson walked in. Honor could picture the female jurors so caught up in watching the handsome prosecutor, they forgot to pay attention to the evidence.

She smiled at the thought.

"What?" He brushed rain from his hair and rubbed his hand down his jaw, the gesture speaking of a weariness that Honor understood only too well.

"I was thinking that you must be a distraction in the courtroom, what with that *GQ* model thing you've got going on."

"Were you?" He smiled, his eyes flashing with surprise and something else. Something deeper and more compelling.

"Yes. I think someone should make it illegal for the prosecutor to overshadow the evidence."

Grayson's laughter was deep and warm, washing over Honor and reminding her that life didn't always have to be a serious thing. That sometimes laughter could make the most difficult times bearable. "I'll have to tell Jude you said that. He'll laugh himself to good health in no time."

"They do say laughter is the best medicine."

"My point exactly."

"How is your brother doing? Have you gotten an update?"

"Marginally better. Lord willing, he'll be headed this way in a couple of weeks." Grayson yawned, smiling apologetically. "Sorry. Long day."

"Don't I know it?" Honor unlocked the door, but stopped short of opening it. "I would think you'd have gone straight home to bed rather than waiting to escort me here."

"I wouldn't have slept anyway. Not until I knew you were home safe. I'm sure I mentioned that before." He took a step closer, and Honor could almost feel his warmth through her coat. She tried to back up, and bumped into the door.

"You can't escort me home every night, Grayson. You know that, don't you?"

"What I know is that you're a woman in danger, and having me around might just keep you safe. That being the case, everything else is moot."

"I keep trying to tell you that I'm not your responsibility."

"And I keep trying to tell *you* that I always keep my promises."

"Are we going to have this conversation every time we see each other?"

"That depends."

"On?"

"Whether or not you stop telling me I shouldn't do what I know is right." He smiled, but there was grim determination in his eyes, and Honor knew he meant what he said. Somehow, he'd convinced himself her well-being was his responsibility. Nothing Honor said would change his mind.

She decided to try anyway, because Grayson's presence was too unsettling, too alarming.

Too addictive.

And it was the kind of addiction Honor wasn't sure she'd want to break. "I appreciate your concern, Grayson, but there's a police car parked a few hundred yards away. I don't think either of us need to be worried about my safety."

"There aren't officers lined up on your route home, Honor. And a lot can happen on a ten-mile stretch of road." He sounded as tired as Honor felt.

"A lot can happen if I do something stupid. Like stop to help a stranded motorist or pick up a hitch-hiker. I can assure you I've got no intention of doing either of those things."

"I'm sure you don't."

"Then stop staying up until all hours of the night to protect me. Not getting enough sleep isn't healthy."

He chuckled and shook his head. "Not healthy? If you knew what I ate today, you wouldn't be so worried about how much sleep I'm getting."

"Should I ask what you've been eating?"

"Today? Since our breakfast was interrupted, I got a doughnut on the way to my meeting, then I grabbed a hamburger and fries while Jake lectured me on keeping out of his investigation."

"He lectured you?"

"I'm afraid so."

"And you listened?"

"He was buying lunch, and I was hungry." Grayson sounded disgruntled, and Honor laughed.

"Poor you. What else did you eat today? Besides fast food junk."

"A taco."

"Fast food?"

"Is there any other kind when you've got a busy schedule?"

"Yes. And you're right, your eating habits are as unhealthy as your lack of adequate sleep."

"Actually, I did sleep. For about two hours while I was waiting for your shift to end. The sound of your car engine woke me up."

"Be that as it may, you still need to get home and into bed. Your busy day will start all over again very soon."

"What I need—" he smiled and took a step closer "—is a good home-cooked meal or two. That'll get me back on track with the right nutrients."

"It'll be good for you to cook one, then."

"And here I was hoping to get another invitation." Grayson's laughter shivered along Honor's spine, making her want to lean in and rest her head on his chest, feel the vibration of it against her cheek.

"Sorry, but I always try to learn from my mistakes."

"Is that what this morning's invitation to breakfast was?"

"And yesterday."

"You mean the kiss that wasn't?"

"It most certainly *was*."

"No, Honor. It wasn't. This—" he took a step closer, closing what little space had been between them "—is a kiss."

And then he showed her, his lips pressing against hers, firm and tender all at the same time. His scent surrounding her, his hands settling on her waist.

And for a moment, she lost herself to his touch. Allowed herself to forget all the reasons why letting Grayson kiss her was a mistake.

Breathless, she pulled away, staring up into Grayson's eyes and seeing her own confusion and worry reflected there. "We need to stop this now before one of us gets hurt."

"There's no reason why that should happen."

"Of course there is. Isn't that always the end result of these kinds of things?"

"What kind of thing are we talking about?"

"Men and women getting to know each other. Dating. Falling…for each other."

"It's not always the end result. Sometimes people build something great and lasting. Sometimes they make a lifetime together."

"Sometimes." But not this time, because Honor couldn't risk her heart for something that might not ever be.

"You don't think it will be like that for you?"

"I tried for a lifetime before, Grayson. With a man I'd known and admired and fallen in love with. We were best friends before we married and best friends after, but even that wasn't enough to make it work."

"It takes two committed people to make something work."

She knew what he wasn't saying—that it was obvious Jay hadn't been committed. She didn't comment on it though, because it was late and she was tired. Because saying it wouldn't change anything. Because it was time to say good-night to Grayson.

And goodbye. "Thank you for the escort, Grayson, but I'd rather you not bother tomorrow. I've been doing things on my own for a long time and, really, that's how I prefer it."

He stared at her for moment, his eyes dark as a storm-filled cloud. Then he nodded. "All right, Honor. But just so you know, sharing a road isn't the same as offering an escort."

"I—"

"You were right when you said I needed some sleep. Go on inside or I'll never get home."

Honor thought about saying a hundred different things, but in the end she said nothing but good-night. There was nothing she could say that would change what was happening. Nothing she could do to convince Grayson that there was no attraction between them. Nothing she could do to convince herself that she didn't want to see him again.

She closed the door and turned the lock, waiting until Grayson's car engine purred to life, the sound slowly fading, before she turned and walked down the hall.

EIGHTEEN

Honor expected both girls to be asleep when she walked into the house, and she crept down the hall silently, hoping to keep it that way. Lily hadn't been sleeping well lately, and the last thing Honor needed was to have to deal with her daughter's imagination. It could take an hour to settle Lily in again if she decided she needed to be up and talking about her prince or her dragon or any other fantastical thing that her four-year-old mind could conjure.

Determined to get into bed as quickly as possible, Honor almost ignored the bright light that was spilling out from under Candace's door. Her sister-in-law might be up studying, or might have fallen asleep with the lights on. In either case, she was eighteen and didn't need to be checked on. Old habits were hard to break, though, and Honor knocked gently, not really expecting an answer, but knowing she wouldn't be content to go to sleep without making sure Candace was okay.

"Come in." Her sister-in-law's voice sounded muffled, and Honor pushed open the door, concerned when she saw Candace curled up on the bed, still dressed and facing the wall.

"Is everything okay, Candace?"

"The sheriff left a message on the answering machine. He didn't want to call you at work."

"About what?" Honor crossed the room and sat on the edge of the bed. She knew her sister-in-law well enough to know that she couldn't rush the truth out of her. Whatever was wrong, Candace would let her know in her own good time.

"Mom."

"Mom?" It had been a long time since Honor had heard Candace mention the woman who'd raised her until she was thirteen.

"Yeah. You know. The woman who was happy to get rid of me. The one who said I was too much trouble to have at home."

"What about her?" Honor brushed thick bangs out of Candace's eyes, trying to read her expression.

"She's dead."

"Oh, honey, I'm so sorry."

"I'm not." A single tear slid down Candace's cheek and soaked into her bedspread.

"I know you don't mean that."

"I do mean it."

Honor knew better than to argue. Candace's emotions could rage as wildly as a forest fire, but they always died down quickly. She'd broach the subject again, once Candace had time to deal with what she was feeling. "Did the sheriff say what happened?"

"He just left a message saying you should call him. Of course, I know what happened. She drank herself to death. She always cared more about her vodka than anything else." Candace's words held a lifetime of bitterness and pain.

"She cared about you, Candace. I know she did."

"How could you possibly know that? She never did one thing to show it." Another tear fell, and Honor's heart broke for her sister-in-law.

"Did the sheriff speak to your father? Did he leave a number where we could reach him?" Chad Malone hadn't spoken a word to Honor at his son's funeral. Nor had he acknowledged his daughter. His wife, Melanie, had been silent, too, her blue eyes faded and blank as if life had taken everything she had to give.

"No. All the sheriff said was that Mom has been dead for two weeks. Even if he'd left a number, I wouldn't want to call my father. Two weeks. And he couldn't even let me know."

"Candace…" Honor's voice trailed off as she tried to think of the right words to say. The fact was, it had been Candace's choice to break ties with her family. There had been phone calls from Melanie during the first year after Candace had moved in with Honor and Jay, but Candace had always refused to speak to her mother. Paid airline tickets had gone unused because Jay hadn't seen a reason to force his sister to visit her parents, who had made it clear she wasn't wanted. Honor had tried to change both her husband's and her sister-in-law's minds with no success.

After a year, the phone calls had stopped. There

had been no more talk of visits. Candace had been relinquished completely, but Honor had known that her sister-in-law had never truly let go of her parents or the past she'd shared with them.

"She wasn't a good mother, Honor. Not like you. She drank to forget and she forgot a lot. But she was still my mother." Candace's words were barely audible, and Honor smoothed a hand over her hair, wishing she had words that would take away the pain her sister-in-law was feeling.

"And she loved you in her own way, Candace."

"You're sweet, but she didn't. Not as much as she loved other things. One of the most important lessons I've learned from you is that true love has no limitations or boundaries. It goes on despite time or distance. No matter what. My mother's love was never like that. If it had been, she never would have let me go."

Tears burned behind Honor's eyes, and she patted Candace's shoulder. "And one of the things I've learned from you is that the unexpected things in life are often the most wonderful. Another thing I've learned is that the best kind of sister is a sister of the heart, and that's what you are to me, Candace. Truly."

"Thanks." Candace's smile was a quick curve of her lips, gone before it was ever really there.

"I'll call the sheriff first thing in the morning and find out what happened."

"I don't need to know. I don't want to know." But she did, and Honor could feel it.

"Maybe he can give me your father's address and phone number. We could call—"

"No!" Candace bit her lip, and then continued more quietly. "My mom was a lost soul. My father was evil. I don't want anything from him. Not even answers about what happened to my mother."

"Candace—"

"I'm really sorry, but I'm tired and I've got school tomorrow. So, if you don't mind, I'd rather not talk about this anymore."

Honor wanted to continue the discussion, but knew it would lead nowhere. She'd learned long ago that conversations about Candace's childhood were off limits. It had been the same with Jay. He'd told her just enough to help her understand why he wouldn't say more.

"All right. If you want to talk, I'm always ready to listen."

"I know. Good night, Honor."

"Good night." Honor reached for the light switch, but Candace levered herself up in bed.

"Leave it on, okay?"

"Sure." Honor closed the door, tears clogging her throat and filling her eyes. It hurt to see Candace in pain and to know that there was nothing she could do about it.

Antsy, anxious and wishing it were a decent hour so she could call Jake, get her father-in-law's number, do *something,* Honor went to the kitchen, made a cup of tea and sat at the table. Rain tapped against the windows and roof, the sound a soothing reminder of spring in Ireland and the subtle scent of grass and flowers drifting in the open windows of her parents' home.

She missed those days, but more than that, she missed the sense of security she'd always had there. Since Jay's death, Honor's life had been about paying bills, paying off debts and keeping the household afloat. Enjoying the simple pleasures of spring rain or winter snow had become more difficult than Honor had ever imagined. Balance. Prioritizing. Those were things Honor was always struggling with. It wouldn't be so bad to have someone share that burden with her. It wouldn't be so bad to believe that Grayson was right and that a lifetime could be made by two committed people. Her parents had done it. Some of her friends had been married for a decade or more.

And Honor had been married for six years to a man who'd never seemed committed to anything more than himself. She'd been so naive, so sure that love could conquer all. It couldn't. It could only open a person up to pain, to heartache and to disappointment.

She rubbed the ache in her lower back and sipped chamomile tea, wishing the past didn't seem so much a part of the present lately. Hearing that Melanie had passed away only added to the worry she'd been feeling. The news would have to be dealt with. She'd have to contact Candace's father to offer condolences no matter how Candace felt about it.

Not that he necessarily needed condolences.

From everything Jay had told her, Melanie and Chad Malone had had a rocky relationship filled with knock-down, drag-out fights. Still, after so many years of marriage, Chad must feel some grief over his wife's death.

Maybe.

But Honor knew enough about her father-in-law to recognize that Candace's words were a little too close to the truth. Chad wasn't evil, but he was empty. The kind of person who needed more and more to fill the hollowness inside. A black hole of emotion that sucked everything in and never let go.

Honor hadn't needed to spend a lot of time with the man to realize that. All she'd had to do was watch how he treated his wife and his children.

She sighed and stood to pace across the room and stare out the window. In the distance, a single light burned through the rain and the darkness. She knew whose it was, and the temptation to pick up the phone and call him filled her.

Such a dangerous longing, the need to share her thoughts and concerns with someone else.

Her fingers tightened on the teacup, and she turned away.

"I don't need Grayson Sinclair, Lord. What I need are answers. I need to find out who's been stalking me. I need to find out what happened to Melanie so I can give Candace some sense of closure. I need to get settled in and I need to move on, but I don't need Grayson." She whispered the prayer out loud, sure that God heard, but not sure He agreed.

Since the day she'd become a Christian when she was eight years old, Honor had understood that God had a plan and a purpose for her. She'd believed that the people that came into her life, the circumstances she faced were all part of His plan. Time and experience hadn't changed her mind or altered her faith, but they had forced her to accept that sometimes she wouldn't know all the reasons behind the things that happened to her.

It was possible, even probable, that God had put Grayson into Honor's life for a reason. Whether that was to keep her safe, or for some other reason, she didn't know. What she knew was that she wasn't comfortable with it.

She'd made up her mind about men a long time ago.

She didn't plan to change it.

But maybe God did.

The thought didn't comfort Honor as she put the teacup into the sink and retreated to her bedroom. She had a lot to do tomorrow. Calls to make. Errands to run. A man to avoid.

Somehow she thought the last would be much more difficult than the others.

NINETEEN

By ten the following morning, Honor had called Jake and gotten Chad's address and phone number. Florida. Honor had never imagined her Houston-born in-laws would move from their home state. Though, in the time after Jay's death they had moved from the suburbs of Houston to a country estate. Honor had lost track of them after that, her Christmas cards had been returned two years in a row. She'd had too much going on to worry much about where her in-laws were or what they were doing. They had known where she lived. She'd made sure to inform them as soon as she moved to the apartment in St. Louis.

The fact that they hadn't been courteous enough to do the same when they'd moved hadn't surprised her, and Honor had spent little time thinking about it.

Obviously they hadn't wanted to.

She glanced at the paper she'd left on the kitchen table, Chad's phone number written in black marker. All she had to do was pick up the phone and dial, but the thought of doing so filled her with dread. She'd spoken to Chad only three or four times, but it was enough for her to know that she'd rather not speak with him again. For Candace's sake, she'd do it.

But not yet.

She pulled stew beef from the refrigerator, poured oil into a pan and coated the beef with flour. Outside, rain continued to fall, soaking the yard so that brown, weed-filled puddles formed. Soft music drifted out of the dining room where Lily sat coloring pictures and listening to her favorite Kids' Praise CD. Why ruin such a peaceful morning by calling a man who knew nothing about peace?

Because it had to be done, that's why.

When Candace came home from classes, Honor wanted to be able to tell her what had happened to Melanie. She wanted to be able to give Candace information about where her mother was buried, offer to go with her to the grave even if that meant traveling to Texas or Florida to do so. Whatever Candace needed to do to find closure, that's what Honor wanted to offer.

But she wouldn't be able to offer anything at all if she didn't hurry up and call Chad. She frowned, dropping floured beef into the hot oil and browning it. Why was she being so wishy-washy about this? It wasn't like Chad was suddenly going to become part of their lives. He'd been more than happy to leave them alone for the past four years. There was no reason to think things had changed.

Was there?

Chad *had* just lost his wife. What if he felt the

need to reconnect with the family he'd been so distant from?

A soft knock on the back door made Honor jump, and she turned to the sound, her pulse racing. "Who is it?"

"Grayson."

"What are you doing out in the rain?" Honor pulled the door open, surprised to see her neighbor.

Her friend?

More?

"Waiting for you to ask me in." He held a large black umbrella, but his hair was wet, his jacket speckled with raindrops.

"So come in."

"Something smells good." He left the umbrella in the mudroom and shrugged out of his coat, laying it over the back of the chair.

"I'm making stew for lunch."

"It's just a little past ten. Isn't it kind of early for lunch?"

"It takes time to make a good stew."

"I wouldn't know. I've never been much of a cook. Though I have to admit to a fondness for good, hearty stew." He moved toward the stove and looked down into the pot. "Is it beef stew?"

"Just like my mother use to make."

"Looks like what my mother use to make, too. There was nothing quite like it on a cold, rainy day." He was begging an invitation, but Honor wasn't sure issuing one would be the best way to protect her heart, so she just smiled, pouring broth over the beef and pretending she didn't notice.

"Mr. Sinclair!" Lily raced into the room, a page from her coloring book clutched in her hand. "Look what I made for you."

He took it, studying the brightly colored picture like it was a masterpiece and he an art connoisseur. "This is beautiful, Lily. I love the colors you used."

"The pink?"

"Yes. And the yellow, blue, green and purple." He glanced at Honor and smiled, including her in the exchange.

Her heart skipped a beat, and she turned her attention back to the stew, trying her best to ignore how kind Grayson was being to her daughter, how sweet his attention to the scribbled paper he'd received. Why did he have to be so perfect? Why couldn't he be impatient with Lily or unkind to Candace? At least then, she'd have an excuse besides cowardice to keep her distance.

"It's a gray day, so I used lots of colors. Like a rainbow. It's for you. See, I wrote your name on it."

Surprised, Honor glanced at the paper again. Lily was precocious for her age, reading books and copying words, but there was no way she could have known how to spell "Sinclair."

And of course, she hadn't.

She'd written "Mr. Prince" in bold letters at the bottom of the page, and Honor couldn't help smiling. "Didn't I tell you not to call him that, Lily Mae?"

"Yes, Mommy, but I couldn't spell his real name,

so I had to write this one. I got it from the fairy-tale book Candace bought me."

Grayson laughed, ruffling Lily's hair and then folding the paper she'd given him and sliding it into his shirt pocket. "This is a great picture. Maybe you can color me another one for my brother. He hasn't been feeling well, so a picture like this might really cheer him up."

"Okay!" Lily skipped away, her curls flying in wild disarray. The room fell silent as she left it.

"I suppose you sent her out of here for a reason?" Honor pulled onions from the cupboard and started chopping them.

"I saw Jake at the courthouse an hour ago. He mentioned that he'd had some bad news to deliver to you, but wouldn't tell me what it was. I had to go home and grab the suit jacket I'd forgotten, so I figured I'd stop in here and see if things were okay."

"I'm surprised."

"By what?"

"The fact that Jake didn't tell you the news he'd given us."

"Don't be. Jake and I are both professionals who know the danger of crossing the line and letting personal relationships influence our actions."

"I know. I'm sorry. I didn't mean to imply anything different than that."

"And *I* know *that*." Grayson searched her face, his eyes sky blue and striking in his tan face. "So, *are* you okay?"

"I'm fine. It's Candace who is struggling. Jake was able to locate her parents. Or her father, anyway. Her mother passed away a couple of weeks ago."

"I'm sorry to hear that, Honor. Candace must be crushed."

"She is. I think the worst part for her is that her mother was gone for two weeks and she didn't even know it."

"Was there a reason why her father didn't contact you?"

"Who knows? I don't know Chad well, but what I know I don't like. He's a control freak given to fits of temper. Maybe he kept the information to himself out of spite. Maybe he did it because he could." Honor shrugged and threw the onions into the pot with the beef, then covered it with a lid.

"Is it possible he didn't know your new phone number? You did just recently move."

"We've had the same phone number for four years. If he'd dialed it, he would have been referred to our new number."

"Are you going to call him?"

"I've been trying to talk myself into getting that over with for the past hour and a half."

"You want me to do it for you?" Grayson frowned, pulling a cookie from the box sitting on Honor's counter.

"Grayson Sinclair, you'd better tell me that cookie isn't your breakfast."

"I would, but I'd be lying." He grinned and bit into the sweet treat.

"You need something more wholesome than that."

"If I had time, that's what I'd have, but I don't. I've got to be back in court in an hour."

"You shouldn't have come all the way here just to find out if everything was okay. You could have called me later."

"I told you—"

"You went back home for your suit jacket. Yes, I heard. But I can't believe a man like you doesn't keep a spare suit jacket at his office."

"Guilty as charged. But in my defense, I thought my black suit jacket would look better with the tie I'm wearing than my navy one."

"I wish you hadn't made the effort to stop by here, Grayson. Your day is already so hectic."

"I care. It's as simple as that." Grayson cupped her cheek. "So, do you want me to call your father-in-law?"

"No. That's a job I've got to do myself. And soon. Candace won't have closure until I give her the facts about what happened to her mother."

"Which just proves that kids can take a lot of abuse but still have loyalty and love for their parents." He grabbed another cookie and walked to the back door, "I've got to go or I'll be late. I'll be in court until this evening, and then I've got meetings tonight. If I'm not done in time to meet you after work—"

"I don't need you to meet me."

"If I'm not there, one of Jake's deputies will be. You've got a serious problem, Honor. Until we solve it, I think it's best to err on the side of caution."

He was right, of course. She couldn't take risks, not when she had Lily and Candace to think about. "All right."

"For once, we agree." He smiled, his gaze dropping to her lips and sending her heart racing before he met her eyes again. "Be safe on your way to work tonight."

"And you eat something besides junk food."

"I'm not making any promises." He called a goodbye to Lily, accepting the picture she'd colored for his brother with solemn thanks before he walked back out into the rain.

Honor stood at the door, watching as he crossed the yard and disappeared through the shrubs.

Talking to Grayson had eased some of the trepidation that had left her unable to pick up the phone and dial Chad's number. In his absence, Honor felt ready to do what she'd been putting off.

She grabbed the phone and dialed the number quickly, bracing herself for the conversation she was about to have.

"Hello?" Chad's voice was as gravelly and harsh as Honor remembered it to be.

"Chad. This is Honor Malone."

"Yeah, I thought you'd be calling after I talked to that sheriff. Guy asked me a couple hundred questions about Jay. Like I remember what my son was doing or who he was doing it with."

The crude statement made Honor wince, but she didn't comment. The easiest way to get along with Chad was to keep quiet and let him do all the talking.

Actually, that was the only way to get along with him.

"So, what do you want, Honor? I hope you're not

going to try to get me to rescue you from whatever trouble you're in. Seems to me there's been enough time between us that we aren't really family anymore."

"I didn't call to get your help, Chad. I called to find out what happened to Melanie. Candace needs to know."

"Then Candace should call herself."

"She's got a busy schedule."

"She's a coward. Just like Jay. The boy slunk away with his tail between his legs the minute he was old enough to leave home."

Honor gritted her teeth to keep from making a rude comment and tried to turn the conversation around. "Candace is in college. I know Melanie would be proud of her, and I'm sure you are, too."

"Melanie had her head in the booze too much to be proud of anyone or anything, but I've got to say it's good to know that my daughter didn't turn out like her worthless mother."

Charming. That was Chad. Unless he needed something from someone, he had no compassion— and showed it.

"Can you tell me what happened to Melanie? It really is important to Candace."

"What do you think happened to my wife? She drank herself to death."

"She died from alcohol poisoning?"

"She died of liver failure. Started having problems last year. Tried to quit drinking, but couldn't do it. Eventually her body just gave out."

"I'm sorry."

"So is everyone else I talk to."

"But not you?" The question slipped out, and Honor didn't regret it. Melanie's alcoholism had stolen her ability to mother effectively. As far as Honor could see, Chad had no excuse for being a poor father except sheer meanness.

"What I feel or don't feel isn't your business, Honor."

"But your reasons for not contacting us about Melanie are. Candace had a right to attend her mother's funeral."

"What funeral? Melanie wanted to be cremated and have her ashes scattered on the Gulf."

"Still—"

"Look, I'm pretty sure you mean well. You were always that kind of person. Too good for us Malones. But the fact is, it's over. Melanie is gone. I didn't contact Candace because after four years of never hearing from her, I didn't think she'd care to know. That might have been a mistake in judgment, but it wasn't a crime. So unless you've got something else you need to know, I've got to go."

"No. That's it."

"Good. Have a nice life, Honor." The phone clicked, the line disconnected, and Honor was left holding the phone and wondering how a man who had borne two children could have cared so little for them.

For all his faults, Jay had been immensely pleased by the idea of fatherhood. He'd planned a lifetime of father-child experiences before his death, and often talked to Honor about undoing the pattern of abuse his parents had created.

If he'd lived, he would have loved Lily desperately. Honor had no doubt about that.

She placed the phone back on the receiver, smiling at Lily who was watching her with wide, wary eyes.

"Well, that's that. I'm off the phone and I'm thinking we should make some of your grandmom's homemade bread to go with our stew. Want to help?"

"Okay."

"Get out the bread pans that are in the corner cupboard." Honor pulled yeast from a top shelf and started running warm water into a measuring cup. Angry for Candace's sake, but unable to do anything with the emotion, she concentrated her efforts on kneading soft white dough, pounding it and imagining it was her father-in-law's aristocratic nose she was hitting.

TWENTY

The sky was already lightening, the first hints of morning turning it deep cerulean as Grayson drove past the police cruiser stationed at the end of Honor's street. He waved to the officer as he drove by, then turned his attention to Honor's small bungalow. Her car was parked in the driveway just as it should be. Satisfied and relieved, Grayson drove around the corner and pulled into his own driveway.

His muscles ached from tension, and his eyes were dry from fatigue, but he'd won two court cases, guaranteeing that two very bad men would be in prison for a long time. He'd also met with his team and planned out a strategy for a high-profile case that was on the docket. It had taken hours, but everything he'd wanted to accomplish had been done. Now he was home for a quick shower, some food and a catnap before he started the routine all over again.

The morning was silent, the cold clear air giving Grayson a quick burst of energy as he hurried to his front door. It was false energy, but at least it was energy. He'd been dragging since he'd returned from New York. Emotional stress, worry about Jude. Worry about Honor and her family. All those things had made sleeping difficult. The part of him that had been raised to believe that God was in control, the part of him that *did* believe it, rebelled at the idea of losing sleep over worry. If God was in control, He'd work everything out according to His plan. There was no reason to spend time worrying about it.

Of course, Grayson wasn't the kind to let others do what he thought he could. Even in his relationship with God, he often spent more time solving his own problems than waiting for God to do it. He was a man of action, and he'd never seen anything wrong with that until recently. Lately, he was trying to back off and let God take control. It wasn't easy, but he had no choice. As much as he wanted to put an end to Honor's nightmare, he couldn't.

That was a hard pill to swallow, but a necessary one.

Honor had said it best—until a person realized faith was all he had, he couldn't understand that it was all he needed.

Grayson ran a hand over his hair and yawned. He'd been up for almost twenty-four hours. He needed to rectify that situation. Now. He was going inside. He was going to lie down. And he was going to forget about everything for two hours.

He walked up the steps that led to his front door, pausing when he caught sight of a white plastic grocery bag hanging from the door handle. Not a cosmetic catalogue or advertisement, as the contents were larger and thicker. So what was it?

Grayson approached cautiously, mindful of the threat that had been made against him. The man stalking Honor could easily have visited Grayson's house while the police sat around the corner. He eyed the bag, leaning close, trying to see its contents. Anything electrical and he'd call Jake, have him send for the state's bomb squad.

The scent of yeast hung in the air near the bag. And something else. Onions. Beef.

Stew?

He lifted the bag, peered inside and saw a clear plastic container filled with what looked like stew. Three thick slices of bread were in a plastic Ziploc bag, and Grayson's mouth watered at the sight. He hadn't realized how hungry he was until that moment. Now he was starving. There was a folded piece of paper inside the bag, and he pulled it out as he went in to the house and flicked on the foyer light

Grayson, I decided to help you out on your quest for more nutritious food and brought some beef stew for you. Lily and I made the bread together. If you clean your plate, there are a few chocolate-chip cookies packed, too. Honor.

Grayson smiled as he read the note. He doubted Honor had meant for him to eat the stew at this time of the day, but it looked too good to pass up. Besides, he'd sleep better on a full stomach. He heated the stew up in the microwave, his gaze drawn again and again to the sunroom windows that looked out over the backyard. Honor's house was dark for a change, but Grayson still wanted to walk outside, cross the yard and go over to see her. It seemed odd that after such a short amount of time, Honor would have become so deeply entrenched in his thoughts.

He'd dated Maria for two years before he'd proposed, because he had firmly believed it took at least that long to get to know someone.

Had firmly believed that.

Now he wasn't quite as sure.

Despite the short amount of time he'd known Honor, he knew her goals and dreams, knew what she valued and what she didn't. Knew that being with her was the most comfortable part of his day. Knew that being without her made him long to be near her again.

He'd always scoffed at the idea of love at first sight. His relationship with Maria had been about mutual benefit more than deep emotion. In retrospect, that seemed like a cold and calculated reason to plan a marriage, but at the time it had made sense. Maria was an attractive, intelligent woman whose goals and aspirations had been similar to Grayson's. After weighing the pros and cons, balancing risk with benefit, Grayson had decided that marriage with her would be worth it.

Maria's response hadn't been any less deliberate. There'd been no tearful acceptance. No speechless nod. Maria had slipped the ring on her finger, leaned forward to plant a chaste kiss on Grayson's lips and announced that their marriage would be the perfect merger.

Merger?

Was it any wonder their relationship hadn't worked out?

With Honor things were different. With her, the relationship was more about emotional need and support than convenience. The kisses they'd shared had burned into his soul, branding his heart in a way no other woman's ever had.

He frowned, spooning up a mouthful of rich stew, and acknowledging a truth he'd been avoiding. He'd spent years maintaining careful control in every area of his life. His days planned, his schedule carefully worked out, his life's goals clearly defined. College, law school, a career as a state prosecutor. He'd had a time line for all those things. As well as for relationships, marriage and kids. He hadn't wanted his careful plans ruined. Hadn't wanted the messy complications a relationship could bring. He'd liked his life just the way it had been.

Until he'd met Honor.

One look in her eyes and he'd seen forever.

He wouldn't let a deranged stalker take that from him.

Honor stifled a yawn and glanced at her watch as she stepped out of a patient's room. Ten more minutes and her shift would end. Good. She'd been distracted and ill at ease for most of the day. Speaking with her father-in-law the previous day had added more anxiety to the boiling cauldron that had taken up residence in her stomach. The fact that she hadn't seen Grayson since the previous afternoon had nothing to do with her sour mood. Nothing at all.

"What's wrong with you?" Will fell into step beside her as she moved down the hall.

"Nothing. Why?"

"Because you've spent the entire shift looking like your best friend died."

"Actually, my mother-in-law did."

"Yeah? I'm sorry to hear that, Honor."

"Me, too."

"Maybe we could go out for a drink or something to take the edge off our troubles."

"That's not my kind of thing."

"I didn't think so, but I thought I'd ask anyway. So, how about we just go get something to eat? A little post-dinner/pre-breakfast meal?"

"How about we just do what we always do? Walk out to our cars together and say good-night."

"If I didn't know better, I'd think you were a cold-hearted witch."

"Will!" Surprised, Honor took a hard look at her co-worker. He'd always seemed benign if persistent, but maybe he was something a lot more sinister than that.

"Hey, I'm kidding."

"It didn't sound like a joke."

"Sorry. I've had a long day. Maybe it's coming out in my tone." But he didn't sound sorry, and Honor wondered if walking out to her car with him was a good idea.

Was it possible Will was her stalker?

She'd bring up the idea to Jake. For now, she'd go on instinct and leave without him. Either Grayson or a police cruiser had been waiting for her after work for the past few nights. She'd be safe enough walking outside on her own.

As soon as her shift ended, she signed out, hurrying from the nurse's station before Will arrived from his rounds. The night was dark and silent, the moon a golden crescent. Honor scanned the parking lot as she hurried through it, searching for and finding Grayson's car in its usual spot at the far end of the lot.

Relieved, she offered a quick wave and got into her car, starting the engine and glancing in her rearview mirror, her heart stopping as she saw a face staring back at her. Dark gleaming eyes. Pale distorted features.

The face in the window.

Something hard and smooth pressed against the back of her head and Honor froze. Afraid to move. Afraid to breathe.

"I've got a gun, Honor. I'd hate to have to use it." He spoke in a harsh whisper. A voice that could be anyone or no one. The voice of every nightmare, every fear she'd ever had.

"Who are you? What do you want?" Honor's voice trembled, her mind blank but for one thought—she was going to die.

"We'll talk about that later. Right now, we need

to get away from your friend. He's really become a problem, don't you think?"

"What are you planning?"

"Just some alone-time with you. So, here's what you're going to do. You're going to drive over to where he's parked, and you're going to unroll your window and get him to do the same. Then you're going to tell him that you're sick of being followed around. You're going to accuse him of being your stalker. You're going to tell him that if he follows you home again, you're going to file a restraining order against him."

"He'll never believe that."

"He'd better. I didn't bring the gun to use on you, Honor. Though I will, if I have to. I brought it to take care of anyone who tries to stop me from going after what I want. So, you'd better make sure you're convincing. I'd hate to see an attorney's brains splattered all over the pavement before we go off on our adventure."

"You don't know Grayson. There's nothing I could say that would convince him to—"

"I know *everything*." The hissed words shivered through Honor and made her mouth go dry with fear. The hard nudge of the gun butting against her head filled her with the kind of terror she'd felt only once before. Then she'd been saved by a neighbor. This time, she might not be saved at all.

"Please…"

"Listen to me, I know your prosecutor friend won't risk his career over you. All you have to do is convince him that pursuing his hero-fantasy might cost him that. He'll take off, and we can be on our way in peace. Come on. Drive. If you take too long and he comes over to investigate, things might get messy. You won't like messy."

Did she have a choice?

Honor couldn't think of one. At least not one that ended with her alive. She put the car in gear, her legs trembling so much she pressed too hard on the accelerator and the car jumped forward, the butt of the gun knocking into her head again.

"Better watch it. These things can go off easily. I'm going to get out of sight, but this gun is pressed right against the back of your seat. It'll be easy enough to make you sorry if I have to."

Honor's teeth chattered, but she did what she'd been told—drive over to Grayson's car, motion for him to roll down his window.

He smiled a welcome and did as she'd indicated, speaking softly into the silent darkness. "Hey, looks like you're out a little earlier tonight."

"Yes. I decided not to wait for Will."

"Didn't I tell you not to walk outside by yourself?"

"Yes." Her mind was blank, her body frozen with fear. She couldn't think of what she was supposed to say. She couldn't remember what she had to do to save Grayson and herself.

"Is everything okay, Honor?" Grayson shifted and Honor was sure he was going to get out of his car, see the madman in the backseat of her Ford and die.

She wouldn't let that be the last thing she ever saw. She wouldn't let his life end so brutally.

"It's fine. Just fine. The thing is…" A hard jab at her back urged her on. "I'm getting tired of being followed home every night."

"It's for your own safety."

"I'm beginning to wonder if that's really the truth. I'm beginning to think something else is going on."

"What?" He frowned, and Honor knew he had no idea the direction she was heading in.

"Everything was fine in Lakeview, Grayson, until you came home from New York."

His expression tightened, his frown turning to a scowl. "What are you implying, Honor?"

"I'm not implying anything. I'm flat-out saying it." Her voice was rising with her mounting fear. He'd hear it as anger. She only hoped it would convince him to drive away.

"I don't think I'm clear on what exactly you are saying. Maybe you can fill me in on a few more details."

"I met you and within twenty-four hours I started receiving flowers and threats."

"So?"

"So how do I know that you're not the one responsible? How do I know that you didn't see me that first day and decide you'd do whatever it took to have me?"

His laughter was harsh and ugly, his eyes flashing with anger. "You have got to be kidding me."

"Kidding? I'm dead serious."

"Honor, you received a phone call from the stalker while I was with you. Don't you think it would have been difficult for me to make it while you were standing next to me?" The question was as harsh as his laugh had been, his eyes narrowing as he stared her down.

"You know plenty of criminals. I'm sure one of them would have been willing to make the phone call for the right price."

"I think we'd better end this conversation. I'll be happy to discuss the subject again when we've both had some sleep. For now, I'll make sure you get home safely, and then I'll get out of your life."

"Get rid of him now, or he gets it." The soft whisper from behind Honor was like a cobra's hiss—filled with deadly promise.

"I already told you I'm tired of being followed. If you choose to ignore that, I'll be forced to file an order of protection against you."

"Have you lost your mind?" Grayson bit the words out and Honor knew she'd done what she'd intended. She wanted to beg Grayson's forgiveness, she wanted to tell him it was all a lie.

"No, but I better have lost my tail. I *will* file the order, Grayson, so don't follow me." She rolled up her window and drove away, glancing in the rear-view mirror, tears in her eyes.

Had he sensed her fear?

Did he realize how many lies she'd told?

Did he know how much she cared about him?

"Crying for your lover, Honor?" The man behind

her sneered, rearing up from behind the seat and pressing his gun against her cheek.

"Grayson is my friend."

"That kiss you gave him looked more than friendly."

The words left her cold. He'd been watching even when she'd thought she was safe.

"Is he following us?" The disembodied voice was louder, the serpent sounding more like a self-satisfied man than a cobra.

"No."

"Good. I didn't want to ruin our party if I didn't have to." His masked face appeared in the mirror again, and Honor cringed. "You must be a good actress, Honor. He seemed completely convinced. But I'm not surprised. You've got so many other good qualities."

"Let me go. Please."

"You're going to beg? I expected so much more from you." The cold barrel of the gun ran down the side of her neck, and Honor had to force herself to keep breathing.

"I'm not begging."

"Sure you are. But it won't do you any good. We've got a date with destiny."

"Where are we going?"

"Into the mountains. You know the Blue Ridge Parkway, right?"

"Yes."

"Drive toward it."

"What happens when we get there?"

"I'll let you know when it's time."

"But—"

"Drive!" The gun butted hard into her cheek, and Honor knew that the night was going to get a lot worse before it got better.

If it ever got better.

She shivered, keeping her gaze straight ahead and praying desperately for the help she was afraid would never come.

TWENTY-ONE

Grayson waited a few heartbeats before pulling out after Honor. He kept his headlights off and his speed down, not wanting Honor to know he was behind her. Not because he believed she'd file an order of protection against him, but because she was a bad actress. So bad that he'd known before she even began speaking that something was very wrong. She'd said all the right things, but he'd seen the fear in her eyes. Had known what it meant.

Someone had been in the car with her.

That was the only explanation he could come up with for the stark terror she'd shown in her eyes and for her bizarre accusation. His hands tightened on the steering wheel and his heart beat furiously as he followed her car.

He'd had another late meeting and had intended to have a police officer escort her home again, but worry had nagged at his gut, pulled at his attention, demanded that he be the one to make sure she arrived home safely.

It wasn't often Grayson saw evidence of God's intervention, but this was one of those times. It would have been easy for Honor to send a police officer on his way. She then would have driven off with a madman in her car and no one would have been the wiser. Not until her girls woke up to her absence, or her body was found beaten and bloodied on the side of some road.

And there was no doubt in Grayson's mind that that was exactly what her stalker planned to do. He'd seen it before. Seen the photographs of crime scenes as he tried men who'd created elaborate fantasies, been disappointed and killed the object of their affection.

He wouldn't let that happen to Honor.

He pulled his cell phone from the console, started to dial 911, but hesitated. If some gung-ho cop came riding to the rescue with lights flashing and sirens blaring, Honor would be dead before he ever made it to her car. He dialed Jake's cell phone, instead.

"Reed here."

"Jake, it's Grayson. We've got a situation on the Blue Ridge Parkway."

"Tell me."

Grayson explained as succinctly as possible, refusing to give in to the anger and fear that were surging through him.

"You're on the Parkway, now?"

"Heading toward the overlook."

"I'm on my way. You back off and let us handle

this." Jake issued the order, but Grayson chose not to hear it.

"What's your ETA?"

"Fifteen minutes."

"A lot can happen in fifteen minutes."

"Back off. If you don't, you're going to get in our way and slow us down."

"If I do, Honor might not be alive when you finally get to her. I'll call you if things change."

"Don't—"

Grayson hung up. He was done talking. Done with rational conversation. They were dealing with irrationality. Stalkers weren't working with a full deck. They acted in ways that couldn't be predicted. Grayson wasn't willing to step back and wait for the guy who was with Honor to make a move.

He pressed down on the gas, closing the distance between his car and Honor's. If something happened, he wanted to be close enough to stop it.

Honor gripped the steering wheel with both hands, her heart pounding at an alarming pace. If she had a heart attack, the car would go over the side of the mountain. She and her nightmare would tumble head over heels until they hit the earth below.

Death. Quick and swift and hopefully painless.

Something told her that wasn't what the masked man behind her had planned.

"There's a scenic overlook up ahead. Follow the signs and drive there. Park the car."

"What are we—"

"We'll talk when we get there."

"If we're going to talk, we should go somewhere warmer. Maybe a nice romantic restaurant." If he really had some kind of fantasy about having a relationship with Honor, maybe he'd like the idea of having dinner with her better than the idea of brutally murdering her and throwing her off the side of the mountain.

She shuddered at the thought.

"Dinner at a restaurant? Why not just go back to your place? You've certainly been entertaining that lawyer there plenty."

"I wasn't—"

"Shut up." The gun pressed against her cheek, jabbing hard enough to bring tears to Honor's eyes.

She did what she was told, her gaze darting to the rearview mirror. She expected to see her captor staring back at her, but saw only the open road.

Or was it?

Had there been something moving in the distance? She looked in the mirror again, her breath catching in her throat as she realized a car was coming up behind them. Lights off, but still visible in the moonlight. Was it the police? She'd been praying desperately that Grayson hadn't fallen for her act, praying that he'd realized something was wrong and called for help.

"The turn is coming up. Don't miss it or we'll have our chat somewhere a lot less comfortable."

Honor jerked her attention back to the road and took the turn a little too quickly. Her tires squealed and slid, and Honor gripped the steering wheel hard, terror filling her. She didn't want to die. Not now. She had too many things to do with her life. Too many memories she still wanted to create.

Please, Lord, don't let me die.

"This is it. Pull into the parking area and turn off the car."

Terror thrummed through Honor's veins, her heart pounding so fast she thought it would leap from her chest, but she did what she was told. She'd fight when she had to. Until then, she'd do everything she could to stay alive.

"Good. Now, we're getting out of the car nice and slow. You try to run and I'll shoot you in the back. Understand?"

"I won't try to run." Yet.

"That's what I wanted to hear. Give me your keys and get out."

She pulled the keys from the ignition, her hand shaking as she placed them in his. He was wearing gloves. She hadn't realized it until now. And she knew beyond a shadow of a doubt that she was about to die.

She got out of the car anyway. Her chances were going to be better outside.

"Walk over to that little railing. The one that looks out over the valley. I picked this spot especially for you."

"I'm afraid of heights." It was a lie she could live with. One that she hoped would keep her far away from any place where she could be thrown off.

"Are you? Funny, I heard you climbed rock walls in college and dreamed of making a trek to Mount Everest."

That *had* been a dream of hers years ago, and hearing it now made her cringe. "How do you know that?"

"I know everything there is to know about you, Honor. And I know everything there is to know about how to keep what's rightfully mine."

"I'm not yours."

He laughed, his breath hot and clammy against her ear. "You? Did you really believe this was about *you?* You're nothing, Honor. Nothing but some transplant from Ireland who thinks she's better than everyone." His voice changed as he spoke, the harsh whisper replaced by something familiar. Something she'd heard less than twenty-four hours ago.

"Chad?" She pivoted toward him, saw a flash of movement.

Pain exploded through her head, driving everything away until there was only darkness and the soft, sweet feel of oblivion.

Grayson lunged forward as the man who'd hit Honor leaned down and grabbed her arms.

He didn't give the guy a chance to react, just grasped him by the back of the shirt and yanked him around, punching him in the abdomen. Not caring about the gun that clattered to the ground. Not caring about anything but protecting Honor.

The man grunted, his breath leaving on a whoosh of sound. Grayson hit him again, this time in the face. Hearing the satisfying crack of bone against bone, the thud of flesh slamming into flesh.

Honor's attacker stumbled backward, landing in a heap, but then stumbling to his feet again, he turned, trying to run. Grayson lunged forward, grabbing his arm and jerking him around, ready to punch him again.

His hand was grabbed midswing, the force of the restraint stopping his momentum. "You'd better cool it, friend. We don't want any charges of police brutality." Jake Reed's voice was as calm as a placid lake, but there was steel in his grip.

"I'm not the police."

"You're the prosecutor. We don't need you getting into trouble, either."

"I don't really care what kind of trouble I get into."

"One punch to the guy, I can ignore. I can't ignore two, Gray. And you're not going to do Honor any good if I've got to cart you away and lock you up for a twelve-hour cool-down."

The words finally registered through the red haze of his fury, and Grayson released his hold on the man. Stepped back, turned away.

Honor lay on her side on the ground, her hair covering her face. Grayson knelt beside her, joining a female deputy who was checking Honor's pulse. "Is she okay?"

"Her pulse is strong and steady, but she's out cold. I'm going to call for transport to Lynchburg General." The deputy stood, speaking into her radio as she hovered nearby.

Grayson ignored her, focusing his attention on Honor. He brushed thick strands of silky hair from her face and saw blood on her temple. "Honor?"

His fingers grazed her cheek, dropped to her neck to check her pulse again. As his hand moved, Honor's eyes opened. Hazy. Confused. But open.

"Grayson. You came."

"Did you think I wouldn't?" Relief made his hand shake as he leaned in to help Honor sit up. He slipped a hand behind her back, supporting her when she swayed.

"I told you not to."

"And you expected me to listen?"

"I hoped you wouldn't. I prayed you wouldn't."

"And I prayed that God would help me keep you safe."

"I guess we both got what we prayed for." She smiled, wincing a little as she turned her head. "It *is* Chad."

"What?" He stared into her eyes, trying to determine if the head injury was causing her confusion.

"My stalker. It's Chad Malone."

"Your father-in-law?" He looked at the man he'd punched. Short, stocky, cropped brown hair and angry, hate-filled eyes.

"Yes. I just can't figure out why he'd want to hurt me, or how he ended up here."

"Jake will find out soon enough."

"Good. My head hurts too much to try to work it out myself." She leaned a little more heavily on his arm, and Grayson tightened his hold, calling out to the female deputy.

"Is the ambulance on the way?"

"It should be here in ten."

"Ambulance. For what?" Honor's voice sounded much weaker than Grayson liked, and the blood from her head wound was beginning to pool on the pavement.

"For you."

"I don't need an ambulance."

"You're bleeding like a stuck pig. You do need an ambulance." Grayson pulled off his coat, using the sleeve to staunch the flow of blood.

"Head wounds always bleed a lot."

"Yeah? Well, from the looks of things, you're going to need stitches. You've got a two-inch gash in your temple." He brushed hair away from the spot, lifting the coat to look at the wound. "It's deep."

"It'll have to wait. I need to get home to the girls."

"I'll call Candace and tell her what happened."

"No!" Honor lowered her voice. "She'll panic."

"Then I'll just tell her you got held up. You can explain things when you get home."

"Explain? I don't even understand what happened."

"I'll go see if Jake has any information." He started to rise, but Honor grabbed his hand, holding him in place.

"Don't go. I need to thank you before I forget."

"Thank me for what?"

"For slaying the dragon." She smiled, her pale face beautiful in the moonlight.

"I didn't slay him. I wanted to, though."

"You did slay him, and I can't wait to tell Lily what I learned tonight."

"What's that?"

"That you really are a prince." She laid a palm against his cheek, urging him closer and placing a kiss on his lips.

Grayson laughed, relief and happiness stripping away anger and fear. Hope replacing anxiety. He didn't know what the next few hours would bring, had no idea what would happen over the course of Jake's investigation, but he knew Honor was going to be okay.

That was enough for now.

TWENTY-TWO

Honor stared at her reflection in the bathroom mirror and grimaced, wishing she hadn't agreed to go out. She had looked bad enough after a few sleepless nights. Add fifteen stitches and a bruised cheekbone and her face was shudder-worthy.

Someone knocked at the front door, and Honor froze, her heart pounding with anticipation and dread. She'd been imagining this moment all day. Now that it was here, she wasn't sure she was ready for it.

Lily's squeals of excitement told Honor that Candace had opened the door and let their visitor in.

"Is Honor ready?" Grayson's voice carried down the hall, and Honor glanced at her reflection one last time.

Was she ready?

"I'll be right there." She dusted powder over her bruised cheek, pulled hair over the stitches and prayed Grayson wouldn't take one look at her and change his mind about their date.

Honor's first in over eight years.

Just the thought made her stomach churn.

"Honor, come on. Mr. Sinclair is waiting." Candace appeared at the bathroom door looking as nervous as Honor felt. "You look beautiful, so stop staring at yourself and go."

"Maybe I should cancel."

"Are you nuts? That man is the best thing that has happened in your life since I moved in with you."

Her words made Honor laugh, and she winced as her cheek throbbed in response.

Two days after Chad had attacked her, and she was just beginning to heal. She could only hope Candace's emotional wounds were doing the same.

She studied her sister-in-law's face, trying to find some clue as to how the teenager was doing. But Candace looked the same as always—sweet and just a little closed off, her expression impossible to read. "Are you sure you don't mind me going out tonight?"

"Are you kidding? I've been praying you'd hook up with Grayson since the first time I saw him."

"You have not."

"I have, too. Now come on. Before he decides you're taking too long and leaves."

"Candace…" She wasn't sure what she wanted to say, but only knew it was there, just below the surface, waiting to be revealed.

"Honor." Candace used the same inflection Honor had, her eyes sparkling with humor and hiding whatever grief she might be feeling. Then she sobered, putting her hand on Honor's arm. "You don't have to worry about me, you know."

"Of course, I do. I love you."

"And I love you, too." It was the first time she'd ever said the words, and Honor's eyes burned with tears she didn't dare shed. "But love doesn't mean worry. It means prayer. And with your prayers over me, I'll be just fine."

"What your father did was awful, but it had nothing to do with you. You know that, right?"

"It had plenty to do with me. He wanted control of the trust funds Mom had left to me and Lily. He was willing to kill you to make sure he got it." Candace's jaw tightened, but she didn't walk away as she had every other time Honor had broached the subject.

"Which had nothing to do with you."

"Honor, a man whose DNA I share waited until Mom was getting ready to take her last breath and then hired a doped-up druggie to kill you in St. Louis. When that failed, he decided to 'stalk' and kill you, figuring the police would never suspect him of the crime. If he had succeeded, he would have effectively gotten rid of the trustee to Mom's estate which was the only thing that stood between him and two million dollars."

"He didn't succeed, though."

"Not for lack of trying. And the way he just blabbed it all out hoping for a plea bargain? What a coward." Candace stepped back, her expression closed off again. "You really need to get moving. Lily is probably making Mr. Sinclair crazy. Ever since you told her he really was a dragon slayer and said you'd seen him slay a dragon, she won't stop pestering him to tell the story."

"Grayson will be okay for another minute."

"Honor, please, just go." The tears in Candace's eyes were unmistakable, and Honor wanted desperately to pull her into a hug.

She knew she'd be rebuffed, so she patted her shoulder instead. "I really don't want to leave you, Candace."

"And I already told you that you don't need to worry. Go have dinner and enjoy being with a handsome man."

"I—"

"Honor, is everything okay?" Grayson stood in the hallway, his hair brushed back from his forehead, his gaze touching on her bruised cheek, then resting on her lips before he met her eyes. Her heart jumped in acknowledgment, all the anxiety she'd been feeling melting away.

"Everything is fine. I'm just not sure I should leave Candace…and Lily home tonight."

"Then we'll order pizza or Chinese and eat it here." He brushed strands of hair from her cheek, his fingers lingering, his touch heating her skin.

"No, you won't!" Candace protested loudly, but Grayson just smiled in her direction.

"Sorry, kid. You're outvoted."

"This is ridiculous. I'm not a baby, you know. I don't need a sitter." Candace huffed the words and stomped away, her disgust obvious.

"Do you think she'll get over it?" Grayson tugged Honor a few steps down the hall, stopping before they got to the living room and wrapping his arms around her waist, his scent and his warmth as familiar as an old friend.

"Get over us not going out for dinner? Yes. Get over what her father did? I don't know." Honor sighed and snuggled close to his chest.

"It must be tough for her, knowing that her father is a murderer."

"Chad didn't actually kill anyone." And Honor liked to tell herself he wouldn't have. That either she would have escaped, or he would have changed his mind. She knew the truth, though. Chad would have done anything to gain control of what he thought was rightfully his—the money his wife had inherited from her parents and had kept out of his hands for their entire marriage. It was the one thing he had never been able to take from her. The one thing he'd been determined to get.

No matter the cost.

As soon as he'd realized that Melanie would not be leaving him anything in her will, he'd begun plotting. When hospice had been called in to care for his ailing wife, he'd set his plan in motion, hiring a druggie to kill Honor. Jake and Grayson both suspected that he planned to kill the man after the fact.

Honor preferred not to speculate on any of her father-in-law's plans.

When his attempt to have Honor murdered had failed, Chad had decided to take matters into his own hands. Stalking Honor became a game that he learned to play well. His phone calls were forwarded from his house in Florida to his cell phone, and neither Jake nor Honor had realized he was in Lakeview until it was almost too late. If he hadn't slipped and mentioned Jay's infidelity they might never have made the connection to him. Whether or not Jake's phone call had forced Chad's hand and made him act earlier than he'd planned, was something Chad refused to discuss.

He'd certainly been willing to discuss just about everything else. Like Candace had said, he'd spilled everything, hoping for leniency that Grayson was determined to see he never got.

And rightfully so.

Just thinking about the terrifying ride up into the mountains made Honor shiver.

"Hey, are you okay?" Grayson cupped her face, his hands anchoring her to the present, his eyes beckoning her into the future. And she knew she would risk her heart to go there with him.

"With you here, how could I not be?"

He smiled, pressing a kiss to her lips, the touch so gentle a tear slipped down her cheek.

"Don't cry." His rough palm smoothed away the moisture.

"How can I not when I'm so happy?"

He kissed her again, stealing her breath and filling her heart so that there was no room for regrets or sorrow.

"Mommy? Is this the part in the story when the

prince gets to kiss the princess and they live happily ever after?" Lily's voice cut into the moment, and Grayson pulled away, smiling down into Honor's eyes, offering her everything she'd ever wanted.

"Yes, Lily Mae. It most definitely is." And she pulled Grayson's head down for another kiss, sealing the moment and their future together.

* * * * *

Dear Reader,

Honor Malone's character was inspired by my grandmother, a widow who raised five children alone. Nana poured her heart, soul and passion into her kids. Perhaps that was why she never remarried. Like my grandmother, Honor is a strong, determined mother who has no intention of marrying again after her first husband dies. Despite her deep faith in God, she doesn't want to acknowledge that Grayson Sinclair might be part of His perfect plan for her life. I hope you enjoy reading Honor and Grayson's story, and I pray that wherever you are heading, God will be the compass that guides you on your journey.

If you have time, drop me a line at: shirlee@shirleemccoy.com or by mail at P.O. Box 592, Gambrills, MD 21054.

All His best,

Shirlee McCoy

Questions for Discussion

1. Why is Honor so determined to remain single?

2. In what way did Honor's marriage to Jay change her perspective on life?

3. How did that change affect her relationship with her daughter, her sister-in-law and even with God?

4. How would you describe Honor's relationship with God?

5. Honor is a strong woman who doesn't want to need anyone. What is it about Grayson that makes her want to rely on him?

6. Grayson has spent years pursuing his career. What things has he put on hold in order to be successful?

7. Grayson has been a Christian for many years, but his relationship with God has waned. Have there been times in your life when you've felt distant from God? What things in your life draw you away from a close relationship with Him?

8. What steps does Grayson take to reclaim his relationship with God?

9. Grayson has put aside the thought of marriage and family, but meeting Honor makes him wonder if both might once again be possible. How does his renewed relationship with God strengthen his resolve to pursue a relationship with Honor?

10. Trust is an underlying theme in Honor and Grayson's story. Why is it so hard for Honor to trust Grayson?

11. Honor's relationship with Grayson isn't the only thing that changes during the course of the story. How does Honor's faith grow during her troubles?

12. Honor has difficulty believing that Grayson is part of God's plan for her life. Have you ever struggled to understand the truth of God's plan? How were you able to finally understand what He wanted for your life?

SPECIAL EXCERPT FROM

Love Inspired.
SUSPENSE

*Morgan Smith is hiding in the Witness Protection
Program. Has her past come back to haunt her?*

*Read on for a preview of
TOP SECRET IDENTITY by Sharon Dunn,
the next exciting book in the
WITNESS PROTECTION series
from Love Inspired Suspense. Available April 2014.*

A wave of terror washed over Morgan Smith when sh
heard the tapping at her window. Someone was outside th
caretaker's cottage. Had the man who'd tried to kill her i
Mexico found her in Iowa?

Though she'd been in witness protection for two month
her fear of being killed had never subsided. She'd le
Des Moines for the countryside and a job at a stable b
cause she had felt exposed in the city, vulnerable. She
grown up on a ranch in Wyoming, and when she'd worke
as an American missionary in Mexico, she'd always chose
to be in rural areas. Wide-open spaces seemed safer to he

With her heart pounding, she rose to her feet and walke
the short distance to the window, half expecting to see a fa
contorted with rage, or clawlike hands reaching for her nec
The memory of nearly being strangled made her shudde
She stepped closer to the window, seeing only blackness. Y
the sound of the tapping had been too distinct to dismiss
the wind rattling the glass.

A chill snaked down her spine.

Someone was outside.

If the man from Mexico had come to kill her, it seemed odd that he would give her a warning by tapping on the window.

She thought to call her new boss, who was in the guest-house less than a hundred yards away. Alex Reardon seemed like a nice man. She'd hated being evasive when he'd asked her where she had gotten her knowledge of horses. She'd been blessed to get the job without references. Her references, everything and everyone she knew, all of that had been stripped from her, even her name. She was no longer Magdalena Chavez. Her new name was Morgan Smith.

The knob on the locked door turned and rattled.

She'd been a fool to think the U.S. Marshals could keep her safe.

Pick up TOP SECRET IDENTITY wherever
Love Inspired® Suspense books and ebooks are sold.

Copyright © 2014 by Harlequin Books S.A.

LISEXP0314

Love Inspired®
SUSPENSE
RIVETING INSPIRATIONAL ROMANCE

FOR THE CHILD

Foster mother Noelle Whitman adores the little girl she's caring for. Noelle has terrible memories of her own foster care experience and vows to do right by this child. But when the girl's father, fresh out of jail for murdering his estranged wife, arrives for his daughter, Noelle is worried. The former SWAT team member insists he was framed. But moments later, someone shoots at Caleb, and the three are forced on the run. Protective and kind, Caleb is nothing like the embittered ex-con she expected. And learning to trust him may be the only way to survive.

TOP COPS

WRONGLY ACCUSED
by
LAURA SCOTT

*Available April 2014 wherever
Love Inspired books and ebooks are sold.*

Find us on Facebook at
www.Facebook.com/LoveInspiredBooks

LIS44

OPEN TO LOVE?

After refusing to give in to an unwanted engagement,
Alice Hawthorne is determined to stake her own claim during
the Oklahoma Land Rush. But when she meets Elijah Thornton,
can the preacher convince her to open her heart?

The Preacher's Bride Claim

by

LAURIE KINGERY

*Available April 2014 wherever
Love Inspired books and ebooks are sold.*

Find us on Facebook at
www.Facebook.com/LoveInspiredBooks

LIH28259

Cowboy, wanderer… Father?

Nate Lyster and Mia Verbeek are in perfect agreement—that letting someone new into your heart is much too risky. Left on her own with four kids, Mia can't let just anyone get close, while wandering cowboy Nate learned young that love now means heartbreak later.

But when a fire turns Mia's life upside down, Nate is the only one who can get through to her traumatized son—and her heart. If Nate and Mia can forget the hurts of their pasts, they might get everything they want. But if they let fear win, a perfect love could pass them by….

A Father in the Making
by
Carolyn Aarsen

Available April 2014 wherever
Love Inspired books and ebooks are sold.

Find us on Facebook at
www.Facebook.com/LoveInspiredBooks

LI87

Love Inspired® SUSPENSE
RIVETING INSPIRATIONAL ROMANCE

THREAT FROM HER AMISH PAST

Eight years ago, a drifter destroyed Becca Miller's ties to her Amish community—and murdered her family. Now a special agent with Fort Rickman's criminal investigation department, Becca knows her past has caught up with her, and doesn't want to relive it. She's convinced that the killer, who supposedly died years ago, is very much alive and after her. Special agent Colby Voss agrees to help her investigate. Yet the closer they get to the truth, the closer the killer gets to silencing her permanently.

MILITARY INVESTIGATIONS

THE AGENT'S SECRET PAST
by
DEBBY GIUSTI

Available March 2014 wherever Love Inspired Suspense books and ebooks are sold.

nd us on Facebook at
ww.Facebook.com/LoveInspiredBooks

LIS44587

LoveInspired HISTORICA

A COWBOY WITHOUT A NAME

The only thing Brand Duggan's outlaw kin ever gave him was a
undeserved reputation. Once he's through breaking horses, he
leave Eden Valley. Staying means risk—and heartache. And he h
no business falling for someone like Sybil Bannerman.

The rugged cowboy who rescues her from a stampede is just th
kind of man Sybil Bannerman's editor wants her to write abou
Yet she has no idea how big a secret Brand Duggan carries, unt
her life is threatened. Despite the evidence against him, Sybil ca
walk away from the man who lassoed her heart....

COWBOYS
OF
Eden Valley

Winning Over the Wrangler

by

LINDA FORD

*Available March 2014 wherever Love Inspired Historica
books and ebooks are sold.*

Find us on Facebook at
www.Facebook.com/LoveInspiredBooks

LIH2